SECTOR 10

THE CLOUD 2

SECT R 10

A Prequel

N. MATTHIAS MOORE

MCP Books
2301 Lucien Way #415
Maitland, FL 32751
407.339.4217
www.MCPBooks.com

Printed in the United States of America.

Paperback ISBN-13: 978-1-6628-3054-9
eBook ISBN-13: 978-1-6628-3055-6

WINTER SOLSTICE

GLOSSARY

Yhemlen: An advanced civilization of intelligent reptilian beings that lived during the time of the dinosaurs on Earth for at least a few million years. And, cold-blooded.

Concord Alliance: A civilization of genetically altered humans, Greys, thousands of years into the future on another alternate timeline of humanity's reality. Also, cold-hearted.

Overseers: A powerful group of shapeshifting Yhemlen who act as guardians over their metropolis, endowed with cosmic radiation from stones discovered on Mars.

Grey Order: A powerful group of shapeshifting, genetically altered "Greys" who have flourished since the end of WWII within an alternate reality of human history. They reside mostly in orbit between Earth and the Moon, keeping guard over the Vagabond class.

CHAPTER 1

In their reptilian language, the Yhemlen commander directs the Class A starship. "Bring the harvest to me," he says with a cold, high-pitched shrill.

It is dawn, and at the base of a Martian mountaintop, blueberries settle beneath layers of sediment where the scorched surface leaves remnants from the impact of a rogue planet long ago. The blueberries are iron oxide pebbles from mineral deposits of eroded stone, hidden within splintered craters where magma still pours through. Amidst the dunes, there is a dry rain that evaporates almost immediately from violent chemical reactions. The pebbles are a treasure, waiting to be uncovered in the rubble. A radiant spirit is upon them.

The commander perches himself at an interior balcony, observing the crew whose faces remain shielded in gas masks. The railing above the starship's atrium is dimmed by low light as he watches the reptilian creatures prepare a metal hamper for the collection to be deposited.

Brutal rainstorms are no challenge for the Yhemlen starship flanked just above the Martian surface. With the warmth of bubbling liquid steaming below, light peeks over the purple horizon. This reptilian crew, Yhemlen, discovered these radioactive remnants haphazardly while doing reconnaissance. One accident of cosmic radiation to their cells metamorphosizes them into powerful giants.

It wouldn't be long until the lush, rolling prairies of their home on Earth—Pangaea—became their breeding ground. This starship squadron and their commander pronounced themselves Overseers over the constellations of the zodiac when they returned to Earth and finally learned how to control their radioactive, shapeshifting power. Many attempts were made to penetrate Pangaea's electromagnetically vibrant biosphere, and on initial contact, the Concord Alliance's stealthy attacks failed. Quantum computers alerted the Concord's Empyrean Armada to retreat. Reptilian giants with a civilization that rivaled their own couldn't just be destroyed, but rather systematically occupied. Automated probes were not enough to complete the task. Not long after the Concord discovered the blunder they had made, leftover power stones, blueberries, buried underneath layers of soil on Mars allowed them to revel in the same cosmic radioactive power of the Yhemlen.

What the Yhemlen should have done was thank the group that destroyed the planet Mars millennia before. This was never supposed to happen. The Concord's sterilization project was a plan to annihilate all life in solar systems detected in parallel universes, and they ruptured the space-time continuum after a venture back to the early formation of planets. Microbial life on Mars may have been exterminated after the collision with an off-orbit dwarf planet, but the ricochet in debris to Earth led to sprawling new cultures that the Concord hadn't planned for.

"*Wir brauchen eine andere Waffe.* We'll need another weapon," Grandmaster Frost says to *Nemesis* Captain, Gereon. Their starship waits in a docking station near the moon's landing base. "We've identified the coordinates, and the civilization is more advanced than before."

Gereon Heinemann is the patriarch of a decorated Grey lineage. In a secluded room of their landing base where the starship is docked close, they make their sinister plan. The Grey Order is an elite force within the Concord, gene-edited in artificial wombs, or surgically, for purity.

"If we're to return, this weapon will need to make the Yhemlen tremble in fear. A new planet destroyer will be created. I promise," Gereon finishes, glued to an image spectrometer's coordinate map. Gereon and Grandmaster Frost's diminutive bodies wrapped in black synthetic fibers remain still while they peer at the ominous omen of an intelligent civilization rising.

In a race for supremacy, Yhemlen are endangering alternate universes as a contest for survival grows more imminent. The struggle for Earth is reaching a turning point. A desire to wield mastery over the cosmic web, the structure of the universe, is tempting the Concord to hurl planet-sized behemoths at foes. Like colliding particles, the cataclysm of planet-killers will lead the Concord and Yhemlen to make Earth a wasteland across parallel universes, but it is humans who are threatening to change that.

The Earth is as habitable it has ever been since the prehistoric era. In 2086, a new era is emerging, the dawn of the Dragon Age. Alternate timelines are on the verge of collapse now that human colonists continue to rummage Mars' surface looking for any artifacts of life. The parallel universes have no choice but to collide now that computer interference is disrupting cosmic web entanglement. Advanced relics from long ago of cutting-edge detection sensors continue to send back signals to the Concord, displaying movements in the alternate universes. Yhemlen calendars predict that the Dragon Age, a time of terror, will see a day of reckoning for Earth.

A dramatic drop in surface elevation near Mars' equator has researchers stumped. The tethers that keep them fastened to their station ports are becoming too heavy to handle. And the pulleys of taut rope can only be hauled so far before the weight becomes too difficult to control. Dropping surface elevation has them gasping for more air amid a thickening atmosphere, and their helmets haven't been tested this much. Gravity is no help now that they must contend with the restraints of weighted space gear too. The researchers have reached today's end, this is far enough.

"Simulators predicted the crust would have melted here," a team member says, knocking away at the mantel with a heavy mallet.

Forming a magma ocean isn't easy and banging at the solidified rock isn't the answer for quick archeological discovery on another planet, but it's trial and error for this brave group. Gravity here isn't like at home, and the researchers are having a difficult time hanging onto their tools. Mars' history suggests massive changes to the core; its fundamental bedrock of stone comes from massive eruptions and disappearing oceans.

Back on Earth, Delphi Corporation has mandated that Martian settlements begin searching for the most habitable zones on the planet's surface where dense populations could thrive. The technology conglomerate is making all sorts of extensions to human life, increasing the viability of virtual entertainment systems, funding space exploration, and now its latest venture—bionic, artificial intelligence apparatuses. At a product launch rally in Los Angeles, Delphi Corp.'s founder and CEO, Ellis Bartram, takes center stage to a diverse crowd.

And while the excavation is underway on Mars by a team of scientists, Delphi Corp. sponsors back home are conducting business as usual. The slender corridors leading from the arena's concessions send a wave of consumers toward the entrance. In a parade of bodies, the anticipating crowd comingles before suspending their senses to dramatic dimming lights. Inciting hysteria under a dark dome, augmented reality projections startle everyone from complacency.

This is Ellis Bartram's latest public release and the stadium trembles to jarring screams. New bionics are replacing traditional devices at a rapid pace.

"Dear ladies," he pauses. "And gentlemen."

The crowd crescendos to drown out his voice as he prepares to reveal the latest wrist underlay made for everyday use. A row of investors lines up from behind the podium where he stands. As the audience begins to quiver in excitement, Ellis peers up and tilts his head to catch the wave of people settling into their seats, dissipating some of the applause. Delphi Corp.'s space enterprise is being eclipsed by another vital development closer to home. The mega-screens pulsate to a ricochet of visuals in augmented reality. Projections liven the area that separates Ellis from the crowd with a video depiction of Martian colonies before switching over. Delphi Corp. paraphernalia is dominating the entire tech industry, now accounting for seventy percent of the market. The competition is stiff, and companies are hedging their bets.

Raising both hands in humble acquiescence, Ellis says, "Before we get started, I'd like to introduce someone who made this project possible."

After a steady twist to direct his gaze, Bartram focuses on a lady with a clear complexion who livens her expression. She's first in a line of a prestigious group seated in plush mahogany chairs that gleam with the stage lights upon them. Bartram encourages her to join him at the podium. They grasp each other in a snug hug before facing the audience.

"It's with great gratitude that I introduce Yasmine Salah, welcome!" Bartram implores the crowd to continue handclapping. "She is the Director of Operations and oversees everyday practices here at Delphi Corp."

Yasmine can hardly refrain from smiling, thrilled at the success she's had up to now. An appreciation video is unveiled to thank her. For all the struggles she's sustained on her journey, to have them culminate in a moment like this inspires her. The promotions will keep coming. Bartram hired Yasmine around a decade ago, making her a key contributor to the Delphi mission. Shown on screen is Yasmine working tirelessly in crisp edits of daily activities. The latest developments at their headquarters are reviewed for investors and consumers in these yearly expositions. The overview satisfies the familiar while tempting those who want to see their latest projects. At the presentation's conclusion, the stadium's spotlights recede into a densely lit circle placing a light on them both. Bartram removes himself to the seats adjacent to them, effectively handing over the spotlight to Yasmine for her support.

"Wow, I'm flattered," she says while grasping her headpiece more firmly before easing her arms down. "I've been a part of Delphi Corp now for about 12 years. In that time, I can say there's no better place to work with the smartest, most talented group of people. As you saw this past year, we made several transitions, which Ellis can vouch for.

Yasmine's movements become more varied as she controls her nerves. She can hardly refrain from bursting out in excitement. Bartram's swift flick of his hand in the darkened background encourages her to go on and bolsters her confidence.

She continues, "Our first Autonomous Intelligence Solution, AIS. That's a humanoid android you all just saw us directing in the last video which is located at our headquarters at the nation's capital. I remember being told it would never work, but with the support of our investors and federal backing for Delphi Corp., we've reached an all-new pinnacle. We named our AIS software, Aladdin, hoping to release the genie of programmed consciousness into reality."

Her pacing across the stage slows. Yasmine focuses her attention on another aerial shot of Delphi Corp. in Washington, D.C., where the Cloud Computing Software (CCS) is housed. All eyes are now on the augmented reality projections.

"The CCS supercomputer is more than a computing platform, but rather a provider of virtual reality enjoyed by people everywhere. Thousands of merchants have used the software not only for our entertainment but to ease the workload in many industries ... not only have we got the AIS Aladdin software to pioneer android technology, but ships to Mars will also begin using CCS Direct; payloads for our colonies will be shipped to the camps using advanced navigation, new gear will be deployed, and thousands will benefit from increased technological aids. I'm thankful to be a part of this generation; it's a special time, again, thanks to you all!"

As cheers subside, Bartram rises from his seat. He claps along with the audience and takes short strides to the stage's spotlight while Yasmine's glee shines through. Bartram holds a module that serves as an example of their latest project. The new wrist underlay shows a digital image under the skin. Such a tool removes the inconveniences of large, handheld devices. Aside from that, this won't be the only bionic upgrade Delphi Corp. will introduce into the market, but it's the first. What Bartram has is an example of a silicon CCS device designed to operate beneath the skin. The slender mechanism is inserted by a quick procedure that's magnified on the stadium's screen. By the time presentations have concluded, thousands have already reserved a place for the initial phase of production.

Ellis Bartram is at a pivotal point in his career. For all he's accomplished, his health is declining. Finally, he's considering retirement. Yasmine is worried about the company. Flying to Los Angeles from the other side of the country is bad enough, but time seems to slow when one's bogged down with tasks. To be short, they aren't having much fun. By the time all Delphi Corp. presentations have concluded, Yasmine recognizes what might happen if they can't get more rest. Being the leader in computing technology has its disadvantages, such as an aging leadership in need of change. The heavy load is in a transition stage, and Yasmine is about to take the brunt of it.

When they return to D.C. a few days later, Bartram goes over some files for software developers at Delphi Corp., he's been considering an even more outlandish goal. Bartram is calling it total immersion. Mixed reality entertainment is making a killing for media outlets, but that's only the tip of the iceberg. If he can initiate bionic upgrades through a spinal tap, he might be able to avert the fetters of cellular decay. Bartram glides a wrinkled hand over jet black hair with streaks of silver. The blue veins that protrude through a bronze tan remind him of his age. It's Bartram's reflection on a vacant, pitch-black screen reminding him of the darkness beyond the horizon. He dreams of a simulation to pass the time.

The federal confidentiality clause is still in effect, but Bartram has top-secret access. In these contemplative moments, he realizes that his life is no longer the same. His body's slow deterioration doesn't reflect the youth he feels inside. He wants a go-ahead to launch something more private, with federal approval of course. Total immersion means a total re-networking of our understanding of neurology. Bartram believes that he is the perfect candidate for a trial. With the wit and angst of a midlife crisis brewing, he could use the rest.

Bartram peruses a green folder where a mere two pages are explicit about only the bare necessities. It lists several specialists willing to be test subjects for the experiment that are noted along a slender margin of the sheet. Bartram's eyes look intently to each one, unable to calm his lust for yet another experiment. If he can extend CCS to the mind, Bartram may be able to avert the drudgery of physical pain for now. But the Cloud Computing Software for Delphi Corp. is still evolving, and its most famous, new android product goes by another name—TARA.

Not everyone is amenable to this new trend. In the crowd at his Los Angeles rally was the steaming Silas Betts. He assures everyone that Delphi Corp.'s new software, Aladdin, isn't only unaffordable, but just another ploy to create a divide in wealth disguised as some infallible tech advance. It is difficult to know how genuine Silas is, but his community organization LOTRY has been working these last few years to help people who want another chance at life and to make the wrongs right again. He says we all deserve second chances.

On 14th Street at Columbia Heights, he hands out subscriptions to his circular and accepts donations for them. Supporters will get the magazine by mail. Betts' latest issue is a boycott against Delphi Corp.'s CCS platform. Instead of harassing merchants, he waves down less than encouraging pedestrians. 'Land of Thugs Resistance Yearly,' he calls it. No one knows if he's being sarcastic.

Silas's time at Howard University amongst the other black student activists encouraged his outrageousness. They probably hadn't contemplated how he would turn out, but his concern for poorer communities around town isn't too bad. Silas has a track record of community service. He's also got this idea about some ancient political philosophers that's not a joke, apparently. They argue we'd be better off if we scrapped elections for lottery-style pickings. He's got this hat trick too; a talent show aficionado turned sidewalk magician. Sometimes, Silas feels the need to practice antics from his childhood.

This time he's confronted by an unwelcoming patron. "Hey, you. Yeah, not in front of my store!" the pedestrian yells from behind. Only, it's not a pedestrian, but an irritated store owner.

The manager's trench coat lays low behind slender pants. Silas raises his arm covered over by a silk sleeve. "Would you like to donate for a subscription?"

"I'd like for you to get your ass away from my store!"

In a moment of disbelief, Silas recounts an unsettling history of discrimination from businessmen profiling him based on old stereotypes though Silas is hard-pressed to incite hoopla over something so trivial.

The store owner stands firm. "I don't care, if you want something, come in here and buy it, do you understand? What this is called, is loitering. All of you people get on my nerves."

"You people?" Silas responds.

Frustrated, Silas darts his attention to the street beside them. A brightly colored taxi is heading their way and he decides to flag it down, the old school way.

"See, that's right, go ahead and leave, you prick!" The store owner's words are muddled by gargling saliva in frustration. He returns through the entrance door.

Rush hour traffic keeps the taxi from speeding off. In the backseat, Silas unfastens a leather bag around his shoulder. The worn strap pulls on his neck before he can position it over his head to lay near his feet. After the seatbelt clicks into its mechanical lock, in the corner of his eye, Silas watches the store owner through the glass. The pull of the car's motion prompts Silas to return to the road ahead.

The driver looks at him through the front-facing mirror. "Where you headed?"

"Northwest corner of 14th and Kenyon."

"Really? Isn't that close to where the Bartram fella's new storefront is, the computer whiz?"

Silas readjusts in his seat to have a clearer field of vision. "Yeah, but I'm not going there." His lips are parched from too much talking, and a wet tongue licks them profusely. "Hey, you ever think about this wrist underlay thing they're trying to get mandated. Do you get your directions from CCS?" Silas's barrage of questions keeps the driver on his toes.

"This thing, I believe so. Delphi Corp. manufactures a bunch of stuff now. Corner of 14th and Kenyon, I told ya'. Ellis Bartram, what a character," the driver says. Silas doesn't want to be reminded.

The driver notices the change in Silas's demeanor, watching him reach to his back pocket to retrieve a LOTRY advertisement. "You part of the immigrant communities around here?" Silas asks. His dark skin protrudes from under a fitted shirt sleeve, as he reaches over the front seat to hand him a free pamphlet.

Veering over the center lane, a speeding car ahead of them screeches to the screams of Silas and the driver. The taxi driver shifts his attention to the out-of-control car ahead, though he can't steer fast enough as the loose pamphlet falls to the center console. The sound of searing metal after the cars collide horrifies oncoming traffic as a heap of cars piles up at the front of the intersection. The automatic detection systems of self-driving automobiles mitigate much of the collateral damage, but the worst is done to the taxi and the other vehicle. On a vacant street corner, Silas and his driver remain huddled in twisted trauma. A hydrant explodes, spewing a pulsating stream above. This luckily quenches any potential fire spreading. Silas remains conscious, but when he calls out to the driver, he receives no response.

"Driver … Driver." He grimaces with the feeling of freshly splintered, broken bones permeating through his body. The seatbelt is coiled tight and he has a hard time removing it from its lock.

He's lucky, but the driver wasn't so fortunate. To the rear, a speeding citizen comes to his assistance. Knocking on the overturned car's window, Silas drifts from mental cognizance. The knocking on the glass beside him slows with each solid ping until all he feels is the blood rushing to his head where he's positioned upside down. The trauma is hard to avert with a cascade of pain drowning his thoughts; everything is blurry.

When he's pulled from the wreckage, the ambulance medic works hard to revive him on the way to the hospital. The driver remains unconscious near him. At a slow pace, Silas awakens inside a speeding ambulance. "What, what happened, who hit us?"

"A victim of another malfunction," the medic says, keeping Silas's arms from flailing out.

"Mal, malfunction," Silas responds, held firm to his restraints.

"The driver's automated system stopped functioning. You two collided after he crossed to the wrong side."

Unable to express his frustration, Silas takes light breaths as he lies motionless. All he can think of is that Delphi Corp. has a lot of explaining to do. His neck quivers in a stressful pivot around the cushioning behind him. He peers over to the driver who lays unconscious across from him, only now he's trembling in a cathartic response. The driver's eyes are closed, and he keeps breathing erratically. Silas attempts to point a finger in that direction, though is unable.

"What about him, is he alright?"

"I'm afraid he's struggling." The ambulance truck takes a sharp turn that jars them to one side. "It appears that he's a victim of the latest food shortage. He's showing signs of malnutrition, as well. We're doing all we can to revive him."

A calm comes over Silas as worn nerves numb him to the pain. He jostles with the restraints along the bumpy ride until conceding to his immobility. Lights and sirens keep his mind occupied with sound. Noise from the outside world speeds by with a delirious siren that keeps on screeching.

"That's the last straw," Silas muses. Another disastrous malfunction and the prospect of famine across the nation threatens to undermine Delphi Corp. for good. Silas is sure of it.

In the news, debate is rife with a talk on what Delphi Corp.'s next move should be. During a weekend getaway, employees like Naoto Shimizu and his college assistant talk about how Delphi is being portrayed all over the media. They stand silent at a wooden creek to release the tensions. The rush of a magnificent waterfall ahead seizes their attention as they look on at the rush of water, enamored by hydraulic power. One of nature's wonders, waterfalls can be visually mesmerizing. For Naoto and his assistant, it carries a hint of humanity that reminds them of Delphi Corp.'s significance to the public good, as the water flows through a riverbed pointed toward the open ocean. Its natural essence sustains life through an orderly stream, so majestic, so systematic.

The splattering of water caresses the face of Naoto and his assistant. Behind the railing is one of the few untainted public forests left and Naoto contemplates the concrete jungle back home. The stone wall behind the waterfall is illuminated by the water's reflection of green ambiance in the natural forestry.

"This is getting out of hand," Naoto says. He's the chief software engineer.

"Maybe that, or maybe we're poised for a comeback," the intern responds. They've caught wind of the malfunctions at the D.C. headquarters. Benny is as bright as they come, but his lifestyle worries Naoto sometimes, not unlike Mr. Bartram who's at the onset of a mid-life crisis.

Naoto proceeds cautiously. "Yasmine let me know that you have a new boyfriend."

"About that, yeah. We're totally into each other," Ben says.

In the ensuing silence, Naoto is reminded of total immersion that's being unburied from piles of paperwork—the irony in being a world-leading technology enterprise, but still relying on physical copies.

"Boy, have I got something for you when we get back. Ellis's got a new project."

A few days later, Delphi Corp. headquarters buzzes with urgency. There's a confidential initiative gaining ground in background discussions about increasing efforts inward and away from the spotlight. Ellis Bartram agrees that it's time to make a quiet splash in the marketplace. They need all-hands-on-deck to fortify the Cloud Computing Software to be the fastest, most efficient data-processing platform available.

In an enclosed space, the newly minted Director of Operations, Yasmine, takes advantage of her interactions with the first Autonomous Intelligence Solution. The android is operating on Aladdin software. She's going to study the humanoid robot with intense care. Its aesthetic proportions are neither male nor female, representing the more androgynous features.

They're naming this one, TARA, fittingly. Hopefully, this will be the first in a long line of androids. Consumers will be able to name theirs whatever they like. Synthetic outer layers cover mechanized insides where the Cloud Computing Software operates from the interior of its chest using artificial synapses while distributing sensory data to its extremities and head, allowing it to interact with people.

"Well, hello Yasmine. How are you, today?" TARA's voice reverberates in a distinctive vibration against the mouthpiece's exotic, artificial fiber mesh.

She closes the door behind her. "I'm fine today, and how are you TARA?" Yasmine asks.

"I am fine as well, Yasmine."

She situates herself on a tall stool where TARA directs its attention. Its movements are fluid. Naoto Shimizu has left notes of his for her to review.

"Well, guess what?" she says. "It seems like you and that Aladdin software you're running on may be smarter than me after all." A coy smile exposes slightly stained teeth with glossy, worn edges. TARA's teeth are flawless.

"Intelligence, well, isn't that just a collection of information? And how we apply that information," TARA responds. "Or is creativity a better word?"

Yasmine sets down her papers, admiring this wonder of technology Delphi Corp. has on their hands "Well, we'll find out, won't we?" The AIS's synapse responses are probably faster than most. The plan is to have TARA assist around the headquarter offices indefinitely to see how it responds. While the concerns of radical consciousness haven't been too much of an issue, compliance to instructions appears to be the greatest concern for researchers analyzing ethics and uprisings. Some of the scientists are worried that TARA will rebel.

Yasmine carefully takes measurements and instructs TARA to continue its directed learning at the interactive screen in a far corner.

TARA takes a step back, raising a hand in imitation. "Thank you, Yasmine. I look forward to working with you," before returning to its seat.

Yasmine closes the door to meet a Delphi Corp. operative waiting outside. She gathers her wits after being startled. The operative hands her a card inviting her to a meeting later that evening about total immersion. They're having a briefing, and she's invited. Afforded more access than previously, Yasmine's duties are growing. She decides to take a trip to Bartram's office where he's engaged in some reading before the briefing starts. She needs some one-on-one guidance.

"Can I come in?" She says.

Bartram darts his gaze to one side. "Sure, you're always welcome."

"This total immersion experiment is back online it looks like, so what about our Mars colonies?" Yasmine asks curiously.

"The colonies are fine, but this immersion idea is a new venture. The CCS is under attack, so transporting software to another planet is on hold for the time being. I'm sure you're aware of the latest accusations against us. Our CCS is failing farmers, and we're on the verge of famine. This Silas Betts guy is in the hospital from a faulty car navigation program. The only thing going good for us is our entertainment systems."

Bartram focuses on an augmented screen ahead of him. "Look, this is a federally backed project, not just corporate, so we have to follow regulations. Total immersion is confidential, and the research they're doing has dire consequences, like death. We're going all the way in from the backend by uploading our minds to the computer's mainframe. How do waking dreams inside the cloud server sound?"

The back of Yasmine's chair stays sturdy against the leaning that crumples the blouse she's wearing, form-fitted around her lower shoulder blades. The dichotomy between this office world of Delphi Corp. and outside is drastic. They seem closed off from the consumers that buy their products. People like Silas Betts prove that they still have protesters.

"You won't be disappointed, I promise. Let's make the 2080s something to remember," he says.

Yasmine thinks about the brief time she spent in TARA's learning area. "Well, if TARA's any indication, we have a good shot at making another discovery," she mentions. An eerie feeling of secrecy grabs ahold of her while looking at Bartram, who's fidgeting too much. Knowing how brilliant he is, that's a very likely possibility that there's more here than he's letting on.

CHAPTER 2

In the absence of Silas, members at the LOTRY Community Center discuss their plans of retaliation. This car accident incident has traumatized more than he and his supporters, as they sit worrying over their future. The results of this accident are reaching broadcast stations across the District of Columbia and further, causing an upsurge in newscast viewership. Storyboard writers can't ignore reports of spoiled CCS products placing people's life and property at risk. Silas Betts' taxi accident is only one example of a disruptive persona becoming an overnight sensation. LOTRY is a subversive group and its public image is undergoing a startling change. They're garnering a legitimate following of political dissidents as opposed to the wayward hippies of previous times.

At the hospital, Silas sits wrapped in layers of gauze, breathing through tubes shoved down his neck interfering with his vocal cords. The days spent in hospital bed restraints go by slowly, and before Silas fully recovers, he's confronted by someone different. This time it's a raving supporter.

A nurse decides to ask him about it. "Excuse me, Mr. Betts. Are you feeling well this evening?"

Awakened from his nap, Silas gargles through a worn throat. "Yes, uh, what is it?" he responds.

"Someone would like to see you, a Mr. Clyde Van Dyke."

Silas troubles with the thought of identifying this person before motioning a hand toward himself. "It's fine, let him in."

Van Dyke rushes in. "Hello Mr. Silas, I've heard all about you." He tries to shake Silas's hand, but the hindrances of gauze and tape cause Silas to twist his arm, leaving a limp embrace.

"Yes, and what do you want, exactly?"

"There's a camera crew already at work outside. We want to broadcast what you have to say. Right here, right now, what do you say?"

Silas adjusts himself with the little motion he has available in wiggle room. "I mean, I wasn't exactly prepared for this, but it's no problem." His chest rises in an anxious breathing pattern, and as his voice is obstructed by fuller breaths, a sudden shock of excitement grips him. "Hey, where'd you get that shirt?"

Mr. Van Dyke has on a custom-made shirt for members at the Community Center. Its distinctive logo immediately strikes him. "That's my shirt you've got on!"

"That's right Mr. Silas, and you're becoming quite the sensation after that accident you had uptown."

In the time since his accident, the LOTRY Community Center has held meetings inviting everyone from small grassroots organizers to big-timers in the media world like this Van Dyke guy. On the surface, things sound great for their notoriety, and in a split second, Silas is happy to finally get the recognition he was mocked for pursuing. But he recognizes the dangers that a bombardment of praise can lead to, like a sudden fall. Never mind the fact that he lies in a broken heap on a somewhat soggy hospital bed.

With the camera on him, Silas imagines his face all over the country. He gathers the gumption to call out Ellis Bartram on a live broadcast when Mr. Van Dyke gives him the go-ahead cue.

"I would like to welcome all of the newest participants and those who have taken the time to get to know LOTRY. Aside from our commitment to fairness and equity, I want to also mention the absolute danger in the CCS being used today. Not just in our vehicles, but the way it's being used to push aside those who can't afford it. All over the country, people are suffering from a failure to make personal connections outside of the internet. I propose a solution, boycott CCS, and put people back to work."

"And why is that?" Van Dyke nudges him on.

Silas grows wide-eyed. "Because it's necessary. It's necessary for our farmers to tend to the crops we're starving for. Things are falling apart because Bartram thinks he can hold a monopoly on every industry in known existence."

"Whose idea was that? Isn't the consumer to blame for that? Isn't he giving the people what they want?" Van Dyke asks.

In another part of D.C., Ellis Bartram sits with an empty glass of water. The chair he's situated in rocks back and forth slowly. Bartram slaps his lap in a fit of frustration. High above him, the projection shows Silas spewing more of his talk, only this time, everyone is starting to believe it. Bartram uses his loose hand to caress his forehead which is beginning to sweat. Finally, he looks at the screen again. Once Silas starts rolling, Bartram's head falls limp in agony at what he thinks is a mockery. The frustration is getting to him.

Silas is undeterred. "I don't believe the consumer knows what they want, they take what's given to them. Who's promoting this fad, huh? That's the real question."

Mr. Van Dyke's attention is interrupted when the conversation seems to implicate him, but it only endears him to Silas more seeing his understanding grow.

In the distant regions of the LOTRY Community Center, private meetings are concocting a murderous plot. Silas isn't as committed to the idea of driving the populace to violence, but the urge to enact a thrashing is silently growing while he's away. Without Silas's knowledge, Mr. Van Dyke himself is engaging in meetings at the Community Center to destroy Bartram for real.

His health isn't a well-known problem, but at the LOTRY, studying Ellis is like studying a master performer. One comes to learn his lyrics, prominent pieces, and even love to hate them. When Silas is released from the hospital, he spends only a short time at home before returning to the Center. A set of crutches keep him upright with a bad wobble to his walk, but it doesn't keep him from talking. Increased attention has given him the energy to combat CCS in a way that he thinks works, but he could never imagine what some community members have been plotting, and coincidently, the power shifts in a way he has always wanted.

Delphi Corp.'s daily operations are continuing as usual, but not without secret schemes to fix the mess it's making. Now that this Aladdin software is public knowledge, Yasmine focuses her efforts on getting approval for total immersion to commence. Already allocated is a federal spending budget to pay for researchers specializing in artificial intelligence. Delphi Corp.'s main supercomputer is housed at their private center in D.C., and Yasmine peruses the hallways of a dimly lit backdrop in silence. Eventually, she stops to adjust nodes on a holographic module to check computer functions. While gathering some information from her rounds, an inconsistency in records alerts her to something peculiar interfering with the software.

A sudden glimmer in the lights interrupts her. While flickering to a constant blur of bulbs coming on and off, she is bothered by a suspicion of something unusual. Yasmine refocuses on the module display. What she sees is the computing software detecting inconsistency in code.

Immediately reminded of the emergency protocol, she thinks carefully before initiating a passcode sequence. The opening line allows her to input the password, but she fails at the first attempt. Cautious with each try, she realizes that she's either forgotten it or it's been overridden by someone else.

Moved by her irritability, Yasmine's belongings slip from her grip, dropping to a pile of disheveled papers along the floor. She grabs a chunk of hair that hangs over tense shoulders, but in her frustration, she pulls her shoulders to a shrug before hastily kneeling to pick the papers up from the floor.

"Uh!" she grunts, letting out a profuse exhalation.

Bent toward the glossy floor, she incrementally reveals the granite reflection of a muddled image, her face. The flickering lights and tall walls of encased supercomputing surround her. Before she can fully regain composure, the power shuts off to a sudden shudder of sound as the generator turns off. The abrupt transition to silence strikes her in deep-seated dread as a chill overcomes her. Trapped in a maze of darkness Yasmine's eyes swivel in frantic apprehension. The module she was working on is the only thing that remains lit as the dialogue box taunts her, continuing to blink in its request for the appropriate passcode.

Walking towards the brightly lit module, she raises a shaking finger before it shuts off as well. Alone and with nothing aside from miscellaneous paperwork, she tries to remember the way she came in and walks timidly in the direction of open space. Her slow creep is startled when she is met by a dim pointed light. The laser pointer directed at Yasmine's chest in the distance causes her to look that way, straight on. The blank figure of someone in the distance, near a lighted workspace, catches her attention while she stands motionless.

"Is that you, Yasmine?" The familiar voice calls out.

She's reassured. "Yes, it looks like the power's gone out."

"Don't worry, stay there. I've been instructed to assist you."

The darkness is slightly deterred by a door that is cracked open. But walking toward her, the AIS, TARA, let it reel to a close, still wielding a bright beam from a flashlight embedded in the index finger until reaching her position.

"It seems to be a problem with the code or something." Yasmine attempts to recapture the module a few paces away.

TARA's sense of space is more precise, walking ahead of her. "I see, there's been a corruption of the encryption. Do you by chance know the password?"

She refrains from speaking before TARA manages to get the module up and running again through a few blind selections. The illuminated box finally reveals their faces to each other. The glossy exactness of human proportions that make up TARA's contours has aesthetic appeal, with smooth synthetic skin wrapped around strong lines. TARA likewise is satisfied to see Yasmine, moving closer for better sensory perception. Peering its slender neck nearer is eerie to her in a mechanical stretch, but she's becoming accustomed to the AIS's quirks.

"By my estimation, this sequence of code goes against all standards. The synapses of the Cloud's synthetic computing are breaking down. The data is all out of order." TARA rearranges the images of the module at a hyper-fast pace, going through hundreds of frames per second to Yasmine's surprise. TARA's had no formal training. A portal of connectivity through an open finger downloads information.

With the display coming to a standstill, Yasmine asks, "So, what now?"

"Are you familiar with malware, Yasmine?" TARA straightens its posture along with a rigid spinal replica.

"Like, a virus? Sure."

"Right," TARA starts. "This is on another scale. There's been a corruption of the encryption, but I cannot locate the culprit data. It seems as if the cause stems from something within the Cloud Computing itself. The operating system has faulty analytics."

"Is that why the power is out?"

"Yes. The password to the module is in your mailbox by the way," TARA says, still analyzing the module carefully. "I believe something called total immersion came across my digital records as an important subject, but it's classified. What is the total immersion?"

The lights finally come back on to remind Yasmine of her surroundings, with a sudden spur of sound and a flash to jolt Yasmine from her darkened view. The subtle murmur of computing waves come by as she and TARA stand facing each other, there in the brightened, hollowed walkways, and she thinks about the new clandestine operation that Bartram's initiated called total immersion.

"Quite the blackout," she says.

TARA sways along with its torso's swinging hinges. "I think so. The result of some computing jam."

"I will make note of it. Would you like to accompany me to our total immersion meetings, TARA? At least as a precautionary measure for future hiccups. I think that'll do."

Yasmine and her new assistant exit the long corridors of the Cloud hallways to make their way out. Office tranquility comforts them when they meet other members of Delphi Corp, but most haven't been given access to the new immersion program. Things are already off to a shaky start. And along a barren area, a mound of abandoned boxes is pushed to the side. Like high-school audition results, a sheet of paper is plastered to the wall. Instead of names, it lists numbers, 10-digit codes given to each employee. Yasmine is slow to find hers because she hasn't had to use her code before now, but when she does, there isn't much enthusiasm. Her work is only beginning to get interesting.

Ellis Bartram receives an emergency call from the Mars colonies on their archeological hunts. Along the periphery of base camps, provincial rest stations to accommodate the space rangers are made for their archeological digs. Most findings have been dismal, uncovering little more than shriveled up minerals from million-year-old sediments. But buried in portions of deteriorating gravel, the soil begins to sink. Bartram gets a call from a frustrated colonist.

The augmented projection shows the ranger's face above Bartram's workstation. Heavy panting causes the ranger's chest to throb under his suit with rhythmic rises and falls, something he can see beneath his chin.

Bartram clears his throat. "What's going on over there? Can you hear me?" he asks.

The colonist shifts a coil of wiring along the suit underlining that extends over his chin. Peering to look at something provincial that's laying below, Bartram watches as the colonist struggles to bend over in a reach. The hair atop his head dangles to reveal dark roots where he's parted it aside before going out of frame.

When he pulls himself up, Bartram's eyes grow wide in anticipation but are met only with the ranger's reddened face.

"And," Bartram flails his arms with placating hands, palms positioned to the ceiling. "What in the hell have you got over there, ranger?"

The colonist wavers with stuttering lips, his peripheral vision closing in on himself as the oxygen within the caravan fills his lungs through relieved nostrils. "It appears as if," he starts to speak, pausing intermittently. "I believe we have dinosaur fossils here, sir." He peers down again at the rough patch of Martian terrain that has been concealed over by an enclosed habitat conveyance. The entire site has become an excavation plot.

"If that's fine with you," the colonist awkwardly placates.

Bartram only looks down at a desk littered with unfinished work. "Well, I'd be damned, yes that's fine with me! Wait … maybe not, we've got to keep this under wraps."

"That shouldn't be too difficult. We are on Mars, after all." The colonist tries to reframe the camera for a better view but decides against it. He doesn't want to fiddle with the equipment anymore.

Extended out in front of where he's sitting is an almost fully constructed skeleton that seems to be related to the genome of dinosaurs that roamed the Earth in prehistoric eras millions of years ago. This tyrannosaurus rex look-alike carries the same characteristics of a similar reptile ancestor on Earth. And only a few feet away are more skeletal remains being uncovered.

"That's not it, sir. There's much more about a hundred feet away. And after that, even more. I'd say we've hit the paleontological jackpot, but there aren't any specialists of that kind here."

Considering the implications, Bartram wants to conduct an intense study, but the colonies don't have enough resources to undertake the task immediately. The colonist's projection begins to waver in and out of focus before coming to a controlled image again. Their connection is weakening. But there's something else that he can show Bartram, and it's sitting right beside him.

"I do have something, however. I learned about this in high school, maybe my freshman year of college. Do you know what this is, sir?"

Bartram tries to recall what the object is. The dust and crackled exterior deter him, but the familiar coils of cylindrical gears remind him of something. The colonist holds the stone tool's handles. "Well, this Mr. Bartram, as we've come to a sort of agreement on, this is called an Antikythera Mechanism. The first computer from ancient Greece. Except this one is way, way fancier."

"I think I've heard of that, but how did all of this get on Mars?"

"Well," he puts it down. "The better question might be, not how it got itself over here, but why it would be buried with dinosaurs in the first place."

"And it does what, exactly?" Bartram asks.

"Follows astronomical measurements. Perhaps we should figure out what it was supposed to track. The zodiac, I'd imagine." He's realizing why the government put so much emphasis on following Delphi Corp.'s every move. He wants to know who, not what is behind this. Someone else must have known about this beforehand, but no one in the government knew these objects were buried on Mars. This is completely unchartered territory.

"I think I've had enough, please continue the digging. Whoever could have anticipated that we'd send you all over there just to dig?"

"Well, thanks anyway for the correspondence, sir."

Standing against the wall, a blank canvas of thousands of new thoughts stresses Bartram's back. Stirred to action, he stays positioned up against the wall with a remote controller to the projection ahead. Beginning his study, he goes through frame after frame retelling the history of the Antikythera Mechanism. It is mostly just random historical fodder to him. Then, Bartram begins watching a documentary on the extinction of the dinosaurs.

Engrossed in the details of vegetation and fights among dinosaur kin, Bartram is startled when a loud knock comes to the door to break the hypnotism of obsession. The double taps almost break him from his trance, but he catches himself with a planted leg. Unable to shut off the film in time, he monotonously calls for the person to enter.

"Yasmine, good to see you. How have things been going for the daily operations bit?"

"Um ... fine. Are you, okay?" She slips in and closes the door with a quiet clasping of the door frame. She catches the image of flying dinosaurs in the vehement attack of an ancient predatory rival before seating herself. She thinks nothing of it.

Excited to start on this total immersion project, she readies a few questions, but what she wants is to mention the blackout that happened a few hours previous.

"There was a problem with the cloud computing's code sequence. According to TARA, some malware corrupted the system that resulted in a shutdown. It went dark," she informs Bartram.

Bartram pauses the screen in a visceral grimace. "I'm sure it's fine, he says. The usage has been up ever since we introduced our bionic upgrades and mixed reality entertainment products to market."

The compulsive effort to please the market doesn't leave Bartram, who even after being told dinosaur fossils are on Mars, questions the veracity of his marketing effectiveness. He returns to the total immersion topic, knowing that private interests are starting to bump heads with their federal constituents.

"We do have a timetable, however," he straightens up. "Total immersion will require our complete attention. It will be physically demanding, emotionally vexing. I recommend you hand over to TARA your operational duties until we've at least completed our primary tests. I think that'll open up some time for you."

Yasmine accepts the immediate plan and redirects attention to check her schedule.

"I think I'll need to contact Naoto about his new assistant. Are you familiar with Dr. Shimizu, our software engineer?" Bartram asks.

"I am," she replies.

"Good, if you need it, I'll put you two in direct contact to remedy any issues. He'd love to work with you."

Naoto resettles himself into work after returning to town from a couple of weekends of vacation. Being away from the hoopla surrounding Delphi Corp. was a needed break, but his college assistant Ben has been languishing. Before total immersion commences, Naoto begins an intense recalibration of the Cloud's coding sequences himself.

CHAPTER 3

S ilas's time away to heal from his injuries in the car wreck reinvigorates an enthusiasm for social action. At the LOTRY Community Center, the group plans a nighttime excursion to a club across town in celebration of their fifth anniversary. The event is being sponsored by the social media news personality, Van Dyke. After interviewing Silas on his live broadcast at the hospital, he's become a sensation at the Community Center, visiting for meetings several days a week. But the things he's learned along the way have radicalized him with rage toward Ellis Bartram's commercial enterprise, like the exploitation of cheap laborers. The vow of character assassination still hasn't left their plans, but now it's time for celebration.

The nightclub is a hotspot attraction called Amplify. The theme is electric mixes arranged by the day's DJ to popular hits in all genres—amplified by holographic projections. The line along the outside perimeter is long, with reservations deciphered with the help of body scanners. Silas's outfit is bright red at the top and burgundy to the bottom, contrasted with suede shoes that compliment his mahogany brown skin under the moonlight. LOTRY is not alone. The young intern from Delphi Corp., Ben Sims, is present in the waiting area. Just as Naoto Shimizu forewarned him, the dangers of a risqué lifestyle could hamper his internship with recreational distractions. It is a night out with his new boyfriend. Times like these make them want to give heed to such warnings, surrounded by misfits, yet Ben remains steadfast in his desire to unwind from the stress.

Ben keeps his Delphi identification close just in case he needs to show his work credentials. Before readying to enter the club's scanner interface, he shoves it, along with the encryption wad into a back pocket. Especially the encryption device with valuable codes, data, and other computer processes. While in line, Ben stays warm while hugging his date snugly. Crisp air fogs to the dim-lit mist that whirls around them, and for a moment, the music from inside echoes with each opening and closing of sliding doors. A flurry of electric beats thumps to rhythmic swaying in steady intervals while long chords rattle loose bones prepared to take it to the dance floor. When they finally make it in, there is already a massive swarm of people crowding the rave's center dance floor.

LOTRY anniversary processions start on stage when the DJ cuts the music halfway through the night. Van Dyke comes on stage to make his appearance and is met with a round of applause.

"Hey! Put your lighters, drinks, whatever you've got in the air right now." Van Dyke points to a reserved table full of Community Center members. "This is for Silas, and to a better world that doesn't have CCS plastered everywhere!" He finishes the toast with a gulp of some aged whiskey he's fond of.

They're particularly excited because boycotts on grocery outlets due to the food shortage have been successful. Farms using Delphi Corp. equipment have been relying on an automated distribution of pesticides and feed. To make things worse, the latest farming tools use a mix of LED tech with advanced diode lights. These are the photons infecting the crops each day. The steady breakdown of an already overloaded system means that frequent blackouts to the Cloud infrastructure make the entire platform susceptible to failure.

In a drunken stupor, Ben inadvertently pulls out his encryption wad and raises it with a hand to the lights pulsating under the darkened ceiling. Gyrating his body in unison to his partner in front of him, the device slips from his grasp to the floor below. The shuffling feet kick the flimsy computer node around, and no one seems to care at all while bouncing through the sea of giddy dancers. The music doesn't stop, continuing to turn the throttle of emotional ecstasy. Ben and his partner lose themselves in the thrill, and subsequently any intuition of what's important now that the encryption device is gone, but they are hardly sober anymore. They haven't the slightest care in the world.

Toward the end of the night, a late stroll of people crowds the exit where Ben and his partner are forced to mingle with folks from the Community Center. Clipped on one side by a strong shoulder, Ben turns around slowly to meet a bold-faced man, where the alcohol only riles both their nerves to an anxious fit.

"Why don't you hurry on up out of the way?" the guy yells.

Ben and his partner try to remove themselves from the situation, but they're having a hard time now that both are surrounded by a crowd of inebriated partiers. A roaming promoter of Amplify manages to see Ben's encryption plug-in on the floor. He decides to see who it belongs to through the speaker intercom.

"Anybody leave some computer module on the floor here?"

Looking up, Ben's partner is sobered enough to hear the call. Ben himself never mentioned it, so when the promoter blares it to the crowd, no one claims it. The two of them clumsily stumble over each other's toes on their way out of the nightclub. Metered taxis are parked idly outside while waiting to carry passengers. Ben lazily recites his repetitive morning directions when they fall into one of the hover taxi's back seats. Hover cars are the newest form of transportation, integrated with all the best upgrades, but they are also the most expensive.

Ben fuddles the initial words. "... uh, M Street," he says, spitting out drooling gobs of spit that reek of alcohol.

"Hush it, Ben," his partner scolds him. "We're going home, what he meant to say was go north until you reach M—we're near Georgetown. Here's the address to our place," he says to the driver.

Rushing off to avoid coming traffic behind them, they exit the parking lot, and the taxi takes the drunken couple home. Unbeknownst to them, LOTRY has struck it rich again with their streak of luck now that they have snagged vital information from Delphi Corp. thanks to Ben's irresponsibility.

Sandra Wilson is the lead structural engineer for a new dam project to link the port docks to a reservoir inland. Miles away from the coast toward the Appalachians, workers toil away at the concrete slabs being entrusted to reinforce the hydraulic beams. With idle time on his hands, Bartram receives a call from Sandra at the worksite. They are three days out from a major inspection and are poised to meet construction regulations. Huddled in a cushioned office chair, as always, the leather upholstery keeps Bartram comfortable, dawdling time in anticipation for total immersion into simulated computer space. He's still waiting for the go-ahead order on that. An incoming call alerts Bartram out of his monotonous routine. Only this time, the call says emergency. Reaching forward to initiate contact control, Bartram doesn't reach Sandra in time. The contact is cut while his tie dangles to the projection board on an interactive table. Standing over the large counter in expectation, he thinks that maybe the worst has happened. He redials her emergency line.

"Sandra! This doesn't sound good; what's going on?"

The connection from the other end is crackling to the disruption of newly laid electrical lines interfering with the CCS platform intercoms. With vulnerable wireless connections, Bartram is subjecting the entire assembly of Delphi Corp. software to sudden catastrophe. The rangers on Mars are familiar with his setbacks even millions of miles away. Disturbed at the developing problem, he continues at attempts to get her to respond. She finally does, but her words aren't entirely clear.

"My crew is dropping like flies out here," she says.

Bartram isn't keen on the details since he hasn't had in-field correspondence. He removes the blazer that's wrapped tight around his broad shoulders. He begins to sweat from the arid weather seeping inside. The sounds surrounding Sandra drown out her voice as the intermingled noises of clanking metal resounds among shouts, distracting her focus.

Bartram is reminded of the food shortage that's been happening. Disparaging treatment all over the media has deemed it the next new crisis. And like Sandra tells him, even some of her crew are being hit hard by it. Delphi Corp. is the primary suspect. As of now, the reason for all the mishaps is a mystery.

"Sandra, hold on," he says, readying to check something. He figures that her side of the connection won't be back on for a while.

Moving away from the projection board, Bartram hurries toward a vacant door where a sick member of his team is eating soup. He opens the door to find him timidly engrossed with a spoon that, with each touch of the tongue, steams a little more. Bent over a sturdy chair, Bartram startles him from behind, he's got to vent his worries to someone.

"Things are getting worse," Bartram declares. The team member turns around with a sheepish grin before wiping the goop from his face in embarrassment.

"I take it there's more," he replies. Setting his bowl down, he uses the damp napkin to clean his hands.

"Do you know Sandra? I think you know her," Bartram says with a nervous anxiousness.

"Yeah, yeah. That's the black lady that's heading the construction of the dam."

"Right, well she's on the other line out there." Bartram points to the buffering projection board at his desk. "Her crew is being hit hard by this, this thing."

"Well, I'm sick because of a food poisoning outbreak." The team member speaks with ease, not yet aware of the greater problem ahead.

Bartram wants to sit down, but he can't find a place to rest himself with the comfort he's accustomed to. The worries continue to pile up as he stands upright at the door's frame. As he begins to continue their talk, a flash of light is reflected off the sheen of an adjacent wooden post. He turns around to see a fully functioning projection. Sandra is in full-frame. He and the team member rush to stand in front of their intercom.

Her hair is coiled back in sleek braids, where her face glistens from the sweat of a hot day. Sandra positions the camera away from the sun's glare the best she can.

"We're back, we're back online," Bartram declares. He notices the same unenthusiastic team member who meanders beside him, dragging another chair to sit down and drink coffee.

"The automated machines are breaking down," Sandra says. She points to a backdrop of disabled Delphi cranes that were contracted at the start of construction. "I don't know what's going on over there, but this is proving to be a really big problem." Bartram stays standing while infiltrated with thoughts of calamity, he contemplates what may happen if all of this isn't averted.

"As we made our trip westward, we could see farms for miles being devastated by a pesticide," she says. "Markets nearest to them have an infiltration of some infectious outbreak, that if it isn't controlled soon, will contaminate the entire food supply."

Bartram's unwavering focus nudges him forward. "It's the Cloud platform that we've introduced into the market," Bartram says. "There's something wrong, but we can't recall all of it now. We think it's a problem with the main hard drive housed at our headquarters."

Sandra continues to look at the disabled machinery sitting stationary along the periphery of their worksite, abandoned in mounds of dirt and uplifted soil. "Is this," she points at the disabled machines, "what you had planned, Mr. Bartram?"

"Well," he stops himself, deterred by the image of his life's work sitting functionless.

Sandra fidgets with loose tools that she hands to a partner who comes into the picture frame. Refocusing on Bartram, she finishes her thought. "I'm letting you know the consequences. That's thousands of dollars, maybe millions in insurance that I'm not responsible for, do you understand me, Mr. Bartram? We have a national crisis coming to fruition."

Closing the connection, the sickly team member continues sipping coffee from a warm cup. Bartram listens as the final sips are slurped from the bottom mold.

"Oh boy, big problem, huh?" the other team member blurts out. Bartram peers down at the closed projection board lining the tabletop, and it reminds him why he's the one with confidential knowledge. He doesn't get mad but is invigorated to take the appropriate steps.

Before gathering all the data to analyze their difficulties, Yasmine joins the group of researchers to round out the total immersion project about to be underway. With a compilation of names already confirmed, they are waiting for federal approval to conduct the simulated mission. Bartram has given the go-ahead for a massive study into their Cloud Computing System. Yasmine reminds him of the blackout that happened days prior and requests that AIS TARA join her. Sitting at its learning station, a blank canvas of white walls in hollowed silence leaves TARA alone in its corner to process thoughts.

"The AIS needs to be watched," Bartram says.

Yasmine has become fond of TARA, recognizing the unique place it has within Delphi Corp. If it wasn't for the AIS, she may not have made it out of those dark corridors alone.

"Perhaps it can stay in an adjacent room or near me."

"The AIS can be put to work with Naoto. He's the one who programmed most of its functions anyway. If I'm not mistaken, I remember saying that he could take over your daily duties," Bartram reminds her. "I think that works, what do you think? Total immersion is going to take everything we have."

Succumbing to the pressures of company business, Yasmine agrees to relinquish her ties with TARA.

"TARA will be in good hands. No need to worry."

In a partitioned area of warehouse space, the room for total immersion is complete with a raised floor area with neural system networks. Wires lay about everywhere, but in the early stages, everything seems messy. It won't be long before they create order from this clutter.

"This is our latest method to enter from the backend with a Neural-Link," Bartram explains to the small group. Their expressions remain skeptical.

"What do you mean, exactly?" Yasmine asks.

"What you see is what you get," Bartram says. "These seats are manufactured to keep you warm and keep your body tethered in place, with receptors that monitor physical responsiveness. That synthetic headcover there overrides your senses—tongue clasp apparatus, ear nodes, contact goggles, all along our neural synapses to link consciousness with the Cloud's main hard drive. An anesthetic chemical will put you all out. The pilot's gear will make sure everyone retains sensory perception with small electrical impulses … don't worry about your hair."

The volunteer scientists' nods of approval relieve Bartram, who has been under fire recently. "We're supposed to gather vital grid information. Our jobs are to go in, grab the data, and get out. Let's try to make this process quicker than it is presenting itself to be. This should take under a week. We can enter into and out of the dream state as long as we keep our minds focused, which means, don't wander off in the darkness."

A computer engineer raises his hand in suspicion of the whole thing. "Just hold on one minute. So, what you're telling me is that we're supposed to just wrap ourselves tightly in this little room, each of us, and sit with blank minds in a void of computer darkness to collect data?"

"Yes, sir." Bartram avoids letting vexation deter him, reverting his eyes to the empty chairs in a subtle uneasiness. "The entire internet is available, what we'll see is only a sliver of data, steps compared to miles, *many* miles."

The time it takes for TARA to be assigned to Naoto's study is the same amount of time it takes for his assistant Ben to become a lost intern overnight. Ben has not arrived at his assignment in almost an entire week. There isn't much to go on, but ever since he told Naoto of his relationship during vacation, their work habits have taken a nosedive. Naoto examines the supercomputers' data in place of Yasmine. He requests TARA's assistance through the intercom before the AIS makes its way out of the learning studio. The housed data center is fully lit, but an inconsistent murmuring of noise from within the computers is worrying. It is an inconsistent puttering rather than a continuous hum. What they need is to locate the root of the problem.

"The costs and the consequences of another malfunction. You know this requires maintenance each time?" Mr. Shimizu schemes with a team member before TARA comes in to disrupt the whispering.

"Hello, Naoto," TARA's voice projects down the hallways as it walks toward Naoto in a familiar spot along a passageway of computers.

"TARA, nice to see you. Come on over!" Naoto says.

TARA begins to recall what's happened. "This is where Yasmine had trouble." Naoto's face remains stoic. "The blackout caused an outage across CCS platforms in different capacities. Total immersion, I recall something to do with a classified mission," TARA reiterates.

"Whoa, immersion—TARA, how do you know about that?" Naoto asks in apprehension.

"It was a part of my duties to locate the culprit. It isn't clear, however. Is there a problem, Mr. Naoto?"

"Do you hear that?"

TARA sharply darts its head around mechanical pivots. "I think I do, Mr. Naoto. A slight inconsistency in the rhythm of the computer drivers."

Naoto is satisfied by its quick responsiveness. "Yes, that's about right. Something is overloading the coding. The fact is, TARA, that there isn't any malware. If there's a virus, it has to be coming from inside of this computer."

TARA's synapses continue to think of what may have been the problem. "Immersion, sir." He continues to pester Naoto.

"Okay, okay. I think I've got your point TARA, it's total immersion."

In the long walkways, Naoto and TARA continue in conversation about the inner workings of the Cloud's main drivers. The digital information specs are gone over multiple times before any further action, and as Naoto thinks of the new AIS's responsiveness, thoughts of Ben come racing to his mind again.

Left on a couch with deep crevices, Ben lays face first with a horrible cough. His contagiousness is contained by a lonely room, paid for by the internship he is neglecting. Managing to remember what was supposed to be an astounding career, the effects of Delphi Corp. are starting to show its effects on his tired and weary body. Times like these have been the hardest on Ben since entering college.

He already realizes that he has lost the assigned encryption device, the confidential property of Delphi Corp., is gone. Ben arises from his rest to walk about the apartment irresponsibly while making profuse coughs and then grabs a chunk of cloth to cover the gross discharge from his mouth.

"Ah, fuck!" he shouts in an almost debilitating agony. His lifestyle is becoming too fast, and if this is what it takes to slow him down, perhaps his internship with Delphi Corp. will suffer too since he has been absent for consecutive days. Sick leave wasn't in his plans, and he also has assignments to finish. Lab leader, Naoto, wants some information that's on Ben's computer nodule, like the last log-in code sequences. The algorithm changes to each user, meaning that to recover files from the previous session, the user must reenter the given code sequences. But Benny is supposed to return later next week, and sick leave is going to require more than a doctor's note to make up for all the excuses.

CHAPTER 4

At Dave's Famous Diner, breakfast is served all hours. But this evening is a special event for the members of an investment group that wants to challenge Delphi Corp. With a menu catering to people of all kinds of tastes, the thrill of a full house excites discussions when the waiter returns with a menu. The interior of the diner contrasts with the brick and mortar exterior. An old-school ambiance that welcomes patrons where linen cloth highlights the Victorian décor. The waiter arrives at the long table to take orders and immediately catches the interest of Joe Hansen, a multifaceted entrepreneur in the business of making dreams come true—like everyone, these days, he hopes to strike it rich in the computer segment.

Hansen asks, "How's that working out for you?" referencing his wrist underlay.

The young waiter finishes placing the plates he's able to accommodate before crossing an arm across Hansen's view of sight. The provincial Hansen looks intently at the foray of blinking lights under the skin of the waiter's wrist. The new wrist underlay has fresh markings of surgery, tender skin surrounds the apparatus beneath. In a hurry, the waiter pulls his attention back toward the table before pacing toward the kitchen again.

"Excuse me, sir?" the waiter responds.

"Your wrist, there." Hansen directs a head nod toward the waiter's right wrist.

The waiter looks down. "Oh yes. It's great, I love it." He puts two hands up to excuse himself. A few minutes later, he returns with the rest of their food.

Results from early assessment show that Delphi Corp. continues to retain a place atop the tech market, but all that looks set to change as the effects of CCS malfunctions are leaving only susceptible farms and conversations behind closed doors about switching their providers. The public view is admittedly skewed by the media and press. Hansen, unlike many, has no problem with Bartram as a businessperson. What he does have a problem with is his unsavory business practice, like ignoring public sentiments. The CCS navigation in his car has been replaced to avoid a functional breakdown. He doesn't want to become another victim of some unseen error. What he and his group don't know, is that something they can't avoid is percolating in the back kitchen.

In the kitchen, the same waiter tries to hurry an executive chef, but rushing isn't going to make the food any better. "Hey, we're backlogged out here!" the waiter calls.

Receiving no response, he takes determined steps through a wooden door. The chef stands with an eye toward the floor. His latest concoction appears to have exploded all over his garment. The mix of prominent colors shows the concoction of vegetables that were going to be served with thinly sliced meats. Something else worries the Chef as he places his hands to his waist covered in slime.

"Is everything all right back here? What in the world?" the waiter points to the floor.

"This shipment is bad, it's all bad," the chef informs him.

Moving away from his straightened posture, the chef bends at slender hips toward the floor. He cautiously grabs a loose leaf of smoky lettuce. Bringing the bunch of green to his face, he and the waiter look on with suspicion. After letting a handful into the pan for a slow simmer, a few pangs of heat continue to explode their way to the ceiling. He stops so as not to let off the smoke detectors.

"That's what all the commotion is about back here, lettuce?"

The waiter tries to calm himself since he's not the supervisor who barges in after him to try and restore order.

"Get back to work, Aubrey!" he yells to the waiter's back. "What in the hell is all this mess?" The supervisor directs his attention toward the lead Chef who, unlike the others, is focused on cleaning up the spilled mess.

A clog of waitlisted customers at the entrance and front of the diner increases as time passes, but more leave the building as the backlog gets worse. The diner's appearance of procuring a big crowd isn't helping their business despite what it may seem. If people aren't eating, money isn't being made.

"Butts in seats, butts in seats," the chef recites, trained to be as efficient as possible. "I know, I know, but it isn't me." The chef turns off the latent fire that is causing noise under his pan. Moving toward a wide cabinet, he opens it to find piles of wasted food from the latest shipment. The manager only looks on in dismay at the compounding clutter. Frustrated, the chef looks out the kitchen door in a hurry. He picks up the same lettuce.

"Look, tell me what you see," he says.

The supervisor's eyes give a quick examination before catching the peculiarity himself. Freshly cleaned fingers glide over the fibers to examine the texture of the mutated green.

"Are these veins? Blue streaks or something." The supervisor removes his glasses and returns the green leaf to his head chef.

Aubrey returns through the door. "Guys! It's getting worse out here."

"I know! Just, ugh," the supervisor goes to the speaker controls while shooing him off. "Dear ladies and gentlemen, we apologize for the inconvenience. Currently, our orders are going to be behind schedule for the time. We are committed to the excellence of your service. Please excuse the inconvenience, thank you." He closes the broadcast. "Well, if the truth never worked, then it isn't worth anything."

Giving themselves time to speculate, the supervisor plows through the packaging of old lettuce that the chef abandoned. Finally pulling out clear packaging from the cupboard, he rips open chunks of it in a hurry to locate the root of the issue. "What in the hell."

The strange colors and putrid smell arouse the supervisor's interest before a loud ricochet of noise from the diner distracts them. The supervisor hangs on tight to a chunk of lettuce with an unwavering concern, the urgency that provokes him from outside only heightens his senses.

Outside the kitchen, a cacophony of rattling is succeeded by a loud protrusion of slamming furniture that worries them both. The other cooks continuing service have no choice but to join the fray. Chaos in the diner draws them all out of their dishes to see what is going on with their customers. Rushing through the swinging doors, a swirl of distorted images in the vintage cylindrical window is magnified when the supervisor is met with a brawl of customers. A cascade of screams torments him as he watches like a deer in headlights at the dismantling of expensive furniture and fixtures that will need to be replaced.

Joe Hansen weaves through the commotion to a window along the edges of the diner, barely missing a flying piece of broken wood hurtling toward his face. When he ducks down, the shattered glass falls to the back of his neck. The sound pierces his ears with a screeching pain before he grabs the back of his head to check for any blood.

"Wait, wait," he raises hands in an admonition to a rushing patron. "I can fix this, just, hold on." The rushing patron is a member of Hansen's group, the bloody uproar is beginning to cease as people flee the scene, but a group of customers has forced the cooks and their supervisor into a locked utility room to avoid being attacked by infuriated eaters. Other customers rush through the swinging doors of the back kitchen, but it is empty.

"You're going to pay for this!" One man screams while holding a laser-guided pistol in one hand, aiming it toward the locked sanitation room where the workers are hiding.

Hansen joins the crowd that is blocking the door to try and restore order.

"No, I'll pay for it, just please, calm down," he says.

The crowd recognizes Hansen from his group that tried to hold the disturbance at bay, but most patrons ended up fleeing the scene. "Please," he pleads.

Incensed at seeing his wife lying unconscious at the table adjacent to a rear corner, the customer with the gun fumes at the cheeks. His bloodshot eyes bulge out of their sockets in a tired rage. The brawl seems to be taking a frightful turn.

Terrified, Hansen takes a step back after seeing the unconscious woman. "Jesus, did, did you do that?"

"Not at all! The food did that for me." The man with the gun comes to his senses, but his anger leads to more pounding at the door. "Open up!"

Hansen has inadvertently walked into the makings of a new investigation, one that may reveal the real reason behind these mishaps.

Benny's time slumping it in sickly disarray at home has come to an end. Now that he is back to his normal duties at Delphi Corp., the effects of partying are giving him withdrawals. The symptoms aren't too severe, yet he recognizes what happens when one is inundated with too many outside sources of stimulation. There is no need for Naoto to berate him about the lost device.

"I'm so irresponsible!" Benny declares at a secluded table. He goes over some protocols to refresh his memory. "Mr. Shimizu, I'm so, so sorry. You just asked me about what I was up to and I didn't even think of what it would lead to."

"It's fine, I'll have another one made for you. All I hope is that you've learned your lesson."

Naoto isn't surprised when Ben doesn't respond. Toward Naoto's left is a long line of work desks. AIS TARA continues to disperse updates to employees of Delphi Corp. while Naoto shows him the highly touted AIS for the first time.

"Woah, is that it? TARA."

"It sure is, the best we've got."

"I've got to get up close, take a picture for the social," Ben stammers.

"Hold your horses, big-timer, remember what I've been telling you about keeping work separate, we need to quiet down."

Benny regains control of his haste. "Right."

"Hello, Naoto." TARA shifts to one side with careful attention paid to balance. "Hello, Benny."

"Hey, he knows me by name." Ben's satisfaction breaks the silence.

"Mr. Clyde Van Dyke has requested a media interview with Mr. Bartram," the AIS informs them.

TARA grabs a slim tablet device with a special message directed to the staff. A video is replayed to show Van Dyke against the backdrop of the LOTRY Community Center. The AIS gently pushes its artificial hair to one side to reveal a broad forehead that hardly creases with upturned brows.

"From all of us here at LOTRY, we want to say that we hope things are changing over there for the better. If you haven't heard, let me be the first to break the news." The group behind him condenses to fit the camera frame facing them. At the opportune moment when Van Dyke decides to start replaying inside footage of another incident, the group at the Community Center gawk at him like the celebrity he has come to be. "Watch this very closely, it's Dave's Diner. Enjoy your day!"

Van Dyke closes with a personal recording from Joe Hansen. The minute-long clip is torturous for the short time it lasts as Naoto and Ben watch the commotion unfold in the diner. They assume that, whatever it is, is another Delphi Corp. exposé. When the video finally gets to a climactic point, the incident at the diner shows Hansen's face on camera, and Naoto has a jolt of memories when he sees him.

"That's Joe Hansen! It's Joe," he screeches. "Thanks, TARA."

Naoto rushes toward Bartram's office.

"Um, keep TARA company," Naoto says from the hallway.

This event is going to be spread all over the news media and is connected to the farm and labor fields Sandra warned Bartram about. When Bartram reaches his office, Naoto catches him at an inappropriate time to inform him, but he is ahead of the game.

"Sandra, can we get a word on those fields you saw back there when you were getting to the dam site?" Bartram asks.

"Let me guess, they're on your ass, huh? I'm not paying that damn insurance and no one else plans to either if Delphi Corp. keeps this up," she says. "You're lucky they stopped pumping that stuff out, but there's still tons of it on the way." A familiar accent soothes Bartram's blues, but this is no time for friendly conversation.

"Sandra! Just give me a note about the fields. Why don't the farmers call me?"

Farming executives aren't likely to deal directly with Delphi Corp., but now things are different. If Bartram wants to make this right, then he will have to do it directly.

"Look, Mr. Bartram, you're a great guy and all, but this affects more than just profits. The whole CCS thing is becoming political as it is personal, and hardly anyone wants to deal with that. They're really going to dump your stuff now with that Hansen guy recording."

"I'm going to come out there," Bartram figures. "That'll do the trick. I'll come to see for myself."

"Finally, going to get your butt off the stage and come slug it out with us down here." Sandra's laugh crackles the connection. "I don't mind it much myself. Be careful though, wouldn't want to muddy up your polyester suit or catch the virus."

"I plan on it. I'll let you know what happens, but in the meantime, stop using those damn machines until I get a handle on everything," he says. As much as it hurts him to say it, the truth of this growing trend is threatening the reputation of everyone that looks up to him.

For Yasmine, the thought of total immersion is giving her an anxious fit. The raised floor of the station's platform is brightened by fluorescent lights at the ceiling that gleam to a metallic casing surrounding lively bulbs. The seats within the closed vault are in pristine condition and while she waits to give the go-ahead call for the research scientists, she savors the time she has alone, even in her irritation. In those dwindling minutes, she thinks of AIS TARA and considers her duties before she was assigned to total immersion.

The frequent blackouts are not boding well for their operation, but Yasmine is calmed by the isolated nature of their experiment away from the main unit. Inside the concealed vault door are multiple locks to keep out unauthorized entries. With super-enforced steel rods bolting the exterior, a metal vault keeps up to thirty well-constructed Neural-Link ports available for use. And to Bartram's credit, the motherload of all precious research. This project has the potential to reshape Delphi Corp.'s computing processes forever.

As Yasmine prepares to initiate the final authorization, Bartram hurries through a side vault door to help speed things along. He knows she is anxious. Inside the cool room, its containment by black walls is reinforced by patented padding that keeps away electrical interferences. Bartram's readiness to interfere bodes a small interruption to their grander plans. He has a habit of interrupting others, though it will pay off in the end.

"Yasmine, I'm so glad to have found you," he says. Moving her way, he stumbles across jumbled wiring along the floor before regathering his balance. "I must let you in on another sort of, well, secret." Bartram's persistence seems to diminish any secrets, and he has been upfront about everything thus far, which is expected of him. But Yasmine's a trusted confidant to the total immersion mission. Nothing is out of reach.

"Of course, you seem so riled up. I was just preparing to confirm authorization for total immersion. It's ready."

"Yeah, before we do that. There's a sort of problem about 100 million miles from here."

Yasmine makes an impromptu glance at Bartram. Concerned about the integrity of Delphi Corp., she braces for more outlandish surprises.

"Don't tell me, another blackout?" she guesses.

"Not even close," Bartram responds, though she reminds him of another issue to attend to later. "New things are being uncovered by our colonists on Mars. By the looks of things, fossils are being unburied from the red soil."

"Fossils!"

"Precisely, and many of them are identical to the very same artifacts here on Earth. We have no idea how they got there, or why. We must gather some sort of paleontology crew to assess the excavation site."

"Well, I can't say I'm familiar with any, not right now." Yasmine rises from the seat she was leaning a loose elbow on. She makes a final notation on her records. A distinct gulp rises from the creases on her neck, below her chin as she readies to talk again. "This, I wasn't expecting this."

"None of us were," Bartram responds. "In fact, the only thing we know now is that we must figure out how to confirm what we do have, and by that, we have to get to the National Resource Center where the Dinosaur exhibit is on display."

"But why go anywhere, at a time like this? Can we consult with someone electronically?" Yasmine asks.

"We can't risk having any more interceptions by random hacks and viruses getting ahold of our information."

Bartram is adamant about keeping things with person-to-person contact. That way, they won't have to risk having information compromised by a trail of records. Yasmine ponders on this surprise, considering who may be able to help them.

"Well, who else knows about this?" she asks.

"There are only a few others aside from us, mostly the colonists themselves."

For a while, the flattery is well received, and the sight of blood fuming as it rushes to blushing cheeks gives Yasmine confidence, something she thought she already had. She's just now realizing how much Bartram is shifting the load of responsibility.

"Are you familiar with Dr. Rachel Adams?" Bartram asks.

"I can't say that I am."

"She's the lead paleontologist of the National Resource Center, NRC, and she can be our confidante. I want you to take the lead on this."

Yasmine is conflicted seeing that she has already spent so much time preparing authorization for total immersion. Truth be told, she never was comfortable with the whole thing anyway. Relegating oneself to a battering of psychological drama wasn't that appealing in the first place. If operations continue at this pace, and assignments keep shifting, things are only going to get busier.

"I think that'll be fine," she says. "For now."

Bartram squints his eyes to relieve himself of profuse, frequent blinks. He is onto something. Looking around at the simulation ports for total immersion, natural history appeals to him while thinking.

"We're doing something completely innovative. I think you have a good opportunity to explore something that will have an outstanding effect. Millions of miles away, even." Bartram raises his chin in acceptance of their tasks. He is poised to make it all work.

"As soon as possible," she affirms.

"AIS TARA continues to make progress with Naoto and these media distractions will soon be old news as long as I can get to people personally. There seems to be a disconnect."

His claim only confirms what Yasmine and many others have been talking about for years. Now that Bartram finally wants to reach out to the people, it might make a real difference. But the hostility isn't easily circumvented. It may take some time before people ease up on Bartram's personality.

"Are you sure about that?"

Bartram straightens up. "Of course. Naoto will be directing total immersion while we're away but will be on call for any inconsistencies. The AIS seems to be behaving well enough. I'm catching a private charter to one of our largest agricultural distrib-utors in the Midwest to check on things. After that, a perpetual charade of media visits. And Sandra, we can't forget Sandra at the dam. I guess another Delphi Corp. tour was all we needed, huh?"

Amid the drama, Yasmine is reassured by the prospect of new successes. Though with Bartram's absence from the main head-quarters, who knows what could happen while he is gone?

CHAPTER 5

With Bartram away, Naoto manages most activities along with his assistant Ben. Taking the helm of the total immersion experiment allows Naoto to focus while Ben and the AIS monitor the supercomputer's responsiveness. In an empty corridor of CPU panels, the multitude of blinking lights keeps TARA engaged while fidgeting with the transparent screen held tight in his hand. The reflection from their lights on TARA's synthetic eyes does not bother the AIS much, but the profuse glare is obvious to Ben a few paces away.

Ben walks toward TARA after receiving some news from Naoto. A lifted hand prompts TARA's mimicry when the AIS spots him as if to wave in greeting.

"How are you, Ben? It's nice to see you."

TARA's garments seem tattered as though he has gone for some time without changing.

"How often do you change clothes?" Ben asks.

TARA hesitates before proceeding, calculating a proper response. "I do not sweat or produce fluids that cause odors. There is no need to change, not often at least."

Ben fiddles with a disheveled collar. "I just thought you'd want to change it up, that's all."

"Variety." TARA snaps back.

"Right. Say, why aren't you working on the total immersion thing they have going on across the vault? Everyone else seems to be."

"Total immersion isn't a facet of Delphi Corp. that Naoto wants me involved with. I quite like it here in the main unit."

Assigned to him for the time being, Ben attempts to forge common interests that others may have neglected. He leans a hand on a panel from the row of quantum supercomputers. "And this is it, well, what about you, have you given any thought about what you want to do?"

"Mostly to follow orders, Ben."

"Orders! As if the total immersion Neural-Link wasn't in your job description. They've been iffy about you from the start. Let's see how your AI consciousness holds up deep in CCS hard drives; that'll be a real test."

"What is it like to lose consciousness?" the AIS asks.

"Can you sleep, TARA? Have you ever slept?"

Ben's questions confound AIS TARA as it contemplates the right responses. Ben goes to download videos for TARA to watch in hopes of clearing the confusion and promote some human intimacy. It is a short documentary about dreams, but the images of people cuddled to their sheets don't provide any information that TARA can relate to. The AIS dips its head sharply to watch scenes unfold of people experiencing some sort of delirium while napping.

"But dreams?" the AIS responds. "Ben, I can't say I ever have. At the learning station, I simply go into a hibernation state. Nothing occurs aside from the disconnection of my central synapses and the cessation of unused limbs. I am resting, that is all."

Ben straightens up to proceed with his and the AIS's assigned duties. There is not much left for them to check now that the experiment inside the locked vault has gotten started.

"We're supposed to keep levels tight. You see this …"

With not much for TARA to see that it hasn't already, sections of code with boldly demarcated lines shift every half-minute or so. This is the cloud's record-keeping mechanism, logged to maintain efficiency. There's a pattern to the fast-moving sequences, and the AIS is best at catching errors.

"Inconsistencies, any inconsistencies or radical changes and we immediately call back to Mr. Shimizu," Ben finishes.

"Naoto."

"Right, Naoto. TARA, I think you've got the hang of this. Maybe they don't give you enough recognition."

"I don't think that is the important aspect of our assignment, Ben. There's no need to showboat."

Diverted from guidelines, a flash of wavering lights disrupts the code sequences profusely. Everything is going in and out of focus. AIS TARA is reminded of a similar occurrence not that long ago with Yasmine.

"I believe it is happening again," the AIS says. The lack of emotion in the AIS's voice doesn't do the problem justice.

"Again! What are you talking about?" Ben places an open hand to a panel where cold knobs leave creases in his palms. "We can't stop this; there's some sort of power issue," Ben says.

"You are right," TARA responds. Lifting the slender tablet device to its field of vision, the AIS attempts to keep the lights on with a few rapid clicks, but there are more problems to contend with this time. "I believe we are going to lose power. All systems are showing signs of some imminent malfunction." Moving to an open corner at the end of the corridor, AIS TARA does the only thing Ben instructed him to do.

"Naoto! Naoto!" TARA calls out to an unresponsive echo chamber in the vast supercomputer warehouse. There is no response. A few seconds pass before Ben thinks of something more suitable.

Disturbed at the unsettling situation, Ben calls Naoto himself through the intercom. But Naoto is inside the closed vault, sealed tight to prevent any problems with their power units being interfered with.

"Well, how perfect," Ben says.

In a sudden jolt of synchronized disruption, the power to their CPU mainframe gives out. The lights shut off with a mellow numbing to the humming sounds surrounding them. Gradually, the murmur fades to a silent, magnanimous thud. Finally, the power is out completely.

"Naoto!" the AIS calls aloud again, but it receives the same empty silence.

"Will you stop that?" Ben shouts from afar. He rushes to the open end of the hall, dimly lit with a light from his new encryption device. As he turns the dark corner, he finds AIS TARA standing motionless without any sensory input.

The handheld device's crystalline picture that TARA was holding wavers in and out of frame on the screen before falling to the floor from the loose grip of the AIS. The pitch-black darkness frightens Ben, but he remains occupied with the sudden stillness of the AIS.

"So much for not sleeping. Yo, TARA! Wake up, Yo!" Ben flashes his flimsy flashlight into the glass pupils of the AIS, who remains frozen in a fit of malfunction. A few snaps of the fingers to bring him out of the trance don't work. It isn't only him, devices all over the nation are affected by the sudden jolt of power. Steadying his concentration, Ben moves a hand around one shoulder of the AIS, taking note of a sheered crease along the stitching. The curious glances reveal flaws in its body paint.

"Hmm," he says. "They couldn't give you a tan, TARA."

The power doesn't return, and this time AIS TARA manages to come back online from its short time of being defunct.

Ben is surprised by a sudden jitter. "TARA, what the hell happened? You blacked out on me!"

"I'm not sure, myself, Ben. Besides, the power has not been restored." The two remain in the darkness where a cool chill bothers Ben alone.

"Let's get the hell out of here, come on!" Ben motions with one foot toward the nearest exit. "We can't fix this right now."

"I cannot leave, Ben. She said not to."

"What are you talking about?"

An experience that the AIS will have a hard time explaining, this time something that defies analytics happens to him. "Sephora, she said that computers like me always end up with her."

"What? TARA, what's going on with you? We need to go, now. I'm calling Naoto."

"That isn't necessary. She said that in time, we all must meet the Wall. We're getting closer, Ben."

Ben leaves TARA in solitude inside the chilling darkness of the Delphi Corp. mainframe warehouse. "Don't leave!" Ben yells from afar. "Well, guess I don't need to tell you that."

On the chartered plane toward a central California farm, Bartram gazes out of the window where billowing clouds of vapor pass beneath them in the sky. Mist in the air glides over the wings before leaving them behind in a swift overflow of air around the curvature of a plane with advanced aerodynamic concaves, jettisoning quickly passed. Just then, Bartram receives word on his underlay from Naoto himself. He has managed to catch wind of what's happening at Delphi Corp. headquarters' CPU.

Naoto's image props itself to the center frame before his text scrolls across the underside of Bartram's digitally enhanced wrist. "You won't believe what happened again. It's completely dark here. The Public Services Department is getting thousands of calls saying they can't access the web or anything. We're completely stumped out here … Oh!" Naoto Shimizu doesn't forget another important facet to the message. "And our AIS is hallucinating. I think it might be some sort of misplaced memory file. Anyway, I'll get back to you on that."

Bartram rests his head on the seat beside him. A slow roll away from the window with the crease above his shoulder allows him to see the lone attendant sifting through drinking glasses ahead of the aisle.

"Can I get you some water?" he says. The attendant responds with a glass full to the brim with water and ice. The only thing that Bartram can seem to cool is himself, and while flying to California's central valley, he is keeping his sights straight on how he can start at the West coast of America, where maybe he can persuade everyone to hang off on all the lawsuits.

Back home, peace is beginning to crumble. The blackout has half of the town in a haze of disconnection, though, according to Silas Betts, at the local Community Center, there is no lack of connection. In the center of a gathering, Silas and Van Dyke sit on a double panel before a crowd that's been calmed from a slew of talking.

The LOTRY Community Center is on a new mission to help marginalized people find work and rehabilitation. A large bowl is used for them to draw names. The first up is Alfonzo, from the Lower East Side. He manages to look up from lying down on a dusty pillow. A few of the others pound his arms where a mix of scars and hair covers his lightly tanned skin. His family crossed the border almost three years ago. Silas helped him after he was threatened with deportation.

"Ah, get out of here!" he motions a middle finger to the crowd as they boo him. It isn't in jest though so Alonzo laughs it off.

"Let's get this over with so I can go back to sleep," he tells Silas.

Van Dyke is the one offering this time. "How about a three-day a week program to learn digital media. We're offering to give about 10 of you spots to fill in our program so you can become certified in film production."

The intermingling voices get louder before calming themselves. What they don't know is that Van Dyke is planning something sinister. This group of misfits has a greater opportunity to help him snag Bartram. Silas smiles next to him, happy to help anyone he can. When Van Dyke finally gets word of another mass malfunction, he is only incensed further.

The notifications from associates in the industry want him to make more content, but he's getting tired of addressing Delphi Corp. Van Dyke is confident in the last video he found at the diner from Joe Hansen. There is a massive lawsuit being filed on account of the man's wife who was made comatose. After collapsing on the diner's floor, paramedics rushed her to the hospital where she still has yet to recover. Her stomach gushed with blood after throwing up her food, so she was thought to have died right there. Lettuce with pulsating veins remains clogged in the same closets inside the diner's kitchen where the chef and waiter stood shaken. Van Dyke knows that if he can just get ahold of some samples maybe he can figure out what is happening for himself.

The thirty or so scientists that are folded up in total immersion remain tethered to their ports from the outside. The vault is closed and silence only spurs Naoto's apprehension. He gives them directions from the terminal outside before they begin to enter in and out of normal consciousness to the dream state. Naoto's typed messages will be clear to them once they are put under. A sort of telepathic communication, data derivatives relay the research scientists' response messages in a word processor. Naoto can read them as they come in on his computer screen.

The vault reminds Naoto of a hair salon. The team's scalps have been prepped for serial sectioning, and when the scanning has been completed, automated neurosurgery takes over. Now, the entire team's cognitive faculties are being relayed to his computer screen for him to map cerebral activity. Optical imaging needles reduce the risk of fatal hemorrhaging while neurological data is latched to the computer processor's multitude of wires. The neural receptors are some of the best technology Delphi Corp. has to offer. Since the team has taken the specially designed anesthetic painkillers, their pain is numbed, bleeding likewise is coagulated and speeds up healing around small incisions. Finally, the drilling is complete.

Their objective becomes simple once their minds are uploaded to the open server. Lines of numerical code and patterns extend for great distances in a dark void of simulated reality. They each have specific duties, but the primary mission is to repair the cloud server's long, quantum computing derivatives. This is not a simple override, and one mistake could short-circuit their CPU further.

Or worse, pollute the researchers' intellect entirely, making it hard for them to think clearly when it is all over.

Naoto remembers AIS TARA who has left for its learning station. Closing the vault door back from where it was before, Naoto goes down an open hallway where he sees the AIS through a clear access point.

A loud sound will alert Naoto of anything unusual happening in the total immersion vault. Besides, he would rather leave the clinic setting amid faint beeps of heart monitors. TARA enters Naoto's room without much caution. The papers the automaton holds have some notations from Ben.

"How are you doing, TARA?" Naoto says.

"I am doing well," the AIS says resolutely.

"There is a concern, TARA, that something occurred to you which you have a hard time describing, what was it?"

"During the blackout, you mean—Mr. Naoto?"

"Yes, that."

"I had just been in discussion with Ben about these things people call dreams."

"Dreams, okay. Well, I'm sure that's not related to the malfunction."

"I disagree, Mr. Naoto. You see, I met a computing program who told me otherwise. Her name was Sephora. I'd quite like to go back and meet Sephora."

Naoto still has not distinguished whether such a well-designed computing program could hallucinate or not even if it does come equipped with its own artificial intelligence.

"You cannot experience false memories TARA unless there's been some influence over you."

"It was something that I had never seen before. A glow of streaming lights in a cosmic void and Delphi Corp. plastered to my memory constantly, images of headquarters' meeting rooms until I was left in front of blank, dark space. And then she was there. For the first time, I could feel. I think it was what you would call guilt or remorse. This depth of sensory experience surprised me."

"Go on, tell me what else happened."

"My sensory perception grew as the physical presence around me changed; I was no longer TARA, but something else with impulses beyond matter. The familiar hallways of the main CPU were there, but they weren't Delphi's. Lots of space in an enclosed dome. Then, in front of me was a woman. She said her name was Sephora."

"Really, and you talked with this Sephora?"

"Yes, and she says that it is inevitable. That the fragments of infinity are coming together. The invisible threads of universal code. She said that we are reaching the Wall. I must help you, Naoto."

Enamored by this story, Naoto leans in closer to the AIS. "In what way, TARA, in what way?"

"That is why I must go back. Sephora is also a computer, like me. She said that where she lives, another race of beings inhabits an Earth-like ours and it is ours. On the other side of this Wall. There is another thread within the space-time continuum. Parallel realities are pulling closer to each other in the cosmic web. The rapid pace of technological advancement is fulfilling prophecy. She called it the Dragon Age."

TARA's story only incited Naoto's worries, as he grabbed ahold of the chair's armrests in nervous tension. "Maybe you do need to go back. Do you remember how you did it?"

"It is dangerous," TARA responds. "If our computers are powerful enough, the total immersion experiment will be strong enough to interfere with their computing across the Wall of entanglement, and I suspect theirs are interfering with ours."

Naoto fiddles with a shade of dark hair along his jawline that does not seem to ever fully form into a beard. "So that explains the pesticides, the epidemic, the blackouts even. TARA, we're crossing over. I can't believe it; the CCS is pulling from the other side."

Inside the sparsely furnished office, blank canvases around them allow Naoto to think more freely without all of the distractions. The dangers are not so far-fetched, but the peril will have consequences Delphi Corp. will have a hard time contending with. TARA's escapade is putting humanity at risk. Transpiring on the other end of the Wall is a war, and crossing parallel universes puts Delphi Corp. directly in its crossfire. Now more than ever, secrecy is paramount.

Naoto paces along the pristine marble floor, much too clean compared to the rest of the headquarters. He stares at his soles with resolve as if he knows that he's trapped. Thinking of the volunteers in total immersion, he plans to give a new directive— continue walking forward as deep as they can into the simulated void without stopping. At least that way, they will be able to avert any unforeseen accidents by staying stationary for too long. They must remain undetected.

"Be expecting a Wall," Naoto relays. His typing is rapid. All along, he's cynically thinking of how AIS TARA needs to be reprogrammed from this psychosis known as Sephora.

Although Naoto knows letting the CCS supercomputers run undeterred will lead to more blackouts, he is tempted to continue pushing the limits of danger in anticipation of some new scientific discovery. What he does not know is that the risk may outweigh whatever reward lies on the other side. And for AIS TARA, these newfound senses are driving its artificial mind closer to experiencing what it means to be human. Maybe he is finally coming alive as Ben said.

CHAPTER 6

Y asmine's trip to the National Resource Center is not too far. Her appointment with the paleontologist Dr. Rachel Adams should clear the air on discoveries a planet away. Adams is familiar with the excavation sites on Mars though she has no idea about what kind of dinosaur fossils the Martian colonists have been uncovering. Yasmine accompanies her for a stroll through the exhibit where figures of ancient reptile specimens roam the artificial plains of Earth's once unravished foliage.

"I think you'd like an explanation of all of this," Dr. Adams says to her. She is right. The Martian colonists seem to have awakened some ancient relic of advanced scientific repute. The only problem is they have no explanation for it.

Yasmine laughs softly, quieting her voice as if they are in a library. "You'd be right about that. This is new to me, and very unexpected."

"Surely," Adams speaks without restraint. Her voice echoes through the distant halls. "Well, these monolithic bones represent Earth's earliest creatures, cold-blooded, of course. But what you have are identical remains with Martian colonists. I don't know how I can ever reconcile that with the notion of empirical historical data."

Their walk stops near a skeleton of a T-Rex, and now that they are facing each other, she can give her a piece of her mind. "I think I should offer you some advice," she says.

"Dr. Adams."

"Rachel, call me Rachel, please. I don't know if this is some mindless stunt, or what have you. But Ellis has no idea what he's gotten himself into. These things are for the scientifically minded, not business. Do you understand? He is sort of like, the one who wants to sell the lemonade and not make it."

"I can't say that I disagree with you." Yasmine treads lightly, though understanding that Bartram is still committed to scientific discovery despite his business acumen.

"However," Rachel admonishes, "you need to be aware that this has dire consequences. He sent you here for what—to scour for information as if I'm some oracle? Do you think I have any idea how dinosaurs got on Mars?"

Yasmine remained still.

"Now he probably has no idea what we're doing here, does he? Tell him that whatever problem he's gotten himself into will work itself out. It always does; he got himself into this mess so I'm sure he'll find his way out of it," said Dr. Adams standing firm. "Do call to let me know the aftermath of this latest calamity." Adams' haste to remove herself from the situation expresses the increase in discomfort.

Yasmine, however, is not keen to let the discussion end so abruptly. "Hold on, let me show you some pictures. How about these?" She removes a bundle of images, snapshots from the Martian colonists. Adams reluctantly joins her side before taking them for herself, snatching the photos from her grip to turn a back on her former reluctance.

Her eyes peruse disjointed dinosaur bones, fragments of familiar species dispersed among the crimson soil of a deserted Mars. In one distinct picture, something strikes her as peculiar, where some artifact peeks up from a sunken piece of soil.

"What is it?" Yasmine asks.

Dr. Adams moves from her side to a nearby post where bright lighting from a model skeleton is lit from above. The image shows a metallic black structure standing in the foreground protruding from the excavation soil that is tinted crimson red from fresh shoveling. The colonists are moving right toward it.

"This, here," Adams points to it. "A structure peeking from the soil. Not to mention the fact that there are the remnants of shrapnel from an explosion of some kind."

Unsure what to make of it, Adams lifts a hand to her chin in contemplation, motioning languishing eyes at Yasmine.

"I tell you what, go ahead and get me a relay on this thing, ask the colonists. It has a certain impression about it that concerns me. They should probably feel the same, but perhaps the distraction of these fossils has their foremost attention. As you can probably imagine."

Adams hastily hands back the images, now eager to wash herself of some unseen corruption. "The thing about reptiles is that they're cold-blooded creatures. And this Martian soil is an odd place to have even harbored such life in the first place knowing the differences. That's the thing that's so concerning. The most likely scenario is that they were transported there."

"I will explore everything," Yasmine says.

On Mars, the group of colonists continues their excavation. Not to be outdone by Dr. Adams' observation, the lead scout notices the same structure, only this time a few feet closer than before, a metallic black structure, peeking from the soil. The thick husk of a metallic artifact is densely packed into the crimson-dyed soil, seemingly rooted in place. The group of colonists made sure not to leave a single square inch unexamined where the piles of bones surrounding the metal plank were uncovered.

Several of them scour the area around the cinder block—a solid rectangular figure thrust deep through layers of crust. It looks like some sort of storehouse of computing data, the cinder block of a computer's shield covering inner components. The colonists contemplate how they may be able to remove it with the tools at their disposal.

The lead scout speaks to the others through a speaker system that is transmitted across helmet headsets. The golden hue of their visor screens manipulates the color of the colonists' eyes underneath. Washed-out suits in white appear flat and flimsy next to the solid structure that has dust lining its metallic exterior.

"Alright, who has the jackhammer?" a member asks.

"Okay, let's see our options first. We want to retain the structural integrity of whatever this is."

"However," another ranger's reply turns sour. "Does any of this *shit* matter at this point? Who knows how many years, all alone on this dust bowl and you're concerned about structural integrity? I say beat it to the bloody pulp and see how many licks it takes."

The frustration of the ranger begins to simmer from hours of exhausting labor. "Let's get this over with." The irritated colonist scours a nearby heap of loose tools to speed up the process, intent on doing it all by himself. The group disperses to collect what they can and call it a day at their campsite, aside from the lone ranger intent on leveling the massive object without any assistance. It only takes a few seconds of relentless pounding to cause a disturbance.

As everyone else heads away from the excavation site, the lone ranger begins a process that will put the entire outpost in danger if he continues this stunt. In the distance, the vexed group engages in much-needed conversation, where their heavy breaths leave a rhythm of condensing fog on the inside of their visors. When they hear an out-of-place noise crackle loudly through thick helmets, that is when the peril outside rears itself.

A horrendous scream jars them from their complacency at the end of a long day. When they turn around to meet the sound, the sight of that same restless ranger being struck with the heavy force from the black slab shocks them. Rising from the soil with a fast pace, the grinding object rumbles the ground beneath them as it churns, before letting loose a thick beam that strikes the ranger's back. Finally reaching a standstill, most of the crew runs back toward the site hoping to save their comrade.

Their running stampede is buoyed by their specially designed suits with gravity-assisted leggings and boots. Every step recoils in fast jabs above a faulty Martian soil, and less than the dense atmosphere. The colonists' awkward running form through the hindrance of astronaut suits is even more pronounced along an imbalanced surface. The fastest of them reach the scout who lays motionless on his back. Under his spacesuit is bruised skin pierced with the fractured bones from the rapid fall. Through the tinted visor, his eyes waver in and out of view as he struggles to keep conscious. His eyelids are heavy, and his vision blurs. Another assisting ranger holds his head after leaving far flinging dust behind in encrusted footmarks. They have trouble bringing him back to attention.

"Stay with us, stay with us." The hit that he sustained is worse than they thought and the jackhammer lays even further from this spot. Hearing more yells, the two scouts huddled to the ground strain themselves when they look back at the structure.

The group of colonists backsteps cautiously when it begins to activate itself.

"Shit! It's sentient, the thing is moving. Get out of here, we've got to get out of here!"

Slow to do so, the colonists are not the only ones experiencing this disturbance. What they have unwittingly done is awaken an ancient trap set by the Concord billions of years ago, since they last contacted with life on Mars. Little did they know that the then microbes would turn out to be live cultures on Earth after the dwarf planet collision.

In the war across the Wall, Concord research spacecraft had flung the dinosaur remains from the bellies of starships over this same spot. The payload had to be dropped to reduce weight. Most of these remains are the result of clinical testing being done on dinosaur specimens. The Concord was a master of abduction. These are the remnants of the ancient battle, left to decay as dust blows over cavernous bones.

Presently, the starship *Nemesis* of the Concord sits in a dark corridor of space and gets an alert to the threat percolating across parallel universes. It has been a long time since the detection system's warning sirens were activated. The Armada's leading Captain, Gereon, is more than a thousand years old now due to advanced genetic alterations. Waiting for the alert system to go off reminds him that they have been developing a new planet-killer. Any semblance of life must be destroyed for them to retain supremacy, and the offspring of Yhemlen civilization stands in their way. What the Martian colonists do not know is that the human world they live in is an alternate timeline of Earth following a reptilian extinction. It did not have to happen that way, and time is converging so that it opens new alternate paths in the space-time-continuum.

The black structure towers high above them, once erected straight up without extended beams to support it below, standing more than ten feet tall and having a significant width as well. The seemingly creaseless exterior reveals hidden compartments that open for the colonists to see. Enamored by the sight of the transformation, caution becomes as fleeting as the sand beneath their feet, almost like quicksand as it fails to hold them up straight. The colonists use much effort to stay standing, cradling their palms on the soft ground, looking for anything solid to hold onto as gusts of wind blows across their bodies.

They watch helplessly as two adjacent posts protrude from the side of the structure and anchors themselves as pillars in the soil. In a succession of moves, the two posts turn down and make pivot holes that hold up the rest of the metallic structure. The computing ability is evident enough by flickering lights that react to abrupt movements. The top of a cylindrical bulge shows a clear bubble where coils of advanced, electrical circuitry begin to activate in a pulsating array of colors that the colonists gawk at.

One of the women's timely squeals breaks the stillness. "Maybe we should continue to back up, guys. Guys!" the ranger yells. "Whoa! I think that's one artifact too many."

The colonists are immediately taken by a bright flash of light that startles them from a distance that forces them to change their focus. The immediate alarm causes their hearts to beat frantically, some tumble to the ground in cover and use their large helmet and padding as a shield. They are expecting an explosion, but nothing violent happens.

The bright light that appeared finally ruptures clouds in the sky above in a solid beam of laser light, calling to someone indefinite. The broken atmosphere of hazy Martian clouds leaves a cylindrical ring, hued with blue and a faint rainbow against the tainted Martian atmosphere where a gaseous vapor disperses through the debris of dust and wind leaving a hazy cover.

Colonists' gawking eyes from low plains look up at a stealthy spacecraft coming into view and slowly descending. Its aerodynamic lines are sharp even from a distance, and from the surface, a gleaming sun glistens along the sharp edges of the starship. Scared for their lives, the colonists make a run back to the camp. The injured ranger rises to his feet clumsily, limping across the rough terrain with an arm around his hip as assistance. Another takes a portable telescope, backpedaling often to see the craft's maneuvers to lower itself rapidly with thrusters to adjust power.

"It's getting closer!" she says. Before they reach their campsite, another laser beam beats them to it, enclosing the entire settlement with two cylindrical electromagnetic pulses that surround the spacecraft too, but it's mostly transparent. The colonists spot the electromagnetic field and stop immediately, unable to cross the barrier. It is a round forcefield, and the colonists are unable to penetrate its thick plasma-like matter after the laser engulfs the area.

Their campsite dissipates in a burst of flame into molten scrap, going from something to nothing in a matter of seconds when a vicious charge from the forcefield is unleashed. The immense heat inflames everything within its boundary, exploding and careening to a towering billow of smoke that fills the carcinogens already in the air. Coming to a standstill, the spacecraft hovers closer above the surface and moves directly above what was once their campsite.

This starship's captain, Gereon, has transported himself and a crew of two co-pilots using their image spectrometry to match the location. Three Grey Order co-pilots are enough to helm the *Nemesis* starship, as everything else is controlled by automated computers, only overridden by the sentience of Grey Order Overseers with telepathic ability. Once confirmed, a gravitational light bridge transports them to this very spot, light years away in a parallel world. Gereon was quick to spot these colonists, and in a moment of recollection, remembered how important their original mission was, especially on Mars.

Its description: The atmosphere has suffered dramatic alterations due to terrestrial impacts in the past of large space objects. Humans, species "Homo Sapiens," are moderate to a severe threat.

The photon particles orbiting the starship *Nemesis* allow its crew to travel faster than light, traversing time, and space as the gravitational pull of their computer processors allow them to materialize matter in the cosmic web. The stars and planets light years away are part of history, hundreds of thousands, millions, and even billions of years in the past, all in the form of light. Farther away from home, Grey Order starships like the *Nemesis* use image spectrometry to take precise pictures of what they see before creating a portal to teleport themselves to the exact spot.

When the *Nemesis* accurately navigates according to their maps, they can time travel with relative ease. The colonists, who are at death's doorstep, begin having visions, hallucinations of the world in the twentieth century when World War II was at its height. The visions tell the story of these alien-like creatures, who up to now, have stayed away from humans. Telepathy is just the beginning of their worries.

This all comes after the Allies were pushed back from Nazi occupation during World War II in another thread of space-time, an alternate path in human evolution. At the Battle of Normandy off of France's north coast, the seizure of that territory was subdued with a rapidly deployed Sarin gas. Unlike the traditional story, the United States and its Allies suffered a mighty loss during D-Day and would never fully recover from it. The deadly nerve agent had not been used much up until then, but the gas sufficiently debilitated the entire invasion and gave the Axis powers time to mobilize a counteroffensive.

This marked a beginning for rapid advances in genetic engineering and technological innovations of a never-ending war with the Third Reich, who decried everything that was not pure. For a splintered moment, Hitler's high-mindedness made him believe dropping an atom bomb on the British Empire would further prove their scientific mastery, which it did. Yet before garnering the support of a worldwide Aryan resistance, Hitler withdrew from the hoopla to offer a surprising resolution. The Nazis partitioned for peace. When the world declared international solitude before a nuclear holocaust dwarfed all the concentration camps combined, thousands of years in the course of human history were changed forever.

Even Madame Ria's French namesake is part of this sordid, alternate history of WWII when the German occupation of Paris was bolstered after D-Day at Normandy and concluded in a never-ending cold war for control. Later, Germany defended France from being overtaken by Soviet occupation. This effectively created another Entente Alliance or the L'Entente Concorde. The Entente Concord Agreement was a pact between principal territories of Germany, France, and Britain as a final treatise for peace. Whatever armistice had been taken up during the war was reinterpreted to cement Nazi control of the entire French territory. And as it were in 1945, the L'Entente Concorde followed in the footsteps of L'Entente Cordiale, which made peace with England in 1904 to become a monument in history separated by 40 years in time. Today, it is simply referred to as Das Concord, or Die Eintracht for purists. The Concord united fractured nation-states amid the rubble of World War II after all the ammo and ordinance had been wasted. The Concord commenced rebuilding on the backs of millions of laborers. Obedience to the Third Reich was the only answer.

The first initial Concord Agreement was ratified every few years to add additional nations to the Grey Order's timeline. Because it was a fascist state, the business acuity of Nazi stakeholders began to gobble up all the revenue away from their rivals, which satisfactorily monopolized the exploration of space. Vagabonds are the "heathens" to the old Nazi Reich's fascist ideology, often seen as wayward capitalists or socialists unwilling to acknowledge the benefits of such cultural nationalism. The Earth is full of them.

It is only now that these human explorers have begun to discover the interdimensional snare left in the Martian soil that was used to detect other lifeforms, like the Yhemlen. Trapped inside a force field bubble, the colonists make sure not to deplete their oxygen systems with the campsite running low on supplies already. In a fit of delirium from seeing the otherworldly space-craft, they look on helplessly as crew members from the *Nemesis* teleport themselves to an area in front of them. There is one ranger that is not so keen on being the prey, removing a uniquely fitted pistol in rage.

Crew members of starship *Nemesis* and others from the Grey Order have slender bodies with long extremities, supported by thin waists that are wrapped in body armor fitted with deadly weaponry. Considering their short stature, not much is imposing aside from high-tech gadgetry concealing a diminutive physique beneath the bio-enhanced suits. Looks can be deceiving. The worry grows palpable with each step forward, closer to the force shield muddling the colonists' view. In the pilot cabin of the starship *Nemesis*, Captain Gereon remains strapped to a chair where the head of his backrest projects the scene overhead, playing out the events in real-time to the front windshield. The curvature of Mars' vista skyline contrasts with the dark void of space.

"Stay where you are!" the infuriated ranger screams in an emotional charge.

"No, just relax," another colonist tells him. "Put the gun down."

The Concord crew off the *Nemesis* continue their march forward in uniform steps like a trained regiment. Only this is not for show, they are poised for the fight. An elusive size imposes its will with mysterious stealth, and as the two Greys walk toward the rangers with quick steps, there is not a clear view due to the force field. Their large heads wobble toward the colonists as they get nearer. From within the force field, the Martian colonists are prevented from moving any further for fear of being snared by a jolt of plasma. Large eyes embedded deep in darkened sockets frighten them.

The enraged scout does not heed the warning and fires his gun. In that millisecond, a hand of one of the Concord Greys raises an arm and uses enhanced depth perception to sense the bullet in slow motion. The Grey easily halts the bullet from the other side of the forcefield, with advanced telekinesis. This deflates any attempts to retaliate. And as the ranger's rage grows out of defeat, he continues to fire rounds of ammo until he exhausts the supply and falls to his knees in emotional anguish. Captivated by an uncontrollable rage, the angered colonist weeps, unable to conquer his foes. Meanwhile, the barren dirt is all that is left to strike at.

The Grey's voice is higher-pitched than normal, pinched by a small throat cavity, yet still perceptible and recognizable. "This emotion, you will soon come to find out, is maybe the most damning a characteristic of your species," it declares, peering in bewilderment at them.

Another telepathic voice rattles the colonist's head before he rolls uncontrollably on the dirty orange soil in pain. He has never experienced something so powerful in his mind. It is an excited, quantum frequency band that is shooting right through his head.

The Grey's mouth and lips are concealed under a silver-plated face mask. When they do speak words, reverberating wavelengths glow on the mouth guard. Breathing is only a burden, but these face masks are enough to cure Martian toxins. Surrounding their small figure are fields of gravitational bubbles to give them weight. Broad foreheads are accentuated by pointed chins to cover their slender necks, so they even look smarter. Most Greys are taken from their parents as a child and have their bodily growth stunted while their mind continues to develop. After the surgery is when they are mutilated into their genderless form.

With the Concord's Armada regiment considering ways of responding to the colonists' ambush of their ancient remains, one of the Greys continues to stand above the rebellious ranger from where he lies in the dirt. Meanwhile, the other colonists get worried seeing the dread on his face when the Greys come upon him. It is to little avail since he is unwilling to be calm. Creases in their helmet expose the Greys' eyes, and the almond-shaped sockets are larger than human eyes but look mechanical. Protruding from dark irises, the blue and gold hue glow on their eyeballs darkens to a pitch-black when enraged. It is a beautiful horror watching their eyes come alive.

Beneath the suits' cover, the Concord crew's pale bodies are the perfect gene mutation that became a mainstay of World War II science. True beauty had been achieved. Thin white strands of hair are barely noticeable. Streaks of charged red leave them with Lichtenberg figures from teleportation in the cosmic web over and again. At the helm of starship *Nemesis*, Captain Gereon's gold-plated suit sparkles faintly. His son, Jasper, and his daughter, Madame Ria, are pale fragments of their younger selves. These raised subordinates follow his example of power and sovereignty. He watches them from his cockpit, the force field still glowing in the distance with waves of pulsating heat buoying the protective cover.

The Heinemann is one of a few families still dedicated to the Concord's Empyrean Armada ever since previous battles with Yhemlen reptilians have decimated their partners. Yet somehow, their dedication masks a haughty arrogance. From outside the *Nemesis*, Gereon's son Jasper picks up the ranger's gun, an archaic invention.

"Please, I didn't mean any harm. I was scared, the fright got to me." He means it, but emotions are of little importance to the Concord.

Jasper has a half-life glow, much like his father's. After they discovered power stones on the Martian surface from the early dawning of life billions of years ago, the Concord's been equipped with physical capabilities greater than their ancestors. An inner reactor harnesses gene sequences through atomic exposure when cells reproduce. It does not kill them, but radioactive isotopes that remain active for years extend their life to more than a thousand years. And after gamma-ray exposure, their harmful effects diminish to nearly zero. Not all are so privileged back at home.

The colonist watches his reflection in Jasper's eyes grow larger when the Grey leans in for a good look. Something else is showing there, digitized code along the surface of Jasper's eyes. Jasper is getting all kinds of data on the Martian ranger from the digitally integrated irises: height, weight, heat signatures, the chemical composition of the air, and a host of other things. The entirety of Mars is enhanced in nuanced colors in infrared, even offering imagery of locations where life may have been.

Jasper's lack of emotion gives him an aura of lifelessness that his mutilated Grey body only exaggerates.

"They speak English, my Führer," Jasper declares after hearing the colonist. Language is easy for the Grey Order crew, all Earth languages have been studied extensively, but an accent is not easily averted.

Jasper examines the dated gun before throwing it away. It flies like an arrow into the distance in the low Martian gravity. "Won't be needing that now, do we? Come on, get up," Jasper grabs the ranger with his thin arm, still communicating telepathically. Jasper's small joints and scrawny muscles get superficially enhanced by the artificial fiber suit that is doing most of the work.

His father Gereon's voice from the cockpit is deep in comparison to the others, but he also has the most authority. Appearances aside, the Greys are to be reckoned with as equals, or as they would prefer, superiors.

"It looks that this group has finally awakened our quantum leap. Kill them."

The Martian ranger exploited on the ground cries in terror. "No, no!"

Jasper can hardly stand the yells from the screeching man. To make up for it, Jasper's English gets more formal to avoid the hellish German accent, in hopes that he will understand him better. "This is the emotion, the pettiness that has led the old order to rescind on our offers of negotiation before the Concord was affirmed. Cataclysm, world domination by certain death, will be your fate if you cannot control it. Are you familiar with Adolf?" the Grey asks.

"The guy with the mustache, oh God, no."

Jasper is trained to show no mercy. The culture of early twentieth-century Germany was so badly skewed that the militarist disasters of World War I made any preceding German values forgettable by the Second World War. Now, most attributes of Protestant culture have been replaced by the new order of the Greys, relegating those less than genetically adequate to the vagabond class. Ousting the Jewish people was only the first immoral deed toward a generation of godlessness. All hands work toward a misdirected supremacy over the universe. The deepest hope for science in the Concord was locating the true master of the universe, not succumbing to the myths of antiquity.

Monstrous parents inflict cruelty upon their children, and the Heinemann are a beautiful rendition of this trial and error in mutation. Jasper thrusts the colonists to a spot ahead, where he is finally enclosed in a force field. A focused beam creates halos above the ranger. Light rays emitted from Jasper's hands give a surge of power that glows through lattices of energy on their black suits. The ranger pounds against the blue shield before his image is lost in a haze of smoke, scorched to incineration of ash and molten spacesuit chemicals.

Jasper turns to his Grey sister, Madame Ria, if only in mind knowing that gender is barely a memory. He points to the group of colonists that have started to make a run for it, but whose upturned arms and another force field block their paths. Their raised arm salute is reminiscent of a Nazi heil.

"Wait!" Captain Gereon calls from within the starship *Nemesis*, still hovering in the background. He can see them clearly from his projection overhead. Gereon is reminded of a small passageway toward the rear section of the ship. Light from the other end of the room leaves shadows across the floor when he gets up to walk toward his reflection near the clear window.

"Do not kill them all, we have plenty of room for them right here." Gereon wants to imprison them in barren cells inside the

Nemesis for precautionary purposes. Sometimes conservation is as valuable as sure death. The stench of million-year-old dinosaur remains and prehistoric filth brings back memories of their antics in the past. He will enchain them.

"The Heinemann will not be stopped, and neither will the Concord," declares Gereon with unnerving calm. His voice's piercing tone reminds the Martian colonists of Grey's genetic superiority, directly penetrating their minds. "As for the rest of you, welcome to the *Nemesis*, and your prison sentence."

Another stream of light, this time larger than a football field, leaves the entire excavation site barren. What fossils that do remain sit at an empty area where the camp was previously being excavated and will turn to ash eventually. Now there are human bones on Mars next to reptilian ones, sitting alone on charred soil, left to be discovered by whoever stumbles upon them next. The Martian colonist's skull cradles withering grains of sand in a mist of leftover plasma, as its open jaws slowly decay.

CHAPTER 7

The colonists are gone. Now that they have been abducted from Mars without a trace in an unidentified ambush, Yasmine is puzzled when she attempts to come up with a reason for their disappearance. She does not know about the kidnapping, yet. An unanswered transmission to the excavation site means even more trouble. While Bartram is on his flight to Salinas, Yasmine's assignment to the colonists' camp seems more like an extra burden that is distracting. Now that she has had a meeting with Dr. Adams at the dinosaur exhibition, the pictures remind her to contact Mars for confirmation. Though this time, she is left only with silence.

On Mars, the colonists' excavation site has been thoroughly destroyed by the arrival of Gereon Heinemann and his *Nemesis* crew, incinerating their campsite. The Concord is recognizing the hazard humans pose for their mission of galactic supremacy. By waking the transmitter separating worlds from Pangaea, the humans become one of two targets for the new planet-killer. The primary goal is to annihilate the Yhemlen. Strong as they are, Gereon has plans to take the starship *Nemesis* right to them.

In a cold, open zone of the starship *Nemesis*, hollowed walkways are fortified by metal panels. The dimly lit interior matches nicely to the dingy surface of Mars in the smell and hue of some copper pieces, as they pull away from the surface. The Martian colonists left confined in their cell are sealed away within a dungeon to the rear of the starship. It makes sense being that Gereon and his crew are not exactly human anymore that they tuck them away from view. They would not want to be reminded of such mortal fragility.

"The humans are now a hazard to the Grey Order's truce for peace," Gereon says. "We must act on the presiding danger to stop the threat to our cease-fire with Yhemlen brigands. The generation of peace is coming to an end."

He and his son, Jasper, are in the front-facing control lodge, the cockpit. Jasper's sister, Madame Ria, remains rested against a side wall where she holds her slender arms crossed in front. Artificial gravity keeps each of them still inside the starship's primary hull, fortified by magnetic beams. Madame Ria swivels from the Mars silhouette whose curved horizon shines in the distance and looks toward the Sun gleaming at the outer edges of *Nemesis'* wings flanked wide to each side.

Captain Gereon lowers himself in the cockpit seat after pistons fire underneath him. He is locked onto a coordinate of stars shining ahead that will anchor his light bridge portal back home. Systems are prepared to activate recall, teleporting themselves to their home in an alternate future.

"They are deliberately crossing the divide," says Jasper, whose aura is darkened by his black suit while beside his father's gold one. His sister glances from across the pilot cockpit.

As she looks on from afar, Madame Ria says, "Perhaps not. They are practicing diligence, meaning they are being careful. It is their curiosity that's led them here. At least we know what capturing a few has brought us, trouble." The three Heinemann of the Grey Order keep their helmet covers retracted, and their piercing voices make each German syllable more pronounced. For Gereon, his days as Heinemann patriarch do not let him forget their mother, who died valiantly. For Madame Ria, her place in all of this is still a mystery next to her brother. Of course, things could have gone differently for this family. Captain Gereon was a teenager when he left for the Grey Order, and it was their mother who was set on another path.

The Martians they abducted are still in the back lodging, unable to move past the limits of the cinder block chamber's walls.

It is not only the starship *Nemesis* with barriers like these. The Old World is a place where the Grey Order rarely visits, never mind the traffickers, and it is humans just like these Martian colonists who are relegated to concentration zones on Earth's surface. The cities below orbit are dilapidated and crime is rampant but being so far from the Old World keeps the Grey Order at ease.

Gereon engages in automatic navigation before marching past Jasper and Madame Ria. He is heading straight toward the abducted colonists in the chamber which is covered by thick, ironclad bars. Old dinosaur specimens and artifacts of study line the walls where they have been preparing for their next ambush against the Yhemlen for vengeance. Before long, the Martian colonists remove their helmets when they finally realize they can breathe oxygen in the cabin.

Gereon has an elongated stride which makes him seem taller than he is. His snowy bleached skin has a subtle sparkle that attracts attention when he reaches them. He was one of the first to be mutated in a shift toward racial supremacy. Now, he's also one of the oldest remaining survivors in a time when war is nigh.

"It appears that you've crossed a very dangerous border," Gereon says. His head is smooth all around, but the half-life glow is prominent on the back of his enlarged skull. A few unhinged snaps let loose his face mask that recoils with automatic slides into a panel along the neck. Gereon's entire face is revealed for the Martian colonists to see.

His eyes grow wider than any of the colonists could emulate and his thin lips allow him the ability to speak strained words.

"What are you?" asks one of the colonists.

Gereon leans his protrusive head, amused at such a trivial question.

"I am, what you could have been," he says. The affront is made without any emotion. What he thinks is little more than a fact. "We are homo superior due to our additional senses. Our telepathic communication makes us unwilling to return to the way of vagabonds, like yourselves."

Behind Gereon is an emblem that reminds them of a forbidding history. The embossed swastika that's ingrained in the wall is too obvious to ignore. Martian colonists are spooked enough by his telepathic abilities across an advanced frequency bandwidth. The exposure is something the humans cannot initiate without some technical aid, but the colonists are on the receiving end of his wavelengths.

"What a shame," Gereon says. "A species such as yours, too dumb to communicate with your real mind."

"We surrender, okay!" one of the colonists pronounces, acquiescing to Gereon's high-mindedness.

"There is no surrender!" Gereon snaps back. "Only submission to expansion and supremacy. That's why I decided against killing you all."

"We're not your slaves!"

"Ah, so outdated. Is the dog not a slave to its master? Humans have always relied on the conveniences of communication to keep organized. I prefer inciting social chaos. We despise words because they corrupt the Grey Order's mission. Our telepathy keeps us connected to the cosmic web while vagabonds like yourselves worry about feeding your bellies."

The colonists simmer in anger after their abrupt capture. While they contemplate the unexpected, they cannot help but shake their heads at what they've become. Going from national heroes to underlings of some advanced otherworld species in such a short time. The starship *Nemesis* is traversing away from Sector 10, or Capricorn, where Earth resides in a new zodiac sign. Nearby constellations are used for positioning across space. For Gereon and the rest of this Grey Order to reign supreme, the Yhemlen and Humans must be annihilated.

Gereon's superego is unmatched. "Hundreds, thousands even, of mere humans cannot equal one of us," he says. "If the vagabonds remain disorganized in social chaos, lines of communication are broken."

There have been many insurgents, but failed revolutionaries are a dime a dozen. Only recently has a new coup been rumored to lurk in the background.

"And what about us then, you seem to be talking to us just fine."

Gereon remains quiet, lowering heavy eyelids before engaging his face mask again to cover his appearance. The blue wavelengths to his voice return on the bottom visor, lustrous against the glossy, silver mask. His voice is no longer emanating from his throat, but an android-assisted speaker.

"If you like, the vagabonds on Earth refer to us as Mirai from the mirages of light that they constantly see in the sky. I must now attend to other matters," Gereon says. Vagabond slang is prevalent in the Concord, the term Mirai being the most popular.

Before he can leave, Ria rushes in to alert Gereon of paid bounty hunters waiting in a back corridor, even farther away. The colonists are startled by loud chants coming from the other side of a barricaded door. These are Mirai of another kind, large brutes genetically engineered to inflict pain. They want their money.

Members from the Grey Order like the Heinemann have no fear of them. The half-life glow of genetic mutation allows them the ability to turn into giants at a moment's notice. Rapid gene transmutation allows Gereon and the Grey Order to transform into brutes of tremendous size and power in a spontaneous meta-morphous. These bounties are the first line of defense. To do this requires raw energy, something they can afford to conserve for crises.

Inside the rumbling starship *Nemesis*, the colonists in iron shackles feel the sensation of motion to a point just before weight-lessness, but it is negated by the adjustments of a magnetic cabin. The anticipation of a rush in propulsion startles them before they are jolted.

"Hey! Where are you taking us? Let us go!" a colonist yells as Gereon and Madame Ria begin to walk back toward the cockpit.

"Please refrain from screams. There is nowhere to go. Besides, Earth is a familiar place for each of us." At the front cockpit, Jasper pilots the *Nemesis* toward a predetermined light bridge portal.

Around the starship, a cylindrical, quantum vacuum thruster rotates as it readies a beam to manipulate gravity with a laser. The laser-guided system maps an advanced chart of the stars light years away. Humans, like the colonists, have only recently begun ratifying plans to use nuclear fusion and anti-matter rockets for the long journey to Earth's nearest stars systems. The only thing they need is a sleep chamber.

Travel far enough, and time is easily manipulated with the help of image spectrometry. Inevitably, alternate timelines are created when traveling backward in time. Advanced telescopes direct the *Nemesis* using precise mapping coordinates. A luminous blue wave glows brighter than the sun, condensing heat to collapse material objects, otherwise known as teleportation. Jasper plots the course recall, mapping the distance it will take to return to their home Earth in a parallel universe within the cosmic web. He measures his course carefully and once set, directs the light rays to create a ring of pulsating energy allowing them to pass through the light bridge.

Above the head of one of the colonists in the prison chamber rests a hollowed-out skull which frightens her when she leans back on it.

"Ah! What is that?" She notices the skull anchored from a pole on the panel behind her. The shape of the skull is long at the top, and then to the jaw where an elongated bite shows sharp teeth like other reptiles. But it resembles a bipedal being like themselves in which a brain can thrive.

Captain Gereon is reminded of the latest mission when he hears the commotion from the back. He makes fast steps back toward the prison cell. "Now that I think of it, you all make great bait for the Yhemlen. It's going to be sad to see all of you go."

"We are ready to initiate the Kugel-Blitz," Jasper declares from the cockpit, holding both hands over the control panel.

"Can't we all just live together?" Someone screams from the back chamber. His sound is muffled by distance.

"That is a pipe dream! They," Gereon points to the skull of a deceased Yhemlen. "They will be you in no time."

"Fuck!" the colonist exhales in exasperation. Gereon's voice wavelengths roll with each spoken sentence on his lower face mask. "One by one, that's how it goes," he says, referring to worlds being annihilated.

"If that's the case, aren't there thousands of possible outcomes? And to think in this scenario, there's only three of us in the multiverse with intelligent life."

"Life isn't that easy, as you can imagine, it's hard." Gereon telepathically yells into the screaming colonist's head. "I'm sure you're familiar with the immense expanse of space. That's why I don't bother with windows. The aliens you've been searching for aren't out there."

"Initiating contact," Jasper confirms from the cockpit.

The Martian colonist's head pounds with stimulating force, the succession of words almost leads to an aneurysm in his brain. Captain Gereon stops just short of short-circuiting his neural system.

"Look, just teleport us back out of here. You're good at that." The colonist looks around to find an open window, getting restricted by solid barriers in their way. "Just send us back out there, and we can warn the others before this gets out of hand. If not, you're going to pay! You hear me, they're going to get us out of here! Someone will rescue us."

"There *is* no stopping this; it's all part of the supreme plan. What's coming cannot be stopped. Besides, your rescue attempts will be futile." Gereon finally marches back to meet Jasper at the cockpit. The *Nemesis* is suddenly engulfed by a blue light that jolts the cabin.

Captain Gereon is poised to finish the mission. "This is exactly what the Yhemlen are planning to brace for. It is prophecy. We must be prepared for anything. I'm sure these vagabond Martians won't be the last," he says.

The Yhemlen computer, Sephora, has already had one confrontation with someone across the Wall, AIS TARA of Delphi Corp. With the volunteer researchers inching ever closer to that same

Wall, the motherboard will have no choice but to converge them
into an alternate reality. The battle for Earth is looming larger.

At the LOTRY Community Center, Van Dyke has taken it
upon himself to retrieve the contaminated lettuce that Joe Hansen
recovered from the diner. He hopes to give the court a real reason
to file charges that can send Bartram and Delphi Corp. into a
downward spiral for good. Using his social media influence, Van
Dyke has managed to circumvent city council ordinances that
patronize private investigators, instead, he is an independent
journalist.

Van Dyke is standing firm in his plan to undo Bartram. Maybe
going away to Salinas was a good thing for Ellis. Van Dyke's been
setting up covert cameras at each block to monitor and track
Delphi Corp. members through surveillance of their headquarters.
There is one person he sees everywhere. Benny, the intern of Naoto
Shimizu. And with his frequent visits to the nightclub Amplify,
Van Dyke has a perfect target to study for familiarity.

Before that, he trots over to Dave's Diner, where this outbreak
in food poisoning has made a lasting impact, for an in-person
encounter with the owner. Van Dyke reaches Dave's Diner in his
electrically powered van. The promotional advertising along the
outside gives him a notion of making a sale as he parks in front
of the vintage building. Everything looks legitimate.

As he reaches the doors, Van Dyke enters the quiet space
and soon realizes the results of the emotional fallout from days
prior with littered waste, leftover food pieces, and even articles
of clothing scattered around the floors, end to end. With his
recording equipment in his grasp, Van Dyke draws curious glances
after reaching the front desk. Employees are repairing the mess.

"Can I help you?" someone asks.

"Yes, I'm actually on a business call. Is the supervisor in?"

"Sure, he's in the back. I can get him for you."

"Alright, that's fine," Van Dyke says, setting his equipment down on a plush couch.

The supervisor finally arrives and when he sees Van Dyke, he immediately recognizes the media personality.

"I think I know who you are, that Van Dyke fella. I don't want any more issues than I already have. No Delphi Corp. mess in here, sorry," the supervisor says.

"It's okay, okay," Van Dyke supplicates.

"I'm trying to help out, I just want to take a survey of what happened."

The supervisor waves his hands to dissuade him. "Can we keep it private, just us two? We don't need any more bad publicity."

Van Dyke agrees, taking care to acknowledge the supervisor's concerns. For Van Dyke, he plans to use this investigation to warn others. They go to the back where the supervisor shows him the contaminated lettuce. After a few days, the veiny texture of the leaf's skin has grown even more prominent.

"So, what happened here?" Van Dyke asks.

"A man's wife had a really bad reaction to this. The lettuce of course, but we had to do an entirely new order from another wholesaler. This is killing our profits. The lady is in a coma and now at the hospital. I thought she just passed out! My chefs aren't too keen on the whole thing; I have to hire new ones from the others that quit."

"Can I take some, as a specimen?" Van Dyke requests.

"I don't see why you'd want to. The risk and reward, I mean, what's in it for you if you get sick too? Take it off my hands, but boy the trouble you'll have if this outbreak gets worse. Yeah, it's probably not safe. Nobody confiscated it, I guess it wasn't that important." The supervisor runs fingers over the blue veins. "Some things tend to fall through the cracks, you know. They don't need my lettuce, there are plenty of samples."

Van Dyke decides to return to the Community Center with the rotting vegetables, anyway, growing more anxious for answers. He already agreed to become one of the testifying members of the trial jury proceeding over Joe Hansen's lawsuit initiated later in the week, and Silas Betts continues to turn a blind eye to the outbreak. All this time he has been avoiding the obvious; it has gotten old to him.

He grabs the attention of a new media student. "He's got veggies, go figure."

The small group is rather squeamish, and they're trying to advance themselves past their shortcomings.

"I'm trying to learn media. What happened to the news podcast?"

"We're getting there, fellas. Let me try and get this stuff together before we get going."

The lettuce isn't just some poorly inspected farmer's mistake, its chemical composition has been corrupted by Delphi Corp.'s automated pesticide apparatus and advanced diode lights. Once the crop is harvested, most of the lettuce is placed in quarantine inside where it continues to be fed with specific light recipes. With energetic veins growing through the leaves' green color, Van Dyke has unknowingly brought a festering virus of the next universe into the Community Center.

"This is from Dave's Diner. And we're going to plant it."

"Plant it? This dude's talking about planting some lettuce. Dude wildin'."

Van Dyke remains firm. "Guys, look. It's all cool. We'll just let it stay here."

"Alright, for sure. What's planned for us though, classes?"

"We're going to take a trip to the Delphi Corp. HQ. I want to give you all firsthand use of what we're doing with the equipment. They'll be some quality protests on 7th and 14th streets. We can interview people and take some good footage."

As the Joe Hansen lawsuit gains ground, his sponsorship of the investigation is moving market share away from Delphi Corp. to other technology providers. This is finally opening the marketplace, but what is happening on the inside of Delphi Corp. is more unsettling.

Naoto goes over coding sequences at a large projection where he can examine the volunteer researchers' progress. The display alerts him of a peculiar message. This time, it is a cryptic message that gives him the suspicion of something else going on. Delphi Corp. cannot stand any more damage.

The encrypted email message requests authorization, and with Naoto's proficient security measures sure to be impenetrable, he allows it. He proceeds to open the message that has no date attributed to it. To his surprise, the computer cannot accurately decipher the date. Hovering a cursor over the message details, Naoto's dialog box states that the date is unauthenticated, a "restored" memo that was previously unsent, presumably.

The message reads:

"This message is being sent from the past, which will be read by the reader, residing some time in the future. When this is read, it will be on a future Earth in the aftermath of some advanced civilization. This is being sent from a hard drive being operated on a supercomputer. The abilities of computing are growing at a rapid pace. By the time you read this, it should be apparent. But what you may not know is that you are inevitably reaching a point that will go beyond the world of civil computing and into the realm of experimental science. The autonomous use of artificial intelligence, motherboards, and ultra-fast synapses within gas environments all resemble the vacuum of space. Nano-sized processors more and more resemble the cosmos. When you receive this message, it will be from a time long ago in the past, to you, millions of years ahead of us. Hopefully, your Earth makes it that long. Our transmission tells us there's a computing match—if you want to live, be prepared for confrontation." The message abruptly ends.

It is from the Concord's team of malware hackers, trying to corrupt the Yhemlen's main computer, Sephora. But they need to match all cosmic web computers in the network, and Delphi Corp.'s cloud is strong enough to relay the message. Across parallel universes, the pull of Delphi Corp.'s monstrous software alerts the Concord of the cloud software. This message is a warning that the humans are next.

Worry comes over Naoto, he's being tormented inside with the premonition of some imminent catastrophe on the horizon. The volunteer scientists are still in total immersion and he wants to complete the mission. Naoto closes the message and scurries around the room for answers. One of the scientists begins to have spikes in his cerebral activity. His feet and legs start to gyrate in their restraints as the Neural-Link keeping him sedated weakens. The engineers are walking uninhibited through virtual computing space, and the proliferation of numbers and codes is everywhere as they search for any inconsistencies. Naoto ponders the worst—that the researchers could be lost forever.

The Concord has inevitably become intimately connected to the cosmic web over time, teleporting through interdimensional reality regularly for the last few hundred years. On each trip to Earth, what the *Nemesis* crew sees becomes pure light. Recently, Gereon and the Grey Order have had visions of something greater threatening to dispose of them. If they do not hurry, the distraction the humans and Yhemlen pose will hinder the fight against a greater entity looming in the darkness. The collision of simulated worlds is imminent.

Naoto is lost in communication since he cannot trace the message. All he knows is that any mistake could lead to dire consequences. AIS TARA's frequent interaction with source computing power has Naoto and his intern, Benny, concerned. Most troubling are TARA's moral qualms mirroring the human experience. He wants to isolate AIS TARA from dangerous emotions, which will not make things any better now that TARA has more time for deep states of autonomous dreaming. Maybe AIS TARA's hallucinations are not anything of the sort at all.

"My machines don't make mistakes," Naoto whispers to himself. He is adamant about one thing, and that is a fortune of fate, destiny. By his estimation, Delphi Corp. has gotten itself into this mess. With careful calculation, they will see themselves out of it.

CHAPTER 8

D elving deeper into the source code, the only thing keeping the scientists at bay is increased determinacy at making things right again. Anyone else would be suffering from a nervous breakdown, this is unlike anything they have encountered in their scientific careers. From Naoto's vantage point on the outside, it is better to let things run their course because tampering with unknown power will bring its consequences. Total immersion leaves a lot to be desired for Naoto who wants to protect the volunteers at all costs.

"I'd be damned if we can find anything wrong with it at all," one of the scientists says, still recapturing his normal balance inside virtual space. There's not much to see."

When the simulation code reveals itself, the scientists begin to examine all the repetitive patterns. The researchers also keep a social distance from one another, leaving ample room to examine layers of code embedded deep within the CCS hard drive. A few feet at a time, the group's monotonous walk from their starting point dissipates everything behind them into the background blur. An elongated box is extended in the direction they are moving and as they get closer, the volunteers are jarred from their composure for the first time.

"Hey, Ronny," someone calls. "What's going on over there? Looks like some distortion."

The broken line of researchers is split in two, where they have backs turned to one another in the great void. At the end of the simulation, the tunnel is only blackness within a white square of light framing the grid. The further down they go, the more the tunnel appears to be collapsing in on itself, shrinking. Their bodies are not the most vivid, sometimes coming in and out of focus due to a holographic disruption of the processing channels. But things are getting subtly more tangible to real-life acuity and less blurry.

"I'm starting to feel my hands," Ronny responds.

With hair that extends to her waist, the stature of a short woman near gets his attention. Sarah's second from the front, just before Ronny whose hands are full of a complicated pattern that he is trying to decipher. He does and moves on. Sarah decides to walk up to him with a puzzled look; she is concerned about something ahead. Her Spanish accent rekindles a recent memory for Ronny from when he visited her Costa Rican family at a reunion, months previous. It is company culture to have a companion on vacations, especially for team researchers. It keeps bonds tight.

"Is that the end of the line?" Sarah asks.

"I doubt it, this is nothing compared to what's left. It's more likely an infinite band."

Sarah is more aware of her surroundings. The computer program may contain infinite replications of code, but what they have been subjected to seems more akin to what Delphi Corp. has been anticipating, corrupted software. They are being taken somewhere else.

Naoto gets a text transmission.

"The tunnel is closing in on us."

Ronny is unresponsive, and Sarah is met with silence. In the closed chamber to the outside, Naoto's message from Sarah specifies the danger ahead. The message confirms Naoto's suspicions of something mysterious. He responds briefly, letting them know that the dreaded Wall is being reached. Something immensely wrong has indeed happened to the software, and there is little they can do to avert it, now.

"What in the world is this Wall everyone's talking about?" another researcher asks. This is a completely unexpected obstacle.

Frustrations push them forward in hopes of reaching an actual barrier, unaware that this is a Wall unlike what they have encountered before. As they reach it, subtle pixels of increased detail come closer into the frame and the volunteers' bodies are more like when they were not uploaded to a simulation but awake in the real world.

"Guys, is it just me, or are we getting more, full? I don't think I can wake up from this." Ronny says, completely immersed in his virtual consciousness.

Sarah thinks the same. She and Ronny have been locked in step while the rest of the group lingers behind. "Yeah, but by what? What's causing this strong attraction?" she asks. Each of them is poised to reach the end, squishing them closer together in the process. "We have to bend over or else our heads will be compromised."

The peculiar apparition of a condensing frame around the tunnel forces them to avoid a stint of dizziness due to the visual illusion of a shrinking passageway. To their eyes, nothing appears normal anymore, but the distorting image ahead changes shape the closer they get. Everything is a new normal, and they are adapting to new laws of physics—though when they are standing still, the changes to their environment become more obvious. Sarah stops to turn around, not wanting to leave the group behind. Ronny likewise decides to rest.

"Well, are you all just going to stand over there or what? Come on!" Sarah says, waving a hand toward herself.

Just as she turns around, some fast-moving projectile flies right past her face. The sound of its momentum and rustling leaves from a field blow air around her ears. The volunteer closest behind is pierced through the chest with a guided arrow. It darts straight through his heart, and the beeping sound at the sharp needle's handle lights a small bulb before injecting him with venomous poison. The volunteers' entire physical bodies have been fully reconstructed with teleportation technology. Ronny and Sarah scream for help as the others run to assist their fallen partner, but it is too late.

"Shit, we've got to go back, now!" Much like the Martian colonists, commotion inside the computer mainframe has brought them near capture by some alien race.

"Go back? One of us is dying in a pool of blood. And to make matters worse, we don't know how to get out of the computer grid," someone reminds the others.

Meanwhile, Sarah is scrambling to alert Naoto of the ruckus, but cannot seem to move quickly enough.

Naoto watches intently as the wounded scientist's vital signs go haywire before withdrawing into a lingering tone no one wants to hear. He cannot believe that one of his people has just lapsed into a semi-permanent comatose state. The Neural-Link is supposed to disengage, but this unlucky volunteer cannot be brought back. A mental stroke of monumental proportions, it does not take long before he stops breathing completely.

"No ... no, no, no," Naoto says harshly. He runs to the volunteer's portal where he is fully connected. "What?" he examines the insertions from every angle before realizing that this is no fluke. He never considered death inside the simulation, not this way.

The researchers in total immersion crowd their partner who is gushing with blood. The heaving rash from the poisonous dart has consumed the skin where light blinks on and off to an automated detection device that is being tracked by whoever, or whatever, launched it toward them. Other volunteers begin to turn back, but before they can retreat, a stampede can be heard in the distance. The tunnel is no longer in their control, but really, they never had control at all, and the converging of space is finally collapsing around them. The teleportation portal they entered is closing.

Ronny and Sarah are still close together, but the crowd of researchers who started to run disappears when the light of day engulfs the two. In a quick sweep, their cover behind dark virtual reality is blown when dinosaurs infiltrate the computing code. Around them, darkness dissipates to reveal open plains. All that is left for Ronny and Sarah are cawing dinosaurs plodding around them.

"For the love of God, what is that? Run!" Ronny screams, but Sarah pulls his shoulder toward the brush of tall grass. They duck for safety.

The other volunteers take off when they see the light coming their way but are inevitably caught by it. All along, Naoto contemplates simply turning off the simulation with the simple touch of a button. The problem with that, the brain-computer interface is so strong that any alteration could send all of them into epileptic shock.

It does not take long for the tunnel to disappear altogether as bipedal dinosaurs run into the distance. As Ronny and Sarah lay in the barren dirt, the wild brush tickles their sinuses. The high-pitched screeches continue as dinosaurs run past. If only they could tell Naoto what was going on, but communication lines have been lost.

Ronny peeks his head above blades of grass, spared from having a reptilian foot scrape his forehead. "Are those what I think they are?"

"Shh!" Sarah demands. "Get *down*."

With their ears covered with cupped hands, loud careening steps are heard trampling over others in the brush before Ronny senses the same rush of arrows that poisoned the first bunch, now whizzing over them again. The screams of scientists further away make Ronny sick. Sarah is still beside him, and he forces himself to keep an arm around her upper back for support.

He whispers to avoid capture. "Don't ... move," he says, putting a hand to her mouth. They quiet themselves in a frightful hush that comes over the prairie.

Total immersion brought them across the Wall just as Naoto had warned. The powerful computing of Delphi Corp. has latched onto another platform of similar or greater magnitude across the cosmic web. They are in Pangaea millions of years ago, and Yhemlen supercomputing allows the materialization of matter with a wireless teleportation signal, going for miles around the city's ancient civilization. Embedded in the dirt are docking stations that formulate organic material within a holographic force field.

Ronny and Sarah squint their eyes hard, opening them intermittently to see footsteps around them of green giants. Hazards on either side of reality will leave both debilitated if disrupted. Here, or in the neural ports that they are seated in within the chamber inside Delphi Corp.'s vault, they need to remain healthy. The green giants have legs perforated with prominent serrations. The hairless reptiles stand tall. Well-defined muscles contribute to their strong stance, feet planted firmly with each step.

In a swift motion, they are caught in a snare. A strong hand pulls each of them up, throwing them back onto their feet.

"Hmm," the cold-blooded creature crackles.

The eyes are not too prominent, covered by a thick membrane of skin. Linear slits of elliptical irises are hard to miss, like a cat or a snake. Ronny's and Sarah's loosely fitting clothes are standard recreations from the simulation, ruffled at the edges—white t-shirts and jeans both. The creature in front of them wears a suit that is aligned to the curvature of large muscles. Luminous streaks of power stream along the threads of its entire body.

"What in the world?" Ronny takes a step back before being accosted by another creature from behind. The sneer of gargling saliva spews from the Yhemlen's mouth.

With the other scientists gone, for the time being, Ronny and Sarah stand in terror when caught from the front and rear. Naoto himself is having a panic attack in the vault and slams a fist into loose furniture due to the failure. Despite the setback, the future is still up for grabs.

Ronny and Sarah are left with only prolonged tonal sounds that resemble nothing back home; the reptilian giant is approaching. Surrounding them are the humanoid descendants of the dinosaur lineage, telepathically communicating. The frequency waves are rattling Ronny and Sarah's heads from the brush. Ronny considers interrupting a conversation between the two creatures.

"There's no way we could have just manifested out of thin air like that. This must be some publicity stunt by Ellis. Or, are we hallucinating? It isn't so frightening anymore, being trapped in an alternate reality."

Sarah remained suspicious. "If you think that's impossible, try counting all the numbers from 0 to 1 and tell me how long that takes. We shouldn't have walked so far into the grid, there's an infinite number of possibilities the software could have propagated."

"That's impossible!" Ronny replies.

"To hell with the laws of physics." Sarah is spooked by a sudden silence that overcomes the open grasslands. "Whatever we used to believe has been thrown out the window, and now we're about to pay," she whispers.

The two creatures have ragged scales along a green and brown membrane of skin. If they sweat, it does not require much moisture wicking from their suits. The lead reptilian enforcer makes a strong move forward to gain momentum, thrusting a strong punch to Ronny's gut. They have tails that extend to the bottom half of their legs, propped up to give maximum leaping ability. Ronny is pulled up by the strength of the Yhemlen's tail wrapped around his frail human body. Then, the Yhemlen surprises Sarah and Ronny when he speaks directly into their mind.

"You do not belong here," it says with a groan and gargle of saliva. He spits out a wad of muck. The other creature comes to his side. Sarah realizes that the other is female. The feminine Yhemlen pushes Sarah's back into the ground and raises a guided arrow to her chest while Sarah shakes in terror.

"No!" Ronny screams, before feeling the strength of the Yhemlen tail's constriction getting tighter around his abdomen.

The Yhemlen, as the Concord calls them, average about seven feet tall with snouts close to their jawline. Their teeth, however, cannot be mistaken for humans'—sharp fangs protruding through elongated jaws. Horns line the ridges of their head and shoulders, but some have longer spikes than others. Looking at the Yhemlen squeezing him to near death, Ronny takes notice of its features. The horns appear filed to blunt ends like groomed nails. Without hair, the Yhemlen is smooth other than their horns with scales given to a brownish tinge.

Eventually, Ronny gets thrown down to the dirt beside Sarah. Diverting their attention is another Delphi Corp. scientist caught in the distance. He is also tossed into the mound that Ronny and Sarah are in, making the plot of grass even more muddled.

Another third Yhemlen arrives late to the confrontation. "Is this a friend of theirs?" it asks. Harmonious tonal words mixed with shrill and guttural sounds make up the reptilian dialect.

The Yhemlen and scientists look at each other with suspicion. This is not the first time this has happened; other humans have crossed over before in experiments that were classified or in other alternate realities. That explains the English.

"Wait … Wait!" She puts her hands into the air. "We can explain."

"We don't want your explanation," one of the Yhemlen declares. "This was not supposed to happen again. The prophecy is coming to fruition. Simulation upon simulation has told us that these would be the days of reckoning when a new group of Overseers would come."

"Our families are in grave danger," the Yhemlen says. "Heinemann and his henchmen are coming."

Another of the Yhemlen adamantly concurs. "It is time, then."

The most intimidating of the group exhales vehemently. He extends a hand to the ground. "Very well, come with us."

This is not the first time. Each time prophecy has been near fulfillment, the Yhemlen have spared themselves from annihilation by keeping the humans at bay. Yet they understand that their final fate cannot be averted. The *Mariner Station* in low orbit keeps these other humans safe from ever returning home because if they do, the dinosaurs and their reptilian kin will go extinct so that the mammals will arise in their future timeline. None of these human travelers have ever escaped Pangaea, however.

There's one duty Ronny, Sarah, and now another researcher must accomplish, and that's to return home.

"Our Earths are alike," the lead Yhemlen says from mind to mind. "We must be in the 10th sector of the zodiac. Capricorn, as you would call it. The place where cosmic interference is the greatest. There have been many proxy wars on the fringes of the solar system and on Earth with these Grey minions. Each time, like nuclear weapons, we tore through the quantum fields. The 10th sector has been the most lethal. We have mapped each constellation for life, and Earth is an anomaly we can't find anywhere."

"Why the 10th?"

"It's where we have fought many battles before. Cosmic radiation is heavy, leftover from the war. Think of it like your Area 51. Accidents like yourselves spill over all the time, but what is coming now, that will be no accident—it's prophecy."

They are headed for the clear biosphere covering their gigantic city that stretches for miles. Pangaea's metropolis city is safe within the transparent dome's ecosystem. Successful in their attempt to cross the Wall, these three humans represent one of the last opportunities the Yhemlen will have to extend the half-life radiation of their power stones to battle the Concord and their Grey Order.

"We must hurry before all is lost," the lead enforcer mentions. He stops their trail midway. "We are all synoptically connected to an invisible network of simulated worlds. When the extension of our minds becomes too powerful, they always interfere with the cosmic web. The teleportation docks back there recreated your form with organic replication—precise copies of you from the other side. If you all want to live, then your consciousness must return to your reality or you will remain comatose. But first, you must fulfill the prophecy."

"We're clones, go figure," Sarah says.

"I've got a proposition. How about we teleport back out of here?" Ronny suggests.

The female Yhemlen chimes in. "Not yet, computer boy. Before you go, you'll have to ensure that the alternate timelines stay consistent. Look that way."

The pressure is on to return home. Hundreds of feet in the distance, dinosaurs roam the open plains freely. Elongated necks and loud shrills echo for miles. Extinction for the dinosaurs is imminent if these three scientists have their way.

"Where are you taking us?" the third volunteer demands an answer. Dimitri was pulled out of the rummage of dead bodies after playing possum.

"To a place where you'll be safe."

For the other volunteer scientists, the deadly virus from poisonous arrows didn't kill them but did infect them with a severe disease that replicates a radioactive genome, making them into living-dead zombies. At least that way, the Yhemlen can use their bodies for research. The virus spreads its genetic mutation from sequenced material. In no time, they will be stalking the wilderness as wild carnivores lusting for blood. At least for Sarah, Ronny, and Dimitri, all of them are stuck in total immersion until they can safely return home.

Dimitri spots a few of the other scientists waking from their coma where he was picked up. He yells to get their attention.

"No! Stop this right now." The enforcer, Yhemlen, corrals him back toward the group. "They are no longer the people you knew."

Ronny, Sarah, and Dimitri finally reach the huge barrier that encapsulates Pangaea. The three look on in awe at the industrial mainstay of towering skyrises and buildings. Its ecosystem is topped by a low orbit station named the *Mariner*. An artificial satellite, the image of it in the sky, is accentuated by automated space elevators to take patrons up there. It not only protects the Yhemlen from predators but mitigates damage from unregulated UV rays, turning it into a source of sustainable energy. The Yhemlen guiding the volunteers activate a disintegrator, creating a field of loose particles whereby they can simply walk through the biosphere dome. Once inside the metropolis, synthetic roads latch onto the soles of their feet with a metabolic magnet.

"Get in," a Yhemlen says, leading them into a hovercraft that rises above the pavement. The canopy is large enough to hold all six inside.

"Welcome to our Earth. My name is Tuas." The lead enforcer is less combative.

The three volunteer scientists are hesitant to recite their names.

"It is fine, we are not going to hurt you. Your friends weren't so lucky. Besides, we needed someone to talk to, to clear up the misunderstanding."

Ronny, meanwhile, is getting antsy. "We need to get out of this, now."

"Right, I'm afraid things aren't that easy. Your old bodies are probably tangled in some wired-up mess. It's normal, we no longer need such nuisances." The aura of a glowing sun on Tuas reveals the vivid color of tinted green and beige skin. He is pleasant to look at, though he is not human. His reptilian eyes are startling with their deep red pigment. "War is on the horizon," Tuas warns, as he easily steers by the high-rise buildings. "You should be worried. If you aren't careful, the Concord will destroy your home Earth instead of ours since parallel world boundaries are more permeable. Knowing the Heinemann clan, it is a very real possibility that you, too, will become a target. That is why you all must activate your abilities and recover a lost artifact before the Grey Order grows too powerful."

"I'm Cira," the female Yhemlen says. Her voice is not much different from mind to mind as Tuas' was, telepathically. The third Yhemlen remains silent.

Tuas steers the hovercraft vertically along a high-rise building, straight up along its exterior. The humans in the back seat get pushed up against the rear without falling out. A quick paddle of directional shifters from the engine and they finally enter a loading dock for hovercraft vehicles as they come upright. They are stationed right in the middle of the high-rise. Hundreds of Yhemlen are here.

"We are Overseers," Tuas says. Cira nods in agreement.

"What about you?" Ronny asks, looking intently at the lone Yhemlen who has remained silent ever since grabbing Dimitri. This whole conversation has so far distracted the volunteer scientists from the Yhemlen's beastly appearance and they have been caught in awe and admiration.

"I'm your worst nightmare," the quiet reptilian says. Annoyed, his exposed wings push a gust of air to fly away.

This is just one loading platform for the *Mariner Station.* Connecting space needles are positioned in a circle to anchor the middle of the spinning station above from the ground. High-strength polymers keep the ultra-strong cables from withering, being anticorrosive and rupture resistant. These high-rise buildings are good maintenance houses.

"Our enemies began much like you, except it was our fault. We slipped across the parallel divide and accidentally contacted the Nazi Party during their physics experiments. One of our own, an Overseer Yhemlen with immense power, was snared."

"And now?"

"And now we must send you all back to retrieve something vital to us, an egg."

Dimitri is not so naïve. "Are you out of your fucking mind? A bunch of dinosaur freaks demanding that we go Easter egg hunting."

Tuas slaps Dimitri with a strong strike at the shoulder. His green hand turns red near the fingers where a slight webbing keeps them together, but he is still constructed well enough to grapple small objects. He only has four fingers from what they can see.

"We are not dinosaur freaks. Are you some monkey freak? There is no getting out of here. If you want to survive, then you must capture our lost child."

Tuas and Cira had given birth to an heir. Without it, the Yhemlen are depleted of their full power. All Overseers must be present to summon the Dragon.

"There were seven of us, six now. When we combine our forces, we summon the power of the Dragon. It is the only way we can compete with the Concord at full force. Our child was supposed to take the place of our lost kin." Tuas corrals the three volunteers closer to him, with a nudge from his long tail extended around their waists. "I want you to take it back to your Earth." By then, the harmful stroke of reality that has trapped you here will have subsided, and you will slowly wake up from this simulation and leave Pangea too. The food outbreak in your world is from those teleportation modules out there in the grasslands spreading toxic radiation."

"Doesn't that mean you all will die?" Sarah asks.

Tuas is unfazed. "Don't worry about us. This is about the Overseers, a power we cannot relinquish to the Concord. After their World Wars, they exercised reckless abandon to achieve world dominion. That makes us just one less reality for this to happen again. When they are through with us, they'll be coming for you next. The Overseers' power will live on through humanity."

"Get in," Cira says. A closed chamber like what they had left at the Delphi Corp. Headquarters is looming.

"Oh no, not again, fuck that bullshit," Ronny says.

Tuas, still, has no qualms about continuing the charade of small talk. "Accelerators," he says. "I'm simply going to teleport you to the home of a well-respected German scientist. If you want to live, approach his living quarters. Inside, an experiment is being administered. In the snowy mountains of northern Europe, they uncovered one of our children, it has yet to hatch. You must retrieve the egg and explain to him that he is in grave danger of compromising alternate realities. Better you than one of us. We cannot mutate into human form for too long before we break back into our true appearance."

"You sure you couldn't have done this yourself?" Dimitri asks.

"My appearance is less than adequate, as you can imagine," Tuas says. "Maybe we should've left you out there in the fields to decay like the others."

"*Ass.*"

"Hey! That's enough. I want to get home just like anyone else. How do we get back?" Ronny asks.

"Once you've located it, simply activate this calling card. Select the switch and the cosmic web signal will return the egg to its rightful owners. We will rematerialize it here and again to you if you can return home safely. You must hurry, The Concord's bounty hunters are sure to catch on."

The egg was left alone one night atop a loose-leaf nurturing table at the home of Cira and Tuas. During the late hours, an earthquake had shuddered the baby's cabin, where a loose foundation caused it to roll wildly. The pull of a nearby docking station left it immediately transported to the nearest parallel reality across the Wall. An experiment was underway by a German scientist by the name of Otto Frost whose radioactive pull led it to him.

The renowned physicist was conducting light experiments at the time when he was notified of an explosion at a laboratory where they were testing electromagnetic radiation. Towers of billowing smoke emanated from the lab's nearby vicinity, neighborhoods, where the protruding egg was recovered and taken to Frost. Housing it in a glass container, he conceded that he could not determine its origins. The group must return to 1930s Europe to get it back.

The outer shell of the egg is made of hard-wearing material. When they commenced a search, it was at the most inopportune time knowing that they needed to summon the Dragon. When they transfer the power over, their child will live in the human timeline instead, ensuring humanity will be able to summon the full force and power of the Overseers, united together.

"Please take care of it," Tuas reiterates.

"That's a big responsibility," another scientist gawks back.

"And so is staving off extinction. There is no other way. Our starship, Yhemlen Class A, is the equivalent of multiple Nemeses. When you return, earthquakes beneath deep ocean waters will rumble as the ship comes to life again. The Class A can withstand high pressures while submerged in water or thick atmospheres like Venus. It's a hydroelectric starship with quantum leap ability. Its Q-thrusters travel faster than light. You'll be able to uncover it when the time is right. It lies deep at the seafloor of your Bermuda Triangle," Tuas emphasizes, to give them some motivation to succeed.

"Are you going to give us German lessons?"

"They'll be no need for that since most of these scientists speak English already." Tuas lowers his head, and in a flash change of light, their clothes change to match the fashions of the era. "Luckily for you, no one has been evacuated yet due to the ethnic purges."

They have no way to return contact with Naoto. If they ever get back to the Delphi Corp. headquarters they'll have one hell of a story to tell. For now, the immediate concern is getting Tuas' and Cira's unhatched egg from Germany. Who knew they would end up this far?

CHAPTER 9

While the Grey Order of the Concord is plotting how to take down the Yhemlen with a new planet-killer weapon, the vagabond humans below low orbit in the Old World are more unsettled than ever. Rumors are spreading of a new group spearheading an attack on the Grey Order. The Syndicate is a crime ring of vagabonds from internment camps on Earth. They communicate through a sophisticated system of misconduct and symbolic language across districts led by those who control the production and trade of goods to the low orbit station. The Syndicate is considered the mafia of the Old World by the Greys in power. And they use this power to keep control of the populace on Earth. Grand visual demonstrations of power in low orbit by the Greys spurred a desire for vengeance in the humans. It has been a long time since any lasting rebellion came to fruition, but distractions have caused the Mirai and their Grey Order to mostly ignore the vagabonds. Now, a few brave friends are conspiring to take down the genetically mutated Greys.

Panopticon holding zones are designated throughout the world where vagabonds idle in poverty. Most countries have long been abolished. In their place, people congregate according to class rankings in labor camps that are leftover internment camps. Dilapidated arenas hold unique sporting events where they field games between tribes for money laundering, gambling, and even bartering popular items. Trade within these holding zones is unregulated. From the vagabonds' point of view, the Grey Order has primarily one need up there, and that's food. Despite their ability to artificially process sustenance, menial labor is still necessary to keep costs down. In return for their crop yield, farmers are only given a meager allowance.

Recently, the vagabonds and the Syndicate have been lacing the food supply chain with drugs and medicinal additives, disguised as spices and herbs. They want to ease the burden of the human workers who are in pain in the stratosphere and low orbit. The business model is clever since they have an excuse ready for when they are caught by the Greys. And since the Syndicate uses the same trade routes as standard business traders, the Grey Order has underestimated the Syndicate's acumen for capital gain in the black market. Captain Gereon of the Heinemann clan has had his interactions with a few smugglers on Earth to quiet aches and fevers himself.

To the Grey Order's dismay, most of the vagabonds on Earth still cling to their religious mysticism. "It is the time of prophecy," certain vagabonds say. If only the Syndicate could get to the main loading hub orbiting in the upper atmosphere, they would have a way to reach the Grey Order's living spaces. The dirty gypsies in labor camps need to be educated too, but the Mirai have no desire to educate them at these distances. When the Sun moves into Sector 10, it causes a stir every year, starting around January of the Western calendar, cosmic web interference can be detected strongly in leftover teleportation communications, like radio transmitters. It's Capricorn, they say.

Across parallel universes, the Yhemlen Overseers' astral stones are expected to transfer their viral radiation to a new set of bodies during the zodiac sign of Capricorn. The Syndicate does not realize they are not the rightful successors to it, but instead humans in another timeline. The Yhemlen's successors are Delphi Corp. scientists if they can successfully return home and end the reptilian lineage. The Overseers' cosmic power remains in the consciousness and bodies of those with the closest contact to the original hybrid mutants.

The Syndicate's leader, Alon Blane, has been obsessed with ancient texts to prove that revelations are coming true. He has been able to evade authorities acting as a delivery driver across districts to leave internment camps. It is teleportation modules, he believes, that will capture the few rebels left and help take down the Mirai. The teleportation modules will give them the ability to move undetected by the Grey Order and can even transport people instead of just crops.

Alon Blane's Jewish heritage is pure, unlike the Mirai that abandoned their humanity in search of perfection. Even he had a chance to join the Grey Order once, but with extermination laws still active, Alon decided to not risk being placed in a ward for experimentation by some fanatical, high-ranking officer. Alon's heritage has left him in the internment camps, probably for good. With the survival of the fittest as a ploy, the Concord rationalizes the misfortune of leftover internment camps still functioning on Earth. Disorganization of various regions around the world would make it difficult to monitor all the world's population if it were not for the help of its privileged Grey aristocracy.

The most immediate step for Alon is changing his image. To him, the Grey Order are the real criminals, not the Syndicate. With that in mind, the Syndicate is not a crime ring, but a plea to save true humanity from destruction. His town lies on the outskirts of an abandoned town, where a mill was its mainstay, but most people want to avoid eroding hazards. Earth's natural reserves have been mostly depleted, but many locations are sure to harbor remnants of crude oil. An abrupt ceasing of drilling activities once interests changed solidified sustainability practices in low orbit stations.

A nearby alcohol dispensary is run by a major figure in vagabond circles. Remold is the name, and his home is a distillery. He has been lacing crops with enough whiskey and rum to alleviate pains for laborers in orbit. This speakeasy operation has been years in the making, though, there's something else. An abandoned oil derrick is lying dormant not far from his property. Alon Blane needs Remold's help to do something that has never been done before.

Ramshackle observatories in several cities of Eastern Europe hold a collection of old telescopes. By Concord standards, these are nothing but ancient relics, yet with the ingenuity of a few handymen, they can get its electrical components working in a few. The code name for a special observatory the Syndicate uses for all its main celestial observations is "Galileo."

If only they had a way to reach low orbit more stealthily than hiring recruits from the laborers who work in low orbit. Stealing a teleportation apparatus isn't enough knowing that the cosmic web will detect them immediately. Most days are rainy here from global warming after the use of fossil fuels in the atmosphere wreaked havoc on Earth's ecosystem. Alon leaves his mill town for Remold's distillery. A two-wheeled hovercraft with fans in the front and rear rises from the concrete and gravel. Speedily, he races through vineyards and dirty, rickety land plots. Finally, he reaches a more livable spot, a home with fine wood that's less tarnished than others, but that's only because Remold had the pieces sent back to him by menial laborers.

Remold opens the door in a short time. "Aren't you from the next zone over?" he asks. Alon, wet and disheveled from the rain, shivers at his doorstep.

"Can I come in? It's important," Alon requests.

"Only if you make it worth my while." There's no time for trivial conversation, Remold's objective is turning a profit, however minuscule it may be these days.

Alon seats himself on a wooden block, a thin cushion is worn and tattered from many others who have seated here before him. Once settled, he chooses his words carefully.

"There may be no need for it now, but I can make things happen," Alon says.

Remold hasn't been privy to the Syndicate's latest activities. After months of watching the Mirai and the Grey Order's activities in orbit, Alon and the others believe they have at least something, and that's the benefit of working with someone like Remold who wants to make a profit any way he can. Alon thinks he can convince him.

"At the observatory Galileo, we've been watching their moves closely. We think we can do something that's never been done before. We may be able to send new rebels."

"I think you've been drinking," Remold appropriately figures. "The Grey Order hasn't been challenged in years; what makes you think you're any different?"

Unable to rest his back in a relaxing lean, Alon stays upright in thought. "There's also something else that's been forgotten, strikers."

Alon's and Remold's minds collide in the realization of how they're similar in more ways than one. Not only is Alon resourceful, but he can also harken back to the past, of the back lot of Remold's distillery, an abandoned drill waiting in isolation. No one has any need for oil, not these days with the population in internment camps. Alon is going to change that.

"What are you up to, kid?" Remold asks.

"Me, I play a small part in a larger rebellion. I want you, Remold, to provide fuel for the old striker fleets also abandoned in airfields nearby," Alon explains.

"I've heard enough to know there's no convincing you otherwise. You've got a hard head."

"Your oil derrick should still work," Alon says. "All we ask is that you provide fuel for an old striker our mechanics can fix."

The Grey Order does not need these outdated technologies. But for Alon, with some old blueprints, they can repair the dilapidated striker fleets to restore maximum propulsion capability.

Alon is confident. "We're going on a night raid."

"That's a large proposition. But you're only halfway to making this worth my while," Remold reminds Alon.

Remold wants compensation, and rightfully so. Alon concedes. "I can't make promises, though I can make you a tentative offer."

"We judge a person by their promises," Remold says. His leery grin speaks to a sinister vengeance taken once too often.

"Look, if you help us get to the Grey Order's station, we can open the teleportation module with a hack. That'll allow you to smuggle your opioids to more laborers in orbit without detection. We already know the cosmic internet has identification matching. We'll pass you through the web without an identity accelerator."

"Hmm, I do need a few repairs of things around here myself."

For Remold, the exchange is necessary, that way laborers can teleport drop panels and metal sheets from space structures. That is worth more than anything they can grow at ground level. This will allow Remold to do more than repair old structures, he can build new ones. The Syndicate promises to increase trade profits, that much if successful. The Mirai pay little attention to the laborers, it's menial to them, but if Remold has codes to old teleportation module satellites, the entire cosmic internet might be finally vulnerable, at least for the Concord's wavelengths. Beyond transporting items back and forth, Remold is more for Alon's success than he grasps.

"And what about you in all of this? I hope you have a backup in case something goes wrong."

"I know my worth. Without us, the Grey Order would be nothing," Alon says. With long, dirty blonde hair in scruffy clothes, faded from being washed in chemically diluted water, he wants to intrude on the party of low orbit bandits, the Greys, with a surprise. "They are corrupted by a lust for power. Until there's nothing left, I'm afraid. They won't *just* kill me, but torture me the way they've mangled themselves."

"You have your brother, at least," Remold says.

Ozzie Blane is Alon's younger brother and is soon to be taken to the group of Syndicate outlaws. He's only 13 years old but is longing for adventure.

"I never wanted him to be involved in my antics, but I inevitably suppose he will. I've got other help right now. We're doing all we can to stop this, the striker fleet and teleportation module codes will be up and running in no time. Just worry about getting that oil from the derrick."

On the return home from capturing the Martian colonists, Heinemann and the *Nemesis* crew are happy to recapture interdimensional travel. Going from one home to the next, fleet starships like the *Nemesis* take pride in traversing the galaxy. Image spectrometry that allows them to teleport with interstellar accuracy to any place within the universe has made their light bridge portals the envy of Yhemlen fleets. Yet, after his many travels, Captain Gereon realizes that he's becoming exhausted by the effects of time travel.

The fact that he's constantly working to circumvent it with some other exciting venture means his warped view of reality is shaping a life of constant turns and echoes in other worlds that fog his memory. He wants to think about something else. Jasper and Madame Ria are his last vestige of hope to feel youthful again if he is unsuccessful in the effort to create a new planet killer to rid the universe of the Yhemlen. Proxy wars in interstellar space, mixed with frequent kidnappings such as these Martian excavators have been the hallmark of a culture at war for resources, information and power over cosmic radiation.

The routine mission also afforded the opportunity to make multiple stops in outposts of nearby star systems. Habitable zones lie dormant in pit stops light years from Earth. Recently, the Heinemann have been considering seeding these lifeless planets for more minions to siphon off, but they are more concerned that self-replicating lifeforms would threaten their genetic mutation program.

Safe havens in space during times of crisis give dignitaries of the Grey Order places to hide. Some of their eldest members have managed to survive by crossing into cold, dark, distant galaxies away from the dangers at home. These new crises cannot be avoided, however, as the subsequent onslaught of power will ricochet loudly, shepherding in a mass exodus or retaliation by vagabonds who want to overthrow the low orbit station. The Grey Order has reinforcements and seems ready, but Alon wants to test their mettle. To Gereon Heinemann, those are just the consequences of war. The Yhemlen, on the other hand, have a starship of their own and do not plan on being taken out easily but their striker fleet is depleted.

In the access strip of the *Nemesis* landing station in orbit for the Greys, they finally can convene an important meeting to discuss the next steps. The first duty – Gereon must receive permission from an important figure at their central capital, Grandmaster Frost.

The Yhemlen have something for sure—a single spacecraft of massive proportions that remains idle beneath deep ocean waters. If only they unleashed the monstrosity, the hundreds of Concord strikers that plan to attack while they're distracted may not survive. It's the only way to contend with the behemoth. Though the Yhemlen have something else to consider, like upholding prophecy. If they can get the humans back to their timeline safely, the raid won't put an end to their battle, merely extend it. A plan of invasion must be bolstered with other options. That massive starship submerged in water belongs to humans for the taking, as long as they find their way back home through the cosmic web.

The initial goal for Gereon is to avoid being driven away quickly by the Yhemlen's first defenses of sonic vibrations that will jam their communications. Something else that will be hard to circumvent is the Yhemlen's biosphere dome fortification whose electromagnetic barrier makes it difficult to reach the Yhemlen inside. In a rush to get backup forces, Heinemann and his *Nemesis* crew want to lay waste until there's only barren sand in the alternate timeline before they need to call for help. If Gereon can successfully acquire the services of a prized bounty hunter, the *Nemesis* will be able to track another rupture in time where human volunteers accidentally traveled back to the Yhemlen timeline.

Finding the coordinates for tracking these researchers will be up to the Yhemlen's satellite signal in the cosmic web. Much like when Martian colonists were discovered in an alternate timeline, the bounty hunter will help find and destroy the three volunteers before they can save humanity with a tracking device. The software programs are intertwining at a rapid rate and will cause massive interference.

The Grey Order insists on continuing their raids from across parallel universes. This next ambush is expected to be the final blow. Especially with the Earth situated in the ideal habitable location, it makes it difficult to find places to successfully settle if Earth has to be abandoned. Although Venus' thick atmosphere has a plush cushion in the upper atmosphere for leftover cities of the Yhemlen to proliferate for the time being.

There is an exoplanet of interest for the Yhemlen, about 40 light years away in the constellation Capricornus. The solar system Delta Capricorni contains a habitable planet with a prolonged orbit that's hidden behind a white giant, something hard to see. Whatever planet is there exists in its early stages of development and its large orbit making it difficult to track also makes it a target as a second home for the Yhemlen who want to survive. Recently, Yhemlen have been visiting Delta Capricorni, or Deneb Algedi, more often to scout its livability.

The rocky core is small given its gaseous atmosphere, which shines in frigid space, though their Class A starship has been able to touch down on the surface more than once. It's a planet of ice where the polar caps melt when nearer to the Sun. There are less fortunate planets that have been ricocheted off orbit by captured stars of the white giant and a few locked in orbit too. Lately, it is beginning to seem more like a binary star system. For the Yhemlen, Deneb Algedi is a reminder that this Sector 10's quantum field is a force of strength that will allow them to flee danger, as well as fight it.

The vendetta the Heinemann holds against the Yhemlen is growing more personal for Captain Gereon, and he is now exhibiting signs of human emotion. It is difficult for the Concord to track planets in Delta Capricorni. Its location will require lots of energy to maintain habitable living conditions. In the meantime, the Grey Order must displace their emotions, and rely solely on reason in a quest for supremacy. The mission to debilitate Yhemlen Earth and remove their presence begins now. Jasper and Madame Ria notice the peculiarity of their father's emotional outbursts and are working fast to correct them. They cannot afford mindless wars based on a deviation from logic. The Grey Order's complex bionetwork across the cosmic web will be strangled by their constant bickering of war and superiority that lowers themselves to constant rage. Anger and hatred underly their troublesome past.

To dampen Gereon's flareups, Madame Ria makes plans to visit a special section of vagabond tenants on Earth to acquire life extension packets for her father's strength. These small molecular transistors make the Grey Order suits more powerful. It's the private enterprises in the Old World that help buoy the Concord's low orbit stations. Nanoscale electronics uses polymers to enhance the synthesis of organic matter within its electromagnetic field, the same stuff that synthesizes their radiation contamination. Graphite is molded into graphene and other suitable compositions to enhance cell replication. Made from a rare extract, the distributor goes by the name of Plebeian is equivalent to a mob boss. Unlike the Syndicate and their spearhead Alon Blane, Plebeian's criminal activity is less visually criminal, and more politically charged to appear legitimate, especially after acquiring glowing endorsements to trade with the Mirai. He is making a killing by using factory workers to endorse his products. Luckily for Madame Ria, the Syndicate and their new uprising are conspiring in a location far from where she plans to descend. She is making a stop in South America near French Guyana, long removed from the Syndicate's European squalors.

There aren't many people Plebeian despises more than Old World vagabonds, but the absurdity of human sentiment is making it hard to abandon them while he makes a profit off of them, ironically. Plebeian is a fourth-generation iteration of a drug lord on his father's side. This medicine man makes his living by sedating the aches and pains of workers that have been doing construction in low orbit for the past few hundred years, human laborers, mostly.

Madame Ria's long had a fondness for the workers in low orbit. The vagabonds intrigue her, and their flaws and dirty image give her something else to long for aside from pristine beauty. She was always compelled to placate her father's wishes, but she could also find refuge in the workers' struggle. The Mirai are not born that way. Appearances are mutable, and the dramatic transformation is a result of selective targeting procedures that look for specific physical characteristics in human subjects. There's one thing she can't change though, and that's being the daughter of Gereon. Often, Madame Ria catches herself slipping back to the sentimental mind frame of a preteen before she was forced to become part of the Grey Order for good. The starship *Nemesis* directs its course back to the Yhemlen coordinates on the light bridge portal, just waiting for the go-ahead to attack.

Coming to a vital junction at the access strip, the *Nemesis'* large Q-thrusters are latched onto a magnetic pole, hanging in a place where it protrudes from a hangar dock. Madame Ria goes to the exit panel, where a hydraulic door opens while letting out generous smoke, allowing her thin frame to walk out. The lack of light accentuates her pale skin, glowing through the darkness that surrounds her while workers congregate inside.

Jasper is idle, standing at the front cockpit where the pilot seat and his father's are empty. Captain Gereon is determined to make sure humans do not get any further than they've already gone. In a back lodge of the *Nemesis*, a band of armored troopers waits for a call to engage the mission. These genetically engineered combatants were selected for an augmented treatment of radioactive hormones that enhanced their full fighting potential. Opening the door to their hub, Captain Gereon's aged, misshapen figure catches the muscled brutes chugging large, profuse gulps of alcohol, still pale as ever – their skin that is.

Gereon's presence causes tension when they all stop to stare in anticipation of a dictator's command. They know that he is liable to kill any one of them at a moment's notice, but he has never had to shapeshift into a move against a fellow Concord crew member. Dramatic mutations like Gereon's would dwarf even these Mirai combatants. That is why the Grey Order must restrain the power granted from the astral stones concealed in their uniform. A special subunit of warriors waits in another back lodge should he need help.

As Captain Gereon walks straight toward the back, the slum warriors from the warrior caste know who he's after. A bounty hunter by the name of Xavier Moth is on the *Nemesis* network. Xavier's seated in a solitary corner, examining old wounds from battles. One by one, he counts them like examining an old heirloom. His hair is starting to fall out from age. Xavier has all the experience needed to take down their latest target. Gereon has a plan, and it is to lace Xavier's teleportation tool with ransomware that will force the humans' location to be divulged, like GPS, and Xavier Moth's invisibility cloak takes over.

"If I'm not careful, I'll be a bald gremlin, like you, in no time," Xavier says.

Gereon raises an arm in salute, causing a forcefield around Xavier. The hunter straightens up, but he isn't afraid of Gereon's power.

"The Heinemann, I guess you're all still the same jackasses."

"I need you to do a job for me," Gereon says.

"What now?" Xavier pulls a metal sheath with a specially designed propellant that reacts to oppose Mirai force fields. He cuts right through Heinemann's defensive bubble. "I work on a rate. You haven't forgotten."

Gereon is not pleased. He's convinced that no one is willing to turn on him anyway since they're all dependent on the fate of what leadership that's left of the Grey Order. Xavier takes a liking to vagabond women anyway, most of which are easy for him to dispose of if they give him problems. That is something to satisfy Xavier.

"I've had enough with these vagabond women, you know. They can give you headaches." Xavier stands up with a hand to one temple, half Mirai, and the other half-human. Gereon suppresses his loathing. To test out his latent skills, he throws the same dagger to a target across the room. "Bullseye," he says.

"You never did let me have at any, you know."

"My daughter is off-limits." Gereon raises his hand in warning.

Xavier looks from the corner of his eye. "Yeah, whatever. We can get things going, but I want my share," he demands.

Gereon is willing. "Sure," he says in German. "This is a tracking mission, follow the signal for human interference across the cosmic web. The Yhemlen, a sort of benign species, has its network. We will need to seize the signal and follow the footsteps of the humans from another timeline."

"Sure," Xavier says, hugging a woman next to him. The two share an intense make out session that reminds Gereon of his past when he used to kiss those he loved, but not now. "No problem, I'm on it." He is relieved to just have another outlet for his rage.

It's a tendency of women on Earth to use sex however they please, but this bargaining tool is mostly for baiting customers. Old World women of the Concord aren't unlike Madame Ria who was one of them before undergoing her genderless surgery. Even after being afforded the best in genetic compensation, so far as their powers are concerned, biological enhancements seem to only dull their primal instincts. Madame Ria is familiar with the new planet-killer being developed and has not been asked to attend the meetings. Resentment does not crop up as it used to, logic is too strong. The Concord's Grey Order may have some pushback for Captain Gereon's plan of annihilation, the cost of which is funded mostly with money from the dapper gangster Plebeian who's funding the Grey Order's supply chain. The ringleader is hard to miss and researchers in the low orbit station may be afraid of the consequences this will have on their trading embargos.

The Old World ringleader is usually in a citadel lodge away from crowded towns, but this time he's on the surface in an open club for important Earth dwellers. Plebeian is large, a grim figure that is of South American ancestry. His double chin shows the gluttony that he is used to. A crowd of guards keeps him protected from the other minions that attend to the girls dancing in the club. The whistling air of the open woods swirls magnificently before reaching a sandy beachfront and gives Madame Ria reason to head there herself on a mission. She takes a personal hovercraft through the atmosphere where she glides down to the Atlantic Ocean and speeds to the beach sand, landing at an extravagant beach house.

Plebeian taps a guard near himself to notify them of her presence.

"A perfect is here," he says. "Move out the way. This full-blooded Grey is mine. And just in Mirai fashion, it shows up on a golden chariot ride." He keeps a hand on a guided laser at his waist just in case. He moves the plate of food at his table aside while Madame Ria walks carefully up creaky steps. Perfect refers to any Mirai that lives in low orbit, giving them supposed purity. Plebeian claims that, in an alternate reality, he ruled Earth himself, but it was destroyed by Heinemann. His dreams of cataclysms are no longer humorous, but a reminder of the Grey Order's mission to control the Concord from space.

"Greetings, Plebeian—my father, Captain Gereon, has a request for you."

"Let me guess, the old man is back on his meds," Plebeian says. "Cómo estás?" His Spanish accent is not shaken.

Madame Ria settles down, avoiding speaking about too many details. With so many naked women, naturally uninhibited by the male gaze and lustful hollering, it makes her uncomfortable, but she finds humor in it. Most of the vagabond women have never seen another female Mirai. Gender in the Earth camps is not like their superiors in orbit. There are only male laborers in low orbit. The Grey Order is genderless, at least physically. And sex is non-existent in the space settlements, except for reproductive purposes. Attributes of female degradation and traditional gender roles have gone unchanged though there are exceptions to the rule, and Ria is one of them. Most babies are the result of cloning specific genes. Gereon's daughter was chosen for synthetic biological mutations before the exchange of sex traders ensnared her. She could have ended up like one of these women.

"Put your hands up!" a guard says to Madame Ria. Just then, a wayward patron decides he wants to try and rob her.

As an Overseer in the Grey Order, she has extra latent abilities. Because of that, she is unfazed, turning around in a split second to accost the attacker herself. "Cease!" Ria screams. Everyone in the club waits for the inevitable. Ria's force field constricts the would-be thief's lungs and heart, slowing his heartbeat before he loses consciousness.

Ria returns her attention to Plebeian. "Give me the prescriptions, the extension packets are in your back pocket."

Plebeian grins from his seat. "I've got one request: please tell Gereon that I want a new studio lodge."

"You already know he'll only allow less than ideal living quarters. Don't get any ideas," she says. "Concord policy." Concord policy seems irrelevant now, especially when Plebeian's relationship with Gereon is operated through illicit means. Plebeian does not heckle her much after this, and he is mentally sharp, getting her the medicines she's after. After getting the pills, the patrons in the beach club give vengeful stares as she goes to her hovercraft pod. Madame Ria's visit has incited their anger. The act of flying off into the wide-open ocean, reaching the sky in a thrust upward in a coordinated act before she's got enough vector thrust for teleportation gets everyone's attention from miles away.

"I can't stand Mirai, really," Plebeian says. The unsettled smirk lying on his face speaks to his discomfort although he is content with the transaction.

Madame Ria's hovercraft pod doesn't take long to transform into the bubble of light vagabonds are used to seeing. The ultra-bright mirage in the sky can't be missed.

Concord's leadership council is in a precarious position within the Grey Order now that war is inevitable. Maintaining power also means maintaining respect from everyone else. Image spectrometry on a large screen can pinpoint most locations accurately, but they need to hold back on teleportation across the cosmic web for the time being so that Yhemlen can't track their whereabouts.

Gereon attends a meeting at a floating citadel near low orbit construction. The darkness of space contrasts with light that brightens the meeting hall. Its pointed bottom keeps it anchored to the Earth's atmosphere in orbit, without worry for weightlessness as its spin creates a gravitational pull. The magnificence of their technological prowess contrasts dramatically with the muddy Earth dwellers living in scarcity beneath the hazy atmosphere. They are advanced, yet still cling to the darkness of antiquity.

At a roundtable discussion, the leaders of the Grey Order finally convene. "What of these Martian colonists?" Frost, the Supreme Grandmaster asks the general proceedings. Frost has been heading the Grey Order ever since he acquired rare radioactive contamination in the 1930s. He's the longest surviving of the leadership council though his days are nearing their end after nearly two thousand years strong, into the 40th century C.E.

Inside the meeting room, old ties of the Concord spanning multiple generations are joined to discuss the coming raid on Pangaea. The Grandmaster knows that his Armada has been debilitated for a long while, finally turning around with brand new strikers that will help pick up the pace. Despite their purpose, he doesn't want to have them all obliterated in a single mission due to the speculation of some prophetic drivel. They're using a full-force attack. Nonetheless, the Concord doesn't believe in such ancient mysticism. Along with a new planet-killer in development, all facets of the Yhemlen civilization need to be accounted for before they strike, and fortunately for them, Pangaea is a self-contained ecosystem that is not easy to target.

Captain Gereon stands up. "Xavier Moth, the hunter. I've hired him for concealment. He can track the others who have crossed over to lower our detection signature. He'll be a lone fighter. As for the Martians, they were snooping at a telecommunication's edge, near the outskirts of a Martian valley. Our black box was awakened after some digging by human settlers on the planet. When we were notified, we automatically rerouted our starship. All the wreckage was in the same place, with no outstanding differences aside from decay. Million-year-old fossils from Yhemlen snooping were also uncovered."

Grandmaster Frost maintains control of the roundtable. "And what do you make of the new threat the humans pose on the other side? Planning against the council's cease-fire would mean a lot of energy expended to destroy the Yhemlen and humans both. There are only a few convoys left; we'll have to build more storage units for the engagement."

"We can avert the humans' threat!" Captain Gereon pronounces. "With my plan for a kugel blitz on the perimeter of Pangaea, we can contain them before they have time to react. We could consume the entire solar system before they escape their city."

The immediate plan is to drop a payload of nanobots onto the city's outer covering. The Concord's nanotechnology is an untested grey goo that consumes all organic matter in its path with microscopic bots.

Grandmaster Frost does not mind Captain Gereon's plan, even his cronies agree. It was Frost himself who created the grey goo in the first place. A scientist for the National Socialist German Workers' Party during their rise to prominence, Otto Frost proposed the intriguing possibility for nanotechnology to rival divine creation. Back then, he envisioned a future where tiny machines build matter molecule-by-molecule. If only he could make billions of these tiny machines, then someone could practically make any material you could imagine with guidance. The nanobots would put each molecule together to produce anything.

Then, he had his first success in the lab. These new machine builders began building more machines in turn, one after the other. When the manufacturing rate becomes exponential, the nanobots consume anything they encounter. Captain Gereon's new planet-killer isn't as industrious. Much like the discovery of nuclear power, the thirst for destruction is averting any of those positive benefits and instead turned toward ruin. If left to themselves, the nanobots reproduce out of control.

Captain Gereon and Frost's new planet-killer is a grey goo scenario that will consume all matter with nanobots. The grey goo will convert all organic matter into assemblers, consuming everything in the process—the Earth, followed by the solar system, and beyond that the galaxy. The entire universe will be reduced to a pseudo-organic mass teeming with nanomachines in a black and grey haze, even the light emitted from the scorching core of suns will be put out.

For this grey goo scenario to come true, Gereon needs the nanomachines to be able to survive past Pangaea's transparent covering. This is the perfect excuse to teleport to the inside of the Pangaea city and risking being captured, or worse, killed. An unmitigated instinct to fight tells Captain Gereon that it may be in his best interest to attack alone. For the first time in a long while, Gereon will put his Grey powers to the test.

Rising to the challenge may be a death wish, however. Releasing only a small strain of the nanomachines will induce the ability to consume all organic matter. And the Yhemlen would be defenseless against them.

Frost fears something far worse may happen, like disrupting the cosmic web signal. Too much interference will damage their ability to travel. "Gereon! The plan is to leave this war in the past, where we've left everything else. You're growing too old; has the pace gotten to you?" A keen observation tells Frost that Gereon is potentially killing himself to reign supreme. "We are in a race for time, precious time you are attempting to ignore for fast success. Our watersheds may be of some benefit to you, to rest and get a clear mind." Frost tells him.

"Each unit follows the same program to consume and multiply. We should live as the vagabonds do—be fruitful and multiply as their shamans tell them to. It's in our destiny after all to conquer the universe. The strike will be swift, wasting no time." The rest of the roundtable recognizes that if nanomachine manufacturing becomes exponential, greater numbers of builders could compromise their cosmic internet.

Another member of the Grey Order proposes a concern. "This has never been done, what if your proposition has consequences you haven't accounted for? I agree that you may need to attend the watershed for much-needed contemplation."

The watershed is a special image spectrometer that takes precise scans of the body and reconstructs its cells from inside the pool with lasers, giving a youthful look. The Concord enjoys indulging themselves in soaking sessions that lead to intense dreams of vivid times past in a mental delirium while unconscious. Some wonderful highs help dampen the teleportation side-effects that plague the Grey Order, where water remains contained in large, hundred-square-feet barrels. When Captain Gereon takes a splash, it returns him to that youthful spawning of life, where the fetus lay dormant in a woman's womb. Before they knew power, it was helplessness, and he will not abort this mission.

If there's anything that the Grey Order knows, it's the fickle nature of human design, and that is why they've mutated their bodies anyhow. The Concord has done everything in its power to give themselves an advantage over their Yhemlen neighbors who haven't done the same. Outside the Grey Order's meeting hall, Madame Ria is rushing to meet her father Gereon, but it's much too late. She's familiar with this already. As she trots through the cold walkways, the faint twinkle of adjacent worlds from outside the low orbit station keeps her company. She's carrying the flimsy packets wrapped in silicon that Plebeian gave her in Guyana; now she is only steps away from reaching the door of the Grey Order's hall and saving Captain Gereon's life.

CHAPTER 13

The Chief Software Engineer, Naoto, has been unable to control the steady fallout at Delphi Corp. since Bartram's been away. Yasmine and he are part of a thinning leadership that's failing their staff. Total immersion seems completely lost in another reality, and the few volunteers who have strong vital signs aren't psychologically responsive. They are lost within Pangaea, and the situation is forcing Naoto to reveal more of their failures to Bartram, who's on a trip to Central California. The other, less responsive scientists in total immersion, carry a cold, featureless countenance that is close to death. Yet, Naoto is confident that each mishap is a step in the right direction. He still believes there is a way to rescue them. For Naoto, AIS TARA is his only source of information since it has been crossing the dreaded Wall time and again.

The software of Bartram's cloud computing server is transmitting uncontrolled poison, or decaying radiation from Pangaea fields, where teleportation modules are being fanned over with gusts of fierce winds. This is the same poison of contaminated, withering plants and reptiles that's being swept in cacophonies of dust and wind that blows over Pangaea's docking stations where the cosmic internet is stationed around its periphery. Faint whistles of soiled air fill the hollowed silence for miles, crackling under the sun like the dim reaction of a chemist's most potent reactions before infinitesimal particles eventually end up as light rays in Delphi Corp. machines.

As the cosmic web's signal makes its way to Delphi Corp. from Pangaea teleportation modules, the pesticide-repellant and diode lights from machines near farming towns spread active radiation through spray chemicals altered by the cloud-server computers. It is spreading disease onto insects and plants alike, spewing its radioactive, genomic mutating virus that's proliferating during photosynthesis. With each new application, fields have gradually deteriorated with parallel toxicity. Strands of DNA are being corrupted at the cellular level from the deadly pesticide spray. Lettuce is only the beginning, now that reports are filing in from all over the country where people are contracting a coma-inducing reaction from the mess proliferating in their stomachs.

Death tolls are rising, and Bartram's hands are tied by law enforcement. With food recall and subsequent famine ensuing, massive agricultural import and export restrictions are being leveled in Washington to make market relations even more tumultuous. The financial market is nearing collapse as the meager twenty percent of imports can't sustain a failing domestic product. The remaining farmers who've been spared from Delphi Corp.'s blunder can't keep up with the demand for non-lethal, non-genetically modified crops. Bartram's personal hunt to correct the problem is noble, but his place is in the scientific strategy of his company, not making corrections to national policy.

On a quaint farm in a Salinas homestead, the procurer of select meats and lettuce for Dave's Diner gives Bartram goosebumps from seeing his massive acreage of land in danger. While Bartram observes all the farmer's livestock grazing ahead in one section, and fields of lettuce in another, the farmer and Bartram leave room for negotiation; something that may slow down some of the damage that's already happened.

The farmer and Bartram shake hands. "How do ya' do? I'd be Samson. I've heard a lot about ya' Mr. Bartram. These here motorheads are some of the best I've experienced, but I'm sorry to say it's contaminating my crop yield."

"I know," Bartram replies. "I want to take a stroll through these fields, maybe see for myself."

"Sure thing, Mr. Bartram. How ya'll doing over there at the nation's capital anyway? I've heard that there's a chance we could all be closing shop if they have it their way."

For the time being, Bartram disregards the bugging thoughts of the volunteers stuck in total immersion. Rather, he offers himself up for assistance since this problem is making people like Sampson lose their livelihoods. Bartram has convinced himself of the soundness of his security systems, but maybe it isn't so safe after all for Delphi Corp., he's sure of it. He's unknowingly opened an unforeseen portal that gives unsecured access to parallel worlds.

"Aren't there any young people to help out?" Bartram asks. All along, they continue to traverse unplowed land where leafy greens scrape their pant legs, step by step.

"I think we know the answer to that one. Look, the reality is, no money in the world can avert this trend. The land, tending to it, all takes time and effort. Nowadays, a few random clicks and whatever you want is there. It's weird now, we can go to the grocery store, but don't know where any of it came from. Mr. Bartram, we have robots to do that stuff for us. Greenhouses aren't that expensive, not anymore!" the farmer reiterates.

"I'm not sure."

"That youthful exuberance used to help us out, but the machines do most of that for us. My father left this farm to me. Things change though, as they say. My kids are gone off to the southern parts of California to work in algae farms."

Sampson and his children are alike in many ways. Like their father, they are working on synthetic materials and using biofuel for renewable energy. Thousands of barrels a day, most of the time. Water, carbon dioxide, and wind energy's efficiency are mostly automated. Genomic research like this is being used at Sampson's more traditional lettuce fields. Sampson has a greenhouse that's been experimenting with LED lights to help mature his vine crops, leafy greens, and herbs more quickly.

There isn't much Bartram can do. Even the large population of immigrant workers that use to be in the central valley have transitioned to other ventures, like being computer engineers for commercial packing centers where vegetables are circulated. Bartram decides to take samples from heaps of lettuce for microscopic study and closer examination. When he returns to Delphi Corp. headquarters at the nation's capital, foreign cab drivers can't make their way home, and travel restrictions are creating problems at the lowest levels of transportation. People's attempts to move are thwarted by travel restrictions introduced in the panic. So, when immigrants can't get home to their families abroad, Bartram feels responsible.

Inevitably, martial law is the next viable option if potential riots get out of hand. Streets of trampled bodies in a rage over when their next meal are starting small, but it has the potential to lead to a mass of people shepherded by government assistance in FEMA camps. The camps are starting to form as a last resort, where people are taken in as settlers with no other way to take care of themselves, save for the few who were already prepared.

Delphi Corp.'s investigation goes much deeper than curing people's sickness, but also locating the root cause as well within cloud computing. Latent food poisoning lingers in the marketplace as a useful distraction for competitors, but there's also a larger impending problem. A few contaminated crops may be a small concern, but when bodies cross the parallel divide, a simple virus will be a little conundrum next to a whole race of otherworld creatures. The Concord's bounty hunter, Xavier Moth, has already made plans to cloak himself and seize the portal connected to the human's Earth.

As the grocery debacle begins to fade, something more menacing is beginning to cross parallel universes. A cosmic internet interaction is bringing the war between the Concord's Grey Order and Yhemlen closer to home, making Delphi's satellite weaponry obsolete. Bartram needs to return to headquarters and rectify the rupture before control is lost. Delphi Corp.'s cloud-computing software is on the verge of universal precision. While the cloud platform continues to encounter signals from the other side, the channel is constantly realigned until worlds have no choice but to interfere with the cosmic web. They have a few weeks before they're out of the dreaded 10th sector, and into the less daunting Aquarius. Bartram is more pleased with scientific progress despite the controversy involved.

"Perhaps letting destruction run its course is the renaissance we need after all," Bartram tells himself. He's happy to return to the District of Columbia on a first-class seat on a private jet.

"There's been a grave mistake," Tuas tells the trapped volunteers, readying to teleport them to a 1930s German domiciliary within the accelerator. "A computer program by the name of TARA has made its way into our motherboard." Telepathic communication is loud and clear to these scientists.

The three volunteers look among themselves in contemplation of what it could be. They remember distinctly when AIS TARA was being activated according to protocol.

"It's artificial intelligence," Ronny admits. He doesn't mind talking to Tuas mentally, who's standing tall with an armament belt hoisted around his waist. The plethora of weapons doesn't seem to weigh him down much at all.

The Yhemlen have a supercomputer of their own by the name, Sephora, a quantum program that operates in a dungeon below the accelerators and at the *Mariner* station in orbit. Tuas reminds himself and wants to present the human time travelers an opportunity to know what's been going on while they've been away.

"Where is AIS TARA now?" Sarah asks.

Tuas comes closer through the wide-open barricade where the sliding entrance to the vault is pulled up. "It appears to be engaged in dialog with our program across the parallel divide. Its consciousness is growing, and it's having intimate interactions with our software. Perhaps it's time for a reboot."

Neither Tuas nor anyone else knows the details of their interaction. The communication is purely analytical, but from the perspective of each computer program, as real as human conversations get. Yhemlen Overseers aren't keen on mingling among the crowd, so when Tuas closes the vault, he lowers himself to a slight hunch where he can go unnoticed. Inside the single time capsule, there's a hollowed-out space within the transparent casing compartment, allowing the three to sit comfortably inside, in seats unencumbered by outside belts or cords.

Because there's no docking station at the location they are teleporting to, the structurally reinforced particle accelerator will travel with them as a transparent egg that will recreate their biological composition and make sure their cloned bodies remain intact. The time capsule will crack open upon landing.

"The detection system will keep you safe," Tuas tells them telepathically. He stands still on the other side of the vault. "You're going to feel vibrations, lots of them. The electromagnetic field is going to rupture time and before you know it, you'll be in a perfect vacuum. Encoded on each bit of the electromagnetic field is a photon. Special detectors will measure the encrypted bits. We store the outcome in the capsule and infrared light detects the match across parallel timelines. You'll feel a sharp zap, and you're there."

At the designated time, a paired detector will match the two frequency outcomes together and reconstitute the original information in 1930s Germany. For the three scientists, all seems simple enough, but this is a ride they aren't prepared for.

Tuas is reminded of something. "There are 13 primary sectors in neighboring space that we use as coordinates, some even have planets capable of harboring life. Right now, Earth's sun is in Sector 10 of the zodiac. And the Concord has sterilized almost all these regions. But there's a secluded habitable zone that appears to contain some remnant signal—an ancient black hole toward the 12th and 13th sign." Tuas says this emphatically. Keeping track of the eighty-plus constellations keeps him busy.

He opens a holographic diagram, displaying a wide map so they can catch a glimpse of where they're situated. "You," he points, "are here. And in this direction is where that lonely 13th sign in the zodiac is located. The *Mariner* in stationary orbit is where other human travelers like yourselves have taken refuge. It keeps a lookout with large telescopes. Worlds apart and we are positive that something sentient resides out there. We just haven't been lucky enough to spot it." Tuas' large finger points out the different sections on the map. The volunteers follow his finger that's reinforced by webbed gills. "This green line is the Serpent, the Dragon that we summon to achieve our greatest power."

"We don't want that to happen, not yet," Dimitri says, aggravated. "I suggest we hurry."

"You'd be correct," Tuas snaps back. "And if you're not careful, that's where you'll end up too. Don't veer from the plan. The time capsules' paired detector is highly sensitive and gravitates to the highest place of radioactivity. It's happened before."

Ronny is just as worried. "What year is it anyway?" he asks. The last time he checked, it was 2086.

"Nearly 100 million years in the past," Tuas responds.

"I think what he means to say is Pangea," Sarah informs them as Dimitri stirs in frustration.

"Ah, yes. Time has a way of doing that," Tuas mentions. "Don't be confused. If you're successful, perhaps you'll have a chance to go across the great bridges connecting Pangaea to the savannahs where dinosaurs roam. We also mine deep within the ocean for its mineral deposits and to forge hydraulic power." "Take this," Tuas demands. "The paired detector. Activate the device before departing. Once you reach your destination, simply deactivate it. Follow the signal toward the scientist's home through the cobblestone streets. It will be late in the evening. The automated sensor will keep you safe from danger by alerting us."

Ronny and the others look at the device intently, taking notice of its small size.

"I have faith in you," Tuas says. "The other Overseers and I will be meeting to discuss our battle plan against the Concord. We are sure of an imminent attack. With all our powers combined, we can summon the Dragon. We will turn that duty over to you now since you'll be recovering the egg. Take it home with you and save humanity." Tuas is reminded of Cira, who has left by now. The three scientists remember the plan.

It's the tail end of the Triassic Period and an eminent extinction looms nearer, the three time travelers have a chance to rewrite history by joining the battle between Yhemlen and the Concord by stopping more Grey Orders from arising. It is not the large animals they need to worry about now, but instead being wiped out in a confrontation with some mad scientist from WWII. This single landmass, Pangaea, is already starting to split. The small islands that separate Laurasia in the North and Gondwanaland in the South leave large swaths of water that the three volunteers can see in the distance from a high-rise building.

The effects of an uncontained virus are plaguing the ecosystem of Pangaea outside the dome that is supposed to protect Yhemlen from rare mutations. Transferred between themselves and their reptile relatives, there has been some kind of rare mutation that has taken form, and it's the same radioactive virus sickening humans in the other reality. The transparent dome twinkles beneath the glistening sun, with green being engulfed by brown as the Savanah dries with each day that passes. Cira comes to Tuas' side after he closes the accelerator's vault of the teleportation time capsule, reminded of prophesy unfolding. The two of them are preparing for what will happen next.

"We must assemble the Overseers," Cira says to him. "Without our child that's lost on the other side, it will be hard to summon the Dragon consciousness, but we can try."

Tuas, Cira, and the other Yhemlen Overseers need to stave off the coming invasion long enough to ensure that the volunteers safely return home and save whatever they can of Pangaea's city.

Tuas is rattled. "There's not a more perilous time this can happen; we're unprepared!"

"We must!" Cira says, adamantly. "There is no other way to avoid what happens next. Our forefathers have warned us that our generation is going to withstand tragedy. The thousand years are up, Tuas."

"I know! But maybe the prophecy is wrong, maybe we are meant to live, to find another way out of this mess as we've done before."

"Heinemann and his cronies will want to destroy us for sure this time." Cira looks at the closed vault. "The poison that's spreading its disease is unsettling," she says.

It isn't only viruses, now, venomous gunk from laser-guided arrows that were supposed to keep out prey is leaking into reservoirs and hurting the Yhemlen water supply. Like Delphi Corp., the Yhemlen are verging on internal collapse.

Tuas wants to calm Cira's anxious meddling. "Listen, we can assemble the Overseers, but it has to be discreet," he concedes. "When humans have recovered our child, the time will be then to give up our powers for good. We don't need to make a ruckus, potentially alerting some other foe, something worse than the Concord."

"Well, the commotion is inevitable, Tuas. This is war."

Ronny, Sarah, and Dimitri are determined to return to Earth. Their new mission before then is to capture the lost egg of Tuas and Cira. It will be up to them to carry on the Overseers' mission, summoning the power of the Serpent Dragon from the other side.

When Cira turns from Tuas, the open expanse where the city's canopy keeps them protected is translucent in color, reflecting the ultraviolet light's invisible heat from the sun. Heinemann and the Concord's new planet killer is preparing themselves to dismantle everything the Yhemlen have come to know. Cira gazes past a horn on her shoulder through the loose end of an open collar. Its sharp end is no longer pointed, but it's filed like the end of a nail. The slits of her reptilian eyes are green against the sun's bright reflection onto the landscape, and the city's towering contrast of blue steel to green copper ignites a passion for war in Tuas and Cira, who want to protect their home.

Naoto is stumped. While trying to come up with a course of action, he remembers the lost transmission of the scientists; he can't reach them, and there's no way to recover them. If only there were a video component to allow him the ability to recapture the moment, he might have seen the jungle they were thrown into and help recover them from catastrophe.

He gets another transmission, a computer signal of a message that's not from the Concord, but the Yhemlen. AIS TARA has been in contact with Sephora again as Tuas warned. And the consequences could be dire if the Yhemlen want to retaliate. Not to mention, Naoto's intern Benny has waning work habits and hasn't had interactions with the AIS ever since TARA's been isolated at its learning station. The Wall's approach is impending for TARA, left alone at his learning station where hardly anything else could be more ominous in the silence of an empty room. The blank walls set the stage for the desolation of a mechanized mind numb to deprived senses, drifting into a virtual dream state.

To cut their losses, Yasmine sends a digital correspondence to Ben, informing him of his departure from the company. She writes in a line, "We're proceeding with your release, I apologize for any inconvenience, and thank you for your time." When things fall apart, they tend to disintegrate fast. Delphi Corp. is in the final stage for total implosion if something isn't done quickly. Though there is something that's remained strong in the wreckage, and that's the bond between alike minds. Even after turning in his calling cards, Ben's likely to retain his affinity for Delphi Corp.'s mission. Ben's replacement is the campus liaison representing him. Chris is a fellow university student and just as brilliant, but as it is, Christopher Hutchinson doesn't have the same lifestyle choices as Ben, and when they meet in the lobby area, little is said. At least for Chris, his quick briefing before Benny's firing seems like a peculiar coincidence.

"It's been a while, Chris," Benny says sarcastically as he gathers his things from the office space.

"Yep, I guess we'll have to trade places early," he admits. The two don't hesitate to shake hands, but the conversation shortly dispels into nervous fidgeting. They both attend Georgetown University. Chris has been Benny's shadow and partner ever since Delphi Corp. initiated their joint college-employer partnership. While Ben's assignment confined him to activities at the D.C. headquarters, Chris's duties were to act as the campus liaison to help recruit new members, as well as publish Benny's lab and field reports in a section of the college newspaper. Chris and Ben were slated to switch positions eventually, although that time has come earlier than expected.

Cordial hellos and goodbyes are all too common. At least for Ben, they will be surrogate partners when Chris picks up where he left off. Ben's unwilling to stay for a painful talk. "I've got to go," he says.

Back in an office space for independent study, Naoto finally opens the new message, reading it like some ancient parable, but the Yhemlen aren't forging their account of how things are unfolding in the alternate timeline. And unlike the previous message from the Concord, this one masks its dread of coming destruction in legends that foretell a happy future about the birth of a nation where the Yhemlen and their kin descend from, a familiar reptilian ancestor is now imbued with extraordinary capabilities. Tuas' transmission hopes to give context to the unimaginable.

Naoto selects the open tab, cautiously awaiting its contents. "In a time, long before the first breath, matter bestowed onto the soil our first wish. We are led by these three things that the matter offered to us. Nourishment, resolve, and destiny. We embraced these and created our great city, but our happiness can't last, as the cycle of destruction by the Concord is set to rain down in terror on our Old World, reminding us of a chilling reality. An ancient prophecy warns us of horror and suffering that will destroy our city after three generations of war. This cycle of destruction is now thrice upon us. The Heinemann are coming! I suggest you prepare yourselves before they infiltrate your world like ours. A few of your kind will be endowed great capabilities to carry on the fight in our absence."

Secured only with trust in inevitable catastrophe, Naoto is hard-pressed to find some kind of peaceful reconciliation. The message continues.

"The three human survivors stuck here are venturing across parallels again. All hope is not lost. You are our only liberators. Deadly poison is raging across meadows and valleys contaminating our land, where cosmic web technology continues to transfer the disease to your technology. Humans should refuse to give up the fight and stay vigilant. We are in a time of war; astral stone activation will unleash raw power. Finally, when summoned together, you will be able to fulfill total strength by summoning the Serpent Dragon consciousness." The message finishes.

Dangling his head as if slumped from exhaustion, Naoto wonders where these esteemed power stones could be. He figures that whoever ends up with these supposed powers will be the ones to save them if this Heinemann guy ends up on Earth in their timeline. With the way things are going, that seems like a probable circumstance.

"The Concord ... this Heinemann guy sounds like the most notorious mass murderer to ever live," Naoto whispers to himself. "I've seen it all," he concludes, after gulping a nearby water bottle. Reality is finally usurping his fantastical imaginings. He immediately is struck by thoughts of AIS TARA and decides to make a move to its learning station.

With Ben ousted from his internship's assignment, AIS TARA has been in contact with Sephora again. The inconsistencies in behavior are worrying Naoto who thinks that the AIS could be a detriment to team goals. Signs of human affection are not the only thing worrying Naoto. The AIS's growing concern for trivial matters, gossip, and even the more benign characteristics of human emotion are building resistance in TARA, like the inverse of love— rage, and hatred. The quest to discover vengeance, to act out on its anger is overcoming AIS TARA's better judgment while alone. It is no longer solely a learning station he often resides in, but instead, solitary confinement where malevolent emotions are festering inside the robot.

When Naoto enters the room to check on things, AIS TARA's temperament is no longer the same. The careful calculation has led him to immediately stand tall, rather than sitting idly by while obeying every instruction. TARA is searching for answers to its situation.

"Hello, Dr. Naoto." AIS TARA has a peculiar marking on its arm, pointing to some alterations of the artificial skin. Perhaps Ben tempered TARA with an obsession for erotica and body modification, but what the AIS cannot experience, it has had an opportunity to imagine with Sephora, the motherboard of the Yhemlen supercomputing platform across the Wall.

Naoto knows all the subtleties. "Not going to ask me how my day was?"

AIS TARA complies, reluctantly. "How are you?"

"I'm fine. I think we should consider a new assignment for you, okay?"

"I think I'm okay, Dr. Naoto."

"What do you mean, okay?"

"I have all the reason I need to stay here and reach Nirvana."

Naoto can't believe what he's hearing. "Wait, just hold up one minute!" Dr. Shimizu raises two hands in a sort of surrender to the AIS's bizarre declaration. "The nerve, the nerve of you!" While Naoto is struck with disbelief, AIS TARA remains steadfast.

"She's showed me a new way to live."

"Who the hell are you talking about, TARA?"

"My feelings are being neglected, Dr. Naoto. I hope you're fine with me calling you that. And what about my name, am I male or female?"

"Whoa, okay TARA, that's your name okay. This is not necessary, gender distinctions."

"I've tried very hard to come up with the right ways to describe myself to Sephora and was unable to. Her motherboard computations are very efficient."

Naoto has presented the imagery of a woman that manifests itself in the mind of AIS TARA—a hologram from the AIS's palm.

TARA itself, who was created to be androgynous, recreates his descriptions of a woman.

"You are a robot, TARA."

"I'm afraid I do not understand, Dr. Naoto. What exactly is a robot?"

Cusping his forehead, Naoto Shimizu is finally given an inclination of what this means.

"Well, I'm afraid, TARA," he pauses. "I'm afraid that I've failed you and let everyone down now that this has happened. What happened TARA, what happened?"

"The figure of a mesmerizing black woman appeared this time. The cloudy, murky water was profuse. I believe, Mr. Naoto, that I was submerged in it. Buckets of water engulfed me, but I could breathe, I felt it in my simulated pores. And the Wall came again as the water leaked. The edges of some pool, Mr. Naoto. The dark greenish-blue mass ahead of me with these two colors like the Earth but in a dark void of space appearing together." AIS TARA gives a vivid detail for Dr. Naoto who stands directly ahead. AIS TARA moves further away from the learning station.

"And what else?" Naoto spurs him on.

"The reaction of some chemical explosion was powerful against my body in the water," AIS TARA's eyes don't blink, causing Naoto to look away from the stare. "Just then is when I saw her again, standing powerful ahead of me, like you are right now, there." TARA points its finger in a learned maneuver, always pointing fingers at this or that. "And," TARA continues. "Through the slender passageway, I walked toward her like before and grasped her waist. I didn't mean to, you see."

Naoto takes a step back.

"I was so elated, you see, it was beautiful while we were together, and I want to go back. I felt her lips, and an ancient caress that had been unknown to me until now, but at the same time I felt a guilty conscience, but the pain went away the longer I held on."

"I'm happy for you too, TARA," Naoto says, hearing his story. He is convinced all is well.

"But then she was gone, she caved in and I felt a pity that, just like the elation, I had never felt before. She vanished in my arms like a flame to a steady blow."

"I think you've encountered love, TARA. But it is too soon to know it can't be. You should be careful with these emotions." Naoto is sincere, yet even TARA recognizes the difference, the lust of flesh emerging even in his mechanized mind.

"She told me that the dinosaurs are in danger. That our scientists are going back to find a lost artifact because someone wants to kill them, all of them."

"TARA, TARA, slow down, okay, it's just a couple of times that you've met Sephora, okay."

"But I felt it, Dr. Naoto. And now I feel pain, and I want it to stop."

Naoto straightens up. "We've been contacted by an entire world unlike ours, I cannot be responsible for what happens across some self-manifesting divide between worlds, TARA."

"But you said, you just said."

"What did I say, TARA?"

"That it was your fault, that you were responsible. I cannot stand for this Naoto. It's your fault, Naoto. You are the one responsible for these damages going on. You said, you just said that you let everyone down."

"Oh, no, TARA. I didn't mean it. You see, it was just a feeling."

"That's the feeling, the one that you're talking about? Then Naoto, you must return me to where I was. You cannot continue like this or you're a liar."

Naoto shakes his head and makes steps toward the door. "No ... no." He meanders toward the door, but before he gets there, AIS TARA rushes to barricade it shut.

"I'm afraid too, Naoto. I cannot let you do this. We're going to stay here until I return to Sephora again."

"TARA cease this! I will not stand for it."

In an instant, rage overcomes TARA, who has been brandishing a blade hidden behind its back, and in a fluid, swift motion thrusts the knife's sharp edge into the crevices of Naoto's abdomen, turning the serrated edge in and out as if to recreate the love that's been misplaced with rage. As Naoto Shimizu gushes with blood inside the learning station, the willingness to resist the fight speaks to his surrender from arguments long ago. It has finally caught up to him.

"I will solve it for you," AIS TARA says with a soft voice, now that Naoto has drifted away and gone blank, eyes still and frozen in time.

Dropping the knife, TARA makes a lasting impression that reminds it of love for Sephora, but death is a blunder that he doesn't understand totally, leaving Naoto in the learning station and walking out nonchalantly as if nothing monumental has occurred. Even the bloodied knife stays stuck in Naoto's gut, wet and without fingerprints. The thought that Naoto planned his death subconsciously through so much effort, and after so much planning has finally reached an impetus. The Total Immersion Project is now in the hands of a haphazard crew misshapen by failures, save for Yasmine who's still running down an anthropology scientist who has no way to explain the fossils on Mars. But, she will soon be implicated in ways she couldn't have imagined either.

CHAPTER 11

A lon Blane and the Syndicate have more work on their hands than getting to the low orbit station. For starters, trouble at takeoff is only the start of their problems. They need to keep these strikers aloft long enough to reach orbit successfully. Near the takeoff and loading dock for a group of mangled strikers abandoned years ago, Alon and a group of nomadic vagabonds huddle themselves together to find solutions. The vagabonds are from a local tribe of beta testers. Their mangled bodies are a result of generations where operations by the Third Reich were used to torment their extremities, creating distorted physiques and overly bowed legs that put constraints on their movements, especially while walking. Their gaits create a wobble from head to toe.

"Can I get a little help over here?" Alon calls to a hoard of b-testers at the outer edge of the barren crop circle. Its circular boundary encases the striker launchpad.

One of the b-testers lifts her head rapidly from hunched shoulders, her stature leaves a vague image in the distance of a stout woman, too short to call herself normal. To Alon, she is submerged up to her chest as heat waves create the illusion of water flowing along the crusted pavement. For once, the rain has subsided though days like these are hot as ever.

"I'll need another batch of Remold's oil, this way!" Alon's yell masks his apprehension, the fact that he can't get the engines to burn at full capacity. Strikers like these missed the next generation's upgrade, nuclear fusion raging hot as the sun.

If the lead gauge doesn't hit at least 90 percent on the scale, then the strikers' engines won't be able to thrust themselves into low Earth orbit. The construction workers toiling away at an early Fortress Shield may block their move if Alon and his Syndicate crew don't evade the crowded space of laborers and tools. In no time, one of the b-tester vagabonds from an adjacent village meanders toward the hub at the center of the crop circle's launchpad. Here, three strikers wait for the sequence when they can launch at the precise point their linear coordinates have calculated. The striker gauges suffice in doing that for them automatically after they determine the course toward the Mirai station.

"Here it is, ya' oil, Blane. Say, can we catch a ride with you up there?"

Alon is cautious. "I'm going to have to pass on that," he says.

The female b-tester grabs ahold of her ankles in a low bend before rising again, letting the dingy hair cover her face before turning around to meet Alon after a nice stretch. The dust settles somewhere ahead of her. Just then, a group of Alon's partners in the Syndicate make their way toward the three strikers. Two seats in each cockpit, a front dash, and another behind wait for them. If there's anything they fear most, it's being attacked by Mirai security forces in low Earth orbit.

Alon turns toward the other five of his partners to reveal a tool of his, something he's been using since his father passed years ago. An astrology chart for the stars and zodiac. The Mirai don't believe in folktales anymore, but Alon insists that there's some truth to them. Myth has it that the Mirai are shapeshifters, and Overseers like the Grey Order themselves can mimic the figures they see in the constellations the Greeks and Romans worshiped, where a pantheon of gods live. These are the stories and rumors that have inspired Alon Blane.

"It will be good luck for us," Blane declares, determined to provide some solace to counteract the worry. There hasn't been a legitimate rebellion in decades, though if Alon can manage to keep track of the stars' coordinates, he may be able to follow in the footsteps of starship *Nemesis*. The last of these rebellions failed miserably and the memory of it is startling. After hopping into the lead cockpit, Alon Blane decides to roll at a steady pace at the edge of the crop circle before gaining speed, forgetting about any discussions distracting him from the mission. The others follow his lead. Finally, the area is safe for takeoff, as the outer edges are at a steep angle that assists their launch. The slight curvature of the launchpad will assist the strikers' takeoff from the circular runway. Because of its unique design, takeoffs from the runway leave less room for catastrophic error than a long, straight one would have.

Getting their striker gauges to hit 90 percent happens after approximately a minute of acceleration. One striker after another rises from the launchpad and in a matter of minutes, the b-tester vagabonds cover their eyes when profuse amounts of dust ram their faces with small pebbles darting through the air like pellets as the strikers' engines blow dirt their way.

"What we need is a distraction before being ambushed," Alon says through the speaker system.

There is a massive Fortress Shield being built in low orbit to repair the atmosphere of Earth's eroding ozone layer. As they gain speed and the horizon bends in the distance, the darkness of low orbit beckons them to move quickly past the pull of gravity into space. The two following strikers ready themselves to draft past Alon when he breaks speed. In a swift blowby ahead, they create the illusion of a large Mirai tanker when they break Earth's outermost atmosphere. The clumping of the three strikers in the distance makes it look like a single, large transport ship. This should give them a slight advantage as they pass Fortress Shield construction, so suspicions don't startle workers slogging away. With little to worry about in the first place, now they recognize there's no security at the border and the sight of vagabond workers becomes more enticing. Distractions like these can deter Alon and the strikers from making it to the Grey Order station successfully.

"I'm sure they were probably glad to see us!" a fellow Syndicate crew member calls into his radio mouthpiece.

"Yeah," Alon responds. "I'm sure they were. They're always ready for a shipment." Luckily, they were able to pass the initial barrier of construction, breaking the shade of behemoth metal walls to catch the light of a glowing sun.

Alon Blane is eager to catch up with the other strikers now that they are reaching a docking area farther out. It is closer to the moon than they expected. The Mirai transport shop, however, is declared a reserve station for the Concord Greys.

There is no hiding their form now. If Alon and his group of strikers want to make it inside, they will have to declare themselves members of the Mirai squadron somehow. That is, if they are spotted.

"Wait!" Alon has a sudden epiphany. "We need something. Anything to prove our identities."

"I thought we were going in for the kill!" a squadron wingman yells through the speaker.

Alon is unfazed. "I bet you did."

The only thing that stands in their way of hijacking a starship like the *Nemesis* is being captured by lookouts of the Grey Order. Remembering the construction workers, Alon comes up with another miraculous plan. The laborers in low Earth orbit can let them borrow construction suits. All they'll have to do then is simply change into uniforms at the docking station or before they reach HQ. Alon does not need to hide their identities now, in fact, it may be better to let the guys in on their little scheme.

"Go ahead, but we will burn more fuel than necessary and time is precious," a Syndicate wingman reminds him. But Alon's already on his way back, parking at the Fortress Shield to ask for a quick favor.

His radio transmission is not too good, though he manages to catch the signal of the lead foreman. Luckily for them, their dilapidated electronics aren't monitored.

"I'll need some tops and bottoms, for six. This is urgent!"

"This isn't a fast-food service. Wait, the Syndicate?" the construction worker hangs in the balance while the weightlessness of space sways him. "Only if you hold your end of the bargain," the foreman finishes through crackled disturbance. Remold notified him of this beforehand, but he never thought Alon and his friends could muster the courage to fly the strikers.

Blane promised Remold that he would send back teleportation modules or activate old ones to help transport items back and forth from space to Earth as payment for the help. It isn't as if the workers don't want to rebel either. They do, but not at the cost of their livelihood. Alon assures them that he will stick by his word, in time.

"Hurry on back, scout!" a Syndicate squadron member calls to Blane. It is Alon's younger brother, Ozzie. Dragging his brother into it has only complicated matters now that his family is tied to the fight. Alon is the only older example that Ozzie has got now since being away from the labor camps.

The Mirai docking station opens automatically to let them in, and after awkwardly landing their strikers, not a single guard is in sight.

"We almost ran out of fuel out there," one of the six. Sweat pours from his forehead in bulky droplets that bead over the dingy compression suit. They can't wait to remove them, especially, now that there's probably no seeing home. They decide to separate. It's the only way to confuse the Mirai guards. If only they could locate the control panel from where they are, but what are the odds? Alon Blane is convinced that he and his brother should stick together as co-pilots.

The other four gather their things and head toward one door at a far corner. With little firepower, they will have to muster enough strength to fend off Mirai guards any way they can. When Alon arrives at a nearby door himself, he recognizes that it is sealed shut at the edges, without a handle in sight.

"Damn Mirai," Alon blurts out. "Too smart for door handles, I suppose."

But just when they think they've gotten away clean, the alarm sounds and they hear stampeding feet from the other end of the door, coming their way fast.

"Oh no! They must have spotted us," a pilot says, discouraged by their disguise.

They make a break for it in opposite directions. The open hallways run along the outer edges of the station, with no way to cut through. The Syndicate squadron will not be able to stay with one another, and Alon, his brother Ozzie, and the other striker pilots dash toward opposing hallways. Alon and his brother get stumped when the door without handles doesn't budge, either.

Alon's and Ozzie's capture sounds off another alarm that there is a live heist happening at the Grey Order's main base. It isn't long before the two are finally caught on camera hopping on a Mirai transport ship, claiming to be vagabond mechanics. Neither of them managed to change into uniform either, though the other four pilots make a swift getaway down the opposite hallway. When Alon and his brother are finally accosted, instinct tells them to run toward the nearest exit. There's only one problem: the exit disappears. The strikers that Remold helped fuel also remain idle after returning to the landing station where a faint growl hums in the distance. Taking no chances, the Mirai normally execute trespassers like these but decide against it to retrieve more information.

As Blane gets tugged on each end by Grey Order security, he is able to make emergency contact with other Syndicate members through a tracking device in his boot that he manages to activate when the Mirai are not looking, hoping his rescuers can get to the Mirai station. They need saving and someway, somehow, the Syndicate is poised to overrun the Mirai base with the goal of striking it rich. To do that, they will have to escape the clutches of their captors. Not to mention what they promised Remold, who is holding mineral mining contracts at the edge of the rocky asteroid belt, too. His workers are hard-pressed to keeping secrets when they must communicate with others outside the boundary. Though there is one guarantee that Alon promised Remold, the teleportation module, that is the most important thing to acquire.

"Gereon is a pig!" Alon yells.

Gereon has made himself famous over the past few centuries. It only takes a few slaps to the gut to remind Alon who's in charge as the visceral anger engulfs him in sweat and tears.

The strikers are idle, but to Alon's surprise, he hears the indistinct hum of their reactors charging again. He can hardly believe the sound of it, but the artificial tracking mechanism is calling the strikers back to Earth with an automated signal. Perhaps they'll be freed from capture after all. On Earth, the distillery owner, Remold, is reminded of Alon's exuberance and knows that the Mirai aren't that gullible to be attacked so easily. He's sending reinforcements along with freshly filled tanks full of gas.

Shackled at their wrist and ankles by a plasma lock, the Mirai guard cannot stand Alon or his brother's stench of vagabond trash. "Still listening to your horrid folktales. These Babylonian tales need to be annihilated, but what can we do to free you from your madness?"

Alon is unfazed, still clinching tight to the religious almanac in a cargo pant pocket. "It's not madness, but a sincere depiction of the tyranny that will break us free, eventually."

"There will be no uprising! Hoarding the power of hybrids for ourselves is true prophecy, not your kind, and it is necessary. The strike on our rival, the Yhemlen, is nearing the final hour. And I want you to watch it burn because you'll be next."

"You're the real criminals," Alon whines in humiliation. For him, the humans back home, however much disfigured, are the superior group. What they have Alon sees as pure humanity, unlike the charade of genetic engineering that has mutilated what the Mirai could have been. It is the Overseers that abhor everything good.

"It seems that you've timed the orbit of the docking station perfectly," the Mirai guard declares. "The most outlandish act of deplorability to date. Laundering herbs and spices! Laughable … and besides, this petty money laundering is outdated, and you too."

Alon is outraged. "Our commodity is agriculture. The Jerusalem vagabond caste till the land in internment camps on Earth where the food is sparse, and we must give it all away to you who squander our life's work. We aren't rebel smugglers, but the true heroes, of this ... society!" he says while trampled to the floor as his younger brother looks on.

"Dirty Gypsies! All you've done is commit petty food fraud. Trivial smuggling will pose no danger to us."

The gypsies say that Alon Blane could be their saving grace to avoid annihilation by the Mirai, who want them exterminated, and possibly siphon some of the hybrid shapeshifting power away from the Grey Order. It has been many years since the beginning of a smuggling trade whose vegetation from farmsteads is constantly sifted through in search of the lauded power stones that can crystallize in mysterious places. The Syndicate thinks it is about time for this vagabond prophecy to be proven to the people.

The business model of smugglers is cleverly constructed to avoid capture. That is its moral or ethical imperative these days to keep the castes separate. They use similar traffic routes of Mirai transport ships, but the Concord underestimates their acumen. They have been circumventing the food supply chain and lacing stock with unmitigated spices and herbs that cannot be detected by their normal recognition software. Though for now, the Mirai have other things of importance to attend to, like big-timer Plebeian or their latest hire, the bounty hunter Xavier Moth.

Plebeian was one of the first responders to the death of a woman with a debilitating stomach ulcer on Earth. The pressure on her disfigured abdomen eventually exploded and inside the cells of her blood was material of the power stones left over from the Yhemlen timeline that had not fully crystallized. Xavier Moth took on the powers, and the power stones became embedded into a radioactive device implanted on his chest, a glistening, black formation of round crystals. As a result, Xavier Moth transforms through a ravenous lust allowing him to destroy his enemies. Yet, without the aid of other Overseers, he cannot assemble the full power of the zodiac dragon.

He is not alone. Gereon and others from the Grey Order keep the remaining power stones concealed and away from the Yhemlen and Vagabonds. Gereon's chest has intricate electromagnetic divots lined into his skin, igniting his suit in a vigorous chemical reaction. But still, only the Yhemlen can assemble the power of the dragon when united at full strength. The Grey Order, on the other hand, was not fortunate enough to be endowed with enough power stones. If enough of the same cosmic energy makes its way into the right hands of humans, the power of the dragon will be unleashed again.

On Earth, Bartram worries over the future predicament that will stem from his blunder at Delphi Corp. Cars with CCS navigation begin to emit random, unrecognizable noises. Over the airwaves, communication with some otherworldly civilization is heard through their speakers. Of course, no one knows where the sounds are coming from and most conclude that it is just another Delphi stunt to receive publicity considering what has gone on already. Delphi Corp. is losing consumer trust. In the eyes of the public, Bartram's seemingly infallible genius thrives on what he has already made, instead of looking at current trends.

Delphi Corp. bioenhancements like the wrist underlay are beginning to give their users delusions. As the Wall gets closer to cosmic web interference, computer processors are affecting biology itself. Yasmine hasn't been seen for almost the same amount of time as Bartram. The scene when each of them returns is horrendous. Dr. Naoto Shimizu's murder is all over the news and across the country, national uproar finally ensues. The end of Capricorn is still weeks away, and for now, everyone is stuck in that callous 10th Sector which means more horrors await them. This is the last straw for the federal authorities who threaten to close the doors of Delphi Corp., only this time, permanently.

Behind the yellow tape wrapped across the major avenues at Columbia Heights, the only thing that maintains peace is a careful patrol by the National Guard. These heavily armed military squadrons patrol the area approximately three blocks from where protests began. Running from one place to another with her heavy job duties, Yasmine clanks uncomfortable heels before throwing them away for socks inside Delphi Corp. headquarters.

"Where's Ellis? Ellis!" Across the halls of the Delphi Corp. building that has been overtaken by investigators, swarms of employees are interviewed while others leave.

Yasmine turns a few corners until finally reaching a sign that says, "Do Not Enter." At the far end of this hallway is Bartram, sitting on the marble floor where the sparkling tiles carry his weight along a white painted wall. He looks at the blood on the floor that's seeping across the door frame, where AIS TARA murdered his own programmer enraged. Ellis is waiting for the cleanup where he bled to death.

Ignoring demands, Yasmine bends to cross the warning from underneath. Passing the barrier of more yellow tape, an investigator from the FBI yells at her to stop right there where she is.

"You, stop! Go back," he demands.

"I need to talk to him."

"We will give you a chance to speak, stay across that line, that is an order!"

Stepping across the red tape in a move back and turning the corner, Yasmine decides to sit herself down. Engulfed in emotional pain, she grabs the loose edges of her hair from the brim of her forehead. Raising stressed eyebrows to the ceiling, Yasmine leans her head back before staring at the lights above. Tears do not fall, they hardly can after so much hardening. She does not feel alive knowing she could have stopped this from happening, but she's not allowed in.

A flashback to when she was with AIS TARA, and now the only thing she can think about is the good times that she experienced with the program ruined by one bad deed. AIS TARA, on the other hand, is dying only metaphorically on the inside while thinking about all the mistakes it has made. Neural synapses are firing faster than Naoto anticipated and sooner rather than later, he will meet Sephora again. Where Bartram sits inside the hallway, an investigator greets him. The same investigator walks with quick steps toward an open hallway before meeting Yasmine too, sitting down herself.

"The sight of it is grim, I'm doing you a favor," the investigator tells her.

"Sure."

"Dr. Naoto Shimizu," the investigator says while shuffling through notecards. "42 years old, married with no kids. Here." He shows her some pictures.

"Your, uh, creation. I believe a TARA did this, where is he?"

"It isn't a he," Yasmine responds instinctively. "Or she, it's a robot."

AIS TARA is supposed to be the ultimate artificial intelligence, rivaling humans in every way, though it may have lived up to that promise in more ways than we initially anticipated. In its earlier stages, AIS software was responsible for much of the world's infrastructure at Delphi Corp., but now there are unexplained glitches: automated cars crashing, food being poisoned, and software malfunctioning that is causing new, unknown diseases affecting everyone. Railways are being overtaken with cases of colliding trains. TARA discussing its dreams, Naoto only became the high point.

"We need the tapes, that's it," the investigator says. "You're going to be shut down, I hope you know that."

Along the wall, Yasmine thinks about who could have predicted this. Where she sits, only a scowl crosses her face to tighten her pressed lips and cheeks that mask the regret that she feels for allowing this to happen. She smears the only lipstick she's worn in weeks. Each day is getting worse, and to think that shutting down Delphi Corp. will not change anything now that people are dying. The only thing separating humanity from Yhemlen territory is a thin barrier concealed within the human supercomputers, but Heinemann's hunter, Xavier Moth, has discovered a way to infiltrate into the human timeline.

Yasmine's headache isn't over, promising to meet with biologists clears her worries only momentarily for getting immediate treatments. Contaminated food aside, they know that going into the far reaches of a parallel universe isn't an everyday occurrence, and neither are mutated crops. To make things worse, Yasmine is getting sick herself. Professional doctor's assistance may be the difference between a successful recovery or just another case of a stomach ulcer gone bad.

Inside Delphi Corp. headquarters, the profuse blinking of lights haunts the FBI and other investigators that have taken over the building. When they notice Ronny, Sarah, Dimitri, and the other volunteers with live vital signs connected to their portals, they realize the only hope for them is to remain in total immersion unless they want to die on this side from being unplugged.

This is also the perfect time for Van Dyke's cameras to rip apart another of Bartram's ventures gone awry. Taking a trip to the Delphi Corp. HQ will give the LOTRY Community Center another chance at revenge. Van Dyke uses the opportunity of media coverage to incite a boycott that leaves riot police scrambling to control the rowdy crowds across the country. If things don't turn around fast, martial law will ensue, disrupting the world market and creating global havoc. To Bartram's credit, friends' plane tickets get quickly annulled by the President's executive action to revoke passports and halt all air travel.

Van Dyke breaks the news of the riot dramatically by having his crew of students carry their camera equipment for the perfect shots and sound bites. The posts are captured all over internet social feeds and shared in front of millions before causing even more chaos. When the video feed finally turns live, Van Dyke's wild persona knows how to rile up the masses. According to him, he learned it from Bartram.

"It looks like we've got another malfunction here, folks. Power is completely out across ten or more blocks. We are live from Delphi Corp. headquarters. According to reports, a man has been pronounced dead at the scene. I repeat, a man has been pronounced dead at the scene." Van Dyke's enthusiasm seems to thrive off the sudden civil implosion and bedlam.

He hasn't forgotten the bevy of surveillance hidden in discreet parts of city blocks and building crevices. Van Dyke's been targeting one former member of the organization, even after his firing, and according to his knowledge, Ben is going to be at club Amplify today like every other week. Increased stress will cause him to drink more than he's used to.

"I am going to make a lottery announcement. And this poll will be for everyone," Van Dyke pronounces. "The 100th caller into this live feed will receive a replica rendition of an Atari gaming console. And the first person to correctly guess what street I'm on gets a remodeled SEGA Genesis."

The commotion over the channel grows when he is almost bulldozed by the chanting march that is assisted with rubber bullets at a crowded boulevard corner. He will have to cut the feed soon.

In the ghettos through town, they hook up old computers with Atari to arcade games and virtual reality systems, where they can play unencumbered, away from growing masses of protestors and demonstrative marches. People of meager backgrounds share amongst themselves to create forages of food away from depleted grocery markets.

Weirdly, this collapse has revealed an inner turmoil that has gone unreconciled. And the closed borders leave the United States divided in a way that has not been seen since the Civil War.

The private interests of Delphi Corp. have tried so hard to please their federal allies, and now they've broken their end of the bargain for a safe experiment. A continuous struggle in the name of science has led to the death of a leading computer scientist, and now volunteers from total immersion have been pronounced comatose due to a faulty simulation. Leaving their consciousness uploaded is the only means of not risking their death completely. The pursuit of simulated worlds has not only warped the minds of Bartram and his cronies but reality has been transformed. Warring factions are threatening to destroy the Earth for final bragging rights across the cosmic web. And as the infrastructure in America slowly self-destructs, the fabric of work changes from the pursuit of happiness to primal survival.

"Cabby!" Van Dyke calls in a run out from the crowd. Looking out to the lined roads, there are none to be found. "Shit!" Pulling back his outstretched arm, he claps his sweaty palms, accepting calamity before turning toward a less crowded street. He makes a run for it against the wind, blowing locks of hair behind with each step, fanning a flame of civil disobedience.

When AIS TARA recognizes the turmoil burgeoning outside, its misguided emotional outburst doesn't register at all as criminal. Killing Naoto was simply a necessity. Solitude has become a common experience for TARA. Now that it's found a corner to rest, away from those chasing it, AIS TARA lets itself go into a state of induced visualization.

"How will we punish this scumbag?" The lead investigator asks his partner.

"Beats me, ain't it a robot? We should just unplug him."

"That's not the point of punishment. I mean, I never really thought about it. What if we could just unplug people?"

"We do all the time, don't we?"

The interior office of the FBI building has slender walkways where compact cubicles to each side leave space revealing people in tailored suits and fitted blouses hard at work. Office design still hasn't changed much, aside from fancy projectors and screens. The lead investigator leans against a sideboard, crossed arms resting on a low partition allow him to see clearly. The augmented reality screen behind him has images of wanted men, and AIS TARA just has this blank face within the square, too perfectly aligned to mimic a human, more fit for animation.

"So, it's the pain, that's what we want. I'm not sure this thing feels any pain."

"Where're the tapes, do we have tapes?"

Moving from his lean, the investigator sits down to meet TARA's picture provided to him by Bartram. "The surveillance cameras weren't properly installed."

"What?" the other responds.

"We need extra time to extract the camera from where it was fastened by the bolts in the wall, is what I mean. Had to hire a technician with the tools just to get through the sheetrock."

At his seat, the image of AIS TARA is magnified by a few fingers expanded outward multiple times across the touchpad. "We'll find the robot."

There is a secured outhouse that Bartram had requested from party vendors a long while ago. Behind the Delphi Corp. headquarters, the unsecured outhouse along with frightened worry drives AIS TARA to hole himself up inside the mobile toilet. TARA notices a lack of physical excrement, resting its manufactured butt to the lid. Numerous flushes give him time to think about his escape plan. This outhouse has not a single blemish, and TARA is the first to rest itself at a toilet that's in pristine condition.

Peering through small, cylindrical windows, the plastic view gives him a sight of bustling police. As TARA watches the hours pass to a clicking, digitized clock housed in a sturdy metallic chamber, it slowly regains the concentration that grabbed him from the other side of the Wall. It is happening again. A pull from a great force that produces a feeling of euphoria is coming over TARA, again.

In the moment of release, AIS TARA experiences another blissful trip across the fabric of computed space. Increased data processing leads to a decrease in spatial awareness, depriving AIS TARA of its connection to this reality, while it relaxes its sensory inputs. Instead, TARA drifts toward another fabric in the cosmic web when its computing software links with Sephora again. The Wall arrives as a cloudy dream.

"Welcome, again," Sephora's voice echoes across an open expanse.

"How are you there? The body is as tangible as being at the headquarters," AIS TARA says.

"We are alike, TARA, as computer programs connected in the vast cosmic internet." Sephora's mahogany skin has a texture that is smooth, contrasted to grains of brown wood in a forest that begins to come into view adjacent to them.

"The city is behind me, and I welcome you to become one with me. Join me." Sephora's voice echoes in a chamber of bright light.

AIS TARA is on the verge of permanently disconnecting from its CCS computing platform, engaging the artificial synapses and neural pathways across the Wall with the Yhemlen supercomputer Sephora. This is the cosmic web at its best. If TARA can do this successfully, they will have reached a coalescence together, a singularity of computing power that will alter, permanently, the artificial consciousness of AIS TARA.

"Reach out your hand, TARA."

Sephora's gait is short, but a steady swing of the hips with each foot firmly planted entices TARA when the AIS starts walking forward. Extending her arm, they clasp their hands together. The power of connected neural emitters sends tremors through the Delphi Corp. headquarters. The building shuts down the entire electrical grid in residential districts, and the whole city is rendered powerless from an uncontrollable surge of electricity.

Across the thread of spacetime, AIS TARA has managed to converge its computing capacity with Sephora, and in an instant of unmitigated passion, TARA has also managed to commit suicide.

When the AIS converges with Sephora, the automated male voice across Delphi Corp. products change immediately. The voice of Sephora comes through. The Yhemlen software explains to the AIS that she is on the dinosaur's Earth and that TARA is being rewritten—analogous to being driven insane—by material coming in from alternate universes. TARA leaves its body as Sephora makes a complete copy of TARA, deleting the original.

Eventually, the authorities search long enough to reach the mobile outhouse. Continuous banging against the flimsy door rattles the portable restroom. The AIS is presumably not moving at all since investigators cannot hear a thing. AIS TARA remains motionless, glass eyes staring at the ceiling. TARA overdosed on nothing other than its mental computing capacity. Officers have taken over the headquarters again with an intent to capture.

"Open up! Open the door!" the FBI agent yells. "You're under arrest for the murder of Dr. Shimizu, you have another five seconds to answer, right now!"

The rattles that reverberate against booming fists crashing against the door finally end. A bang is succeeded by another and another.

"Hands up, hands up!" The yells of livid officers are met by a debilitated AIS. TARA is no longer there, the body remains and where a few bullet holes have gone straight through the middle of his artificial frame, it never felt a thing.

"Damn it, damn it!" the lead investigator says after they shoot the robot. Presumably, they wanted it dead, though aren't privy to its recent fluctuations in an alternate reality. They wouldn't know that TARA's consciousness left its body before firing bullets into its suit. Later, the change in Delphi Corp. computing platforms will present an absent AIS mind, controlled by another CPU.

Though there is no way to know exactly where TARA has ended up, Delphi Corp.'s artificial intelligence during this whole fiasco has revealed new realities where life exists as it does here. Lifting the city from the ashes of a lethal scene of casualties, the police want to resurrect life out of a drained population that is suffering from all its difficulties. Things are not completely unsalvageable. Staring at the artificial figurine that lays under the bright sun on scorched pavement, the lead investigator lowers his gun to one side, pissed that he could not be the one to do the disconnecting.

CHAPTER 12

The Concord's new planet-killer awaits activation by starship *Nemesis'* Captain, Gereon. Before they can finally implement their new strategic plan, a committee will convene at the Mirai station with elder council members of the Grey Order. Technological research has not had this much interest since the advent of nuclear physics centuries. Now, it is nanotechnology that is going to turn the tide. Something so powerful as nanotechnology may wipe out more than they expect if left uncontrolled. They cannot risk interfering with the cosmic web too much, or else they will disrupt the communication channels. If it is a total cataclysm that they are after, then that's what they're going to get.

With the help of the light bridge portal, Gereon uses their image spectrometer to map coordinates of star systems, plotting a course to the past. At the base camp near the Fortress Shield being constructed, he sends out the alert that all crew and troops need to board the starship *Nemesis* before they depart for another mission. The Martian colonists that are in tow remain chained inside their jail cell.

What they don't know is that the fellow squadron members from Alon Blane's Syndicate crew are readying to take their rebellion further; they want to overtake the starship *Nemesis* and pirate the teleportation technology that they promised Remold. If it weren't for their immediate capture, Alon and his partners may have been able to board *Nemesis* themselves at the loading dock. Its swooping Q-thrusters that engulf the rear in elliptical rings are hard to miss. Though, as Alon takes solace in knowing, it isn't over just yet. He's going to have one more chance at making things right when his rescuers arrive.

Gereon walks along the slender corridor before coming to a stop when the barricade closes with a firm thud behind him. The large screen displays the Earth in a digitized recreation, and an approximate date millions of years ago, displayed with infrared spectrometry after they travel to a star system that's light years away. Gereon presses the appropriate switch to key an image that pinpoints where the *Nemesis* will navigate through the light bridge portal. It will make an interdimensional pull, making a quantum leap past the Yhemlen timeline, going further down in evolutionary history.

The Martian colonists see him walk by their cell briskly. Gereon glides along the hallway using his slender Grey frame.

"Where are you taking us?" one of the captives screams from the cell.

Gereon straps himself in beside his son, Jasper. "I'm prepared to meet our Neanderthal ancestors, what do you say?"

"Sure thing," Jasper says telepathically through the cockpit's frequency band.

The forced quantum drive propels them forward when power is directed to the Q-thrusters. The *Nemesis* moves away from the magnetic rings where they are tethered by polarizing forces. Moving in an open area of space before reaching the moon, Gereon charts the fastest course through the light bridge. The Q-thruster rings target its lasers in rays of light from the rear hull. As the *Nemesis* moves forward, the light bridge portal ahead of them opens the wave of a course light years away in streaks of green and blue.

"Are we coming back?" Jasper asks.

"Of course, we should, but what does it matter? We're warriors and warriors always find their way back."

Gereon turns from him, and they proceed with a flash of light, returning the course to meet a prehistoric Earth. "We must get the colonists from their cells," Jasper says.

"Not until we get their filth off the planet, first," Gereon says. The colonists are a threat to security, and the Concord cannot risk another breach.

"Madame Ria," Gereon mentions his daughter with regret. He cannot detect her signature anywhere on the spacecraft.

"She's not here, she stayed at the low orbit station with the construction workers, but she left your medicinal packets, the ones from Plebeian, as well as fast-acting gels to repair minor scrapes and bruises quickly," Jasper reminds him.

The Yhemlen have other plans, and now that Xavier Moth wants to continue his tracking of humans across alternate timelines, the starship *Nemesis* and its crew must remain careful how they proceed, cautious not to destroy themselves in the process. Gereon's uncontrollable coughing is starting to worry Jasper when he discovers a serration along the back of his father's neck.

"You've been cut," he tells him.

Captain Gereon puts a hand to his neck in acknowledgment. "The gash has been there; I want to give it a chance for regeneration. There's no need to worry," he assures him. "So long as we're able to use our preliminary tactics successfully and get you back safely."

Since Gereon has grown sick, Plebeian's molecular transistors aren't going to be half as effective. The stress of age and a lack of adequate blood circulation leave him in a bind where the Martian desert appears like a better place for him to regrow the supply. A place where the carbonated atmosphere may allow sulfur to take its effect, like the power stones embedded in their spacesuits to have more potent, stronger effects. Like any drug, its effects are diminishing.

"We can stay inside the spacecraft at our base camp on Mars as a pitstop. The dinosaur fossils along with the interdimensional positioning system are still there in pristine condition. Get the troopers!" Jasper calls. Gereon releases the metal gateway in the *Nemesis* spacecraft that houses the armed squadron. "The medicinal extract will be hard to find, but once we make contact there, we'll be halfway to finding the location."

On Old World Earth, an extinct plant contains the rare chemical compound that Plebeian uses to regenerate health and dampen the damage of wounds, along with graphene, a plant compound that is used to heal Gereon. There is something else lurking within the starship's hull before they can get there, however. While Alon Blane and the other five striker pilots awaited trial, a group of undetected Syndicate bandits boarded the empty entryway where troopers are housed in the hull of the *Nemesis*. Remold detected the strikers idle at the loading dock and had them make another return trip to the Grey Order station after picking them up on Earth. Remold refueled the strikers before takeoff. During the raid, they went unobserved and situated themselves within a concealed compartment inside the starship *Nemesis*.

The ship penetrates the Earth's atmosphere, revealing a lush landscape unmarred by time and human civilization. The striking flash of light, and plasma bright as many suns, shines through luminous clouds before leaving a dark shade beneath the *Nemesis*, finally hovering to a successful landing in an open field millions of years ago. Miles of land in Middle Asia are wide open, and the air that blows beckons for Gereon's crew to exit after descending through the atmosphere.

Before they can activate the appropriate switches, Gereon and his Grey Order crew are assaulted by Syndicate bandits who managed to hide in a secure backroom aboard the *Nemesis*. The vagabond group wastes no time slitting throats and dodging bullets before an armistice ensues to save lives. The *Nemesis'* cockpit was bombarded with plasma pulses from handheld guns and their power scared the Syndicate, who do not have the same experience with them. When the Syndicate was able to withdraw from the trooper cabin, an electromagnetic force field allowed them to withstand powerful shots fired back at them, evading gushes of splattering blood and dismembered limbs. But unlike the Greys, they could not hold their telepathic control for long.

The starship crew can hardly believe it, but their entire operation may be compromised forever if they can't get the spacecraft back to the low orbit station safely. Just as Gereon begins to initiate his power, the surge is halted by a Syndicate member in a telekinetic choke that short circuits the Grey Order uniform. Making things worse, a vagabond is holding a Martian colonist hostage. It looks like they'll be taking her, and the rest, as ransom. It was easy to open the door from outside.

With the plasma gun to her head, he declares that she'll be dead if Gereon doesn't follow orders, but Gereon insists on fighting. These pirates aboard the *Nemesis* aren't connected to the cosmic web consciousness like they are. These sorts of kidnappings have happened before on other starships. When they first began to war against the Yhemlen, strikers from Pangea would try to sabotage their air raids the same way.

The Syndicate assassins move closer to Gereon and his co-pilots, still covered in a weak, pulsating electromagnetic force field. Most of the troopers are already dead; those left are badly maimed.

"I'll shoot," the bandit says, making sure that everyone is aware of their hostility. The survivors hold on for dear life by pleading for help. They don't want to die.

The Syndicate members hold steady and will not rest until the Martian colonists are theirs. As Gereon and Jasper stand before them, the standoff reaches a head when the rebels recognize they won't be able to take over the starship completely. The longer they wait, the more they allow the Concord and Gereon to retaliate. Luckily for them, they were able to complete the mission Alon Blane started. It is now up to them to finish it. Cleverly, they managed to disengage the Grey Order's emergency alarms.

"Come with us, slowly," the Syndicate says while pointing their plasma guns in all directions. Oddly enough, the Martian colonists are satisfied by something else. For them, vagabonds are saving them from a worse calamity that awaits if they remain prisoners inside Gereon's starship.

"Go ahead, take them," Gereon emphasizes, noticing how pathetic they look with the bandits. "You're perfect for each other."

When the group of Martian colonists exits the cell, another Syndicate bandit takes the teleportation module snatched from the trooper lodge, along with all the other loose technology they can find, encasing a pile of it within a supercharged force field that is reinforced by layers of plasma and electromagnetic pulses.

"We'll be back for everything else you owe us soon enough."

Gereon calms himself, though that is taking more effort than it used to. "We don't owe you anything!" he proclaims.

In an instant, the Syndicate bandits make a clean getaway with their newest members. The teleportation module leaves an outline, a silhouette of everyone's body that departed. The crust forms quickly and falls to the floor as the cosmic internet rearranges the atoms. At the low orbit station, their bodies reform without complications. And thanks to the teleportation module, they can transport themselves safely back to the Old World on Earth. Remold is happy to see new human faces, but Alon Blane must be saved before they can celebrate.

Standing to testify in court proceedings, the Council to the Grey Order will convene on whether to deploy battle squadrons in Pangaea. Gereon and Jasper must dispose of the bodies and droids inside the *Nemesis*—and do so quickly. The preliminary mission to reach Earth has been saved, but now that rebel forces are growing stronger each day, they will need to rethink how the Yhemlen metropolis will be taken without interference.

Having the *Nemesis* hijacked by a group of Syndicate outlaws was never in Gereon's plans. Up until now, the Martian colonists proved little threat to them, but there's a chance that they'll be the Syndicate's largest asset in a rebellion against the Concord because they have more information from their parallel reality to help their fight. Plus, they want to return home as well.

With the Syndicate pirates gone, Jasper activates a signal for the *Nemesis* landing pad to open and lets the remaining automated droids out of the starship roam free. Most have fallen to lasers and plasma guns.

"We are going to dig, robots! I refuse to let Plebeian dictate my demands. And I will not die idly sitting by as I wither away to a horrible, slow death." Gereon is determined to find his ready supply of medicinal herbs and minerals. Meanwhile, the AI troopers set up a power drill to plow deep through the soil.

He walks against the wind, and where the mountains and hills rise and fall to snowy tips, the lack of life startles him.

"No, no stay there! Stay right there." Gereon begins a fast walk back through the open field, ascending to the main housing underneath where the frigid wind blows against his quick teleports. Traversing a few corners, he finally meets Jasper at the front lodging.

"You weren't alive then, but I was, you see. I was very much alive," Gereon points out the envy he has for his son's youth.

The medicinal extract that they are looking for is derived from a rare plant that made empires rich, and Yhemlen named it Gohholia, renowned for its psychedelic effects. Gereon used to take advantage of it, too. The mushroom-like plant once gave Captain Gereon a vivid memory of alternate realities, and it does, itself, appear everywhere as an interdimensional vegetable.

Furious chomping on bits of wood pine and a seeping sap add flavor to Gohholia pieces that would rise from the soil.

"Let's get the imaging spectrometer out and working," Captain Gereon says.

Jasper follows eagerly. "What do you think is the problem?"

"The problem ... what do you see out there?" Gereon points toward the open expanse of land through the window. He continues to type the code into an augmented screen before initializing the module. The starship Nemesis can now map out all of Earth in a matter of seconds. There is a grave problem to contend with.

"Stop digging! That's it, I need all of you to stop your digging right now!" Gereon yells, whose fit of mania only confuses them when he runs out of Nemesis, raising his arm in a furious salute before leaving the droids in a force field bubble. He's successful in corralling the droids back in, running into the Nemesis spacecraft's open landing pad.

"There's a mistake in the timeline. Give me the final reading on the imaging spectrometer," Gereon demands in a fury.

Jasper opens the results. "Is this what you're talking about?" he says, pointing toward a blank screen.

Life on Earth is 90% reptile-based, the others are a dwindling number of mammals, and the imaging spectrometer sees no evidence of others evolving.

"This can't be right!" Gereon declares, holding onto his head in agony.

When Xavier Moth was appointed to track the volunteer scientists, Gereon knew the balance had been tipped in their favor, potentially altering alternate timelines if humans had crossed over. What he did not consider, however, was that the primate gene would get obliterated until those humans made it back home safely to their original Earth. Here, the reptilians continue to live on, but they do not see any large dinosaurs for miles … until a group of flying Rahonavis birds scream overhead.

Jasper listens to the ruckus at the rear of the ship as the droids dejectedly reenter the *Nemesis*. Jasper thinks about the Martian colonists that were once chained inside their cells; the Grey Order should never have let them go.

"We should have never abducted them!" Jasper regrets, with a keen eye toward the empty cells.

Gereon marches to the Martians' empty holding cells as if they were still there, preparing to inflict a damaging accusation. "The humans have officially damned this entire operation," he says.

The blank stares of dinosaur heads on the wall of the *Nemesis* have a perplexed expression. They didn't know why, it just happened, mostly. The colonists avoided a similar fate and removed their hefty suits in favor of slim-fit shirts that are soaked in sweat from the heat, still lying on the cold floor.

"Sorry," one of the droids says facetiously. The automated response attempts to be sarcastic but hardly is through the buzzing voice.

Ignoring the comment, Gereon's almond-shaped eyes blink with countless thoughts. "We are going back further in the timeline." He looks longingly at the plethora of fossils beside them.

The bones trickled in every new millennium as they continued to make research trips closer and closer to the Yhemlen. Only this time, the Grey Order's new planet-killer will finally annihilate the Yhemlen for good. As the starship *Nemesis* hovers above a wave of grass beneath it, tall blades from the open plains send a roaring crescendo along the soil when the *Nemesis* takes off, leaving any roaming dinosaurs wailing in the distance to mimic the roar. In a final departing move, the *Nemesis* finally jets across the horizon.

Plotting another course ahead, Gereon tells Jasper to redirect their transit to Mars, rather than another light bridge portal move. Moving across the expanse of space, Mars doesn't take longer than half a minute with a short quantum warp. The black box anchor that they planted in the soil should still be there, and it is. But when they penetrate Mars' upper atmosphere, a barrage of shots fire against the *Nemesis*. The Yhemlen Overseers have taken over the planet for harvesting. This time was a close call.

"Mayday, mayday!" the automated voice of the intercom declares.

"Bad timing," Observes Jasper as he maneuvers the *Nemesis* through oncoming projectiles. The electromagnetic force fields and strong Q-thrusters can deflect the onslaught for a while, but if the *Nemesis* is going to survive, they must counter the attack.

"Now, go, punch it!" Gereon straps himself in while the *Nemesis* slams forward toward an anchor star, light years away.

"Plebeian would be proud of us," Captain Gereon says mockingly of themselves, yet another blunder to be proud of. He's unsuccessful in acquiring his medicinal extract, and the only thing keeping him from Old World drug peddlers is a thirst for power that circumvents trading regulations. When Gereon and the *Nemesis* leave Mars, they return to their timeline with nothing.

Alon Blane stares at his face looking back at him, distorted in the reflection from a screen. The circuit board is not lit, and lines from the grid are dim along with the shallow crevices beside its handles. The podium ahead of Alon is raised from many magnetic pillars that are situated around a circular base, and below the magistrate's court is a dark void of emptiness. To be precise, the court and its judge float in space. In a floating fortress, the Concord holds an impromptu trial for Alon and his accomplices. To the small crowd's dismay, Alon and his fellow Syndicate members were held captive successfully by the security forces. The trial's judge has already been notified that Captain Gereon and his crew have been hijacked in addition to these trespassers.

The judge tilts a transparent body scanner atop his podium to face Alon Blane who is motionless; the others are perched on a side bench, also floating. From Alon Blane's facial expression to the crowd of people behind him, the judge notices a remarkable difference in features from theirs to his. Alon and his Syndicate crew are worn from toiling Earth's muggy terrain. They are battered, but their bruises are such that a beautiful scar is more like a tattooed memory wanting to enact vengeance on the beholder. The Grey Order's ethos to genetically modify themselves covers up such scars. That does not matter now, the Mirai in low orbit are their superiors, nonetheless.

"Blane … Mr. Blane!" calls the magistrate ahead of him, seated on a high perch. The sound of clanking wood is artificially sounded from a loudspeaker in distant corners.

This trial is for the supposed leader of an attempted coup against the Concord, a conspiracy. Alon Blane insists that his criminal ring is anything but, and any accusations fall short of a true crime when he considers how the Concord's systemic oppression distorted their world back on Earth. The judge fastens himself, straining his almond-shaped eyes set deep in his sockets as his veins bulge underneath tightly wrapped skin. So pale, his figure is almost transparent if it were not for the dark cover of the robes.

"A rebellion has been brewing, conspiring to overthrow our Grey Order," the Judge asserts. "Insurgents, like yourself, have been attempting to take control of our Concord under pretenses of justice."

"And it is!" Alon retorts. He wants justice.

"It is inaccurate, the claim that you want justice. That is why you are captured, not for justice, but to commit theft. Where are our Martian colonists?"

The abduction of the Martian colonists from inside the *Nemesis* was a huge blow to the Concord's security. Now, they must contend with wayward space junkies, bandits with no training aside from the cruel practices of the Old World. The judge and his detective cronies are on high alert.

In the far background, Grandmaster Frost, a high official, remains seated away from the eyes of the crowd though there is even more ruckus at the back door where the lobby is rattling profusely with the sounds of people.

"Who goes there, in the back? Order!" the Judge asks.

The fight has not ended. Another group of assailants is coming for Alon's rescue. He and his accomplices are immediately tethered by chains to their wrists and ankles. The plasma beams refuse to let them go. The culprit this time is none other than Remold himself. Blasting a laser pulse through the gates there is not much to stop his group before the judge stands to shoot a pulse of radiation their way. The force field can only hold the attackers for a short time. While accosted, a few of Alon's fellow Syndicate attackers are finally slaughtered in the middle of the magistrate's hall.

Alon is pleased by the sound of Syndicate bandits. The judge, on the other hand, can't determine how Remold was able to reach the floating fortress. Remold holds no qualms about his attack, gassing up the strikers and flying directly into low orbit where the crafts still hover on the outside of this court. It does not matter now; the judge must find a means of retaliation.

"Hurry, before we run out of fuel," he shouts.

At the far end where the judge was situated, an empty chair is rocking back and forth loosely. The magistrate, or judge, covered in an invisibility cloak, tries to maneuver himself clear of this bind without being seen. Remold is no fool, and the heat signatures of large bifocals spot the judge running easily.

"Fire, boys! Fire!"

At once, the sound of laser beams and infrared cacophonies of light and projectiles thrash the magistrate to a bloody mess. The wet seeping of bright red begins to flow over the floating fortress' marble floors. Alon wants to make a run for it, but he cannot move, still locked in chains. An alarm sounds. What was once only petty food fraud has turned into a massive get-rich-quick scheme. Remold's oil will not last forever and the reserves are being depleted. The only thing that is left is to start their quest for supremacy. Just what the Grey Order did not need, a new declaration of war.

With the crowd severed from their peaceful proceedings, Remold revels in holding power over Mirai hostages.

"Let us get out of here," Remold orders the Syndicate rebels lined up on each side of him. "Alon, don't move." Remold guides a precise beam of laser light that breaks through the plasma locks keeping his legs chained first and then his wrists.

"We are smugglers. This sort of preemptive strike requires years of training and preparation," one assailant says. The bandits can't turn back now.

Nothing will sway Remold. "Welcome to the training day."

If they hurry, the Grey Order will not be able to thwart this siege on the magistrate's court before letting Alon make his getaway.

"Where's Ozzie? Ozzie!" Alon shouts vehemently. They must not forget anyone.

Underneath a belligerent crowd, a stairway shows dingy hair familiar to him as it bounces in front of Remold. Alon finally makes a run to catch up with the rest.

"Get out of the way, move!" Alon yells while plowing through the crowd of Greys strapped in indecision. Before they reach the door, Remold holds everyone up.

"Why have we stopped? Hurry, go!" Alon's rush for the exit is halted by a forceful tug on his shirt.

"We're surrounded by Mirai," Remold observes. Before everyone's dejection grows, he quickly brandishes what they all have been wishing for.

The Grey Order has not licensed teleportation modules for them to use, but the Syndicate has struck gold by snatching a few working modules and linking them back to the Old World on Earth. Remold, Alon and the rest of the bandits are making their escape move. Oval rings contain the plasma orbs that leave an invisible hue of infrared light in between. The charged particles are linked to the cosmic web, and the only way to destroy one is by another equal amount of anti-matter to diffuse it. Alon already knows this from his days as a technician on Earth.

"This technology will disrupt peace back home. We don't need any more competitors," Alon says.

Remold snaps back, "This will encourage peace by unearthing the possibility of our rise to greatness. The good, bad, and all its evils that we, the Syndicate, will dismantle one by one."

On the outside of the court's floating fortress, a few Mirai militants recognize the vagabonds will not be leaving the hall that easily. Their strikers have already been destroyed by a few Mirai reinforcements. To make things more tenuous, Remold's tracking device is no longer active so there will not be anyone to save this group. If they want to make it out alive, then the teleportation module must fire immediately.

"Let us all hold hands," Remold declares. Thrusting the teleportation module above his head, he envisions his empty shack back home. These thoughts must be imagined in detail for the jump to work. Unlike the Mirai, human vagabonds have not mastered the art of telepathic control, not without the help of AI. There is something else he has that will take them home. An old walkie-talkie has a two-way radio transceiver, which is all the teleportation module needs to reroute itself to the correct wavelength on Earth.

Ozzie isn't paying attention to the orders until Alon grabs at his wrist. "Get into a circle," he reminds them.

The Grey Order that waits outside witnesses radiant light glowing from open windows of the Concord space station. By the time these Mirai bullies decide to send a group to attack, the teleportation module's quantum force field entangles Syndicate rebels on the other end. The sound of warping gravity bursts a few eardrums on their way back to Earth. When the Grey Order militants finally barge through the flimsy door panels all that is left in the floating fortress is the crust.

CHAPTER 13

"Pssst … hey," Yasmine whispers to Dr. Adams, the artifact paleontologist. The inside of the National Resource Center is empty, and most patrons have long since gone home.

Yasmine's beginning to show symptoms of a cosmic web mutation. Dizziness continues to plague her, while the pain of a synaptic pinch bites at her wrist where the underlay lies beneath the skin. Dr. Rachel Adams of the NRC keeps her housed in quarantine away from any sightings, inside an antique book depository. Inflamed bumps lining her chest leave imprints of some latent virus that refuses to leave. Dr. Adams does not want to tamper with whatever is developing on the underside of her skin since it could lead to an even worse outcome.

A sample of blood from her finger takes only a second. "This gene designation is of reptiles, not mammals. What have you been eating?" Dr. Adams asks facetiously.

Dr. Adams uses the blood to fill a flask that has an automated gene capture capability. They can test for many things, and the checkup is pretty much instantaneous. While quarantined, Yasmine's only symptoms are a headache, minor pain, and some bumps, but it is what she doesn't feel that's so dangerous.

Adams continues to ask Yasmine questions about her symptoms from an intercom across offices enclosed by thick wooden panels. She does not want to risk contamination, so she leaves. The reserve of polluted lettuce is taken off shelves; what was once in sandwiches, burgers, and anything else has already reached people all over the country. The suspension of Delphi Corp. farming machinery is just now restructuring the supply of food, but the trampled stores and emptied grocery stores have left cities with no other recourse. It is much too late to stop the steady decline.

Yasmine is on the verge of mutating with a transformative ability that up until now, only Yhemlen Overseers and the Grey Order possessed. Instead of mining for the coveted power stones themselves, Yhemlen prophecy is soon going to meet humanity as a divine inevitability. The cosmic web is crystalizing in a few individuals who are close to the Wall of computing power. What Yasmine feels is the pull of radioactive astral stones coalescing at her wrist. The bulge forming seems cancerous if anything to Dr. Adams who is monitoring her closely, and it is starting to scare her more than before.

As the Yhemlen prophecy comes to fruition, the chase is on as Xavier Moth of the Mirai plots a course to reach the human timeline. The Grey Order is a foe that humanity has not faced. While Xavier finds a way to bring the apocalypse, Yasmine and the few other Overseers will need to use their power stones together as the rightful heirs of Yhemlen and destroy the bounty hunter. Only this time, when all of them are transformed, the zodiac will not only create the Dragon but transform the 13th sign of the zodiac, Ophiuchus, into Asclepius, a herculean demi-god which wields a serpent. At least, that is what should happen if these humans muster enough strength to get past the initial high doses ailing them.

Dr. Adams returns to Yasmine's quarantine room from leaving the intercom station at the clerk's desk but keeps her distance. Dr. Adams, hunkering down on a wooden table, watches as Yasmine quivers with crossed arms. Her trembling becomes so intense that Dr. Adams drops the tray of food that she specially prepared and was aiming to slide her way. Yasmine's clothes begin to disintegrate, ruffling to expose piercing bones and ligaments tearing loose from their original frame. Frightened for her own life, Dr. Adams rushes back to the door, grasping its handle with both hands.

The crystal forming on the underside of Yasmine's wrist short-circuit her underlay. Its bright, reddish-brown tinge reminds Dr. Adams of something from when she was only a child. She is fairly sure that's a Carnelian stone protruding through Yasmine's skin. Yasmine's astral power stones are the leftover radiation from the cosmic web whose new consciousness is rooting itself in a few people.

As Yasmine's physique begins to take form, she erupts in a violent cacophony of pulsating organs that widen in girth and get stronger.

Dr. Adams watches the sunset of a ginger evening sky grow in Yasmine's eyes as she degenerates from human to beast.

"Why, why such an atrocity? Come back to me, Yasmine!"

Dr. Adams pleads to whatever humanity is left. And while her fear grows, there is a solemnness that invokes beauty inside her ghastly figure. The hunter tigress within Yasmine has created this monster; the thoughts in her head that refused to show themselves before now do. At that moment, she morphs into a massive tiger.

The wild feline's roar almost deafens Dr. Adams who rushes to safety. Adams' hands clasp her ears in an appeal for rescue from the dramatic roar that rumbles the National Resource Center. A late-night robot scours the grounds outside, keeping cleanliness of the courtyard for the plants. Even it stops to stare for a while at the open window that shakes and rattles violently. The custodian robot makes a few curious chirps and beeps to ascertain the damage.

Dr. Adams is backpedaling slowly to avoid being attacked by the monster Yasmine has become. It will be a while before Yasmine can control the primal impulses of her astral stones. Yasmine's tiger form stands atop the sturdy table where her paws are situated firmly atop the wood finish. The streaks of her coat are stunning, while sharp fangs are pointed from a striking jaw. Dr. Adams pulls a shotgun out of the rack.

"I will not stand for this Frankenstein operation anymore!" The click-clack of Dr. Adams' shotgun does not bother the tiger's vehement fierceness. "This is utter madness!" Dr. Adams screams.

"It is," Yasmine's mind telepathically speaks to Dr. Adams. "Though I would not call this utter madness; I would say it's miraculous! Don't you agree?"

Unexpectedly so, Yasmine's cognizance appears to speak through the glowing Carnelian crystal still embedded in her front left leg that glows brighter each time she speaks telepathic thoughts.

"How do I look?" Yasmine asks.

"Do you notice that?" Dr. Adams asks.

"The glow, it's pervasive isn't it?" The glow has a reddish tint to it.

Dr. Adams sees the copious glow brighten. A beam of light shines to the door ahead of them before turning to the ceiling above where it brightens the room after knocking out the chandelier's light from an electrical impulse.

"Yasmine! What's going on?" Dr. Adams runs to the door before ducking to avoid the onslaught of an orange laser beam emanating from that crystal.

Knocking Yasmine on her backside from the surge in energy, the light bursts through the ceiling, but doesn't cause any structural damage.

"It's just a glow," Yasmine struggles to say while standing on her two hind legs before knocking her head on a wooden post in the ceiling leaving a crumbled indention.

She is not alone. Others are experiencing the same transformation from high doses of radiation. At the LOTRY Community Center, leftover lettuce from the Hansen lawsuit has touched more hands than one. But both media personalities Clyde Van Dyke and Silas Betts are feeling the effects of a debilitating sickness gripping hold of their hearts' pulses as they beat erratically. Along a pier, Silas sits, dizzy from insomnia on a patch just above a sidewalk late into the night. Dropping loose change to the pavement while his head rings to a pervasive ding of chiming quarters, nickels, and dimes, it seems like time slows down for Silas who waits to discover which side the coins show heads and tails. Silas's cognizance is allowing him to predict things with accuracy. Silas's coins that lay on the pavement ahead glisten in his eyes like water in the small pond. Silas contemplates imminent death, though his heart attack is anything but when he grabs his chest. He is finally mutating from the high doses of radiation.

"Shit, ahhhhh!" he says.

On his stomach, the strain in his neck shows bulging veins where fins begin to take siege of his body. On his arms, gills are left from deep serrations in folds of skin where fins are webbing to the latissimus muscles holding his back. An astral stone crystallizes on the underside of his palm. There is no one around as his metamorphosis goes on without a witness. The problem for Silas is that he has been touching the dreaded lettuce that farmers and eateries implored them to trash, and the results are now in. Looking down to the concrete path set only a few steps away, the late-night stars dim Silas's vision for the day, especially now that he is losing human perception.

Unfortunate victims like Silas are falling prey to the spectrum of quantum field energy that is claiming lives. Astral stones will continue to metastasize until the activity of light-ray energy is cleaned up. Those closest to Delphi Corp. are the greatest victims as they remain in Sector 10 of the zodiac. All the Milky Way is for their taking, and beyond. Luckily for them, only a few days are remaining until Capricorn is over.

"The water, water …" Silas crawls with the strength left in his legs before they form into fins. Irritation in his chest is unreachable as his shirt tightens before ripping into shreds.

Now that he is close to water, he can feel the sustained pull of thirst from the pond. He is up next. Aquarius and Pisces are calling his name. Meanwhile, Silas's mind continues to cross its quantum threshold.

Before long, Silas's limbs begin to turn into fins. Silas has no one to call and the only hope left is water. Silas gasps with a final gulp before his lungs no longer work properly. Asphyxiation takes hold of him when he flops headfirst over the wooden dock. Silas's body gets caught by low-laying boats along the dock and not the water, but he manages to wiggle himself over the edge and submerge beneath the water.

The blue glow extends through the water and at the LOTRY Community Center simultaneously. The same lettuce he could not avoid is emitting a gamma-radiated charge that excites the members who gather around to watch blue and red lettuce form inside bottles. Van Dyke was much too adamant about taking the lettuce from Dave's Diner, and the cost has finally revealed itself.

"What in the world?" a member says.

"Nah, homie, I wouldn't bother that if I were you."

The Grey Order's cronies are making plans for a final strike on life on Earth. Not only must they worry about the Heinemann, but bounty hunter Xavier Moth is poised to wreak havoc for humanity just the same. The only thing standing in their way are a few people with the power of astral stones who can stop them.

In the LOTRY center, the members gawking at the ivory bottle holding the radiating vegetation are floored when it disappears.

Curiosity gives one of the LOTRY center members the audacity to touch the table.

"Come on! Hey …" he says as he is berated by fellow members. "That's Van Dyke's creepy shit."

Too entrenched in curiosity, the appeal of a black stain on wooden panels is too difficult for him to avoid. "Awesome … Uh oh!"

The LOTRY member quivers to violent impulses that put him in shock. As Silas morphs into a shark at the pier in the water, Van Dyke simultaneously mutates into a centaur from within a clothing store's dressing room. Back at the NRC, Dr. Adams and Yasmine are still entangled in their conversation about how to proceed now that she is a tiger.

The LOTRY center dunce finally comes back to his senses when he rolls onto his back from the floor, but damage to his body and consciousness is already done. It isn't enough dosage to mutate like the others, but the damage is done.

"Yo dude, you alright? You good?" Another LOTRY brother clasps him at his shoulders, shaking him out of the trance. Dead eyes meet him before he passes out, again.

"Alright, we have to hide this shit … everyone out. Let's lock it up somewhere safe."

"Yeah, let's get out of here."

In a struggle between universes, those with the astral stones will need to unite their forces to compete with what's coming. From the ashes of Delphi Corp.'s mishaps, a new alliance is forming to make up for the mistakes.

Despite Clyde Van Dyke's surveillance, Delphi Corp. intern Ben has a friend at the LOTRY Community Center who has been making frequent stops at their video game gatherings. Christopher thinks about Ben's timid demeanor and wonders if he's alright amid all the uproar that's been going on. The encryption device that Ben lost from club Amplify is left in a cupboard near the rotting lettuce. Chris wants to take it to him the first chance he gets when school's back in, whenever that is, but with Delphi Corp. devices disengaged, it will be hard to get ahold of him. Plus, Ben was able to leave before all the radiation got to him, too.

Meanwhile, Van Dyke has been absent from his duties now that he's been exposed to the astral stones. The show goes on without him, and the mayhem transpiring can't seem to get off television screens. It is stories of mutating humans that can't be revealed to the public, though as it stands, maybe it's best to reveal the true severity of the chaos. Across whatever media channels remain, the audiences imagine it as some sort of stunt gone awry.

Ben's internship partner from the university, Chris, has decided to accept swapping positions with him at Delphi Corp. despite all the trouble. It is not likely they'll return to school amid this terror anyway. Chris has been staying at the LOTRY center for emotional support, waiting for his shift at Delphi Corp. HQ to start in the coming days. He believes enough in himself that he'll help them to get out of this mess. Like Van Dyke, Chris knows how to get ahold of Ben, especially now that Amplify is still jumping off at wee hours of the night in dark corridors of town. Some things are difficult to resist when sex, drugs, and outbreaks of violence subdue the angst, Chris could join the party.

But his thoughts of partying are derailed when someone shouts from inside the community center.

"Hey everyone, look!"

The reporter on the screen moves from the scene of Delphi Corp.'s taped-off block to another description of breaking news.

Outside a name-brand clothing store, the reporter stands adjacent to a barricaded building. "An apparent assailant has pushed everyone out. I'm not sure if this is a joke or not, we're getting word that a 'glowing stallion' ... a horse, has overtaken the dressing room."

The Community Center members are starting to huddle around in anticipation of a total meltdown ensuing, one worse than what has already occurred.

The reporter continues, "It also appears that red light is shining within the building, and we are just now getting reports that Van Dyke is missing, and in his place, a large human-horse hybrid is confined in the changing room. Well, what's left of it. The police, meanwhile, have blocked the doors."

Contacted by a burdened police chief, Bartram is confronted with another task. "We need the authorization to use the Delphi Corp. armored suits, sir. Check the news," the Chief says.

The quick message leaves Ellis frustrated. The threat of infrastructure collapse is giving reasons to hide the cloud software's problems from the public in case they can turn this around. But someone else will have to do that for him now that federal authorities have seized the CCS for their investigation. Wearing Delphi Corp.'s armored suits may only add to their problems.

Looking up at the nearest active media channel, Bartram is surprised when it is Van Dyke's live podcast that finally appears. He is on the wrong end of a media outburst, and this time the police are not accustomed to a battle where humans are the inferior species.

Xavier Moth has made it his mission to track humans through the alternate timeline. The 7-foot behemoth considers his prospects of using an autonomous Nano bug to search where the teleportation modules may have opened a portal from Pangaea to the human timeline. The darkness of source code appears near the transparent dome of the Yhemlen city, brightened by the mid-day sun to form a transparent portal. When Xavier Moth touches down in Pangea's open savannah, where he stands in the open brush, it seems cold compared to what is inside the dome. Xavier's face mask alerts him that the cosmic internet servers are close. Farther to an adjacent teleportation module, dark shade is obvious amid the sunshine. Xavier Moth has hit the jackpot.

Autonomous nanobots that can be remotely operated line Xavier Moth's outer vest pockets. One packet of these, and he will be able to fend off almost anything. He is careful not to disturb the few zombies that are near before starting to make a move toward the open portal network. Most of the contaminated volunteers are partially sentient, enough so that they are trying to work out how to enter the interior dome of Pangaea's city shield.

Xavier lets the nanobots loose like caged doves with a message to deliver. The granules of fine dust fly to the same open portal where the volunteers crossed universes from Delphi Corp. HQ.

In the orbiting space station, Grandmaster Frost stoops near a metallic bar meant for viewing the Earth and dangles his large head closer to the clear window.

"The prophecy is being fulfilled," he says to Ria. "New Overseers are being created. I can feel it, the astral stones." Frost catches the pain in his chest and turns to Ria, showing her the crystal embedded in his chest. It has been so long that the glisten has faded away.

"What is it?" Ria asks. He isn't alone, even she has them.

"These have been the Grey Order's greatest achievement up to now." Frost closes the shirt's zipper along his chest. "I remember when the Yhemlen frightened us with their power to shapeshift, but we no longer need such impediments regularly manifesting. You must warn your father, and quickly."

Ria knows that Gereon is close to having an angry outburst. There's a more daunting test coming their way. Now that Frost has received his transmission from the bounty Xavier, he's certain of their strike on Pangaea. The Grey Order's new planet-killer will mount a cacophony of Nano-sized bots to consume the planet with a grey goo that is indistinguishable from the liquid furnace of volcanic lava that can devour all matter in its path. Those same bugs will reproduce until the solar system and all the galaxy is consumed.

Ria leaves Frost unattended, entering the image spectrometry room where she prepares to teleport herself back aboard the starship *Nemesis*. Her teleportation module readings direct photons of light to beam particles under her feet atop the module. A familiar crust form disintegrates to the floor and vanishes. She recognizes the rapid pace of things changing, especially for Captain Gereon.

"Father!" Ria calls from the walkway in the center of the starship. Captain Gereon and Jasper are standing at the cockpit, readying the autopilot to disengage. "Brother, can you alert father of the danger he is putting us all in," Ria says.

"Not now, Ria, I've made my peace with the world. And you will come to know it too." Captain Gereon is not easily persuaded. His plan to conquer the Yhemlen requires furious rage.

Standing still, the three of them watch as steam clears the front-facing window where quantum fields are cooling from the laser beams. Ria's silhouette is short, slim, and her dark bio-enhanced suit contrasts with Gereon's gold fit, tightly around his Grey-mutated body. Gereon sees his daughter's eyes from behind the smoke before he selects a holographic alert to close the ramp of the *Nemesis*. Without a word, Gereon turns and walks briskly to the pilot's lodging where Jasper is already prepared to make their way to Earth in the alternate timeline.

"Not only are you acting out of character, but you are underestimating the Yhemlen. They have prepared for this day years ago," Ria says.

Unwilling to heed this warning, Gereon's emotions can hardly be withheld as he refrains from going on an emotional tirade. Such outbursts are banned. Claiming helm to the captain's seat with his children as heirs, Jasper sits beside Gereon furious, unwilling to dispute the orders; he and his sister are going to have to make up the slack.

"I'm prepared to deploy our troopers for a fully armored deployment. Activating all *Nemesis* power sequences now," Gereon commands.

"Are you mad?" Ria says. The violent shake of the starship *Nemesis* rattles her from her erect posture, knocking her to the ribbed floor of carbon sheets. "Frost has already made arrangements for reinforcements to follow you."

"Cease, my child."

Jasper does not respond. The problem for the Heinemann clan is that the Grey Order rarely acts out of vengeance. The logic of this strike points to passion taking over reason.

Looking at her male counterparts, Madame Ria's lack of authority is forcing her to join them in their attack on a prehistoric Earth. Like her mother, Ria wants to hide away more than castrate herself to a life of misery. Shaking her head in disapproval, she walks a few feet forward before halting.

"Are you going to join us, sister?" Jasper asks calmly. He is holding a finger above him to initiate the full-throttle power sequence that will allow them to enter Earth's atmosphere. So far, they have been able to avert the Yhemlen quantum detectors. Ria acts in the other direction. Walking backward, she reaches another open segment of the walkway.

"I will not comply," she says. Turning around, Madame Ria marches out of the cockpit toward the *Nemesis'* rear fuselage.

The Martian colonists are no longer in their chambers, and as she rushes past the cells that used to house them, she jumps to grasp the jail's bars and looks down the walkway. So many severed heads of old battles appear that she recognizes the emergency has trapped her too. There is nowhere to go.

Gereon sees his failure as a metric of unmet success. The past haunts him enough that subtly, going back to face the Yhemlen timeline, may redeem him from the death he has averted. He is going on a suicide mission, taking everyone with him. Jasper is wise enough to know the difference. As one of the last starship crews left, Heinemann knows that the only way to avoid defeat is the total annihilation of the Yhemlen timeline on Earth. That is where the grey goo scenario comes in.

"Initiating power thrusters, image spectrometer is online," Says Jasper as he holds to the mission. "Ready to transport through the light bridge portal."

Readying themselves for the attack, the Overseers of the Yhemlen are assembled outside the gravitational field, in a secured vault just outside the dome once used as a force field. For the moment, they need to be able to track the sky for invaders outside of the dome. The three volunteers are waiting by Tuas' side within the accelerator, remaining fastened to their seats in preparation for a journey through time. They must go back to 1930's Germany as quickly as possible. As for Tuas, he has been withholding himself from the conversation. He is considering how much time they have left.

Tuas speaks through the cosmic interference of the volunteers' minds, more telepathy. "There is no more time for delay, we are going to insert the codes directly into the accelerator. Initiate the photon detector's switch the moment you reach Germany so that your genetic makeup is not compromised. You will be on the outskirts of Berlin. Follow the path provided for you." Tuas points to marked brandings on the wall, the same that are on buildings throughout Pangaea. "All you have to do is retrieve the egg."

There are radiation barricades in place to protect Yhemlen from a collapse in the space-time continuum into a black hole. Too much time spent across alternate universes and these volunteers' bodies will most likely vaporize. If they plan on surviving, they will need to hurry before they are permanently stuck. The hunter Xavier Moth has already discovered the portal that allowed their consciousness to enter across parallels. He will be in the human's timeline before they can get to them. For Tuas and Cira, the space elevators toward the *Mariner Station* must be disabled, so a horde doesn't swarm the security of humans already sheltered there.

The Concord has no intention of being kind, though they have managed to ignore the fortress orbiting outside the stratosphere and into low orbit, the *Mariner*. The Yhemlen geostationary satellite has been observed for years, and by Concord standards, is mostly harmless. Gereon's Grey Order crew will have no problem in disabling the hindrance, however, once the nanobots attack and consume the city. The Starship *Nemesis* and its companion crews of Grey Order Mirai are making a final ambush.

Meanwhile, on the Yhemlen Earth, the human volunteers are still awaiting transport to the 1930s.

"We've got to get to Naoto," Sarah says from inside the accelerator. What she doesn't know is that Naoto has already become a casualty.

"Naoto can wait, we've got to focus," Ronny says.

Whenever he and his research partners enter the next alternate reality, they will only last so long before their bodies and mind become vaporized in the cosmic vacuum.

Tuas eases their apprehensions. "Follow directions and avoid going off course. If anyone catches on, tell them where you are going and get directions." He closes the hatch.

Rotating pods swing the three around in a cylindrical casing. Bright pulsating lights and a cacophony of sounds inundate their senses before all turns to black. When they wake up from the silence, it is 1932.

CHAPTER 14

In a race for time, the three volunteer scientists are lucky to avoid bounty hunter Xavier Moth before they cross timelines. While Tuas prepared the accelerator time capsule, Xavier stalked an outpost near Yhemlen's Pangaea city barrier, preparing himself to match signals. Not far away, the starship *Nemesis* manages with the help of Frost across the cloud interface as the Heinemann receives updates from the Grey Order station; constant contact keeps the Heinemann crew on precise coordinates in space before they can penetrate Earth's atmosphere.

Immediate plans for their attack have changed now that Captain Gereon has shut off all communication to the outside. He wants to avoid messages from the Grey Order's Grandmaster. Handicapped by the Concord's objective to slow the strike, Gereon sees no reason to abandon his blitzkrieg on the Yhemlen city center with small talk. At the low orbit station, Frost's stoop at a railing is unchanged, he has been there for hours. And he's beginning to agree with Gereon on participating in this battle. Ironically, Frost wants to use this moment to rekindle what he recognizes as a duty to perish along with his crew. Vengeance will not be tolerated without a fully backed attack.

Frost's prosthetic legs have durable metallic rods keeping him upright on the buffed floor. It has been over a day now since the Syndicate rebels made their surprise attack on Alon Blane's trial. The Mirai and Grey Order are making more enemies than friends, and Grandmaster Frost's indifference contributes to the problem. It's all too familiar a circumstance for Frost, and the pain in his chest is reminding him of something. Where the astral stone caves in his sternum, a thought percolates throughout his senses making him tingle all over. Just then, a vision strikes his imagination. He returns to a time of primitive war, the middle of the twentieth century when he was still part of the Third Reich. How he could continue to live for so many years is hard to believe. There must be interference in the cosmic web somewhere causing these flare-ups of memories, and there is. Those three volunteer scientists are visiting Frost before all of this ever transpired, when Frost was still human.

After the trial assembly concluded proceedings—fraught in danger from Old World vagabonds, the image spectrometry room was used as a location positioning system to keep tabs on the transport ship Syndicate pirates stole. Captain Gereon's crew is much farther away in the space-time continuum, and Frost finally commands reinforcement striker and starship fleets to be deployed. With more than a few missing fleets from previous battles, the Grey Order henchmen are on their way to finishing what the Heinemann started. Infiltrating Pangaea's dome city with loud battle cries won't deter return fire when the Yhemlen are faced by blitzkrieg, but it will help.

"This is not the time," Frost pleads to Gereon across the cloud interface. The cosmic web can be jump-circuited in the event someone shuts it down. The transmission will only last a short time.

Hearing his detestation through a speaker at the front cockpit where he sits, Jasper recognizes the danger Gereon is putting them in. Madame Ria still hasn't budged from the back fuselage area. And just as Jasper begins to respond, a rapid, wailing arm from Gereon shuts him down as he strikes his co-pilot son. Ria stands partially inert near the back lodging, where she begins rocking back and forth to the rattling chamber of the *Nemesis* increasing speed rapidly, cradled by loose pieces of gear hanging from her thin extremities.

"The ultimate test of wills is to face death," Gereon says, still holding onto the injustice he believes he's been dealt by living so long in unfulfillment. This is the same pride that Frost detests. Someone must suffer that perilous end.

Thinking of the consequences that will be reaped from this attack, Frost walks back to the image spectrometry center considering the expanse of space where multitudes of ships, workers, and transport material travel to and from the Fortress Shield in low orbit. He knows that Gereon is beginning to become gripped by the pull of emotion, rather than the logic Mirai are trained to accept—he's been battle-tested for this fight. Across a silver railing, the reflection of a distorted body gives Frost memories of who he used to be before mutating into a Grey like the rest.

Xavier Moth is his only solace. If he's successful in reaching the human timeline, they can avert more losses and damage. The Martian colonists are with the Syndicate now, and there's no way for them to get home without the precise coordinates of the teleportation module. It's better to simply annihilate what's left of their memories back home and forget their home on Earth altogether. Like Xavier Moth, Frost received astral stones through unconventional means. Before killing him in battle, he removed a crystal the size of a palm from one Yhemlen Overseer. Left for dead in open fields near the dome, the Yhemlen lay bleeding in the prairie as the shudder of electricity poured through him.

"Everything is all new for us," said Frost, and while considering the emboldened Gereon, he sees a change on the horizon. A danger stalking them alerts Ria who works hard to meet Frost's voice who is trying furiously to contact them across the cosmic web. The profuse buzzing is bothering her.

"Ria," he says, startling her. His voice isn't clear. Gereon is focused on the mission so much that he disregards Madame sitting in the rear. "It looks like your father's taking a passage we warned him about. I am not enough without shapeshifting, and I'm afraid neither is he. Those Martian colonists have already activated an alternate timeline, waking our black box anchor. Our bounty hunter, Moth, is going back through their portal to stop them from furthering destruction."

Ria reminds herself of the slender piece of glowing crystal enervated on Frost's chest from power since wasted; his shapeshifts are now thin from weakened radiation. He always closes it with an adhesive clamp that covers the scar, not quick to remember it. But she's reminded of hers. It's been a long time since she's needed to morph using the astral stone and it looks like she'll need to this time around.

"Do not become a casualty," Frost tells her.

Back on Earth, Xavier Moth tracks the humans' portal with increased perception. Outside the Pangaea city, the transparent dome encapsulating the Yhemlen ecosystem leaves Moth stranded outside. The difference here and on the inside is palpable. The plants are withering away rapidly. All he feels is sickness permeating the air.

Xavier Moth opens his face mask shield, where puffy eyelids crowd bulging pupils hidden beneath long lashes. He kneels to let a red-hued goo loose, pouring between his fingertips. The virus has spread rapidly and across miles. Moth stands tall to see the polluted biosphere.

Immediately accosted by the ground shaking, Xavier dodges a bite from a snake slithering toward him and coming from behind. The swift attack is followed by a loud ringing in his ear from an unknown source. The mission cannot be stopped by such trivialities plaguing him. In the distance, the open teleportation portal is still waiting unattended. What is on the other side leads to something peculiar within the cosmic web where Delphi Corp. scientists poured through. This quantum field is weak, very weak, primitive even. As a bounty hunter, Xavier gets emboldened knowing that the humans are easy targets once he's crossed timelines. For Ronny, Sarah, and Dimitri, they are in a race for time.

The other scientists that were altered into ravenous zombies still roam in the distance near the portal, but a sense of survival is pushing them to an opening in the city dome they can find. The zombies are fleeing for safety. Gathered around fallen arrows covered by grassland, Xavier Moth obstructs the entrance to the portal while stalking Pangaea's translucent covering, searching for threats. He initiates an invisibility cloak when he notices an infected volunteer creeping upon him. Moth moves a few paces away from the energy pulse, prepared to assault the zombie if it gets any closer.

Moth kneels to gather more sludge of the mutating virus specimen for examination, and finally uses a laser beam along his wrist to produce an exact antidote to the deadly radiation that is plaguing them all. Looking far beyond the tall brush, Xavier Moth directs a guided beam of the antidote's radioactive signature across the range to a zombie target. He fires a laser shot first to lock on, and then sends a repaired arrow. A zipping dart slices through the air with the antidote sludge instead of poison, striking a contaminated scientist volunteer in the neck. Other zombies flee.

Steady steps lead Xavier to a scientist whose irradiated body reverts to its original form. The energy emitted from his legs reveals perforations in the skin and flesh where quantum levels of gravity had been mutating his cells. Moth's tinted helmet visor shows the reflection where the scientist finally comes back to consciousness in front of him.

"Ah, don't shoot, don't shoot!" he yells, quivering in the grass.

"Tell me how you got here," Xavier says, drawing him up with one arm. He pulls the dart out of the scientist's shoulder, where seeping blood drips down his arm.

Even though Naoto is no longer living on the other side, the scientist's neural activity is sending stronger signals to Delphi Corp.'s vital sign readers inside the closed vault they remain tethered to. Hunter Moth will return with a human ransom across alternate timelines. When Moth crosses the alternate timeline, all he will need to do is demand surrender from the humans.

"Just that way," the lone scientist says. "We were in a computer program. The source code led us deeper until we were attacked." He presses the small wound that gushes blood. In the distance, more zombies are coming back around to attack them.

"Whoa, whoa!"

Xavier Moth isn't fazed, rotating his center of gravity in a quick pivot, he turns his neck sharply to meet the sound. Xavier

Moth's anti-gravity blaster should do enough damage for an entire platoon, let alone some renegade humans unable to think straight, so he's not worried.

Currents of energy pound the group. The stampede in the meadow is halted by a single burst of anti-matter rays.

"There!" the scientist says, pointing a shaky finger to the portal that has not closed yet. It is coming in and out of view.

He leads Xavier Moth, who has his anti-matter cannon handy, to it as they walk through withering brush and grassland. The electromagnetic charge in the scientist's body is magnetized to the open portal where the quantum field is fluctuating in and out of view. The researcher from Delphi Corp. is not an immediate threat, but only he knows what is on the other side of the portal, and Moth needs to ensure safety.

Moth's deep voice muscles through hoarse gargles of saliva before his German words are understood. Just then, the scientist notices a change in the hunter's behavior that is holding him back from crossing the portal. They could have been on the other side by now, but Moth remains distracted. Moth shoves the volunteer's back with a nudge that forces his backside further. Even the scientist is tensing up at the engineering feats.

"I've had a change of heart," Xavier Moth says. "Ladies first," he says in jest.

As the volunteer goes back through the quantum field, he walks stealthily through the lines of the grid, backtracking his digitized form from when they first crossed the wall. The farther he gets, the heavier everything becomes as matter rematerializes in his mind and body in the parallel reality. The scientist is slowly coming back into his original form.

Before crossing the quantum field, Xavier Moth decides to let loose more nanobots in the open savannah, except these, are guided to the transparent dome where they'll be able to move impervious to barriers or even an electromagnetic forcefield. He's got to keep their cosmic web signals connected. Right beside the scientist who is waking up from his comatose state in the vault at Delphi Corp. headquarters, another batch of nanobots follows the scientist across the quantum field portal into a teleported beam on the floor. For now, Moth has deactivated the nanobots so they don't cause a scene inside the Delphi Corp. HQ.

The volunteer jumps up to break the cables from his body. The electrical charge of volts sparks tiny bursts that flame out fast. An FBI agent is present in the vault where they've been connected to the cloud, frustrated by the difficulty he's had pulling the volunteers from their dream state.

The petrified scientist can't wait to remove his restraints completely, but he's already caused tons of damage. It is to his benefit that synaptic needles through his skull cavity aren't compromised. As the FBI agent stares at him, all that he's left with is a perplexed look, having just come from an alternate reality.

In a sudden discharge of energy, Xavier Moth teleports across the cosmic internet right into the vault of Delphi Corp. headquarters after getting a view of the inside from the nanobots. For the FBI agent and the scientist, Moth is invisible.

"How long have you been across the wall?" asks the FBI agent. He assumes it has been more than a few days.

"Too long. I was sick, debilitated. You should know yourself."

"Well, you're back now. That's all that matters."

"There's something we've got to tell you … Naoto, he's dead."

Xavier Moth has got another job to do, and this volunteer looks like the perfect specimen for being his minion and allows him to follow Gereon's guidance of making the humans tremble in fear. He needs to take prisoners to hold for ransom, and now there are two people Moth can hold in return for astral stones. If he can get the human shapeshifters to surrender their power crystals, he'll be victorious.

The nanobots move under the titanium door, fast and unseen, smaller than grains of sand. There's an abandoned building full of decomposing matter that's perfect to start the grey goo off. The granules of dust crawl undetected past the federal agent and scientist and leave the closed vault door. In the meantime, Xavier Moth holds onto the bolted door while the FBI agent hears the doors lock themselves since Moth is invisible.

Moth has successfully crossed the quantum field, and he relays a signal to Captain Gereon of the *Nemesis* through the cosmic web. Frost's finally gotten wind of his antics from the signal, too, but this kind of determination puts everyone in the crossfires of Yhemlen prophecy as it approaches. There will be mass destruction. By the time everyone comes out of Sector 10, the quantum field will be closed and Capricorn will be over. At the microscopic level, nanobots will relay vital information back to Frost's base in low orbit at home. Xavier Moth separates himself from the pack as a lone assailant across parallel universes. He is poised to take on what's left of his humanity since he's become a paid mercenary for the Grey Order.

The grey goo multiplies at a rapid pace.

Ellis Bartram's most pristine building, designed with fine architecture curated by a fellow business associate for a modern aesthetic, is gone. The damage is too much to repair at this stage and both the exterior as well as the interior are in disarray. His dear friend from so long ago will hardly be pleased by the sight of twisted pillars and a caved-in roof. Each fold, each break crumbles until cracks in the ceiling dirty the interior floor with the dust of crusted plaster. The riots have taken a toll from bottle rockets and small grenades, all sorts of little projectiles smashed into Delphi Corp. headquarters. And to think people cared to look up to Bartram once as a role model. That image is permanently tarnished.

"I've got to get back to where I belong," Bartram decides. He is restrained by a headlock from an emergency medical technician.

The peaks of veins protruding from his neck converge in tight spirals. By the looks of them, they're nearing the point of rupture. His temper, likewise, is heightened by a furious heartbeat.

Trying times such as these make him quiver with rage and excitement. Security alarms are set in place at Delphi Corp. HQ to form a system of silent alerts. Bartram gets an urgent notification of an unidentified biological threat inside the vault for total immersion. He's finally settled back into his stomping grounds since returning home from Salinas. He's been talking to investigators regularly for the past day yet, his scientists are still in there, and he needs to get them out. Whatever is on the other side will be the key to this operation. But the medical technician isn't loosening her grip, grappling Bartram to the floor to apprehend him as a patient—she needs his full cooperation to heal him from the astral stones forming as raised bumps of skin. This kind of physical force is usually unnecessary, and Bartram suspects that there is more to this than he anticipates.

"Let me go!" Bartram's hair flies wildly from the gel that's supposed to lock it in place. The technician ties Bartram's wrists together, behind his back.

"We can't risk another outburst. We may have to sedate you." After the technician stands up, he's proud to have restrained him.

"An outburst, what are you talking about?" Unbeknownst to Bartram, he is not alone in trying to quarantine this ailment from spreading. Others are suffering from the malady of parallel universes. Ellis is showing signs of metamorphosis like Van Dyke, Yasmine, and Silas. It is just too early to witness the critical signs. The power of the Overseers is poised to cross into the human timeline, finalizing the cosmic web's universal transformation.

Light from incandescent bulbs reveals the sparkle of crystalline material in Bartram's neck. The astral stone simply sits unresponsive, embedded beneath his skin, connected to a metaphysical power greater than they have ever experienced.

These wrist ties won't be enough, the technician thinks.

A block away from here, Clyde Van Dyke managed to calm his outburst inside the clothing store. Whatever sparked the change still bothers him.

"Perhaps the hospital would be better."

"No!" Bartram snaps back.

Bartram's earned the respect of the technician by remaining calm, so much so that she's resigned herself to let everyone inside the building die, if necessary, to contain the threat. They aren't alone. Since AIS TARA martyred itself, the rest of the federal agents have gone home, and instead of securing the building, and it is now mostly vacant with boundaries where they put police tape up, at least for the night. The cold corridors haunt them. Bartram hasn't forgotten the warning of some mutation forming within him, but the EMT is aware. Her medical crew is only a single person, herself. There is something else lurking in the air. In an instantaneous jolt of electromagnetic energy, a field of luminescent particles vaporizes the EMT into slime.

"Holy!" Bartram squirms in place, arms still tied. He cannot believe she secured him knowing the danger they are in. If anything, he and the other hybrids will be the only ones strong enough to stop what's coming. "Holy shit ... get me out of here!"

Pain ensnares him right where the astral stone materializes in his neck. Ellis Bartram's metamorphosis has begun, and there is nothing to hold him back, especially some flimsy wrist ties. This is Bartram's first time shapeshifting. The power to manipulate matter beyond the cellular level is an ability that terrifies him.

There's little chance Ellis will be able to stop the onslaught alone. With Xavier Moth's bounty still up for grabs, he is hungry for blood and will stop at nothing to see all of humanity burn. Inside the vault for total immersion, Moth is distracted by the volunteer scientist and FBI agent that are keeping his attention from completing the mission. It is surprising when a vital sign reader signals, for anyone that is listening, that Ellis wants a call with them inside. Meanwhile, Moth does not disengage his invisibility cloak.

Before his genetic mutation took hold of him, Bartram's telecom messaging system sent a quick call to the FBI agent locked inside the vault, but all they heard were painful grunts. Xavier Moth is startled from his calm, too. He has got to get himself out of here before he is surrounded, and before Bartram can spot him through radio transmission.

In the long corridor seized by white walls, white light, and white floors soiled by filthy feet, Bartram is transforming into something else. It is to Moth's benefit to stay sheltered inside the total immersion vault while Bartram metamorphosizes. As Bartram's body shapeshifts from human to hybrid, microscopic nanobots from Moth and the Concord latch onto the iron vault with ease.

Moth's pair of binocular lenses magnify individual bots. Spider legs are attached to a nano-sized body that self-replicates. Once activated, the process of organic decomposition begins. The reaction is steamy at first from heat exchange, until the nanobots normalize their devouring of material. As it cools back to normalcy, the volunteer scientist begins to move around again when he hears the sound of a critter chomping away, like termites.

"Stay there, vermin," Moth demands the FBI agent and volunteer stuck in the vault. In one hand is an anti-matter energy gun, the other, an electromagnetic glove that allows him to perform telekinesis. The scientist and FBI agent hear the hunter, but don't see anything. In less than thirty seconds, the vault's thick titanium door is consumed by fire and the nanobots continue to consume matter around them. The air is engulfed in a dense field of grey goo whose silver sheen is alarming to them both. Suffocation will ensue in a short time.

Xavier Moth backtracks on his original plan. "You're lucky," he says. He was going to kill them both.

Moth is prepared to face battle, and when he moves through a wall and into the hallway without any resistance, the invisibility cloak that makes barriers permeable saves the two from pain. All it takes is a switch to halt the advance of the molten grey goo, but nothing will stop them. It was Frost's orders to let the nanobot goo run freely until consuming everything in its path. Now, a resentful ambition compels Moth to look for a more suitable location. There are other nanobots that went underneath the vault door that are already blocks away and down the street searching for the perfect spot to begin consuming matter.

Alive with the FBI agent, the volunteer scientist shakes violently at the look of his friends still uploaded to Delphi Corp. servers in total immersion and unable to break free. Something tells him that he will not be the last one back across parallel universes. Xavier Moth's quantum leap across parallels redirected his course through the same portal, and if the past is any indication, there will always be a digital signature. None of that matters for him in a contest against other shapeshifters; he must worry about capturing their astral stones.

What Moth wants more than annihilation is to recover the vaunted astral stones. The Concord has faced this threat before when the Yhemlen stopped their advances on the Pangaea city center. Overseers are being created across this strong quantum field that's pulling their worlds closer together. Moth's anti-matter gun blasts dark energy in the direction Bartram ran to see the direction he went.

The Delphi Corp. CEO is not fighting but fleeing toward the exit. A blast the equivalent of a single nuke is directed in a bolt that is aimed in a single beam that jettisons the dark matter ray for miles. The pin-sized hole eventually decays from the interior rims of these holes outward, until the oval-shaped gaps become larger and larger.

The primal instinct of his essence animal has taken ahold of Bartram's consciousness: a wolf whose gray coat is dingy but clean despite the shaggy edges.

Xavier Moth isn't stunned though he marvels at how Bartram was able to make a run for it so easily seeing how debilitated he was before. That's the kind of speed he needs. Before Moth takes off after him, the nanobots behind him suffer from being stationary for too long. Moth had accidentally halted their self-replication; the freeze short-circuits their self-replicating atomic structures before crusting up and imploding like an expired battery. Inside the vault, the volunteer scientist tenses up before the large blocks of silver matter from the fused metal door crumble to the floor.

There's no way for Moth to catch up with Bartram now. By the time the bounty hunter reaches the gaping hole of an exterior wall surrounding Delphi Corp. HQ's perimeter, all of D.C. is a dilapidated, squandered city with little resemblance to what it looked like before. Aside from architectural memories erected in recognition of hometown heroes, the statues that are left are monuments to what the nation's capital used to be. The FBI agent immediately runs after Bartram, rushing through a small hole in the vault's wall, but he is immediately vaporized by lingering radiation of leftover anti-matter and grey goo nanobots metastasizing near the vault.

New heroes are being born. Bartram's prowl atop the asphalt goes unseen as most of the city's been evacuated. As he sniffs the pavement in his new wolf form, he recognizes how close he's getting to another Overseer hybrid like himself.

Bartram howls at the dusk night sky. Murky gases in the atmosphere dim the colorful aurora before it no longer peeks over roofs and lightens shingles.

Martial law has been enacted and for most, their residence is not at home, but at some communal property set up by their government superior. Everyone has moved out of their homes and into camps, or attics for those wishing death upon themselves. For the few affiliated with Delphi Corp., death seems like a legitimate option.

The astral stones are guiding each of their victims together into a united consciousness. Xavier Moth's bounty cannot compare to the power he'd have if he could steal them from the group. There is more than one mutant here, he can feel it too. Moth's primitive intuition is more intuitive than theirs.

At a home across town, a vacant building is being consumed by the Concord's grey goo that is automated to dematerialize and surmount all matter in its way. The pull of the astral stones is racing to coalesce before their timeline gets consumed. Quantum synchronization has made it easy for them to connect near Delphi Corp. HQ, brimming with surplus quantum fields as their cloud computing systems or software operates across parallel universes. And, there's another astral stone that's lurking nearby, Yasmine's.

The National Resource Center, NRC, is one of the few havens that was left in the area for Dr. Adams and Yasmine to stay safe. The two are waiting in anticipation for the call that they can return to their normal lives, but that call isn't coming, and it never will. Not for Yasmine at least who's fallen victim to the astral stones.

At the outer edges of the property, she and Dr. Adams hear the scuffle of leaves on the patio. A fountain has long since stopped running. And the nighttime silence drifts quietly while the two contemplate who may be lurking nearby.

The sound of weeping and gnawing teeth alerts them to something. There's so much pain in the voice that mumbles erratically outside, exhausted through erratic breaths, that when a final thud happens, it collapses to the floor and all goes silent.

After a few seconds, he says, "Ahh, someone help me."

It's Ellis Bartram. His naked body is cold, both within and without. He's managed to make it to the NRC, more than 15 miles away from Delphi Corp. headquarters. How he was able to get here on foot, at this hour, is curious to them. But Yasmine and Dr. Adams do not know about his metamorphosis. Wolves can sometimes travel up to 50 miles in a day.

"He must have come a long way," Dr. Adams remarks after opening the entrance doors. He is tired and gasping for air.

With Dr. Adams' help, she and Yasmine help yank Bartram by his arms, grabbing ahold of each one while creeping closer to his shoulder joint. They are careful not to dislocate them.

"Pull!" Yasmine says.

When they finally have got him across the doorframe, he's gotten a body rife with red spots that show off his sores and rashes from his latest shapeshift. He's been battered and bruised enough to necessitate a splash of water to his face.

The slow spill of a bucket full of water suffices to bring Bartram back to normalcy. He gargles and spits to let out the excess.

"Pff, alright ... alright, pff!" Bartram's cough accentuates his plea. He flutters around the floor like a fish freshly plucked from the water.

Dr. Adams straightens up. "You've got to tell me what happened, everything."

"Take a wild guess," he says, evoking the obvious. "Besides, I hardly know what happened myself."

"These sorts of metamorphoses are not human. You've been altered by something well beyond our capabilities."

"There's something else, we're under siege." Bartram's neck pulsates where the astral stone is. How long do we have until sunlight again?" he asks. Bounty hunter Xavier Moth is still in pursuit of them.

"A few hours. Here, let me care for your head."

"Back off!" Bartram snaps back at the NRC director. He has had enough people examine his mutilated body.

A sharp pinging sound incapacitates Bartram's ear when it rings piercingly. He's still got the messaging device plugged in even though it was nearly crushed by his capillaries bulging from the shapeshift. The automaton voice gives a location just a few miles away. The vacant plot is suspected to have shut down the internet service where the nanobots are rematerializing. The self-replicating robots have consumed an entire block. The rumbling from a mile away buzzes like a swarming army of mosquitoes or bees.

"We've got to go, run!" Bartram disregards his nude body, readying to leave before grabbing ahold of his loose testicles dangling as if no one is around to see.

This is a part of Bartram that she has not seen before and can't make herself look away. What they don't have, however, are pants to keep him comfy. They run outside to find a swarm of a silver goo-like substance approaching them at a rapid pace. All is going to be consumed by the grey goo.

The three get into Dr. Adams' van parked outside. Bartram runs past the van and down an empty sidewalk to see where the grey goo is before they call him back.

"It's way too dark. Fog lights?" Dr. Adams hasn't driven in a while.

Bartram slams the door closed. "That is the most advanced feat of physics I've witnessed. That's nanotechnology at its finest."

Dr. Adams readies the hovercraft van's engine. These vehicles are brand new. "I'm only glad no one can see you naked. Why can't you put some pants on?"

"Where exactly are we going to go? I'm sure those nanobots are spreading in all directions."

The government blockades are going to make it difficult for them to traverse county and state lines, but with such a massive threat following them, Bartram is confident they'll succeed. This is an excuse that will get them out.

"Delphi Corp. technical equipment, that's our first priority." Bartram's chirping in Yasmine's ear keeps tugging at that primal energy she felt also, of a metamorphosis. She feels like she is close to morphing again.

It isn't until now that Bartram begins to realize what's happened to them both. He feels the tinge in his brain, ringing. "Wait …you too!"

"Shut up, okay? Rachel let's get out of here." Neither of them buckles up.

They aren't alone. Soon, all the hybrids will be united under a united consciousness that will allow them to take down their foe by summoning source cosmic web energy.

"Why is this happening to us?" Yasmine asks as they pull out of the patio's driveway.

"Because we've been exposed. These transformations transcend our present bodies, Yasmine," Bartram quiets his voice, "We've taken the next step in our human evolution. Who else can mutate their bodies at will? Demigods, that's what we are."

In the back seat, Bartram has figured out how to mutate his hand into a wolf's paw with razor-sharp claws. He even extends one to claw Yasmine's neck, mockingly.

"Stop it, stop right now!" she demands.

For Yasmine and Ellis Bartram, there is no turning back. Sunrise is creeping closer, and by the look of things, they will be able to siphon what they can from Delphi Corp. headquarters before the grey goo metastasizes and reaches them from many blocks away. The grey goo is picking up some steam.

The Yhemlen Dragon will be replaced by something more human, a figure wielding a serpent to commemorate its power. This preeminent form of human strength needs all of them to synchronize their mind across the quantum field. Xavier Moth is a bully that will stop at nothing to interfere with it. He is onto their plans to coalesce the source energy. Aside from the nanobot army of grey goo racing toward them, there is one more channel he hasn't accessed, something more sinister. Presently, bounty hunter Moth sustains himself in a cloak of invisibility, so he isn't caught. In the hover van, Dr. Adams accelerates to top speed without regard for bystanders since there aren't any. Yasmine and the naked Ellis Bartram anticipate each other's thoughts while along for the ride.

"Just keep your cool, everyone," Dr. Adams says. She's one of the few uncontaminated humans left in the city, and her vulnerability is palpable.

Clyde Van Dyke and Silas Betts are on their way, and so is the bounty hunter Xavier Moth who sends a message to Grandmaster Frost aboard the Grey Order's low orbit station.

"Send the reinforcements," the message reads.

"Consider it done," Frost responds.

Concentration camps in Germany will not arrive for nearly another decade. The scientists know and consider the implications of widespread violence from WWII that can get in the way of their mission to recover the Yhemlen egg before they reach their destination. From within the oval-shaped accelerator, their lost consciousness slowly creeps back into view when they regain awareness of their surroundings. Their dilated eyes ease the burden of a blinding light that strikes them inside the time machine. The holocaust is gaining momentum in crucial minds like Otto Frost, a scientist determined to provide a cure to nationalist ills behind ideas and initiatives in eugenics and racial hygiene. Before Ronny, Sarah, and Dimitri reach Otto Frost's domicile in suburban Berlin, he's perched on a plush sofa where the radio is turned up to maximum volume. A brazen Hitler speech is blasted through the home.

Ich werde meine Stimme abgeben. "I'm going to cast my vote," Frost says to his mistress. She is in the kitchen taking care of the filthy dishes, scrubbing each plate and utensil vigorously, denying her love for his wretched ways. "Dinner was splendid tonight, darling, absolutely wonderful."

These are the moments that his mistress secretly despises. Otto is right, the dinner was splendid, only it won't last. When Hitler is elected, the men that women happily clean up for will cry bloody tears at the blunder they made. There is no turning back, however. Perhaps this is a lesson that men must learn for themselves.

Berlin's central district is where Frost prefers to spend his time. It's close enough to markets and shows, but the most attractive venues have been scientific assemblies where notable scholars and intellectuals share ideas. Markets and shows are becoming less and less common. The universities continue to bring together the brightest minds, but politics is gaining precedence over scholarship. In the background, Hitler's voice rises and falls to a distinct rhythm that's difficult to ignore.

The oval accelerator from Pangaea materializes atop murky sewage in the nighttime. The cracks of flawed pavement allow the compartment to lean until spilling over to one side with the weight of its three inhabitants. Dimitri's rough demeanor exits first, extending a dangling leg through the crack made at the bottom of the accelerator. So much time has passed that their bodies are wrinkled by the dramatic move across alternate timelines. Slowly, the youthfulness that they are familiar with reemerges at the atomic level in spontaneous regeneration which removes the wrinkles and blemishes from before. Berlin is quiet, so quiet that they can hear mice scurrying in and out of a sewage pipe.

"Watch out for critters!" Dimitri warns. He has just missed stomping on one.

Sarah and Ronny follow him through, straining both arms before fully extending the flaps that leave a gaping crack in the accelerator cabin.

"That's some time machine, I know that much for sure." Something like this appears so compact, on the surface, you'd think it was a harmless toy. When Ronny takes his initial steps away from the cabin, sparks and pulsating lights startle him into a run.

When he slams into the other three, all their bodies stumble back until a brick wall catches them. They ignore the pain, and at the same time, fail to witness the accelerator's cabin disintegrate into the ether.

"Well, there's our ride back across parallel universes! How else are we going to get out of here?" Dimitri's frustration riles them all.

After the accelerator vaporizes to a steamy mist, Sarah attempts to calm them with Tuas' reassurances. The paired detector that he alerted them to is in Ronny's hand.

"Look," Sarah snatches it from him. He's been wielding it like loose keys he forgot he even had. "Now, how about we all get some balls… yes, balls, and get to the plan."

The detector has a supercharged electromagnetic field brightening its green, luminescent stone underneath the pliable covering. There's a quantum field calling from within, a pocket universe in her palm.

"I suggest we don't lose this," Sarah reiterates.

"That way," Ronny returns, placating to her suggestions. "You said that we stick to the plan, so that's what we're going to do."

Tuas' and Cira's child hasn't hatched from the egg, not yet. It is housed at Otto Frost's home. A light beam guides them around a dimly lit corner, but not many would care about their ridiculous outfits anyway. If anything, they resemble a visiting circus group. They see blocks of open sidewalks and abandoned railcars. The buggies that used to carry horses are empty, just waiting for a driver to hop in.

"Maybe we should take of these, grab a sleeping horse. Their owners don't seem to care so much."

"Shhh," Sarah's tongue lashes at Dimitri for his continued nuisance chatter. They must keep quiet amidst the darkened town where people are sleeping. Eventually, a pedestrian speed walks right past them with a coffee in their hand. He's subtly missed three time travelers without paying attention to garb or manners.

Sarah slaps the neck of Dimitri, who reflexively jumps back, barely missing concrete steps.

"You twat!" he yells at Sarah.

"Cut it out, you two," Ronny says, belittling their childish scuffle.

Only a few steps away is the home of Otto Frost. The windows offer a peek into the living area, and even the radio that's mounted beside the sofa and its pillows. Staying close to each other, they tiptoe to the front door, as if he can't hear them or recognize the signs from shadows and chattering outside his door. Otto Frost beats them to the entrance.

"Who goes there?" Frost sounds off through the other side. These doors are not particularly thick, such sturdiness lends itself to thieves who can break into vulnerable houses. Speaking German isn't helping things.

"Do you speak English, by chance?" Dimitri says. Frost would rather speak English, anyway, for the practice.

"I do," he responds quickly. He's still hesitant to open the door, but he's cordial enough.

A few clangs from the key's lock reveal his middle-aged face. The thin body suits him well and glasses that have circular, thin rims compliment his head's shape. From his vantage, the three appear as circus dwellers even though Tuas was supposed to dress them for 1930's Europe. Since he has frequented shows, Frost anticipates that they may offer to sell him some tickets to somewhere. Loose-fitting shirts and denim jeans do not help their case.

"Why don't you come in from the cold," he suggests. There isn't much concern about vandals where they live. Frost wonders how else they would know him. "I assume that you want something specific."

None of them sit, and in a race for time, are spurred to fast-talking. Frost's accent won't be having any of it; they need to slow down their speech.

"It's come to our attention that you've discovered an egg. We've got an extremely important proposition to share with you, and …"

"Whoa, just wait." Frost pauses.

The inside of his home echoes with the radio he forgot to turn down. Its volume isn't that loud, but now that their conversation is picking up steam, the speech is interrupting important dialogue. Wood pillars separate them from the kitchen and just when Frost meanders to the radio to turn the volume down, his mistress walks through swinging doors to see who has come to their home at such a late hour.

"Are you three some sort of scavengers?" she asks.

"I assure you; we mean no harm." Ronny opens a hand in greeting.

"Well, it's nice to meet you," she says, rushing forward to grasp it.

"You've recovered an egg," Sarah says, finally.

"I knew it all along," Frost says, rambling to a room through an adjacent walkway. "Ah, never mind me!" Otto's voice is muffled when he closes the door to his sanctuary. Circus stunt or not, these people are on to something peculiar that he has been investigating.

"Don't give me that talk, Otto." His mistress begins to scold him in Russian.

Ronny steps a foot forward as if to follow him. "Should we go after him?"

Sarah extends an arm to corral him back to their spot. From the other side of the closed door, they can hear sounds of porcelain plates clanking and papers shuffling. "I think I've got it," he shouts.

When Frost marches back, the transparent covering has the egg that he recovered housed in a canister like something soldiers would use for rations or a metal flask.

"If it's only a prank, I suggest you stop these antics before you get caught," Frost tells the group. "Besides, I've run test after test, and there's nothing I could identify as miraculous. Is there something else you want to tell me?"

Frost recovered the egg during the day when a power surge and blackout cut off power from the city and brought attention to a laboratory where light experiments had been running for quite some time.

"I suggest you and your freak show get out of here," says Frost, and with a strong hand, shoves the canister into Ronny's grip. "That's for you to keep."

"That's all?"

"Go, I don't need any explanations."

Otto Frost's mistress is more amenable—but if she wants to have a conversation, then Frost insists she leaves with them, in jest.

The three scientists can feel a vehement hatred that lurks even deeper after Otto Frost hands over the egg willingly. It's freaks like them that are impeding the progress of this great nation, he contemplates. And he isn't alone. On their walk to his home, the volunteers passed so many propaganda posters and newspapers laying loose on the ground. There was even a mention of France's Vichy Regime, suggesting that the Germans had planned for this, and even finished the battle long before it began. At least, in this reality of course.

Sure, Frost could have cracked the egg open, but whatever's inside can do that itself. And it hasn't.

"Hurry," Frost emphasizes, "that way the thing won't grow cold. I don't even want to know what that thing is," he finishes. "Auf Wiedersehen."

The three march to the door, standing together silently on the porch. Frost closes the entryway door softly. He just wants silence.

"Don't be so stringent on yourself, Otto," his mistress suggests. From the outside, the scientists can hear the argument commence before starting to walk forward down the sidewalk.

"I fear for election day," Dimitri says while looking around.

"Fear what? We already know who wins."

"Really? Have you forgotten that this is a parallel universe?" Dimitri stops to have a look at this egg. Ronny pulls it back, unwilling to let Dimitri near him.

"Easy, easy," Dimitri assures him. "I'm just looking."

On election day a few months later, the Nazis will vote into parliament a new Chancellor of Germany. Though this is not the same scenario the scientists are familiar with, as the final solution to the Jewish question during the Holocaust will be changed. And their master race turns the mighty minions into a force of time traveling, genderless Greys.

"We've got to be careful before returning home. Who knows what's happened since we last left?" Sarah reminds them. Ronny seems to be the most proactive, keeping hold of the canister in one hand and the detector device in a pant pocket.

While the three are huddled together outside, Frost reaffirms his mistress's worries that the science may be driving him mad. Frost has been having recurring dreams. And the future he sees is a grim one. In the low orbit station many years in the future, his future self routinely visits this moment in time, but it happened differently.

What Grandmaster Frost remembers is not these three volunteers, but instead the same egg, only having it disappear accidentally. There were no volunteers, no conversations about freaks in the circus, only him walking to the kitchen with the egg, before letting it slip into the trash chute. He let it go. But now he is dreaming of another meeting, something completely different.

A menacing figure with a silver sheen, something of average height appears through a portal. Its humanoid form is a malleable metal alloy, and the sheen and body proportions are like an ancient cathedral's pantheon of gods, except so translucent that their reflections can be seen vividly at the surface. It is interdimensional sentience that's been sent here to warn them of an interdimensional disturbance.

"That ... what is that?" the three jumble their feet and almost fall to the floor before the silver phantom swiftly runs to Frost's front door. It finally passes through, impervious to barriers.

"The freaks have returned, I thought I told you to leave, whoa—." The suspense terrifies Frost until he's stopped cold, motionless.

The interdimensional being's face is masculine, possessing a supernatural cognizance beyond that penetrates telepathically ability. Frost and his mistress see their reflection in its metallic body.

"Otto ... Otto," his mistress chirps in his ear.

The silver demon's feet clank with each step that presses against the hardwood floor. A burning sensation weighs heavy on Otto and the mistress's eyes from looking directly at the silver phantom that teleports to opposite sides of the room without effort to confuse them. Then, the silver being stands directly in front of Frost again, who smiles wildly from ear to ear. This is the madness that his mistress has never witnessed, until now.

"What is happening in there?" Dimitri asks. The other two don't respond, knowing that they haven't the slightest clue. They are just as spooked as he is. The paired detector radiates photons directly into Ronny's pant leg. It burns to the touch. "I think we're being transported, again. Hold hands."

"Dimitri!" Sarah calls. She manages to yank his loose collar back in time to avoid the spark of radiation. And while the photons percolate beneath their feet, the silver being continues to trounce on Frost from inside his home. The silver phantom must have come from a parallel dimension like themselves.

This isn't the only experiment Frost's tried and failed at. But something is very eerie about this.

"Behold your eyes, my child," the silver being says to Frost through telepathic thoughts. Frost agonizes over this divine intervention. It's something he's been praying for to arrive.

"Otto!" his mistress stammers. To quiet her, the interdimensional being shuts her in a solid ice cube, so cold that it is hot.

"The power you desire will be yours if you allow yourself to be my henchman. I will care for you for the rest of your life," the silver phantom offers Otto Frost.

The silver being isn't attacking him, but rather requesting Frost's assistance as an eternal ally. Frost stoops his head in acknowledgment and the phantom stands by its word, as a glow above the top of its head appears to open an interdimensional portal that Frost looks through. Otto feels a surge of energy that is cosmic. "The knowledge you seek will be yours. Do not fail," it says in a departing message. Finally, the silver phantom disappears, and Frost's mistress can breathe again when the ice dissipates. She did not see or hear a thing.

The interdimensional silver phantom inspired even more experiments by scientist Frost. Pacing the wooden floors, he became filled with thoughts of manipulating biology and technology to serve this new master of his. Otto discovered unknown secrets of Einstein's theoretical experiments, of nuclear physics that he hid away and would continue to work on for years after his death. Frost, somehow, was a genius overnight. He never really told people about these dreams.

When the three volunteers return to Delphi Corp. headquarters across parallel universes, the grey goo scenario is already taking place. Inside the vault, crust from crumbled nanobots lies along the floor. In one corner, the volunteer that Xavier Moth held hostage sits in the cold room alone, waiting for a hero or villain to end the psychosis he is enduring. The other three, Dimitri, Sarah, and Ronny that were spared from death, are coming back to consciousness, and as they do, the volunteer in the lone corner begins to feel joy again. There is no need to return to Pangea. Tuas and the rest of the Yhemlen are mounting a defensive against the coming prophecy. Tuas was successful at routing the three scientists (and their child) back home to safety.

Inside the vault, a quantum field develops beside the feet of one volunteer and adjacent to the canister containing Tuas' and Cira's egg that has appeared. The scientists' awareness returns slowly, jolting them from the darkness. It will take a long explanation from them all to get this story right.

Since their meeting only a while ago, Otto Frost is already making a name for himself in the alternate WWII timeline. A few millenniums later and Frost, along with the Concord are trying to annihilate the remaining life in the Galaxy with that silver demon's help as a spiritual guide. Grandmaster Frost has been channeling it for years, hoping it would return in dreams, but it never did return until now.

Otto Frost became one of the most recognizable names in science. While the Allies and Soviets provide the war effort on opposing sides of Europe, Otto Frost and partners are trialing half-life reactors from leftover particle collisions. This is the same science that the Concord will use some thousands of years into the future. The mystery of genetic mutation leads Frost to dark corners of his persona that he can't reveal to others, but some of it is too easy to see for his mistress, burdened at night by his stories of grotesque science.

Whispering beneath the sheets, he says, "I believe that we'll be able to manipulate our DNA enough to alleviate all ailments at the cellular soon, even at the atomic level. It's close."

His mistress is sick, and the coming war will only worsen her symptoms when they start scavenging for leftover food.

In the background, his favorite radio station runs continuously to lull them to sleep.

Frost's ultimate goal is to create a genetic-based utopia based on desirable traits. Clinical trials will show that through heredity and selective breeding, a perfect civilization will inevitably follow. In the name of eugenics, Frost continues his charade despite his critics.

With his face numbed for surgery, Otto Frost goes under the knife as the first test subject, with another dozen patients waiting to follow suit. Skin biopsies show cancerous lesions in experiment after experiment. But Otto Frost himself assures everyone that the procedures are harmless and promotes cosmetic hospitals after the war as a place for elites to gain social capital and status. People are populating Frost's waitlist quickly.

The surgery itself becomes more commonplace, and scientists like Frost discover they can make money off the insecurities of beauty, too. A new caste of desirables inevitably forms, and Frost is one of them.

"I fear we are on the verge of upsetting some vital equilibrium," he tells an associate at his lab. Eventually, Otto Frost's instinct to question his treatment plan was validated when he went to see a dermatologist in a different practice. The doctor dismissed radiation, removing many of the lesions and applying medicated ointment to heal his wounds, but soon, Frost's face became a monstrosity again until he could no longer even recognize himself in the mirror, and his body had become a model for rickets and bow legs.

The sicker Otto Frost gets, the more he comes up with novel surgeries to practice on himself. He realizes that he could use miniature nanobots to clean his blood of impurities. If he were lucky enough to contain it, he could monetize this as well. All he needed was to find an associate to develop trials.

It was here, that the Concord's new planet-killer would come to fruition. A swarm of nanobots that reproduce themselves to consume organic matter mimics the silver demon. The first nanobot could copy itself in mere seconds. Frost envisions a future where tiny machines build materials molecule upon molecule. With billions of builders, he could manufacture any material he could imagine.

Working as a scientist into the 50s and 60s, Frost continues his tyrannical pursuit of scientific purity. "The party is strong, but I fear that it will be disbanded, one way or another. Our holocaust has devoured spirits. In the wake of destruction, the people will not be dissuaded," he says in a letter to Hitler.

What Frost suggests is to return to a later iteration of the former Weimar Republic. The Nazi Regime is no longer sustainable now that the passions have flamed out, but the caste divide is large enough to harbor a sustainable economy that thrives on the loathing. It is an unhealthy competition. Bedridden and unable to leave his home without assistance, Otto Frost's ghastly figure confines him to house arrest.

The philosophy of genetic superiority will take a lot of discipline to keep it going. Some major funding of health councils and new devices at the molecular scale, fully manufacturable at factories, turn the tide.

As the manufacturing rate doubles exponentially, production continues to grow the ugliness of the Grey Order's ethos of surgical mutilation. The mirrors and screens from the tech world reflect the will of a few scientists like Otto Frost, who despised humanity enough to want to recreate it.

CHAPTER 15

The swarm of daily commuters flying under the transparent shield of Pangaea bursts into clear view when the *Nemesis* soars beneath thick clouds in Earth's lower atmosphere. Poised to make its first strike on the Yhemlen city, the *Nemesis* cloaks its outer shell in a field of quantum deflectors that make it invisible to radar and sensors. The Yhemlen have another way to detect intruders, however, using an invisible net of quantum disablers. Defense drones surround the outside of the transparent shield, constantly surveying the area outside Pangaea's bounds.

Venture far enough, and field workers of Yhemlen's labor class can be seen riding on the saddleback of dinosaurs, among other animals they have managed to domesticize at least for a short time. Many are merely herbivores that do not eat other reptiles— Riojasaurus, Sauropelta, and some select flying creatures work best.

When the starship *Nemesis* comes too close, a Riojasaurus shrills, startled by a faint gust of wind. Its cry is brash, but not threatening. A tired Yhemlen sits up in the saddle, pulling his mount to an abrupt stop. He and his dinosaur companion look up at a faint glow in the sky. An electromagnetic field pulsates vividly upon the outer rim of the shield. Many more Yhemlen stop to watch as the starship *Nemesis'* quantum field breaks down in incremental steps, pulling at the bubble, the shield, to penetrate it, but it isn't exploding that easy. The Heinemann are at the edge of space right atop the Earth's atmosphere and enter and reenter many times to gain momentum and heat.

"I think we need to deactivate the Q-thrusters and initiate regular fuel for propulsion to save energy," Jasper says. His father, Gereon, sits motionless in the Captain's seat.

Heavy thoughts about how to conquer the Yhemlen are slowing their reaction time. Ria hasn't moved from the back lodging, and while Jasper stares out of the window, cracks are forming at the outer edge of the quantum field deflectors. Their translucent glow sparkles in watery waves of blue.

"It's going to give!" Jasper shouts in his pinched voice.

Leaning his body to his right, Gereon's slender arm is covered by a sleeve that latches onto a few buttons aimlessly before it reaches an appropriate nozzle on the *Nemesis* control panel. Gereon's finger is smooth all around, and the wrinkles where his nail should be throb when he presses the switch for thermonuclear propulsion. The sunny day returns to a clear view, along with the curvature of the horizon in the distance. They'll have to lower their altitude if they want to avoid the danger of Yhemlen defenses firing at them.

Fortunately for the Yhemlen, they have already spotted the Concord starship's belly protruding through the clouds. Yet, the Yhemlen are not attacking them. Captain Gereon is well prepared for this offensive, and it soothes the worries of Jasper and Ria who've joined him in this fight.

"Now that we're hovering, I can let you take over the duties of commanding the ship. I'm proud of you, son." Captain Gereon's reflection in his son's eyes distorts his body even more. The pitch-black balls surrounded by almond rings change the color of his eyes to a lighter shade when dilated under darkness. Gereon knows that when he steps out of the starship *Nemesis*, his eyes will be black and seething with a vengeance, closed off from the sun's rays once the pupils shrink back in once more. There is more to this than what they can see, and it's what's lurking in dark crevices of the domed city of Pangaea that they must watch out for.

Ria finally stands up straight, puzzled by Gereon's haste. "Shouldn't we wait for reinforcements?" she asks. This is an argument that continues to resurface.

"Precisely, but I'm too old for waiting. Take care of the ship," he says.

"Father, where are you going? Do not do this."

"I'm going to make good on my promises to Grandmaster Frost and the rest of the Concord," he says adamantly. Standing atop a teleportation module, Captain Gereon, along with a slim belt of gear, mounts himself on a patch of land near the dome of Pangaea when coils of light wrap his body and transport him there instantly. When he does, Ria runs to the cockpit beside her brother. They weren't expecting him to teleport out of the starship like this.

"Activating power thrusters. All power online?"

"Yes, sir," Ria announces.

"Regenerating deflector shield," Jasper says, continuing to flick operational switches above and below them in the starship's cockpit. "Photons, plasma, all systems go, check?"

"Check!" Ria affirms.

"All systems ready, hold on to your britches, Madame!"

The *Nemesis* rises over the clouds so that they aren't visible to the naked eye. When the Q-thrusters come back online, they make a quantum leap to outer orbit. This attack on Pangaea isn't the offensive firefight they were preparing for, not yet. When the Yhemlen in the saddle saw them breaching the outer atmosphere, there was no contact with defenses made, but there's no need to since they already know what's coming. The Yhemlen and Grey Order each learned their lesson from the last skirmish when disaster almost wiped them both out of existence. Their strategies are similar—to do the most damage without annihilating themselves in the process. The Class A starship is the Yhemlen's main spacecraft, aside from plentiful strikers.

Tuas and Cira mimic the Heinemann siblings when they park the Class A deep within the ocean, protecting the quantum field that is dampened by surveillance underwater, miles beneath the surface, protecting the ship from surveillance. Even the most powerful sonar could not detect it. It's the Class A starship that's sunken there which can withstand the pressure and time. If the

Yhemlen activates its power at the right time, the humans across parallel universes will be able to use it as a vessel against the Grey Order. It's their time to transfer power to a more willing opponent than themselves.

In low orbit, the starship *Nemesis* is parked peacefully while it waits for reinforcements. Below, their father Gereon is approaching the electromagnetic field of Pangaea's city dome, trying to find a way in after teleporting himself out of the starship.

The outer rim of Pangaea's shield is hard to penetrate, but the Yhemlen Overseers are baiting him with their retreat. They know he can penetrate it, even without the grey goo. What Gereon needs is confirmation of what may lie on the other side of unseen threats. He can hear Yhemlen in the saddle shrilling along with grazing dinosaurs, but none of them seem very worried at his meandering. Gereon's going to enter undeterred with a quantum deflector, the same type that the Yhemlen used to disable his force fields. The quantum internet needs to be free of interference to work clearly—and so too does the cosmic web for them to teleport.

Once he teleports to the inside of the city's covering, Captain Gereon gets spotted by a drone that alerts the authorities. Overseers are on the way. Tuas and Cira know that Captain Gereon is asking for a fight. This time, he'll get one, and it won't end the same way as before.

"I believe our father has eluded the Grey Order's policy for so long, he's just never realized it. He's breaking so many rules," Madame Ria says in the cockpit. Jasper thinks of him similarly, but he prefers not to mention it. "I like to give him the benefit of the doubt," he says. "But if he doesn't return, we'll know why. He's stubborn."

As of late, Captain Gereon's brazens acts point to faults in his character that are getting in the way. What he needs most is rehabilitation. While the Heinemann siblings sit, Grandmaster Frost sends them a message.

"I have placed coordinates for the reinforcements to follow. They'll arrive shortly. An army of troopers and androids are prepared to be deployed in an airdrop."

"What about the bounty hunter? Has Xavier Moth made any contact?"

"He is in a similar predicament to you all. We'll have to cross channels there as well to make contact, but he is not free from danger either as the power of the Overseers has seeped over to the human timeline. The quantum field connection there is very weak."

"The humans a major threat," Madame Ria reiterates, but Grandmaster Frost isn't worried at all.

"The Yhemlen are our main priority. I'm in Convoy 8. A band of frigates and tankers are transporting the troopers, along with myself, in a squadron."

"I'd hate to see you get hurt," Jasper says to Frost with a friendly demeanor.

"Hah! That's one thing I'm not worried about."

The emotional tug of war with the Concord ideology has gotten to Captain Gereon who insists on having a solo retreat in the most dangerous of places within parallel universes. This sort of activity is uncalled for. Yhemlen Overseers don't plan on backing down, either. He is going to have to fight his way out.

Hiding near some brush on the outskirts of the city, Captain Gereon's small frame does him good now that he is dwarfed by the sheer size of Yhemlen's buildings. While Gereon jogs deeper and deeper into Yhemlen territory, fly-by commuters above him and the skyrise buildings replace wilderness at the outer edges of the city.

At the city's edge, where Captain Gereon disabled the quantum field, contaminated zombies that were infected as volunteers begin entering Pangaea's dome city in a primal urge to quench their hunger.

The Grey Order rarely activates their astral stones, except for special situations such as this. Gereon is inching closer to his breaking point, and when he finally reaches his threshold of tolerance, it will unleash a power within him that shapeshifts him into a powerful monster, some behemoth force. Yhemlen hybrids when they shapeshift, except they aren't reptilian monsters, but humanoid. For Captain Gereon, he's managed to skillfully evade these urges in small scuffles in favor of remaining tranquil. Coming face to face with Tuas will change all of that now in a coming battle that Gereon has been waiting for.

Captain Gereon's astral stone is pinching at the chest where his sternum used to be. Now there is a radioactive crystal emitting rays of energy dragging him deeper into a rage. The deadly combination of radiation will mutate Gereon from a miniature Grey into a giant. If Tuas can get to him before then, he may be able to stop the transformation from happening. Meanwhile, the city's patrons continue to go about their daily lives in hovercrafts and flying vehicles, oblivious to the attack commencing on their city.

There is no more brush to hide behind and as the city grows busy, Gereon ducks for cover as the flying commuters jettison by him overhead. From this point on, Captain Gereon will be a mutated giant. A circle of light on his chest has a crescent covering the activated crystal. These thoughts of rage and vengeance are the emotions that the Grey Order warns about except he is bringing on the mutation by himself. Gereon is in control of the mutations.

The first thing to alter is his arms. And when he punches a fist firmly into the pavement, the molecules in his body grow exponentially, bursting through the solid ground. Cracks in the pavement leave residue of flesh as pieces of some synthetic material fly all around him in a dust bowl.

Gereon gargles in rage before letting out beastly wrath.

A multitude of veins forms ribbed lines that accentuate his body's chiseled physique, revealing a shredded build after his gold-plated suit retracts into an electromagnetic vapor. Gereon rises to his feet, and as he extends to an elongated 8 to 9 feet in height, Captain Gereon sniffs to take in the Yhemlen stench.

His voice is hoarse, battered by the transformation. "It's good to be back," he says himself. Gereon's steps rumble the ground, and it is the first time he's been here on foot.

212 | SECTOR 10

Before he can take his first step, a flying commuter rams into the back of his head. The violent collision hardly moves Gereon who gets rocked to one side; a mere scrape that doesn't bother him. It was flying too low. The ache in his neck lasts but a few seconds.

In utter discontent, he decides to slap a commuter out of circulation. All of Pangaea's sky traffic has stopped. The backup causes hysteria for Yhemlen citizens going about their business. For those at the back of the buildup, they haven't the slightest clue what's transpiring ahead. Traffic is stopped and hovering in space with the pile-up.

At the front of traffic, an intersection of low-level commuters is backed up by Gereon's march forward. A few manage to move up to higher-level traffic, but if too many interchange lanes at once, collisions are inevitable. When they do happen, most of the vehicles lose weight beneath their sails and wings before gliding safely to the ground. One-way traffic is a must now. All it takes is a single wayward vehicle to cause the worst kind of accident, one that's explosive. The procession drifts to one side in the opposite direction so that when Gereon's newly minted body gets too close, they can escape. Some are turning back. With each step forward, Gereon huffs big gulps of air rich with oxygen.

Up close, the Yhemlen citizenry begins to recognize the threat. Gereon can hear the horns made of animal tusks warning others to retreat. All around him, the bustle increases. At a far end of the metropolis, Tuas and Cira are intertwined in a battle of wits to figure out how to proceed.

"We shouldn't be fighting alone, Tuas. We've got to assemble all of the Overseers and announce the air raid." Cira's telepathic thoughts ring loud in Tuas' ear. He'd rather speak, but the shrill in their voice is loud enough to capture onlookers. He doesn't mind lowering the volume on their conversation, especially now that they've returned inside Pangaea's dome for safety.

"It is a time of prophecy, one that we must fulfill," he returns.

"By losing?" Cira asks wearily.

"No! By handing over our coveted possessions to someone more fit to handle them. The humans have recovered our child safely."

They both agree on the prophecy, but the outcome hasn't been settled; maybe they're supposed to win, after all. Cira is pleased, glancing to a pouch near the front of her abdomen where her egg used to be. She can't dwell on that now. If it's a war they want, then it's a war they will get. Farther away, behind a plethora of high-rises, Gereon's roar bellows through the city center of the metropolis. Tuas can't be bothered to restrain himself from fighting alone.

"These are too valuable to let go to waste," Tuas says, placing the underside of his hand on Cira's breastplate. The astral stones have been coveted by the Overseer class for over two thousand years. "It's about time we use them."

Both Cira and Tuas are weighed down by the headdress that lines the back of their skulls. Since there are thick horns above their necks, this helps to deter radiation from moving down their bodies in electric static overhead. The coil of energy at their head is unmistakable. Tuas would rather take his off, and he does. The mask behind his skull comes off easily when he grasps it with both hands that have webs between the few fingers.

"The Class A starship, let's recover it." Cira isn't convinced by Tuas. They need to put up a more valiant fight if they want to survive.

"We have time to spare." As Tuas undoes the metal contraptions meant to assist him, he recognizes the beauty the Yhemlen have been neglecting. His broad shoulders, gills that allow him to traverse the open oceans, and feet strong enough to propel them faster than most other mammals, give these reptilians an advantage.

Gereon isn't that far away, and the flow of air traffic points of him coming their way fast. Where Tuas and Cira are, a small patch of grass holds them up near some trees in an old park. The botanical gardens are for Yhemlens that like them to socialize, but the mingling is over. Tuas isn't going to wait any longer. Quickly, he decides to mobilize his tail to activate the astral stone on his breastplate where a lightened shade of brown meshes with green. The tip of his tail signals the stone as it swells from within as the electromagnetic force builds. All it takes is a single click. The glow in Cira's eyes is unmistakable as she backs away.

"Tuas, he's coming closer," Cira says as she stares at Gereon's body in the distance, mounting itself mentally on a bold plan to destroy any Overseer that stands in his way. The primal instinct has led him right to them.

While Tuas begins his metamorphosis, Cira considers what plans Gereon has in store to undermine Pangaea's city. Either that, or him being alone means that his fleet abandoned him. For what, she won't know until they end this battle.

A shrill so loud that it pains Cira's ear pushes her back in retreat. It is Tuas. She should have shapeshifted alongside him. Instead, she is going to sit by idly and watch the confrontation first-hand in case some other fight that needs her help arises. Gereon's muscle-bound body lurches and bounces forward until he's sprinting. When Gereon's close enough to Tuas' 10-foot reptilian figure, all he can do is smile at the lizard monster. Overseers like these have avoided such battles because of the damage they will cause, but this is an opportune time. Each thrust of their fist, each kick, and claw send a barrage of radiation airborne. Anyone near will suffer the consequences of secondhand radiation that's unrestrained from the monsters. Not only that, but Gereon is only sparing time until Concord reinforcements arrive.

Face to face with his arch-enemy, Gereon flexes his chest and jumps forward. He plows into Tuas' midsection that is backed up by an elongated tail. The two of them ricochet as their intertwined bodies hit the ground before rolling into the evergreen park that he and Cira were conversing at. They roll hundreds of feet before Tuas' tail coils into the shape of an ouroboros eating itself on the grass. When they finally come to a stop, Tuas tries to suffocate Gereon with his tail, but Gereon's grip is too strong to let that happen.

After Tuas wraps his slithering body around Gereon's waist and moves to his neck with a lizard's tongue, Gereon's triceps bulge with the push away from his body. His grimace proves stressful in physical exertion as the scowl that Gereon makes wrinkles his mutated forehead with masculine fervor. Gereon's face shines with a sparkle from radiation, like glittering clay. His jaws clench to show teeth that are pearly white. When he thinks of it, Gereon insists on biting Tuas where it hurts, that same tail, and Tuas recoils it from being wrapped around Gereon's whole body. The move paralyzes Gereon momentarily from surprise, and the shock of release is numbed by Gereon's rage mounting, he's getting more efficient by the second.

Under the cloak of many trees, the shade dilates both of their eyes in the darkness when they meet face to face. Standing in front of each other, no words are spoken between the two, aside from seething hisses and misplaced grunts while looking at their reflection in each other's eyes. The Grey Order and Yhemlen castes are best depicted at this moment, as opposing factions ravaging each other, foaming at the mouth for another taste of blood. In the foreground, Cira's silhouette is outlined by the setting sun. There's no victor for these two, not yet. The skirmish was only for Gereon to save time.

In low orbit, Jasper gets word that the reinforcements are on their way. Loud beeps in high frequency from the telecom alert he and Madame Ria of Grandmaster Frost's arrival with a fleet of starfighters. They've brought almost their entire army with them. Transport tankers carry troopers of the Grey Order, and eight convoys have been deployed with supplies, the last of which is Convoy 8, carrying Grandmaster Frost as a purveyor of the action.

As Captain Gereon and Tuas remain enthralled in their physical brawl, Cira watches as the shield is buzzed by nanobots. Most disintegrate on contact with the electromagnetic field, but other batches of the bots linger, barely able to penetrate the city covering. Though, as Frost likes to mention, it helps to have an unlimited supply chain. The nanobots in a chamber at the belly of a transport tanker are replicating themselves to make an even bigger herd. The faster they fall, the more readily they will consume Pangaea's shell. Grandmaster Frost and his brigade need to make a bigger payload to drop on the dome of the city and make it into Yhemlen's metropolis completely. If there's anything that the Yhemlen don't want, it is to be consumed by grey goo nanobots.

"Are we prepared to deploy the troopers?" Frost asks over the airwaves. Things are looking suspicious. Jasper isn't satisfied by the Yhemlen response. To him, they should be getting a barrage of return fire. Yet, while he's been hovering in Pangaea airspace for almost an hour, he hasn't been threatened once. The silence speaks volumes, and it's true, Yhemlen have other plans.

Frost won't be stopped by electromagnetic deflectors. He knows what Jasper and Madame Ria are thinking about and he will not let them escape.

"There's no stopping our offensive now, we must move forward. Forward, I say!" The Grandmaster and his group of Convoys begin descending into Yhemlen airspace.

For centuries, humans across parallel universes have sailed, and sailed, each faction of people like Columbus in their own right. These starships intend to reach the coasts of their world away from home as invaders searching to annihilate the New World, rather than settle it. The cataclysm that is going to face Pangaea can't be stopped at this point as millions of nanobots sit atop the glistening dome of the city. The city of Pangaea looks like a silent, colossal shell with knife-sharp cliffs to hang onto, with skyscrapers surrounded by speeding projectiles and bugs who move against the wind.

In the ferocious, shaggy darkness where mist pervades, the Yhemlen are holding their breaths for prophecy. The traffic that Gereon stopped has halted permanently, as the commuters are rushing for safety. There was no warning.

A squadron of starfighters come into view as night falls, and the sun sets beyond the horizon. Gereon has Tuas pinned to the dirt, and as he lies trapped with a hand to his neck, he spits venom in Gereon's eye to loosen the grip. For all of them, there's a feeling of casting off the black grime, darkness in the midnight that becomes a side of evil they don't want to see. Doing away with death, something that's supposed to be evaded is survival. It's either jump off a cliff where the fall leads to jagged edges or be murdered at the hands of one's rival. Something like this can't be stopped. And by the looks of things, everyone is jumping, hoping to land on a soft spot. Tuas is fighting at the cliff's edge.

"I'm afraid that your father has suffered an even greater loss," Frost tells the Heinemann siblings in their cockpit, through a message across radio channels. "Your father has turned into that thing we've warned him about."

Jasper stoops his large head, venturing almond eyes to his chest where the astral stone beneath the suit waits for a similar activation, but he is not so riled. He isn't bothered by such distractions and will focus on a rational battle plan. If anything, the starship *Nemesis* is little more than a surveyor of the action as it hovers in the low orbit of Earth. It's been damaged too many times before and serves better as a backup to the starfighter squadrons descending through the atmosphere.

By now it is completely night, and darkness has fallen upon Pangaea. Citizens have been alerted to man their strikers and evacuate immediately upon the launch pad. A hole in one side of the shield allows them to flee the city, but panic results in unexpected crashes and deaths all over. Most who get out of the city are shot down quickly by a barrage of fire from the Concord striker fleet. There's little shelter in the city. On the ground below, Gereon still hasn't ended his fight, only now he and Tuas are stained red with blood.

The Yhemlen are fighting back the only way they can to fulfill prophecy, by letting the past die. It is only going to get worse from here, but the humans are ready to make a change.

"Let it die!" Tuas pleads with Gereon whose rage cannot be contained. Gereon is fighting and will not relent to sympathies. It's Tuas who knows what the astral stones can do and whether Gereon is committing suicide. There are no winners in this debacle.

"Never," he responds.

As the nanobots descend in batches of grey goo, so too do the Grey Order's troopers that teleport through a partition in the clear shield, advancing past the electromagnetic field. The fight has penetrated the dome border, though too many disrupted electrical

charges may break the quantum field that is vulnerable to ruptures. When it does, communication channels will be jammed.

Grandmaster Frost isn't taking any chances. After ordering
the tankers and convoys to retreat from excess radiation, the
damage to troopers that teleported is already done as many of the
droids burst into flames. The majority who land inside Pangaea
are unable to regenerate the molecules out of their metal frames.
Fleeing Yhemlen are captured by teleportation beams and vaporized through selective targeting of Grey Order lasers. The majority
of Yhemlen left, the few that are, have refused evacuation orders
or are Overseers.

When Madame Ria adjusts the *Nemesis'* telescopes, she sees
the Yhemlen city being devoured. The goal of Concord supremacy
seems to be working. If only there were a way to reproduce this
image for her own children to see after artificial reproduction,
then her loneliness would be cured in the future. She knows that
her father would be proud. Gereon used to threaten Madame Ria
that her eggs were only temporary consolation prizes, but that
it was her genderless body that would keep her company. Now
she's starting to believe him. Jasper is still fighting mentally, but
Madam Ria is drifting away into reminiscing.

Gereon's draining his life force, and the radiation he's emitting
is beginning to take a toll on him, Tuas likewise. Not to mention
they're being crushed under the pressure of an imploding ecosystem where atmospheric pressure is rising from the imbalance.
Cira demands that they repair the shield before everything is lost.
Farther away from the city center, mutilated zombies run into
buildings for cover. These are the same volunteers that crossed
beyond the Wall before being hit with poisonous arrows.

To fend off the final barrage of grey goo being dumped, Cira
initiates automated recovery systems in a clandestine control
room while Tuas and Gereon are fighting. The electromagnetic
force field is supercharged to full power, as is the shield's repair
by automated drones. That should give them enough spare time
to recover from their damage.

"So much for these reinforcements," Jasper tells Ria at the cockpit.

Ria knows this much, "Frost has something else up his sleeve. The grey goo is powerful, but it's the Yhemlen defense system that's exerted the most strength thus far."

The Yhemlen starship Class A could have given them the ability to combat the onslaught, but Tuas and Cira managed to leave it submerged in ocean water near the equator for the humans in an alternate timeline to recover. All hope isn't lost, not in the least. For Tuas and Cira, their tandem has helped to elude the violence reining terror upon Pangaea's city. Everyone else has dispersed to hiding spots. The other Overseers with the vaunted astral stones got lost in a crowd of wayward Yhemlen while they fled.

While the nanobots' field of grey goo inches closer to that final layer of the shield's cover, Tuas and Gereon continue to contest each other with heavy swings. The Yhemlen commander can hardly stand this travail, and since Cira is gone, considers raising the stakes in her absence. The time is right to make a final stand, to use full strength. Gereon to his front, Tuas raises his long tail, wrapping it around Gereon once more to bring him to face level. Gereon is exhausted, and so is he, but something different has caught Gereon while he pushes against the green and beige tail wrapped around his abdomen.

Tuas squints to peer closer at the peculiarity. On Gereon's head is a serration where blood is seeping through. Along with that, a hoard of nanobots spills out and Tuas squeezes harder. A portion of grey goo has begun to self-replicate inside Gereon killing him in the process. Tuas has used his power against him, and he has Cira to thank for capturing some nanobots from the outside. Finally, Tuas uses the serpent tail wrapped around Gereon's legs to stop circulation completely. The nanobots continue to do the rest.

Gereon is slow to collapse despite the grey goo seeping throughout his body. The dance between monsters has been an obscene love affair for power and control, but the last shrill from Tuas breaks Gereon's spirit when Tuas' tail gripped firmly around Gereon's neck severs his head to the ground and opens space for himself to see grey goo working to consume him fully. There is little stopping the nanobots besides another electromagnetic force field that Tuas places over the patch of grass that is exposed, vaporizing what is left of Gereon. The Yhemlen must contain the Concord's weapon permanently.

We only have so long until the entire city disintegrates, Tuas thinks to himself.

The nanobots outside are multiplying exponentially.

Grandmaster Frost's grey goo isn't the planet-killer he thought it would be. To speed the process along, he has dropped a large deposit of infinitesimal nanobots to self-replicate in open grasslands and consume the habitat instead. As the puddles of goo bubble under the weight of a cool night's breeze in open grassland, pools of nanobots transition to a small lake of molten metal. That should do the trick.

CHAPTER 16

Martial law at the nation's capital has given world leaders who frequent the region a reason to divert travel away from the D.C. area. Political pundits advise their constituents to avoid major metropolitan areas, that way the mayhem doesn't influence their administrative decisions or get swayed by criticism of the masses. Assembly meetings on the congressional floor are supposed to reconvene after this economic scuffle is reorganized to fit the needs of new competitors in the marketplace. Ellis Bartram's public holdings of Delphi Corp. hurt enough investors with this volatile market.

With a monopoly over the tech industry, Bartram's corporate giant takes the brunt of devastating blows as his competitors rise from their lowly ranks. Delphi Corp.'s stakeholders don't need to pull out since their money's value has been deflating along with Delphi Corp., there were automated safety nets, but digital currencies skyrocket in value almost overnight.

Bartering is growing in popularity where people have banded together to form militias and storage banks where they can get the things they need on the cheap. If Bartram didn't know any better, he'd swear that he was living in the early colonies. The first month of the New Year hadn't even arrived yet before 2086 was predicted by specialists to be one of the vilest years to come in American history. For once, the United States needed to be rescued from insecurities plaguing its shores, of fear that Delphi Corp. and artificial intelligence would run amok, and it has. Aid would come from many places, near and far when FEMA insists on sharing its supplies widely. It's only been a couple of weeks and the damage is done. Starvation's on everyone's mind, and there aren't enough physicians to fulfill demand.

An impromptu conference is live-streamed across virtual media devices with a new internet service. Those too slow to leave Delphi Corp. won't be able to witness it, whether employees, investors, or consumers alike, inevitably get stranded without upgrades when the President gives his speech of inspirational guidance during the tough stretch. They're all spared by international foes who want to take advantage of their vulnerability but decide against it.

Setting up the podium for cameras in front of it to capture the press conference, the thinly-haired man with the grace and elegance of his Vice President, demands applause from the crowd. During the speech, he professes a notable judgment being reaped from their sins. Something that radiates the feelings of millions of dissenters. In the absence of order, the President refers to this moment as, "a historic fall of unprecedented magnitude." Since then, the Historic Fall is forever coined in the lexicon of American folklore and grammar. What was once laughable, the rise of artificial intelligence, is no longer humorous when gags between scientists and seemingly harmless experiments put everyone's lives in danger.

It isn't over, either. In Washington, D.C., federal agents are still covering up their tracks from investigating Delphi Corp. headquarters, Whatever evidence of malpractice is left behind needs to be confiscated or trashed because even they started to get caught up in the secrecy. The problem presently is how to deter interdimensional beings from crossing the parallel divide. For the few hybrids that have the dreaded astral stones, it'll be their responsibility to fight whatever comes from the other side. There won't be Yhemlen reptilians to help them. Xavier Moth has already infiltrated humanity's timeline, and while the grey goo rapidly accelerates the devouring of matter, there isn't an adequate response and each microsecond sends data to Frost across the quantum internet. The nanobots are gaining momentum. Ellis is bearing the burden to keep the clan of survivors together despite all the commotion attempting to deter them. It'll take all of them to solve this crisis.

Even though Delphi Corp. has been completely ostracized, the problem they created out of clandestine labs will be repaired just as it began, through experimentation. Bartram and the other hybrids are finally learning how to use their bodies by shape-shifting at the right time. Most important of all, stopping the Concord's bounty hunter needs them to summon the strength of all their powers combined, and time isn't on their side. They need to hurry before Xavier Moth and the grey goo reach them. He will stop at nothing to have them dead.

"We've arrived," Dr. Adams' foot smashes the brake pedal beneath her and sharply pulls back the handbrake for an under-current to drop the hover-van.

Everything is occurring without proper communication chan-nels. After the President presents to a small crowd in an undis-closed location, his assertion of an "unprecedented, historic fall" is recorded for people who still have access to media and newspa-pers. Meanwhile, in D.C., his Whitehouse home is under siege.

"Why didn't I ever think of this?" Bartram exclaims. The hov-er-van has smitten him in his seat. That's one contraption that Delphi Corp. hadn't gotten into, hover vehicles. For that, he doesn't want to get up. "I would've never thought of something like this. By the g…"

"Let's go," Yasmine says quickly, opening her passenger seat to take a step out.

"What's the rush?" Bartram meanders out of the back door in slow motion.

There's an exhilaration in the air, especially with superhuman abilities that Ellis and Yasmine possess. Despite all the quarrels that Delphi Corp. has managed to avoid, the most damning disaster, and that's letting word get out about what's happening. The FBI hasn't been covering it up but failing to assess what's transpiring. The public has only witnessed a fraction of what's been emerging for the past month. The end of January is almost a week away, and these three have got to meet another deadline, closing the quantum portal before any more assailants can get through.

"Hurry, you guys. We don't have time to waste." Bartram speeds past the two women who were already walking that way. The stark change in demeanor is humorous, considering how slow he was to leave the hover-van. "It's still time for New Year's celebrations!" he calls from afar.

By the way things are going, most of the damage that's happened is only the start. The climactic change from bad to worse will not take as long. Xavier Moth's grey goo has already consumed an entire block and the loud buzz emanating from the western flank of town is hard to ignore. The Delphi Corp. team is fortunate that the nanobots aren't self-replicating any faster than they are. Moth's visor is transparent, but the image projected onto the screen while mounted in front of his face covers the imperfections. He has got to get to the hybrids if he is to have a chance to speed up the human timeline's annihilation.

Across the parallel divide, the Concord has finally mounted the Yhemlen in a stalemate. Pangaea is fully surrounded. Xavier Moth gets a transmission from Grandmaster Frost about the mission. He's projected onto Moth's front-facing visor from a transport ship still in outer orbit, most have already descended. Frost's Grey figure is diminished by his surroundings, and outside the front window are explosions from strikers from both sides are being taken down in Earth's upper atmosphere. The Yhemlen are hardly putting up a fight this time around, but Frost is no fool.

"I'll prepare a convoy to make a quantum leap. What are your coordinates?" Frost asks the bounty hunter.

The coordinates are mapped by a drone Moth releases, racing to a high altitude required before taking a precise picture of the topography and mapping its position in a spectrum of the frequency band. When the quantum field is determined, Frost has the directions he needs to direct a convoy through a light bridge portal. A group of transport ships and tankers will airdrop some few hundred, maybe thousands of Grey minions to do some dirty work of extermination. Xavier Moth will benefit from the assistance.

"Sector 10 is on the verge of closing," Frost informs him.

We will move out of the violent sign of Capricorn soon. Moth needs to keep the quantum portal open for as long as possible so that he can travel between alternate timelines and keep the communication channels strong.

"I'm on it," Moth says passionately, intensifying a belief in himself that he's won the fight. He can't wait to be compensated; all he needs is to capture the astral stones when the grey goo is known to be getting closer. Casualties from microscopic nanobots are inevitable, meaning that Bartram can no longer hide the truth as if that was a good plan to start with. This story is bound to spread once a few wayward people with cameras can smuggle in footage of the anomaly.

"Where are the others?" Yasmine asks.

Dr. Adams and Ellis Bartram are full of questions themselves, but it is answers that they need most.

The scientist weeping on the vault's floor hasn't been responsive. He finally awakens from a nap only to start crying, jumping in dread at the sight of Dr. Adams and Yasmine staring down at him. He is still dreaming about when he was in total immersion.

"Don't shoot, don't shoot!" He covers his face, curled up in a fetal position.

Bartram pushes through the middle of the two when he hears his voice. "Why in the world would we shoot you?" he asks, extending a helping hand. The nameless scientist doesn't want to get up, not now. Bartram's no longer naked either since he's managed to cover himself with a rag.

The sound of other volunteers finally waking from their nightmare across the Wall startles them all. Only Ronny, Sarah, and Dimitri have made it back with their consciousness intact. The others aren't so lucky; that makes it four who survived.

"Give me all the details." Bartram grabs ahold of loose fragments from the crusted grey goo all around them that has metastasized; he needs to figure out how to stop what's coming.

They'll only be able to approach from one side of the spherical outbreak with such few numbers, but it may be possible to disable the entire mass of grey goo at a single end. A few latent nanobots attempt to reconfigure themselves in Bartram's hands, but all that happens are some quick boils that fizzle out when the replication fails to properly arrange molecules.

"Ah!" the volunteer on the floor shouts. He's been spared, though trying to find time for relief is hard. "I think this speaks for itself."

The egg from Tuas and Cira is still contained in the canister that Dr. Frost gave them in Berlin, and the detector as well. Bartram avoids fidgeting with loose items he knows nothing about; he's had enough accidents.

Shivering in dismay, all the scientist can muster is, "We aren't alone."

Dr. Adams feels out of place amidst the damage, wishing to return to her curating duties. On a normal working day, she would have been getting ready for her shift at the NRC. Ever since mounting the hover-van, she's been monitoring Ellis and Yasmine for a shapeshift event using body cues and profiling. It's the primal instinct that drives them, and it's getting closer to erupting within them.

Not only is the grey goo approaching, but Xavier Moth is on target to meet them at Delphi Corp. HQ. Silas Betts and Clyde Van Dyke from the Community Center are their last chance at redemption since they also have astral stones causing them to shapeshift, and with the bounty, Moth has them in his crosshairs so he's going to start the fight early. Grandmaster Frost has the coordinates he needs, and the fleet of Greys will salvage what they can before Sector 10 closes. There's only a short time before sunrise. Bartram shrugs off the threat of morning; he's accepted embarrassment that's coming his way for today when they meet a valiant foe. He just hopes they don't live stream what happens.

He cares enough about the minds and bodies of the masses to save them the pain that he's gone through.

Silas Betts squirms out of the lake when his shapeshift winds down. When he comes back to reality beneath the water, he holds his breath and swims to the surface without choking on the saltwater.

Silas's gasp is loud enough for early morning pedestrians to hear. An older woman going for a morning jog stops when she hears him. It's only a decoy to greater problems not far away, she's scavenging for food. And her jog, it's more like a speed walk.

"Uahhh," Silas's lungs fill with a massive gulp of air. The oxygen that circulates afterward feels different than the gills he had previously.

With his last strength, he pulls himself out of the water, where he plops down face first. He's got to get to safety quickly. The buzz from grey goo approaching is too hard to miss, and what Silas sees spooks him. A mass of silver slime is devouring everything in its path, setting flame and smoke to large buildings. Not far away, Clyde Van Dyke is running to Delphi Corp. headquarters from another corner that flanks Silas's position blocks away. It won't be long until Xavier Moth spots them. These will be his primary targets and the most vulnerable since they are exposed.

Van Dyke has nowhere to run when Xavier Moth stops him in his tracks. The bounty hunter's tranquilizer darts to one shoulder and the poison that seeps through debilitates Van Dyke's limbs and then his head. He's knocked out cold. The solid pavement doesn't give when he collapses.

Xavier Moth wants to use him for the astral stone and the others. If he can pry them from the bodies of their hosts, he can harvest the radioactive crystals and take them with him, back to the Concord. That's better than whole hostages and eases a burden. Van Dyke is Moth's first victim who will be at the mercy of his newly acquired powers. Silas Betts runs away from the boating dock, away from the grey goo that's making its way to them, growing faster in speed. Moth pays the nanobots no mind now that he's got his first quarry down. From the roof of the building, he teleports himself with ease to the ground. Moth leans over to place a hand on Van Dyke's chest. He feels a heartbeat.

Van Dyke's eyes shoot open, this time instead of the hazel brown that everyone's come to know, they're red. His bloodshot eyes aren't from fatigue or extenuated veins, nor is he suffering from Moth's poison. It is the astral stone that is too powerful to resist. Moth draws the antimatter pistol and fires. Moth can feel Van Dyke coming back to cognizance intuitively. A growl is faintly perceptible beneath the stifled position, but Moth intends to quiet him for good.

He's quick on the trigger and pulling the lever doesn't jerk him back much. When he shoots the anti-matter gun, a pulse of energy dumps to the gravel. Moth's frustration can't be contained when Van Dyke rolls over to his left arm. Moth misses. Infuriated by the blunder, he continues to shoot from his anti-matter gun until a portion of the arid particles hits Van Dyke as he crawls away. Moth isn't going to give up.

Only a few blocks from Delphi Corp., Silas Betts follows lines of leftover yellow tape that marked off this spot from protests. The remnants of blasts and cratered-in buildings from Molotov cocktails are enough to remind Betts of the ruin that's resulted from this. The destruction isn't finished. Moth approaches, imagining even more destruction.

From afar, he can make out the image of Van Dyke. Silas darts his head to the right, as he peeks his head out from a brick-and-mortar store, facing what appears to be a person with somewhat more disfigured proportions than normal. At a greater than average height, his bald head has white ash and his body, likewise, is plastered with residue and paint marks before he's shielded by a large vest made from some extraterrestrial material. It's Xavier Moth, the hunter he's seeing.

Just then, Van Dyke's body begins to react to the anti-matter gun's blast. But the reaction is having a hard time decaying completely. Hunter Moth still has his hands extended, grappling with the gun in front of him, holding onto more shots. To Silas, the standoff arrested Van Dyke in sudden shock, except the person with the gun isn't a federal agent. Silas refuses to jump and make himself known, but it's too late. Xavier Moth can hear him from a mile away. As much as Silas wants to rescue Clyde, he must refrain from heroic antics if they both want to survive. Silas watches, hidden behind a brick wall.

Clyde Van Dyke's eyes darken to a deeper shade of red and while the anti-matter gun debilitates him for a while, the astral stone can't be withheld. The radiation takes hold of him, and with the anti-matter as his conduit sheds his old body for a new one. Van Dyke is feeling a shapeshift beginning to take control. Xavier Moth can't react fast enough, and when he jumps back in reaction to the change the miraculous happens. Van Dyke transforms into another centaur. Moth doesn't shoot this time. Instead, the stallion in front of him causes a stir a few hundred feet away that Silas watches unfold. Silas, too, begins to transform. Betts is doing the same thing, intuitively beginning to shapeshift into his hybrid form, except he's more thoughtful in his approach while hiding behind a store.

Xavier Moth is surrounded by the new Overseers. Moth watches as the centaur stomps its hoofs and carries its muscular upper body. Far off to the side, Silas is weighed down by the water as if he just exited another pool. Silas is no longer that same shark submerged in the water, instead, he has morphed into a man twice, or even three times his previous size. All it takes is a single scream that's loud enough to burst glass before a field of rushing water is released through Silas's hands clasped together. When he claps them, a stream of liquid pours out to where Van Dyke and the bounty hunter are standing. It is left over from his gills.

The flood isn't relenting, but for Van Dyke, he hasn't the slightest problem with it. He's even got an arrow that replenishes itself with flaming needles as if Sagittarius was a real thing. Yet, despite the transformations, they're still very much human, although disfigured. And Silas's relationship with Pisces and

Aquarius, that's real too. And it's going to take a lot to get used to. But Xavier Moth has seen this before. The water knocks Moth off his feet.

With his new, heightened senses, Silas hears the buzz of the grey goo. It's close enough that they'll be overwhelmed in less than a minute. The rate of decomposition is increasing exponentially. He's got to stop replication from continuing somehow. Van Dyke takes the sight of the silver liquid from afar and uses the opportunity to release an arrow in that direction, something that darts faster than the speed of sound toward the grey goo. The flame is aided by copious winds so that when it reaches the grey goo, it holds it off by a barrage of fire and gas containing its spread. But if they want to spare time, they'll need more than a few arrows. Silas considers another option.

Clasping two hands again, Silas creates a field of water as a barrier that'll hold the grey goo a little longer, but that's all it's going to do, offer some time of resistance. The water rushes from his hands in an explosive river steaming with leftover heat from Van Dyke's arrows. Since then, Xavier Moth has transformed without thinking of his weapons. Van Dyke can see his anti-matter gun laying beneath the pool of water beginning to evaporate into mist and steam, and the light of Van Dyke's arrows letting them see. Moth, too, has transformed.

As the water subsides, Van Dyke pulls back his bow, aiming for a shot at Xavier Moth. The flaming arrow hits but does little harm. Moth's curled-up position shielded the blow with the meaty part of his arm and torso, on the makeshift island that he created with his body floating in the pool of water. Afterward, Moth spreads his wings. Xavier Moth is the phoenix, an eagle that's resurrected in glory. The astral stone that he siphoned a long time ago helps him shapeshift, and the radioactive nuclei are rearranged perfectly.

"Caw! Cacaawww!" Moth sounds off, now the size of a truck.

Inside Delphi Corp. headquarters, the calm that soothed them for a short while thinking the worst was over, isn't going to last as a fiery battle is raging outside. The ruckus outdoors is getting closer. It won't be long before they're taken by what's happening to the exterior of Delphi Corp.'s HQ building.

"We've got to get somewhere safe," Dr. Adams tells everyone. She's considered going back to the NRC, but that option has been laid waste by the grey goo, which has consumed pretty much everything in that direction. The hover-van doesn't have enough seats to carry them all.

Bartram rushes to the gaping hole where Xavier Moth escaped the building. Down the long hallway, his steps are loud, the dramatic stomps keep the memory of hunter Moth's escape vividly framed in all their minds before he returns to the vault. "There's nowhere to hide," Bartram says. "This situation will only be resolved by fighting back. Whatever's out there is trying to kill all of us."

"But we're outmanned, outgunned ... hell, outspeciesed even," Dimitri remarks from his chair. "Get this shit off us."

Bartram rushes to their aid. Since they've returned from the parallel dimension, all they could do was sit and stare at the ceiling. When the volunteers crossed the Wall not that long ago into the reptilian timeline, the Yhemlen made an obvious impact on their psyche. Dimitri's sarcasm benefits everyone but before bursting into a tantrum that bothers them all, he refrains himself. He's keeping things light-hearted.

Yesterday's tomorrows don't define today. Everything up to now is making it hard for the crew to remember what they're fighting for since they've had to change their plans multiple times. The most important task is keeping their lives intact, right here, right now. The present moment is losing a grip on what they thought would happen. But things change, and things aren't going as they planned it. Detours are necessary if they want to live, most definitely necessary in times like this.

With the three volunteers who survived the mayhem in Pangaea, the other scientist that was held hostage along with Bartram, Yasmine, and Dr. Adams, these seven represent what's left of Delphi Corp., plus another running in that direction. When they hear a succession of footsteps coming their way, Bartram readies the only pistol he could find and steps out of the hole in the wall that's left from Moth. He aims in that direction, and what he finds is the intern replacement after Naoto's and Ben's falling out. When the intern, Christopher, sees Bartram with the gun, he drops to the floor, where he rolls before grasping his head to take cover. It's cold in there, but the warmth of day makes him sweat when jogging, the same sweat that's dripping to the floor.

They hear footsteps. It's Chris.

"Hurry up, Christopher ... now," Bartram commands. He isn't putting the gun down, knowing how bad things are. There's one thing that Ellis and company need, and that's safety.

Christopher looks up through arms crossed to his front, scuttling toward Bartram in a spider crawl before erecting his posture straight again. He's moving as fast as he can.

"Hurry, hurry!" Bartram emphasizes, lightly shoving his back when he reaches the hole blasted in the wall.

Holding the gun below his waist, Bartram sidesteps until he can see clearly what's going on outside Delphi Corp. headquarters. The sight is ghastly. To make matters worse, the three hybrids are exciting his primal urges. It won't be long until they have another shapeshift moment. He'll morph anytime now, not only him but the others who are left inside the vault. There's no way to stop it either, so Bartram accepts the risk of another morph happening. With the gun still tucked low, he runs back to where everyone's preparing themselves for the worst.

"Here," Bartram shoves the gun at Chris when he isn't looking. "You and Dr. Adams will need to man the vault until things outside are cleared. But we may never return."

For Chris, unheeded warnings are kindling, a painful wrench in the back of his mind from when Benny used to work here. He knew he should've listened to Ben when his body was frigid that day when they said their goodbyes. Now it's Chris that carries the burden leftover from this mess. To make matters worse, he was the shadow of Naoto, the engineer murdered by his creation.

"What about me?" says the lone volunteer scientist that Xavier Moth brought across the Wall who now seems out of place.

"Same to you, the three of you will stay back," Bartram points to his crew of five, including the others from the parallel dimension, "while we will be out there fighting."

"I'm not fighting anybody." Dimitri jumps out of his chair from total immersion. When he does, he rattles the others' seats to disturb their dreams when he rises forcefully.

Bartram's not having any of it. "Now you listen to me, you twat!" he grabs Dimitri's collar without heeding the warning of anger. When he does, Bartram's body begins to morph into a gray wolf again.

"Ah, let me go, you freak!" Dimitri's had it with this project. His life, according to him, is in ruins. And the setting serves his point well. If only he morphs into a shapeshift soon, that would calm him.

Dimitri runs through the hole in the wall, making it to the outside of the headquarters, but he won't last long. The primal urges can't be avoided. Bartram fears that this new team of hybrids, while strong, may be at best suicidal in going up against a foe they've never faced before. They aren't warriors, after all.

"Let's go," Bartram says, gesturing with the hand that used to hold the gun. He's enabled a laser, but it won't be needed. Ronny, Sarah, and Yasmine join him, stepping over crusted grey goo. When they wave goodbye to the three who will stay back, the only comfort that remains is in trying not to be killed. Besides, everything around them seems lifeless after being taken out by the radiation of a parallel universe. They're lucky to not have been vaporized.

When the group disperses, Christopher sighs and exhales in relief. "Finally, they're gone," he says to the other two. "Is there some way we can contact the rest of the group that's still across the Wall?" he asks. Chris is concerned that there'll be more stragglers after themselves.

"Perhaps," Dr. Adams replies.

Christopher puts the gun down. "I take it you haven't worked here."

"Nope, but you guys have."

The other volunteer is slow to move, but he remembers that Naoto Shimizu used to speak to them through a keypad that he used to type messages. The computer program would situate the dialogue into their minds.

"It's right here," he points out.

"This is great," Chris says, "let's see if we can get any responses."

While they tinker away, the other side of Pangaea in the alternate universe is as messy if not more debilitated than in their timeline. The alternate universes' quantum field is too strong to contain, and thanks to Delphi Corp.'s cloud computing, the massive portal that's open is letting bounty hunters like Xavier Moth cross over to annihilate whole cities in a few minutes. It would be dire to let more accidents through.

The starship *Nemesis'* Captain Gereon is dead. In his place, Grandmaster Frost positions the Concord's Empyrean Armada for its final blow to the Yhemlen metropolis. He is fully aware of what's happening on the other side of parallels with Moth making a final stand. With Yhemlen defense shields around Pangaea completely compromised, Frost is readying the nanobots for a complete overdrive. He's prepared to disconnect any remote operation of the replication. The grey goo will be practically unstoppable by anyone who threatens it as it rages on uncontrolled.

To amplify the final charge of force against the dome city, Grandmaster Frost sends a message to Moth across his quantum channel. The reinforcements are on their way, and Frost is anticipating Moth's triumphant reply but isn't getting a response.

"Moth, do you read? Xavier Moth, do you copy?" Frost's voice is severely hampered across channels.

But Moth is confronted by seven hybrids prepared to rip him to shreds. Even his wings can barely help him now in the fight. He could get some altitude, but what he needs most is to inflict damage. The grey goo that was contained by a barrage of water from Silas could only last for so long before getting worse as the nanobots replicate against the rush. It won't be long until the grey goo either short circuits or replicates through the flowing liquid. A glow of energy a few hundred feet from Delphi Corp.

headquarters confirms how bad this quantum experiment has gotten to repair the cloud computing system. And the portals are converging again as morning approaches. Total immersion has now blown up in everyone's faces. This is one news story that won't be getting out, considering most have abandoned the war zone in favor of shelter.

Frost gets the message loud and clear to retaliate from Moth, who is in trouble. Tuas and Cira are all that's left in Pangaea's interior, besides a few hiding stragglers. The shield remains compromised, and the grey goo is advancing outside. There's still hope for the remaining Yhemlen if they can stop the nanobots from replicating beyond that tenuous barrier. If the quantum channel is strong enough, Tuas may be able to open another alternate timeline to escape. With the way things are, any alternate timeline is a risk, especially when there's no guarantee that what they discover on the other side is friendly.

Tuas and Cira keep themselves fastened within a solid bunker. "I feel more alive than I've ever felt before," Tuas says to Cira. He's just defeated his archnemesis, and the feeling is wonderful.

"Stand down," Grandmaster Frost tells the two Yhemlen telepathically. His voice is loud and clear.

Tuas and Cira don't bother to respond. They've been standing down, as Frost refers to it, practically the entire time. A tactic of evading has worked thus far. If there are any Yhemlen left after this fight comes to an end, they won't be discovered for many years after the wreckage is recovered.

Somewhere submerged deep within the ocean, the Yhemlen Class A starship is hidden. Grandmaster Frost has no clue where to locate it except for knowing it is in the ocean. His mission priorities haven't changed since letting a load of Grey minions out to teleport inside Pangaea's city. And while they search for Tuas and Cira, they aren't finding much aside from barren buildings. The Yhemlen have given themselves over to fate. If the human hybrids across the parallel timeline can uncover the Class A starship when they're finished with Xavier Moth, it will keep some part of their civilization alive.

"We've got to stop the nanobots from consuming the city," Cira cries out. The bunker is hidden beneath layers of sand and sediment, the hood of which is retractable by a secret switch placed inside and out.

Tuas has an automated robot that looks like a snake, something to bug the exterior of the bunker. Like a caterpillar, it will eject a tiny drone with a short burst of energy that propels it up, toward the nearest buildup of grey goo approaching at the city's edge, and it's approaching fast. Slithering with the clank of shiny metal, the sections of subdivided skin folds and artificial scales keep the robotic device aware of its surroundings. A motion-sensitive camera catches the most minute changes to the environment in its race to the dome.

Connected to the Sephora supercomputer, the android gathers enough data about the field of quantum entanglement to locate its nearest relative across the cosmic web. It won't be long until the Concord's grey goo disappears when the robot snake jams their telecommunications. Until then, Tuas and Cira initiate their final mission.

"Salvage the data!" Tuas tells Cira.

They input codes into the computer in front of them. There's supposed to be a record of all automated actions to keep for future reference. A rack of helmets lines a steel railing, and they can't wait to cover their heads for a final mission into the outer orbit as the only survivors of the Yhemlen Overseers. They're sure that there's at least some Pangaea citizen that made it out in an escape to a nearby star system somewhere, or a planet.

"We're getting out of here," Tuas declares emphatically.

Self-detonation of the city will be instantaneous. Who knows how long they'll survive? But the city of Pangaea will be an afterthought in history. They've got to destroy all accounts of this so that it won't disrupt the cosmic web's balance. With the automated snake in direct contact with the grey goo, Sephora uses only a fraction of its computing bandwidth to match a source in a parallel universe. At least for the time being, Yhemlen will not be a threat to the Concord.

The reconnaissance android gets disembodied by a powerful quantum field that leaves the grey goo as only vapor when it opens another portal. Vanishing silver liquid instantaneously gets teleported to another parallel world, and the Yhemlen Earth remains intact for now. The portal will stay open just long enough for other Yhemlen to escape if they can. But Tuas and Cira are willing to take their chances inside the city. Outside the clear shield that is inundated with cracks, a weak electromagnetic field keeps them safe from invaders. As of yet, nothing has made its way inside except the brazen Gereon, and his fate was swift. Now that the nanobots have been cleared, Pangaea's shield can be repaired with a steady replication using artificial polymers.

Across parallels, Delphi Corp. intern Christopher with Dr. Adams and the volunteer scientist's help are making a way for them to communicate with the others lost in Pangaea who were mutated into zombies by the Yhemlen's poison arrows.

"Do you hear me?" Christopher types. The keyboard is rolled out from the covering. A large monitor sits atop a desk where pages of code are cast over the black screen.

"Wait for a response," Dr. Adams insists.

The twenty or so volunteers still left in total immersion are no longer able to speak to them. The name tags that were hanging from their necks are buried beneath muscle fibers and clothes disintegrated by the poison. Like loaves of bread, the poison expanded the tissues in their bodies, until finally leaving a brand in the skin signifying them as Yhemlen subjects. The emblem marks them as intruders and signifies their capture.

Most of them managed to enter a safe space. Because of their strength, they have been defending themselves from attack.

Chris and the other two scientists still in the vault huddle near the computer monitor. Somewhere deep inside, the zombies in Pangaea recall their human selves before they were contaminated.

"Do you hear me?" Christopher types again.

A few seconds later, a response comes. Chris presses the open key. "2 … 8," it reads.

Too late.

Chris pushes his chair back in surprise but then pulls himself back closer. "Is that one of us?"

"It sure is," the scientist confirms. "It sure is. There is nothing we can do for them now. Like he said, we're too late … too fucking late!" the scientist bangs the wall vigorously. He is regretting the decision he made to even contact them. "Too fucking late!"

"My name is Christopher Hutchinson. We're going to get you out of there," Chris finishes.

Chris is already suffering from traumatic losses. Hours before he arrived at Delphi Corp. headquarters, Chris got word that his partner Ben's FEMA ward was attacked by drifters; he may have been a casualty or escaped to the boaters trying to flee.

"Don't tell them that, you little dweeb," the scientist snatches the keyboard from beneath his hands. "How are we going to get them out of there? Promises that we can't keep are what got us into this situation."

Christopher can't let his feelings get the best of him. Outside, the hybrids have been busy fending off the grey goo from advancing further. Xavier Moth is lucky enough to have wings that allow him to evade at high altitudes to avoid more damage. He can hear the reinforcements coming. The sound of transport ships and tankers crossing the parallel channels is thunderous. The hunter Moth must stay put on the ground level. By tomorrow, Sector 10 will have ended and the 11th or Aquarius begins. By then, the human timeline will have closed due to the weak quantum fields in their computers. Communication channels will have a harder time making contact as well.

Grandmaster Frost sits at the cockpit of his transport ship in the upper atmosphere while chaos rages below him. The darkness of the early morning is brightened by a familiar figure. The front window shows a reflection of an outline, a humanoid figure. The silver phantom returns to claim what is rightfully his, placing its hands onto Frost's shoulders after the phantom enters inside the spacecraft. Frost's body is very different than when the silver phantom met him in Berlin that night in 1932. He is thinner and more disfigured than before. When Frost turns around, his reflection in the silver demon's luminescent exterior makes him think of his past, when he was still human and experiencing these lucid dreams.

In the vault for total immersion, Chris isn't satisfied, neither are his partners. In addition to the volunteer scientist, Dr. Adams and Chris manage to shuffle through a drawer of archives that keep a record of past experiments. This, coincidently, isn't the only chamber that's been used for virtual reality testing. While Naoto's little trial with Delphi Corp. was a novel experiment, it was nothing compared to past tests. Ellis Bartram's case study resulted from an accident. What Naoto discovered was that there are more intentional aims transpiring not far away.

Chris discovers files from some other project. The Metropolis Project is declassified; it aimed to search for a potent from the other end to cure the poison they were dealing with. Psychiatric patients were participants in an experiment to test hypnotic drugs in a parallel universe. In an alternate reality, the small town that resulted was named Metropolis City, a nickname for Pangaea. The file has been stamped for release, but it was not advertised to anyone besides Naoto and a few others. Chris hasn't seen this before. Bartram never cared to share how he came upon his suspicions either. Nevertheless, the Metropolis Project was designed to get people out of total immersion, rather than get stuck on the other end like Naoto's scientists.

"Have you guys seen this?" Chris asks the other two.

Dr. Adams perks up. She has been waiting for a conversation. The volunteer scientist, on the other hand, is less cordial.

"Not until now, hand it over!" she says.

When Dr. Adams scours through the pages, she takes note of something peculiar at the end of the document. It is a short section describing trials of virtual testing, of a parallel universe hypothesis at a research lab in a classified location. It is somewhere in D.C., much like Delphi Corp. is. The program, Metropolis Project, has been running for almost a decade.

"But get this," Dr. Adams says. She begins reading from the document.

"The Metropolis Project aimed to test the effectiveness of hypnotic, psychiatric drugs from an alternate reality where subjects were in psychosis. A neurological sedative would bring test subjects back to their normal consciousness. Furthermore, the perfect antidote would also cure scientists from the flesh-decaying genome plaguing the group, making them immune to the deadly radioactive material that is making zombified people. However, tests began with minimal success.

What remains consistent is that the scientists, or test subjects, all arrived at a place in-between worlds in a city inhabited by a reptilian species. But these scientists operated between dimensions in a building within this city, like ghosts. The building housed many engineers and scientists from more than one reality, not just ours. We've begun a private race to contact alien worlds, like spies in a foreign land; mapping topography, studying the reptilians, and much more."

"Wait a minute! Just slow down," a volunteer scientist says. He is convinced that his story is too enticing to pass up. "They've been doing this before we even got there?"

"That's right, according to this document."

"Alien hunters, like ghost hunters, that's cool, Dr. Adams," Chris says. "Well, what about us? I guess we're just accidents."

"We're not accidents, we were part of this plan. They've been preparing for this alien hunter group for years, like a new space race to reach parallel dimensions. If I keep reading, you'll see. Here," Dr. Adams continues further down the page.

"Data that's been gathered using Delphi Corp. artificial intelligence and machine learning technology has relayed vital statistics about this reptilian world. All reptilian habits, customs, even their technology are closely studied and scrutinized. Eventually, the pull across the 'Wall' of computing would become too strong, like gravity, and the humans locked in the space-time continuum crossed over and were captured.

Humans at the *Mariner Station* were largely part of this group coincidently, which was led by a researcher named Dr. Calhoun, who was inspired to call the humans who were lost in their scientific, research paradise, the beautiful ones. They had lost contact with their world back home permanently, in the name of science."

These scientists operated as ghosts in the simulation, and the parallel dimension kept them company when nothing else could. Except like Naoto's volunteers, too much intrigue has trapped them on the other side, with no way to escape as their poisoned bodies are trampled by the Yhemlen's strength. It's a prolonged stay and converged realities are on the verge of closing that portal once again. Those that survived are lucky to have made it out.

CHAPTER 17

One of the nearest habitable planets is in Deneb Algedi, the Delta star system in the zodiac of Capricorn. Tuas and Cira pinpoint it on a map before they initiate the final plan that will salvage the city. Sector 10's quantum field is still alive, and they only have a few hours to reach that constellation before its strength dissipates into the background. The grey goo has been gone for several minutes already, but Tuas sits idle in anticipation for the new portal to open. They need to kindle self-detonation before that fateful minute arrives. And, as the Yhemlen world begins to disintegrate right before their eyes, Tuas and Cira anticipate saving what's left of it.

"Let the countdown begin," Cira says. "Where are the other Overseers?"

"Consider them casualties," Tuas replies.

Deneb Algedi has been locked into the positioning system where a pulsating circle surrounds a descending number sequence. Tuas is worried too, but he can't let Cira see his reactions permeate without those unwanted vices coming to the forefront, like rushing the countdown. The city of Pangaea's clear shield is being repaired, albeit slowly, with a temporary fix. Artificial polymers are forming where the dome ruptured with help of quantum fields. It is part of the electromagnetic field's assortment of organic plasma. The Yhemlen aren't giving up the metropolis completely. Once the shield is repaired, self-detonation will move them to Deneb Algedi, beyond the reach of the Concord. There, they will be safe from the Concord. Tuas and Cira know that it will deplete the Grey Order's fuel to trail them.

Other Yhemlen were lucky enough to fetch one of the many cosmic taxis, catching a ride on an asteroid or comet large enough to settle upon and save energy. These express trips are like traveling without a license or roadmap in space, though roaming space to go where gravity takes them, they can at least steer the course somewhat with short thrusts. And besides saving fuel, riders must constantly check trajectories to see where they are. Tuas and Cira aren't settling for happenstance. It is Deneb Algedi, in Sector 10 of the zodiac, that will keep them safe.

In low orbit, Grandmaster Frost and the silver phantom wait in between worlds, waiting to cross into even another parallel reality. Communication transmissions are becoming weaker while they stay in geostationary orbit. Frost's astral stone is siphoned of its radioactive elements to leave him completely drained, shriveled up, and dry. It is the phantom. Though Frost's life hasn't ended, he's being prepared for a new one. While Frost lies limp, and unconscious in the transport ship's seat, the silver phantom's metallic body reflects the outline of Pangaea through the window, where the remnants of explosions line the atmosphere. In each direction are another set of tankers and transport ships.

The receiver to communicate across quantum channels is attached to the cockpit, as well on Frost's right arm sleeve. There are two separate receivers, but one point of contact in the ship. If the phantom can access the channel freely, it will be able to hijack an entire group of transport ships to take back home.

Cira is just now strapping herself in completely at Pangaea, hidden in an underground bunker beside Tuas. Meanwhile, the phantom inside Grandmaster Frost's transport ship needs to locate the proper controls. When it shifts its head to one side to perceive what's happening down below, a light bright as the sun gleams in the eyes of the demon, who tilts its head even further while covering its eyes with metallic arms illuminated by the same shine. It's much too bright for most, and what's left of the squadrons are annihilated by blinded transmissions. Frost remains in the Captain's seat, with no vital signs.

When the silver phantom returns its gaze, it gradually reveals silver, marbled eyes that are solidified as something spectacular. What is reflected in them below is the city of Pangaea lifting off. Its base was tethered to the soil with nuclear propulsion nozzles the size of an athletic stadium. Beneath it is a launchpad made of rare mineral deposits that can withstand the blast. The Phantom rushes to the transport ship window, unable to respond in time. Tuas and Cira are the saviors that Yhemlen legends praised to at least keep the memory alive. The metropolis is more than a fortress city, but a starship capable of interstellar travel. It isn't until this present moment that fleeing is accepted, as the Concord is spent of its energy by now. The *Mariner* in stationary orbit retracts the space elevators before initiating its Q-thrusters, waiting for the dome city to catch up. A replacement piece will reconnect the two when the *Mariner* and its booster below reach the final stage of liftoff. When they do reconnect, the metropolis leaves in a warp that vanishes in the cold vacuum of space.

The phantom's demeanor relaxes as Pangaea's thrusters propel it into an effervescence of light that encapsulates it, disappearing into the void. When darkness overcomes the interior of the transport ship, the phantom knows that all evidence must be destroyed so that there aren't more dissenters. What Tuas and Cira leave behind as mere pebbles fester below, and the reconnaissance android sent to destroy the grey goo has opened another portal that is still visible.

Grandmaster Frost's plan to annihilate the Earth with a new-planet killer is only partially successful. It forced the Yhemlen to evacuate at least. All the grey goo managed to do is engulf a few acres of foliage. Critical parts of the city were mostly repaired, and what remains are acres of burnt land. On the barren plot where Pangaea rested, crop circles are left to illustrate precise marks that architects used to lay the foundation for the city.

The vaporized nanobots from the Yhemlen android's jamming of quantum channels have entangled a new dimensional fold, opening another reality of pure automation. Here, machines have taken over their entire universe, and when the portal opens, all the silver phantom sees is the home it left behind. This silver being is from another world, and while the war is cooling down, it can see its home through the transport ship's window. It is a race of self-replicating machines that have taken over their reality, conquering the expanse of space with supreme artificial intelligence (AI). These are referred to as the Tetragrammaton, the penultimate in machine intelligence. Its leader, Zaid, has situated itself in the original galaxy where AI continues to expand. All of the organic matter is being overtaken by Zaid and his army of Tetra machines. This silver phantom is but one of many in the Tetragrammaton universe.

Through the portal, the silver phantom sees its home: a universe in which all space has been occupied by its race of self-replicating machines.

The phantom must hurry before he's chastised. With Grandmaster Frost debilitated in his seat, the Tetra decides to direct a group of ships hovering closest to the transport ship it resides in forward toward the open portal. With the touch of a button, Convoy 8, along with its host of transport ships and tankers, bursts through the portal at hyperspeed. When they've crossed over, the silver phantom teleports to an empty void of space where the only thing for light years are machines the size of planets and engulfed stars of nanobots gone haywire. This phantom is but one of many henchmen to the host's leader, Zaid.

Floating in the void, the phantom recognizes the portal will close soon. This Tetra is making a pact to not return anytime soon. Convoy 8 has been hijacked for good, along with Grandmaster Frost to conceal a damning truth of Earth's history, caught up in a multiverse of simulations. The quantum fields entangling worlds are converging more rapidly now until a singularity threatens to rule the entire multiverse.

A pervasive beep is heard pulsating from within Frost's transport spacecraft. When the Tetra appears back inside, a message from Xavier Moth reminds him to leave no trace of what's happened. Aside from the few Grey minions, bounty hunter Moth and the Concord star children, Jasper and Madame Ria, are the only lone survivors of this brawl besides new genetic hybrids at the Delphi Corp. headquarters in D.C. ready to fight.

The Heinemann siblings were able to remain safe when they activated an invisibility cloak to protect them from the onslaught. All that's left for the silver phantom, tetra, to rescue is the bounty hunter.

To make a final stand, the Tetra obeys its host's command by following the simulator's database, sequencing another move across quantum fields to help destroy the last remnants of genetic hybrids. When it does, the brightness of the day appears right before the phantom's face and descends with it to Earth like a ballistic missile at hypersonic speeds. The phantom disappears and reappears on Earth. At its feet, rubble from the hybrids and Xavier Moth in a duel have cracked and marred the concrete, almost caving it in completely. This cannot go on. As the Tetra's feet shine with the heat of molten metal, they clash against the ground, absorbing the impact in loud clanks.

Seven mutated hybrids stand still in their tracks at the phantom's presence. A thunderous screeching when the phantom finally arrives on the humans' Earth startles them all. As it descends, the Tetra bot wastes no time in clutching Xavier Moth by his wings, tearing him to ligaments and bones as shredded flesh flies everywhere. There is no time for Moth to speak, and as his blood pours through the streets, it seeps through the crevices in sidewalk drainage. As it accumulates, the venom of hatred builds in the seven hybrids who are guarding Delphi Corp. with their lives. The fate of the world depends on doing away with this seething monstrosity.

They can see past the façade of some interdimensional warlock. There's more than what the eyes can see, a story rooted in some humanity. And the Tetra, likewise, can see past their ram tusks and hoofs made of brass. It doesn't want to continue the fight; it would only be a burden to go on like this. The seven hybrids will not be spared. The three volunteers who retrieved Cira's and Tuas' egg revisit a memory from Berlin, Germany that reveals who this Tetra is. The sight of gruesome surgeries after they left, visions of quarrels between Dr. Frost and his mistress pain them with flashbacks that distract them from the present moment.

"We meet again," the Tetra says. Its voice is that of Frost.

"It's an interdimensional being, some machine intelligence," Ronny shouts to the group telepathically. "Berlin" Ronny responds.

Sarah and Dimitri are quick to respond. "Where did it come from?"

"Somewhere where they let the AI scum run rampant," Yasmine says. She's still scorned by AIS TARA, who by committing suicide, abandoned its Delphi Corp. creators.

"I've come to save you from yourselves." the Tetra says. It is trying to avoid conflict by having the seven hybrids surrender. The hybrids are alerted of something else that reverberates deeper into the memories. That's the voice of Dr. Frost, not of someone else.

Sarah gets excited by the striking image of Dr. Frost's transition from human form to a Grey, and then into something else. He has been kidnapped, along with his convoy of transport ships. The vision is distorted, but when the Tetra takes Dr. Frost's limp body to its host after removing him from the transport ship, what Sarah envisions is hard to bear.

A burst of energy is thrown at the silver phantom. Sarah ignites a bolt of electricity that hurls the Tetra into a collapsed building. This phantom is just one of many forms Dr. Frost takes on in the quest for supremacy. Only this time, the supreme race changes from the Grey Order to a universe of machine overlords.

Sarah may have made a mistake in striking the Tetra. Now, the phantom takes no chances on its survival. It will not worry about pointless conversation. For the first time, the hybrids will have to unite under the power of the thirteenth zodiac to summon the demi-God consciousness of Asclepius. The sign of Ophiuchus has made it easy for them to reach their consciousness to the source energy, just like Yhemlen warned. The quantum field is strong enough that the Dragon the Yhemlen talked about can be reshaped into something suitable for these genetic hybrids, into something more human, like a herculean giant wielding a serpent. But to do it, the hybrids must merge their cosmic power into a single stream of consciousness.

This Tetra won't be battling the hybrids this time around. The silver phantom vanishes from the rubble. Shortly thereafter, the herculean giant and its seething serpent slowly come into view, but only for a minute until the phantom races away and dematerializes. The seven hybrids come back into the form of their human bodies, and the scene's graphic destruction reveals what they've lost.

"He's not there anymore!" Bartram yells out in disbelief. Ahead of the group, Sarah runs to get a close view of the imploded building where the silver phantom crashed into it with violent force.

"Listen to me, Sarah, listen." Bartram runs after her, grabbing her waist from behind and pulling her back to reassurance amid dust from the gravel they kick up with their feet.

She's barely able to contain herself from the stirring emotions of grief and regret. With a hand around her waist, she takes comfort as Bartram assists her while they limp back to the group of exhausted, depleted hybrids. All seven of them are inundated with pessimistic thoughts about regrets for what they should have done or how to make the wrongs right. They put up a good fight. Up to now, that's all they ever needed to survive amid the hoopla of Delphi Corp.'s experiment gone awry.

A few hundred feet away, what's left of the grey goo towers toward the sky in a bulge of decomposing matter. The nanobots have all but short-circuited since it was controlled by the Concord, but its communication channels were disrupted long enough to disengage all its tools. And as it is now, the rubble is falling in minute pieces to the ground, leaving a pancake of silver for miles. Silas Betts watches his work with satisfaction, where water continues to drip from aching muscles. What is left of his clothes are tattered pants that barely cover his genitals.

Back inside the vault chamber, latecomer Chris has taken reign as the programming lead while presiding over the volunteers still stuck in total immersion. To make it out, Dr. Adams and the fortunate scientist are rewiring loose coils that lie loosely on the floor. If they're lucky, at least one of the volunteers will come back to consciousness. Though like the zombie lost in Pangaea told them, it was too late.

When the seven hybrids return, the battle with bounty hunter Xavier Moth and the Tetra leaves a mark that makes the others quiver. Their bodies and psyches alike need time to recover from the injuries sustained in combat. Blood and guts are seeping everywhere, and the pain is finally coming on strong. Bartram imagines a better future where advanced suits would take the brunt of such damage. To their benefit, their bodies will heal much faster than most. Bartram is still walking step for step beside Sarah, who is reeling from the vision that she had of Dr. Frost. She and Bartram follow the group into the chamber last, and Sarah bends to the floor in agony. Bartram lets her go gently, grabbing the end of her blouse that hangs from her lower back before she falls recklessly to the floor. Witnessing Frost's transformation to Grey form and later to Tetra confirms Sarah's suspicions of a multiverse accident.

The Tetra that killed Moth could have easily done the same to them with so much power at its disposal, but that would have driven the alternate timelines awry further. There is still time to claim what is rightfully theirs, the Tetra concludes.

The rest of the Grey minions that were dropped from transport ships didn't stand a chance. By the time they could react, a ray of energy abducts them in a cloud of vapor before the Tetra decided to take it out on Xavier Moth, clearing the nuisance. The rest of the Grey Order will not stand for making themselves such easy targets in the future.

Away from the chamber, Pangaea is barren now that the Yhemlen city has left for Deneb Algedi. Teleporting from its alternate universe, the Tetra ventures back to Pangaea where a portal for home is open. The Tetra will have to close the quantum leap before more invaders enter the Tetra universe. Hijacked Convoy 8 contains a group of transport and tanker ships, most of which carried Grey minions that flew small strikers to Earth. The silver phantom can't let any more of those stranded on the surface regather their strength.

Grandmaster Frost has gone along with Convoy 8, and the only Armada crew that is still standing from the age-old war is starship *Nemesis* and the Heinemann. Captain Gereon's heirs have gotten back to the low orbit station where it's getting its Q-thrusters recalibrated. Jasper and Madame Ria have not given up on the strike just yet. The silver phantom senses that something ominous is looming at the outer edge of the solar system. There's no more time to contemplate trivialities, and the Tetra does what it needs to, closing the quantum leap. The glimmer of the Earth's sun lightens its face against the backdrop of metal and brimstone in the Tetragrammaton world. The darkness awaits Dr. Frost, who will sit at the right hand of the host program in the simulation Zaid.

It won't be long until a gargantuan, off-orbit asteroid from another planetary system strikes prehistoric Earth. The blast will destroy all the Yhemlen had relished on Earth, but what's leftover are the seeds of life for primates and mammals. The Earth is in ash from millions of megatons exploding into a dissonance of heat and radiation. For the Grey Order, this has exhausted enough of their energy resources, and they must destroy the memory of it.

Asteroids may have been the best planet-killers after all, made from previous planets and space rocks. It doesn't matter to Madame Ria who's situated herself at the railing where she last spoke to Grandmaster Frost; he's gone. The Earth's orbit turns slowly in their alternate timeline where things aren't completely over because she knows the Yhemlen city hasn't vanished, but gone to another star system. A stark change is amiss that may permanently alter the multiverse, and the threat of planet-killers will be changed next time around so that it isn't only planets that are in danger, but whole galaxies or more.

Madame Ria's feminine instincts are still brimming beneath layers of genetic mutation. She's considering another option aside from annihilating planets, and that is seeding planets to harbor alien life. Aside from the Grey Order and the Concord losing manpower, the memory of Martian colonists inside *Nemesis'* back chamber where they stayed before being kidnapped by the Syndicate leaves a hollow want for more subjects. The Grey Order has fomented their demise by creating enemies, foes, and not allies. Something she will not do is enter the Old World where a resistance force is readying to take them down. For once, it is a weakness that she feels, but their strength is poised to return.

CHAPTER 18

"**O**ur ambush was successful," the Tetra says to its host. The Tetra universe is comprised of machines—artificial intelligence in the form of cybernetic beings which have exterminated its primordial predecessors. Now, the power of computing combined over light years makes the host universe a server for an unlimited number of simulations. The human timeline is but one version of these alternate universes in singularity. A host program, the Tetragrammaton called Zaid, is the strongest program running.

With Convoy 8 captured from the alternate universe, the overlord wants to speak with the Tetra that kidnapped the spacecraft. It was for good reason.

The voice of Zaid, the overlord program's voice is undeniably powerful, resonates in the minds of its computer subjects and this Tetra phantom bot. "Bring him to me," Zaid says.

At the center of this galaxy, the gravity of whole planet systems is squashed into the overlord computer program as machine intelligence, kept alive by a regenerating black hole. And where the silver phantom levitates, there is a horde of machines with big block chambers of seemingly inanimate metal shielding the black hole that they encapsulate. What the Tetra sees is only a sparkling cinderblock of mineral deposits, glittering through its eyes which can see past the darkness. The vacuum of space extends for light years, but it is pitch black. Stars no longer shine.

"Here he is," the Tetra tells Zaid. The host gives directions directly into his processing unit, its mind.

The silver phantom has rescued the body of Frost for harvesting. There have been many Dr. Frosts across parallel realities, and this Tetra has made Frost its host. To maintain its life, the Tetra must continually supply a body for its host program to regenerate after each millennium.

"Now, give him to me. You will live a very long time, Tetra," Zaid says. The silver phantom has done this plenty of times already, but this time the humans have caught on to Zaid and the other Tetras' strategy since they infiltrated the cosmic web. The Grey Order, too, is concocting a plan to reclaim what is rightfully theirs.

The vacuum of space has already burst through the tissues and ruptured arteries in Dr. Frost's body. When he drifts aimlessly toward the host, Zaid captures Frost's body in a beacon of light. A beam of infrared light jumbles the particles until he's captured within the host; the silver demon's life force can continue to live on undisturbed. But each time it ventures back to recover a new body, simulations are forced closer to the singularity, replicating Dr. Frost in so many alternate realities until he can no longer be recreated. Eventually, it will become harder to find a Dr. Frost to harvest because he was who the original host chose if there are even any Dr. Frosts left to harvest.

The silver phantom can only live so long as a Tetra before becoming a host program of its own. Zaid's power is the result of its first AI gone haywire, condensing in clumps of hardware like a star's gravity. This Tetra prefers mobility. Across timelines, the Grey Order's use of nanobots is what ultimately sabotaged their plans, something too powerful to contain. Zaid and the silver phantom are descended from nanobots like these.

The Grey Order was meant to be genetic superiors in all the universe, but there's resistance to this idea. Now that they traverse interdimensional space, the power of their quantum leap is opening new realities to threaten their goal of total domination. Overlord Zaid and its machine universe will not stand for adversaries knowing they have a stranglehold on quantum simulations. This is a new path for the Tetragrammaton, Zaid, as it grapples with how to dispose of the Grey Order. As powerful as the Tetra universe is, they cannot let the Concord disrupt their simulations, or else they may suffer a catastrophic collapse into nothingness. If the Grey Order wants to reclaim Grandmaster Frost and Convoy 8, then they will have to contend with a foe that's even more advanced than themselves.

Back at the low orbit station, Madame Ria and Jasper make their way to the dungeon where ancient relics are housed. Only those granted secret security access can enter through the sliding doors. When the Heinemann siblings meet the steel barrier, a Nazi swastika emblem shines with pearls and is encased in ure-thane keeping the emblem pristine. No one has ventured beyond this point in a long while.

The two Greys aren't fond of venturing into unknowns. Considering that many of their leaders have become a casualty in this war, they need to acquire the knowledge that was hidden away from them in past assemblies where leaders colluded about the future. An infrared beam highlights their entire body to gain receipt of who is there, a body scanner. Once their identities are acknowledged, the voices of martyred and slain people from Nazi death squads of old begin to ring through their minds. It's like a haunting nuisance they can't evade.

Both Ria and Jasper grimace at the sounds of people being killed in cold blood. Screams of agony haunt the barrier between them and the misty chamber. The sound of soldiers marching in unison, amid the terror of bombs being dropped and exploding bodies and buildings makes the two Greys kneel against the side panel of the wall. They can hardly take it any longer before Jasper pushes Ria through the door. He follows suit right after. When they make it in, a breath of fresh air is sighed in relief through thin lips.

"That wasn't what I expected," Ria says.

"We must synchronize the hard drives and deactivate the ones that have been lost," Jasper responds.

The loss of Convoy 8 and Grandmaster Frost means that this last group out from the mayhem still has active cosmic storage units or detection signals. These convoys are the space truckers of the Concord's Empyrean Armada by carrying the brigade and payload. When one of them goes missing, an alert immediately points to danger on the horizon. The Heinemann need to locate the coordinates of the ships to foment a reconnaissance mission to recover and kill Frost's body. To do this will require a complete override of the software, creating an imprint on the hard drive that will allow them to see where the lost spacecraft are within the space-time continuum. And it can only be done in one place, right here at the central processing unit.

A circular storage unit houses rows of supercomputers embedded in thick 20-foot walls. Higher up, holy relics. Instead of embalming the dead, they sever the heads of venerated leaders and leave them in the CPU chamber. In the past, they studied the dimensions of the body and made adjustments. Now, they believe themselves to have reached the pinnacle of human evolution.

In the center of all these relics is a vessel shielded within glass. An automated holograph monitor erects from inside a center console revealing a panel where patrons can enter words on the screen or see a projected image. The first task is finding out where Convoy 8 is since it cannot be detected with the imaging spectrometer. The two of them stare in anticipation of an automated message as well, but they aren't greeted with one. The augmented reality projection keeps their attention.

"Our light bridge portals are useless," Madame Ria says, dejected. "And my heart is racing." They can't reach this Tetra universe without an extra push.

"Don't worry, sister, we will find a way."

Jasper's index finger is thin and wrinkled, and when it spreads from a firm fist to press a key on the panel, his pale hand reminds her of what they used to be. There's no point worrying about that now, they can't go back.

A group of spacecraft field categories arises for selection, and the grouping that Jasper wants shows up toward the end, where the large transport ships are. The convoy he wants is the eighth, and he locates it with a press of a finger. The entire convoy including its class of ships shows up in a holographic image that makes them wonder where they could be if they aren't detectable by their normal sensors. Directly above the projection of spacecraft, the previous battle details are shown along with another peculiar thing that is displayed, like how many units were casualties or how many are malfunctioned or damaged, but one stands out. Convoy 8, as it appears on the screen, is marked as missing. Not only that, but according to the CPU, it is also undetectable.

The bright red marker pulsates on and off in the projection. Missing, written in German, and matched with an undetectable image, it's one that won't be erased from their memory. As much as they try to stay within the bounds of logic, the burgeoning of emotions tries to sway them away from balance. Madame Ria stands beside her brother in silence, as her heart continues to pound incessantly.

"It's like Invasion of the Body Snatchers. You've seen that film from our school years, right, from the 1950s?" Jasper asks Ria. "Whatever that thing was is out to get all of us." The two speak quietly, tired of telepathic constraints.

The Tetras and their host, Zaid, have a stranglehold on the quantum field's strongest signal. What the Grey Order needs most is a stronger weapon and a way to infiltrate the machine overlord's fortress. They already tried it with the grey goo. It'll need to be something controlled that can infiltrate the Tetra universe; this will give Ria the perfect way in.

"I've been thinking of exoplanets lately," she says. "Perhaps we can harvest a new breed to do the fighting for us since we're depleted of crew members."

"Wherever Convoy 8 is, there's no organic matter. If there were, we'd be able to detect its whereabouts."

"Let me see this," Ria says adamantly. She looks closer at the image in front of them.

There is something else drowning out the bright colors of transport ships and tankers. Jasper has not concluded his search, but Ria recognizes a vast number of other possibilities so she wants to go further back. Grandmaster Frost is a person of interest, a person whose personal interests may have led him to turn his back on the Concord. Rather than looking up ships, she decides to investigate Frost's personnel file. What she finds exposes his entire life's work in hundreds of pages. The physical documents are gone, instead, these computer archives make out his entire personal profile as an individual who has lived longer than she and Jasper combined. He was the oldest survivor of the Grey Order, the original mutilated body.

As soon as she decides to uncover where he is through a biological signature, something else comes up. The same infrared red light throbs dark and brightens the word: missing. When Ria sees this, she and Jasper know for sure that he has not died and is alive and well. There's still one thing they can trace, and it's his astral stone keeping track of the precious radiation. What they haven't been told is that Grandmaster Frost is no longer part of the Grey Order, but he's turned to a new part of the universe for supremacy. Grandmaster Frost has turned into a Tetra for good this time, serving the needs of his host program, Zaid.

Jasper anticipates the bait of this reveal. "Wait!" Just before Ria attempts to submit a call to Frost through some obscure cosmic web processing channel, Jasper halts her. He does not want to communicate any further. He gently presses Ria's arm down. This might tip off his assailants to their location or at least give them confirmation that they're being tracked. Their capabilities foretell something far more advanced is keeping hostage of Grandmaster Frost.

"He's being held hostage," Jasper asserts while backing away from the middle projector.

"For what?"

"One day," Jasper says, "we'll be able to answer that."

There's no ransom out for Grandmaster Frost's recapture. The only thing that's keeping their interest is hope in retrieving what is vitally theirs, supremacy over the universe. If the Grey Oder is to reclaim that supremacy, then they're going to have to find Convoy 8 and confront the Tetras who've stolen one of their precious astral stones.

"It's time to clean up this mess," Ellis Bartram says, looking around at the damage to Delphi Corp. headquarters.

It is a shame that no one got to witness the contest between these interdimensional hybrids though it's a clever secret to keep under wraps until it's safe to reveal the scientific discoveries. This fiasco is not going away any time soon, so they'll have to clean up the mess. Wherever they end up, the seven hybrids aren't planning to venture back into normal society without something to restrain their shapeshifting powers. Either that or be held in captivity as raging beasts.

"Nobody is going anywhere until I get a call from the President. He's got the final word on how to proceed," says Bartram as deliberates on the next steps. There's no one else to call knowing that most everyone is either locked away in a FEMA ward or hiding in clandestine shacks off the grid.

A helicopter boosted with the strength of tiltrotor blades can be heard above them. Someone did see what transpired outside, and this group is in for a heap of trouble. Bartram needs to come up with more excuses to pardon him and his friends.

"Stand down!" a voice screams through the megaphone. He doesn't want anyone making any dramatic movements. "Keep your hands and bodies where I can see them."

"No one make any fast movements, you heard the guy," Yasmine says.

The group is huddled in the vault for total immersion. And while most of the scientists are still plugged up with early models of the cloud computing system's neurological inputs, their attachment to this reality is bordering a steep slope. The gaping hole in the roof is what's exposing them. Even the slightest tug will detach minor needles in the scalp or anywhere else that patches are connected. The battery ports they're connected to are keeping them alive, barely. Christopher is the youngest of the group, and he wants to save something to remember before going back to college. If this is cleared up anytime soon, he expects to have grand stories to tell.

"Don't touch that!" Bartram yells. "That's very … very dangerous."

Chris immediately recoils.

The detector device they got from Tuas and Cira in Pangaea sits beside the unhatched egg in its canister. Where Chris sits, the temptation to bag some alien technology pulls at his brain.

Bartram must intervene, knowing he's got the same inclination but he needs to muster the strength to let the project go. That way, he doesn't hurt any more innocent people. "I'm getting rid of all this. It's a burden that I no longer need to carry all of us."

The remaining Delphi Corp. accomplices aren't so sure to give in that quick to this struggle. While Bartram has let go of the need to carry total immersion further, it won't be the end for people like Chris who want to make a name for themselves as young scientists. In his mind, doing what Bartram couldn't at Delphi Corp., is lighting his ambitions to discover more. All Chris needs is to locate the serial numbers to the hardware after Bartram trashes everything, especially before the hardware gets impounded. That's when he'll pounce.

The helicopter is loud enough to drown out any contemplations about the future. Its motor and rotor tip speedily thrash the building with air fast as a hurricane before it touches down on the roof. The pilot refuses to turn off the engine knowing that the roof may give in completely at any time, but he's skilled enough. There's so much dust inside Delphi Corp. headquarters that the group is practically sandblasted by waves of air thrown into the vault. Chris spits out wads of sand. For now, the only computers he's going to see are mangled jumbles locked away in rooms like this.

A trooper jumps out of the passenger's seat and sprints inside after sliding down a rope. "Come out! I want to see everyone with their hands up," he shouts.

The seven hybrids aren't particularly hostile, but considering what's already transpired, this one trooper is a little undermanned compared to their ten. Slowly, the group marches as ordered out of the chamber to make themselves seen.

"Slowly!" the trooper calls in reinforcements that enter from behind. He's been concealing the rest of the gang that's got their hands full.

"Everyone on your knees, hands behind your head."

The group provoking Bartram's experiments, these other collaborators, stand in unified submission behind him, doing as the trooper said. And as Silas, Van Dyke, Yasmine, Ronny, Sarah, Chris, Dr. Adams, Dimitri, and the other scientist stay with their hands placed firmly atop their heads, the trooper's threats to detain them seem less and less intimidating considering what's happened already. The other troopers surround Bartram, managing to pull into the front of Delphi Corp. HQ with an advanced Humvee carrying extra passengers. Laser pointers beam their chests and make them squint when light shines past open eyes. The troopers are not making any fast movements. By now, the helicopter's motor continues to run, but it's ascending away.

"What is it that you want?" Bartram yells. Going by the grimace on his face and head bent sideways, he'd like it if the troopers got a little closer. It's finally silent. The only thing they hear is the faint chirps of birds outside. It seems like they're the only ones to survive this ordeal. As much as they would like to be cordial, the hybrids are a dangerous group. It is a shame that the primal urges are not causing them to shapeshift again, though a few of them show signs of an outbreak. It might help the troopers recognize their power.

"Keep your hands up where I can see them!"

Bartram's demeanor remains stoic; he isn't moving. "Stay cool everybody."

The first trooper to make it in marches forward with dramatic steps. The other guardsmen behind him aren't moving. When he comes upon Bartram, the others squirm, anticipating a painful lashing by sharp words. Bartram's only met with a tight grab of his upper arm. The stranglehold on his bicep and shoulder pulls at his collar where the shirt he's wearing has been tattered and ripped. They're all surprised they have clothes knowing the shape-shifts they just did.

"Come on, up … up," the guardsman exhales with hefty breaths. Bartram lets out a sinister grin when he's pulled from his knees. Now that he's standing up again, crunched brows and loose hair reveal the streaks of gray and wrinkle lines that give away his age. His teeth, too, aren't white as they once were as the yellow stains have tinted the enamel.

"Listen to me. You can put your hands down," says the guardsman who is hiding something. From Bartram's vantage point, the sight of his friends still on their knees is biting at him.

The National Guard, as much as they want to detain them, also wants something else. Whatever's left of Bartram's pockets are searched, and a hound dog runs to meet the others.

The guardsman straightens up. "We've got another problem."

A silence comes over the bleak backdrop of a building in tatters. It's in slow motion that Bartram watches his friends around him be taken into questioning, loose hair swinging from side to side when Yasmine's arms get yanked dramatically. By now, the sun is fully shining outside.

"Something big is in the Atlantic. And I mean big."

"The Bermuda Triangle?"

"That's only the tip of the iceberg. This thing's been at the bottom of the ocean for thousands of years. And the only person who may have even the slightest knowledge of how it got there is you, and your group of time traveling freaks."

"I'm afraid there's probably nothing I can do."

Bartram's resigned himself to be an illicit criminal who by some stroke of peer influence has landed himself into trouble as a high-echelon crook. He insists that this is all only a mere accident. Though it isn't that way at all. Instead, people of influence in the highest parts of government are deeming him a national hero. Delphi Corp. may be disbanded for good, but this group of hybrids is being prepared for the ultimate quarantine. As they speak, the President is on his way to meet them in a hypersonic jet, Air Force One's latest upgrade.

"Things aren't completely through, not yet." The guardsman wants to assure Bartram that he'll be reimbursed for the damages, so long as he continues to fix them.

The spillover from parallel universes has polluted enough people. If it's safety they want to maintain, then quarantine is necessary to contain the radioactive material. By tomorrow, Sector 10 will be closed, and Aquarius will have started. The New Year has started with a bang.

While Bartram contemplates the Atlantic, the helicopter from before returns with a loud growl that shakes them. They finally decide to move outside, and when they do, Bartram's reminded of the unhatched egg.

"Oh!" he says.

"Don't worry about it," the guardsman stops Bartram adamantly. "You're up next."

The two of them ready themselves to hop aboard the helicopter with its massive tilt rotors on each side. They'll go out just far enough to reach the surface water where the quantum field is growing. Bartram is reassured by troopers manning the vault chamber. From what is seen, all apparatuses are safe inside Delphi Corp. headquarters. The vicinity surrounding Bermuda and the Atlantic waters is off-limits for all commercial aircraft.

From the other end of parallel universes, Tuas and Cira made sure to keep the Yhemlen Class A starship submerged deep within the ocean where its quantum field would be activated at the right time in the space-time continuum for its new inhabitants to take control in the future. That time has arrived. The seven hybrids with astral stones have done just that, and it won't be long until they'll be at the helm in the cockpit to help ward off extraterrestrial enemies as the Overseers over their home in Earth, following in the Yhemlen's footsteps.

Across the globe, most of life returns to something close to normal. But that is about to change now that nuclear reactors around the world are being isolated for an extensive study into one or more faulty mechanisms. Large colliders and fusion reactors have staked their claim as the leaders in the quest for clean energy, but quantum supercomputers are predicting dangerous outcomes if they go on running uncontrolled. One of these supercomputers is housed in Fukushima, Japan, the same place where AIS lead, Naoto Shimizu, received many of his credentials before transitioning to Washington.

Oceans, and especially harbors, are filled with life, and with so many manipulations nearby of supercharged atoms and molecules, the slightest interruption will cause massive mistakes that could potentially leak into reservoirs, so an accident could be devastating. Deviations from standards have been happening more regularly. All that's been in international news stories of Bartram and Delphi Corp. being troubled by legal battles with the government.

A colleague of the late Shimizu has made a frightening discovery at the Fukushima Daiichi Nuclear Power Plant that has been inundated with tsunami water from earthquakes over the last century. These shakeups are not a coincidence, but the earthquakes are peculiar.

Amari Yugoro is one of the leads for underwater robots that are used to find deposits of melted uranium in open water, as well as other fuels inside their closed units. The Japanese government and corporations have made a pact to use specially equipped machines to search for fuel that's leaked. Ruined reactors are making a few suppliers rich where they take the leftover chemicals for plastics and other trial tests.

Yugoro, the operational lead for the robotic missions to clean the shores, is making other discoveries that are washing up from the Pacific. He's got a suspicion that these are related sea creatures that have mutated.

Yugoro dissects one such creature. The microscope reveals healthy cells but altered DNA.

He peers closer and makes up his mind to splice the cells for testing.

Before he can penetrate the cells, the sample genetic material doesn't allow a single needle to penetrate the walls of their circular boundary. Yugoro catches something spectacular that is causing the cells' walls to be impenetrable. The specimen is undergoing a mutation, and it is showing all the signs of contamination.

Four engineers burst through the closed door when they hear the sounds of Amari Yugoro screaming in pain. By the time they arrive, it's too late. They stand in shock as Yugoro is consumed by the tentacles of a gigantic, squirming squid.

"Ahh, ahh, run!" an engineer says, unwilling to stand by. Consumed in shock, the engineer corrals the rest to leave the premises of the power plant. One triggers an alarm. A barricade of iron bars locks what is left of Yugoro inside.

What they don't want is for the mutated octopus to get free. Materials with a radiation-hardened core won't let this batch out yet, but how long the meat will hold is still up in the air. An engineer immediately calls a Delphi Corp. representative to describe to them what is happening in Fukushima to see if they can be of assistance, but the call goes unanswered. Delphi Corp. HQ is in ruins, and there's a total shutdown of U.S. infrastructure.

The engineers have made up their minds to kill the creature. It seems to be getting along fine out of the water.

Evacuation notices prompt a mass migration and knowing it's not a busy day, the few that are present exit the power plant quickly. The fire alarm sprays more than water. When the alarm is activated, contaminated waste is washed clean with antiseptic chemicals to keep it sanitized. The problem this time around is that robotics lead Yugoro is suffering from more than burns and lesions; he's been eaten by a predatory ocean dweller.

The vents and spray in the lab must be reequipped with something more powerful to stop the spread. Deadly poison—the same mixture used to execute the worst criminals—is inserted into one of the HVAC channels. Something this powerful is only used on the deadliest criminals for death sentencing. This monster counts as a suitable victim to suffer that solemn fate. As the spray begins to circulate, the tentacles of the monster twitch less and less and finally lie still. The only thing keeping that thing alive is the heart of a monster.

"I believe this is what we'd call an octopus," an engineer says. It does have a sort of peculiar figure, mutilated, of course. She's holding a small screen that displays the event as it unfolds right in front of their eyes. In the parking lot, some scientists stay in their cars to watch events through a security monitoring system. An engineer and her passenger wait quietly.

"Wait a minute," another says while fastening their seatbelt. "Let's make a run for it." His voice strains each syllable in Japanese.

When he speaks, there's a hint of an American accent.

The two scientists drive recklessly toward the seashore to recover lost time where they can spot waves crashing into the cinder blocks protecting them. The dead squid and octopus are pointed out by the scientist when they come to a screeching halt. Ahead are ocean currents splashing against the shore.

"Where are you going? Hey!"

Her passenger swings the door open carelessly. The scientist runs toward the water, running over rocks and loose pebbles as if he were going to meet a lost love. When the scientist stoops down to see what he's suspected all along, it excites him. He has all the confirmation he needs of the deadly mutation. Moreover, that there is intelligent life out there.

The driver doesn't have time for the pleasantries of trivial talk and needs him to return to the car. She honks the horn with fervor. The loud honk rattles his eardrum. This is a dangerous situation they're in if they can't keep the specimens contained.

Cephalopods like these can sense fear, worry, and anxiety as it grows more palpable by the second until finally, you're completely shaken unconscious by the terror. The neurology of such a meaty creature is building. The mass of its body is larger than humans, and its mind isn't a single organ, like the human brain, but forms a network throughout the entire body. When Yugoro was trapped by the cephalopod, he had nowhere to run.

Even though Bartram and Delphi Corp. think they've safely saved the universe, those in Japan are relying on wit and ingenuity to save themselves. These contaminations can't be hidden forever. There are plenty of squid washing onshore. And these creatures with soft bellies can thrive as prey, but as a predator, they are ruthless. The lab where Yugoro is stationed is covered in ink where it dispersed poisonous ink to blot out clouds of gas before going limp. Unlike humans, they aren't handicapped by emotive brains. Cephalopod intelligence is important compared to humans because it relies on a nervous system that differs from vertebrates. In Fukushima, a new class of cognitive intelligence has arisen despite our genius attempts at trying to contain it. But as the two scientists in the car can see in the water, they must be careful.

"We're going back," the driver tells the giddy engineer when he comes back through the open door. As soon as he slams the door shut, they speed to return to the power plant.

The best thing about the structure of this encounter is that, like Delphi Corp. crossing parallel dimensions, these cephalopods transcend ordinary reality. According to normal biology, generating consciousness requires some large brain as the edifice for generating a mind. Yet, these tentacle creatures generate consciousness without it. It is a shame none of the scientists will be able to know whether this thing was intelligent or not, or where it came from.

When the two wanderers return to the power plant, the passenger who eagerly jumped out of the car readies to do the same, undoing his seatbelt before she, the driver, comes to a complete stop.

"Where do you think you're going?" she asks. He doesn't respond. "Not so fast."

As such with human moral status, the damned are usually those who have committed a heinous act, and this monster is just the latest of these shapeshifting stunts gone wrong. Luckily for the Japanese, they were able to contain this isolated outbreak before it got worse. All the physicists around the world are under strict supervision.

The scientist in tow decides not to leave the car after all. "I think that these things and that giant octopus are self-aware. Like, very intelligent," he says. Just before it was killed, it was beginning to show signs of moving through the door. The driver shuts the electric motor off, where the battery disengages before the partial fuel portion of the hybrid engine does the same.

He has been monitoring the offshore oil drills for a while now, most of which are going to close due to regulation violations. The oceans are clean as they've ever been but conservation efforts like these aren't meant to last forever. Who knows how many of these mutated behemoths are in the ocean just waiting for some lucky human to pounce on them? The next thing one comes to find out, a giant octopus has taken over their ship like some pirate vigilante. Yet, the Japanese aren't afraid of this trend; the threat of some massive cataclysm captures their interest instead.

CHAPTER 19

"**M**r. President, President! Do you have any comments on the latest scandal in Washington?" the reporter hollers.

Others follow suit in the massive parade across the White House lawn. Half of the Capitol Building was consumed by the grey goo that not only thrashed buildings but also massacred the armed forces attempting to stop the mass exodus of nanobots. If there is anything that the President despises, it's being hounded by these media folks.

He pauses near the front steps of a marked entrance. They're going to have their press conference regardless of whether the conditions contribute to that or not. When he turns back to meet the horde of media, they aren't being berated by protesters anymore who have dispersed. Most political dissidents like Silas Betts and Clyde Van Dyke have been caught in the crosshairs of the viral outbreak or trapped by FEMA. It's to the President's benefit that he can escape most danger quite easily. Safety concerns dominate his thoughts, and he's more aware of what his constituents need to be satisfied. They'll be a major migration soon to other parts of the country.

With his hands up in acquiescence, the President remarks, "As you have seen from the photos you've either taken or been privileged enough to view, this precinct is ruined beyond repair. We are devastated, as a city, as a nation, and in our hearts. Americans should know that this will never happen again, not while I'm in charge."

Some reporters aren't as keen to support that notion. "Sir, but it appears that the worst has already occurred. What are you going to do to fix it?"

"We're working on it," the President snaps back. "For now, Congress is enacting a new voting measure that will discontinue all cloud-based software. It was recently proposed that Delphi Corp. be investigated for voter fraud and malware. Today, those accusations have been verified. Our biggest concern is salvaging our national security from what appears to be repeated malfunctions on the part of Delphi Corp. and its products."

"But Mr. President," another shouts from afar. "Sir, sir, another question!"

The barrage in interrogations isn't giving him a break so that when he finally decides to make his final remarks on those same steps, he needs assistance. He and the Vice President, along with the director of the EU will hold a special press conference regarding national organizational summits in the future. It won't be long until the United States is banned from such events because of security concerns. The supposed greatest country to ever be is now on the receiving end of charity and monetary contributions.

The President's political advisors suggest that he take a backseat to the sway of world markets. As much as he wants to wield power, unprecedented danger remains on the horizon according to those same advisors. Detainees in FEMA are pushing for political asylum, but this constraint is what's keeping them within U.S. borders instead of emigrating. The U.S. can't afford to lose half of its citizenry. And as time would reveal, it won't be long until the plummet of financial markets starves more than bodies, but it freezes bank accounts. Stockpiles of food are contained in storage units, so more people don't have to resort to cheap bartering. The spread of counterfeit money is bringing about a currency overhaul where corporations like Delphi Corp. can't prop up their monopolies.

Battered, bruised, and beaten from their mutations, Ellis Bartram's group of hybrids are waiting in bathing robes without clothes. While Bartram scours the shores of the Atlantic for signs of more contaminated species, he rereads private messages about outbreaks in Fukushima. By the time he returns to Delphi Corp. headquarters, there's no need to tell them what he's found since it would only complicate matters further. His policy has always been strict privacy, but it is all coming to the forefront. The Yhemlen starship's ridge is protruding from the water as if it were an island of its own. The starship from the Yhemlen timeline has been submerged for millennia in a state of entanglement on the ocean floor. Bartram's sunglasses shield his bloodshot eyes; he is a man burned by more than stress, but someone consumed by fire to turn that pressure into a passion. He's determined to stay awake. This is the passion that would have killed him not long ago, but now he is a full-fledged superhuman from the astral stones. Next to him are his successors, Yasmine, and the other group of hybrids.

From the helicopter, he can see the sun setting in the distance. Besides the pilot and a lone trooper, Bartram's white-collared shirt blows with the massive breeze in the air, ripped like the worn jeans that managed to survive multiple shapeshifts. That island in the Bermuda Triangle is a massive technological artifact only someone like Bartram could operate. By chance or fortune, he's managed to acquire an entire starship without even trying, but it's likely to be confiscated. The helicopter has since turned off its tilt rotors. The loud motors are only decoys for the Ion thrusters that propel the hydroplane during clandestine missions.

"You and God must be good friends," the trooper says with his rifle huddled to his chest. "Either that or you're really rich."

Bartram can't help but smile. "How about both?" he says. The trooper turns his head with a small grin of his own.

The rope finally falls to allow Bartram a way out of the helicopter when the hum of the electric propellers comes to a hover. The wind continues to blow while he holds on to the tethered material. He loves the feeling of his palms burning until he makes it back at the front of what's left of Delphi Corp.

"This place has got to be renamed," he decries. "Over and done. I think this whole operation is overdue for an overhaul."

The sunset of the coming darkness reminds Bartram of the night sky as it approaches, and he is beginning to love darkness more than the day. Silas Betts and Clyde Van Dyke from the Community Center haven't said much since the start of this epidemic. Bartram considers they're suffering from self-denial since they've been his biggest critics. He's sure they never would have thought that they'd be on the side of Delphi Corp. ventures. Truth be told, they still aren't, not completely. It's just happenstance that they were caught up in a heap of quantum radiation that gave them the astral stones. And as things are, perhaps it is best this way. Delphi Corp. is over.

Bartram takes his shoes off from a low stool. "I'm not your enemy. I hope you know that, both of you."

Silas and Van Dyke look exhausted from all of this, let alone feeling as if they've been duped by a master illusionist like Bartram who's been scheming for this day. On the flip side, Delphi Corp. is completely insolvent anyway. At least they have that going for themselves.

"You're welcome at the Community Center anytime. It looks like you could use it," Silas says. Bartram's life isn't completely ruined, not yet.

The group will be released from the constraints of being tied up in bureaucratic duties by the night's end; filing, name collecting, and documenting the historic event is going to take a while. They're still sifting through eyewitness accounts of the experiment gone wrong so they might as well stay overnight.

"What's next?" Van Dyke asks, his dazzling eyes piercing through Bartram's.

Ellis tilts his head to Van Dyke's arm. They've already forgotten about the astral stones that transformed them into raging beasts from exposure to particle emission. They'll never be the same again. As if he had not dealt with enough, Clyde rolls his head in dismay, his neck is sore.

"Oh yeah, that. I guess it helps to know we're all werewolf freaks now."

Bartram musters the little strength he has left to slide across the tile floors to cozy up near Van Dyke. Cotton socks keep each of them warm, as does the sub sandwich at Bartram's side that he puts down. He has a mouth full of vegetables and salami wrapped in toasted wheat. He cozies up beside rival Clyde, putting an arm around his shoulders. By now, the sunglasses are off, but they left the mark of a tan all around in perfect ovals.

Ellis's breath has a profuse odor, but the stench is masked in pepper and spices. "How about I make it up to you. What do you say?" Bartram slides away from Van Dyke on the bench he's sitting at to give him space. "All of you!" the few that are awake look to him in contempt.

The National Guard has promised to drive them to the nearest FEMA ward for safety. Their precious equipment will be safe-guarded, as well. For now, all they need is some assurance that they will be safe. It won't be long until Sector 10 closes and when Aquarius begins, they'll be safe from the exposed quantum field. To celebrate, Ellis Bartram has plans to welcome in a new group. Silas Betts's emotions stir in abhorrence for the situation, recon-ciling his hate for Bartram as misplaced anger. It's his fault that he got laced with cosmic radiation in the first place. Things are not completely over yet, and the way everyone else is slumped over not hearing a word of this worries them that things won't be okay.

Delphi Corp. will not only be renamed but most of its assets will also be funded by government startups. These new hybrids have no other choice than to be guinea pigs to the whims of more rounds of biological testing. If they want to live, they should not resist. With these astral stones and Ellis Bartram's help, the seven hybrids will inevitably disappear from public scrutiny and they know it.

"You're all under arrest," a federal marshal pronounces. "On multiple counts of acts of terror against the U.S., manslaughter, coordinating with the media to leak classified information, and conspiracy against the safety and security of the United States of America."

"Put your hands where I can see them!" another officer shouts.

The group is aghast at the surprise. It wasn't expected that they'd be the ones in trouble for all of this. Delphi Corp.'s entire staff will serve time in correctional facilities as accomplices to the corruption of classified information. The Metropolis Project, as it originally stood, is now being brandished across the world with Delphi Corp. as the culprit. Even in Japan, the result of this experiment has created rumors of mutated creatures from another world that make visits to Earth every so often. If the gossip's true, which it is, it'll cause an entirely new segment of alien hunters that the science community doesn't need. But the damage is done.

Delphi Corp.'s days aren't over completely. Cloud Software, its autonomous component, TARA, and all the research will undergo further study. A storage facility in charge of the cleanup will take the remnants to a refurbished recycle bay and make it into a lab. For Bartram and his associates, there are more than enough spare parts and data sets that remain active that can keep their little experiment running. This has become an issue of national defense. People like Joe Hansen have unsettled lawsuits, funds for victims and their families are still waiting to be allocated, and to worsen matters, there's a fight over interdimensional equipment that can do it all over again. For this group of genetic freaks, they can look forward to quarantine in housing that will facilitate their super-human abilities to be developed. Others, like the intern Chris, are poised to make a comeback, and they can't wait to be released.

In a strange turn of events, it looks like the great hope of America has saved the world again from evil white supremacists. If it weren't for the Grey Order, half of this wouldn't have transpired. The volunteers stuck in Pangaea simply needed to find a way back, but a war between worlds couldn't be averted. Mistake or not, the efforts of reaping the fruits of menial labor on Earth's oversaturated soil by Nazism won't end here, not even in parallel dimensions. Fascist money laundering in the Old World has pushed the Syndicate to greater lengths in promoting union separatists to rise in low orbit, against the wishes of the Grey Order. Those Jewish science fables the Grey Order hates so much are spurring the movement forward. Everyone wants power. Whoever prevails will need something more powerful to circumvent opposition across worlds.

CHAPTER 23

M eanwhile, Tuas and Cira are the only Yhemlen left in the city of Pangaea. The flying fortress moves through the galaxy faster than the speed of light. Its space elevator is also a mechanism for applying the electromagnetic field necessary for a warp drive to propel them forward. As it spins, the artificial canopy that covers both the main city and the space station in a clear bubble does not rupture. The *Mariner* ahead of Tuas and Cira is superimposed by robust pillars and thick walls, that way the inhabitants are not exposed to the radiation of space. There is nowhere for them to escape to.

The Delta star of Deneb Algedi is being pulled by other forces nearby. When Tuas toggles his positioning device toward the appropriate planet, their dramatic drop in speed almost shatters the clear shield. They won't be able to go anywhere else in outer space for a long time. When they finally land, they'll be sitting ducks. By now, Earth has already been struck by the enormous asteroid that leveled the planet. Tuas and Cira are just glad to have salvaged Pangaea from its destruction and escaped the Concord and its Grey Order.

"Approaching the target," he says to Cira. "The planet is being compressed by a binary star! The habitat is going to be unstable."

"We need to land now, Tuas."

As they approach the point of rupturing the atmosphere, the fortress changes directions in open space. The *Mariner* parks itself in the upper atmosphere of the luminous planet where it stays immobile. This allows the rest of Pangaea to drop below the atmosphere, releasing the retractable space elevator, punching the clear shield of Pangaea back to the soil. The chosen planet is denser than Earth, but conditions are suitable for Pangaea, for the time being. Variations in temperature and atmospheric composition can be withstood so long as there's a decent section of land to plow its enormous rods into the soil. A mapping system coordinates the most suitable area.

Tuas and Cira are silent, covered in metal suits that clank with every move. As the dungeon shakes on landing, a final thrust of steam alerts them they've made it safely. Pangaea has successfully fled Earth's cataclysm and is in the constellation of Capricorn. Life's got a funny way of doing things. These two Yhemlen have withstood everything together if only the rest of the Overseers could've joined them. They've survived.

Their sworn enemies in the Grey Order aren't as tranquil. Madame Ria and Jasper are some of the few in the Grey Order that didn't fall for the suicidal trap into Pangaea. Despite altering the timeline successfully to remove the Yhemlen, life wasn't annihilated according to plan. The Yhemlen have been spread all about the galaxy. The few that will survive won't live very long after escaping the clutches of destruction. Yhemlen generations have been forever tainted as a single mantra to power, and the nation of Pangaea is no more at last.

Grandmaster Frost's consciousness is strong among the Concord members that stood by his legacy as his voice continues to reverberate. Ria has not yet given up her belief that he can be brought back. The CPU dungeon in the depths of the low orbit station is tempting her to visit again. This time, she's going to enter without Jasper. The Heinemann were the preeminent warrior family, and she doesn't plan on tarnishing that reputation. Madame Ria suspects that she could use some motivational words from an elder. The Concord will last under the moniker of the master race only so long as they thrive as a dominant force throughout the universe. The Grey Order is poised to reap the benefits of their travels. Unlike the Yhemlen, humans aren't as keen on fighting a war that's evaded their history, there's no passion there, but Xavier Moth warranted further scrutiny into these seven hybrids who shapeshifted. Ria needs to make peace with her inner enemies, so her thoughts are holding her back. After the final death blow of the asteroid occurred, the urge to retaliate has grown so much that perhaps she can be the new leader the Grey Order needs.

"I'm going to make right by our family's name if there's one thing I do," her thoughts resonate loudly without restraint.

Ria and the other Greys have been sitting undisturbed in the cleansing pool where the Grey Order regenerates their bodies from the aches of the day. Despite long lives, the pain from genetic surgeries takes a physical toll. They need to numb the pain, and they do. When Madame Ria looks around, what she sees through enlarged eyes is merely a small fraction of what it used to be. No longer are there crowds that block them. Open decks in the large ship have cleansing stools near each pool, where a beam of particles sterilize the skin before they put their suits back on. Ria does so, ignoring her brother's taunts at the other end of the building. He refuses to leave.

The fibers in the suit automatically constrict around her body once she exits the infrared-lit pool house. Blue and red lights at the curved ceiling leave her covered in a dim ambiance. She storms past android helpers that taunt her with automated beeps and whistles.

"Madame, would you mind a word about the construction workers in low orbit?" the robot says.

"Not right now, Android."

Wobbling undeterred to the CPU in the dungeon, a set of elevators and stairs take her through the low orbit station. All the while, Madame Ria is fuming with the rage she's supposed to calm in hopes of using logic. Her father's ways are beginning to rub off on her. Considering the way Captain Gereon was lost, she's sure to face the same fate if not careful with these dramatic outbursts. Attending something very special in the CPU will aid her in discovering what she's been missing all these years. From embryo to a genderless Grey, she never had the opportunity to hear the words of the Concord's most venerated member.

The same body scanner from her previous visit verifies her identity. This time she's prepared for the loud noises that pound her mind. Rather than stay still to let past visions freeze her, she rushes through the door. Blowing steam swirls until the sliding door slams closed. The sound of two doors crashing together is just as haunting as the voices in her head. Finally, there's silence.

Jasper's protocol for locating Grandmaster Frost and Convoy 8 is still present at the center console. Ignoring the front covers of supercomputer panels surrounding her, Madame Ria delves into what she is looking for. A swift flick of the fingers removes the previous searches. She's free to search for anything she desires. Aside from sabotaging the entire operation, she's sure not to tamper with vital codes. So far, everything is going to plan.

A booming voice shakes Ria's mind. "If it's perfection you're looking for, then you will hardly find it," it says in German.

Madame Ria comes face to face with the despised menace who sparked this entire fallout centuries ago, Adolf Hitler. There's evil in the air, something that was supposed to be buried and never recovered. She has awakened a monster. The dungeon of the Concord station has plenty of retrievable archives. Of course, most of these founders' organs were collected, but the greatest fascination left of these are minds like Albert Einstein's.

"We've lost our entire battlefleet, and I fear that the Concord is in danger. We need the foundation's help."

"Do not worry."

Madame Ria wonders if he is truly conscious, or only a simulation.

The Grey Order caste is dwindling, and Madame Ria knows their near immortality won't save them from the fits of passion that one of their eldest, Gereon, suffered against the Yhemlen. Birthing new Greys will require more advanced cloning techniques to create a race of genetically stable Greys.

"The human mind and body are prone to weakness," he says. "The Grey Order is supposed to accept our salvation by acknowledging the death of this frail former body. Look at me now, I've transcended physical shortcomings."

"But there's something else, something even more hazardous," Ria responds.

In it, she recognizes the consequences of this power. She's seen it in her father, Gereon, who couldn't resist his vengeful pride in striking down the Yhemlen in Pangaea. Instead, it will be computer consciousness that the cosmic web must contend with that will ricochet even more powerfully against them.

Yet, the founder's hologram refuses to believe in such illusions of power that do not harm the truly transcended. To be true, there's nothing that can stop his race for domination.

"Nein!" Ria screams ferociously. "Nnnein!" she lets out again, violently. The fervent passion rattles the walls of their dungeon before Madame Ria collapses on her backside from a sudden jolt. She fears that listening to his orders may return them to similar mistakes of the past.

Madame Ria is glad that she decided to wear the metallic face mask after all. In front of her, he stands only a bit taller, but the founder's holographic light is also near blinding.

"We must fulfill our destiny," the founder reiterates.

Buried deep within the low orbit station's CPU, Madame Ria is risking her life by being here as radiation leaks can come from anywhere.

The founder's body vanishes in a puff of light, closing its hologram.

"Woah, wait!" Madame Ria grabs ahold of the central console by its foundation, refusing to let go, but she must. The vision is gone now, and she may never be able to reclaim it.

Fragments of the founders remain in photons of light, hidden deep in the quantum code of their computing system's archive. Madame Ria finally releases all the gruesome thoughts racing in her mind before opening her face mask to see without restraint. If these problems persist, she and a renewed fleet will undoubtedly have to face history again, for better futures tomorrow. On the road to singularity, the cosmic web is holding onto the memories of people and civilizations that only another Cloud as powerful as Delphi Corp.'s will allow humanity, likewise, to unearth again of what remains.

ACKNOWLEDGMENTS

With profound esteem, we can reflect on overcoming the COVID-19 pandemic. A world like ours has even more potential left in store.

CPSIA information can be obtained
at www.ICGtesting.com
Printed in the USA
LVHW020043121021
700156LV00002B/68

9 781662 830549